ROBERT BLAIR KAISER went through ten years in the Society of Jesus, then, three years shy of ordination, left the Jesuits to pursue a career in journalism. He covered Vatican II for *Time*, worked on the religion beat for the *New York Times*, and served as journalism chairman at the University of Nevada Reno. Four of his eleven published books deal with Catholic Church reform. This is his first novel.

Kaiser won the Overseas Press Club Award in 1963 for the "best magazine reporting of foreign affairs"—for his reporting on the Vatican Council. Editors at three newspapers have nominated him for Pulitzer Prizes, and the book publisher E.P. Dutton nominated him for another Pulitzer for his exhaustive 634-page book on the assassination of Robert F. Kennedy, a work that will be revised and republished next year.

From 1999 to 2005, Kaiser was a contributing editor in Rome for *Newsweek* magazine and a Vatican consultant for CBS-TV. He lives in Phoenix and Rome.

Readers can e-mail him at rbkaiser@takebackourchurch.org.

CARDINAL
MAHONY

A NOVEL

Robert Blair Kaiser

Humble-bee Press

PHOENIX, ARIZONA 2008

FIRST EDITION JANUARY 2008

Copyright © Humble-bee Press 2008
14249 N. Third Avenue
Phoenix, AZ 85023-6282

rbkaiser@takebackourchurch.com

ISBN 978-0-9646642-9-6

Author Photograph © Julian Wasser

Printed in the United States of America
By Bookmasters in Ashland, Ohio

One may order books or get quantity discounts
from Bookmasters 1-800-247-6553

Or go online for autographed copies at
www.robertblairkaiser.com

Book Design by Sue Knopf, Graffolio
Cover Design by Bookcovers.com

10 9 8 7 6 5 4 3 2 1

Dedicated to the memory of a famous
Connecticut schoolteacher who had the grit
and the gumption to write her message novel.

Harriet Beecher Stowe

Uncle Tom's Cabin, first published in 1852,
changed the thinking of Americans, and—
eventually—of the whole world. It was the
second best-selling work of the nineteenth
century (next to the Bible), and was translated
into twenty-three languages. You can still buy
it in most book stores; on Amazon you can
buy used copies for a penny (plus shipping
and handling).

Daring ideas are like chessmen moved forward.
They may be beaten,
but they may start a winning game.
JOHANN WOLFGANG VON GOETHE

The best way to predict the future is to invent it.
ALAN KAY

Satire is a sort of glass,
wherein beholders do generally discover
everybody's face but their own.
JONATHAN SWIFT

CONTENTS

PREFACE

THIS IS A RELATIVELY NEW kind of fiction—what some commentators are now calling "reality fiction." It is a mixture of fact and fiction that uses the names of real persons, living and dead, to tell an entertaining tale and to make a point.

There is, of course, a right way and a wrong way to do this (as, indeed, there is a right way and a wrong way to do almost anything).

To do this the right way, I must be fair to the real persons in the scenario—give each of them, in justice, their due, and, at the same time, give myself, in charity, permission to let my imagination soar.

The Cardinal Mahony in these pages is both real and fictional.

• The facts brought out at his mock trial in Mexico are real.

• The conversion story is fiction. Obviously. It happens in the future.

In the narrative, I try to keep all the characters borrowed from real life "in character." Benedict XVI has to sound like Benedict XVI, not Martin Luther—not only in the way he speaks, but, as the story plays out, in the substance of what he does. And if he acts out of character, I try to set up a scenario that makes the fictional pope's actions plausible.

I have tried to do the same thing with Cardinal Mahony. In putting him on trial for his sins, my fictional prosecutor must stick to the facts. She (and I) can document everything she tells and shows the jury.

Obviously, I cannot "document" what a new, transformed Cardinal Mahony might do in 2008 and 2009. I do try to keep him "in character." I can't have him competing (to use an absurd example) for a place on the U.S. Olympic swimming team. But I can imagine him falling in love with his kidnappers. And I can see him trying to lead the American Church into a new way of being.

I invented this scenario to help seventy-five million American Catholics see the possibilities—to help them understand how they can be Catholic—and aggressively American as well. And why they should.

Utopian? Yes.

CARDINAL MAHONY

A NOVEL

• ONE •

SNATCH

"¡*HOLA!*" SAID THE WOMAN. She was smiling, but there was something about her sudden presence—and the two men with her who were not smiling—that troubled Cardinal Mahony. In the summertime, there were hikers aplenty here in the High Sierra. Now, on this snowy morning in early November 2008, no one on this trail, and no one back at the cabin. The cardinal's aide and his visiting seminarians had schussed off on their Nordic skis only an hour ago and left him quite alone.

He tried not to look frightened. Since the woman had greeted him in Spanish, he judged it was politic to speak Spanish, too. He said, "*Buenos días*—I think."

He eyed the men. They were wearing white ski jackets, Levi's and cowboy boots, as she was. One of the men carried something that looked very much like his own Loyola Marymount University sports bag. The other shouldered a large, folded wood-and-nylon contraption. A stretcher?

"We won't hurt you," said the man with the bag. "Much." He gave the cardinal a karate chop to the Adam's apple that sent his glasses flying, then smothered his face with a terry cloth towel soaked in chloroform. The other man and the woman caught him going down. In an instant, the two men strapped him to the stretcher and trotted him off. In less than five minutes, they came upon the small frozen lake that served as a winter landing pad for Mahony's own helicopter. Soon, they were easing him into the cabin, cuffing him and tying him down in one of two large recliner chairs behind the pilot seats.

1

Roger Michael Mahony had raised few eyebrows some years ago when he persuaded the three Southern California billionaires to give him a $395,000 blue and white Hughes 500D four-passenger jet helicopter. How else could the shepherd of more than four million souls get around the huge Los Angeles basin? Certainly not in his mere Mercedes. Certainly not on the creeping I-10 in the morning. Certainly not on the Pasadena Freeway at any time of the day or night. He'd been taking chopper lessons. Indeed, he already had his first-class license by the time he took delivery of the whirlybird on the rooftop of the Bank of America building at Third and Flower and soared off with his three benefactors on the machine's maiden voyage.

"There it is," he told the land developer, the banker and the mayor. "Your city—and mine—the city of Our Lady Queen of the Angels." He added a salient fact. "And almost every one of the hospitals in this city has a heliport on the roof." Mahony began using these landing pads, and LA's 287 pastors soon grew used to his unannounced appearances at their early Masses—or their late sumptuous dinners. Steve Lopez of the *LA Times* wrote, "The cardinal has given a whole new meaning to the word 'skypilot.'"

Now as the chopper headed south, the woman was taking the cardinal's blood pressure and monitoring his heart. "You gave him too much dope, Rodrigo," she said to the co-pilot.

He shrugged. "He's a big man. What? Two hundred and twenty pounds?" He smiled. "Without his scarlet robes?" Mahony, of course, wasn't in his scarlet robes now. He was wearing a black nylon jogging suit and a pair of white tennis shoes.

They were crossing the Mexican border unchallenged when the cardinal finally opened his eyes. Still groggy, his vision still out of focus, he asked the woman, "What are you doing?"

"We'll be landing at a private airport in a few minutes," she said. "To refuel."

"And then where? And why?"

She eased his glasses on his ears, but did not respond. She was not surprised to find he spoke with such authority. A lesser man might have been cowed by the capture, the chloroform, the cuffs. But she realized this was a man who had learned long ago how to take charge, ask questions, get things done. Now, as the archbishop of Los Angeles, he headed a half-billion a year corporation. His net worth as corporation sole of the Archdiocese of Los Angeles was possibly $15 billion, much of it in commercial and residential real estate that had been left to the Church by rich widows from San Marino and Bel Air and Rolling Hills Estates. He had built his own $193 million cathedral. Even bound as he was, he had a certain dignity. His question, she thought, deserved an answer. She raised an eyebrow to Rodrigo, inviting him to tell the cardinal.

"No," the co-pilot said to Mahony. "No questions. You will know soon enough. You can have some water though." He reached under his knees and passed the woman a small plastic bottle. She unscrewed the cap, apologized to the cardinal for the handcuffs, and held the water to his lips.

He nodded and took two sips, also swallowing his anger at being told "no questions." He said, "I need my pills."

She nodded and reached for the Loyola-Marymount bag. "We were in your cabin. We brought along your pills. And your toothbrush. And some other things." She paused, then smiled. Mahony noted her very white teeth. "Even your Macintosh Powerbook."

Nice of them, he thought. His anger rose, to think how well they'd planned everything. They even knew enough to grab his Prozac.

When they stopped to refuel at a landing strip in the middle of a saguaro forest, the woman strode to the airport manager's shack and fiddled with a TV. "Nothing on the news, yet," she said to Rodrigo when she came back to the chopper. "I checked CNN and Fox and Televisa, too. Tomàs, do you think we have done it?"

As the chopper rose, the pilot said, "I think we did! I think we can relax now." He offered cigars all around. He got no takers. "With luck," he said, blowing a big smoke ring, "no one will know the cardinal is missing until at least midnight."

"Why even then?" asked Rodrigo.

"Because the cardinal's an e-mail freak. His half dozen minions expect his 'midnight missives.' If they don't get 'em, they will know something is wrong. But they cannot confirm that until they get the Mono County Sheriff's Office to check his cabin." He turned in his seat and regarded Mahony. "Isn't that right, Your Holiness?"

The cardinal tried to rise higher in his seat, furious that these, these terrorists had pulled off this caper with such ease, even more furious to think they knew so much about him. Finally, the anger he'd buried burst forth. "Fuck you!"

3

"Did you hear that, Rodrigo? María? His Holiness said, 'Fuck.'"

THEY SAID VERY LITTLE AFTER THAT. The fall light had almost faded by the time they faced into a clearing in the middle of a mountain jungle. They'd eaten only a few tortillas and some cold, refried beans for lunch. María whispered to the cardinal, "The worst is over. Soon, we will be eating warm rabbit stew and washing it down with some red wine."

He shook his head. "I cannot believe this."

Tomàs turned and said, "Believe this: the worst is not over. For us, maybe. But not for, uh, not for you."

They blindfolded him, then untied him and removed his handcuffs. He uncoiled his six foot three inch frame and made his painful way down the narrow ladder to the ground while the rotors were still whirling overhead. Tomàs, Rodrigo and María each had a Jeep waiting for them, with two debriefing officers in each of them. A new set of escorts took Mahony in hand, pushed him into a rusting Chevy Suburban, and followed the Jeeps up a rocky road as the setting sun cast the jungle in an orange glow.

THEY SERVED THE CARDINAL SOME STEW in a small metal bowl, but he did not have the pleasure of María's company, nor any red wine either. He ate alone in his cell, a windowless room in a corrugated metal shack, furnished with a cot, a blanket (no sheets, no pillow), a chair, a table, a pitcher of water and a chamber pot. When he finished eating by the light of a stubby candle, he said to his guard, "I have no cup." The guard did not understand. "*Una taza*," said the cardinal, in Spanish and with a gesture. The guard reached into a small pack and produced a paper cup.

"*Gracias*," said the cardinal.

"*De nada*," said the guard.

Mahony drank, not worried that the water might make him sick. He was already sick, with worry and with fear. For the first time in perhaps twelve hours he prayed, but his prayer was the reproach of Jesus on Golgotha, "My God, my God, why have you forsaken me?"

Before he went to sleep, he was allowed a visit to the latrine ravine. The guard watched him, then gave him a sheet of newspaper to wipe with.

4

DANNY ZAPIEN, THE VETERAN SHERIFF of Mono County, led off *CBS News in the Morning*, live from Bridgeport at 4 AM California time. "We took our own chopper up there near the cardinal's cabin," he said. "We didn't find the cardinal. We didn't find his chopper either. But we found lots of footprints in the snow where the chopper was parked on Mirror Lake."

A spokesman for the U.S. Border Patrol in Tijuana named Gordon Proud told another CBS reporter in San Diego, "We had reports late yesterday morning that a blue and white helicopter, probably a Hughes 500D, crossed the border at Calexico. We didn't tell officials from Homeland Security until about an hour ago—when we heard that the cardinal and his blue and white chopper was missing."

In Washington, D.C., Defense Secretary Robert M. Gates faced a press gang outside his home in Georgetown. "Yes, if terrorists have taken the cardinal to Mexico—or wherever—this is definitely a federal case, but until we find out who they are and what they want, we cannot tell you a thing. Yes, the president has been informed. Yes, we have notified Los Pinos. No, we have no information yet about any demands." A reporter asked Gates why he thought Mahony had been taken by terrorists. "Who else?" he said.

HE'D SURMISED CORRECTLY. By 7:00 PM, Katie Couric was reporting on the *CBS Evening News* that the kidnappers were asking $49 million ransom. Couric waved a sheet of paper. "They chose the cardinal's favorite form of communication—e-mail—to make their demands, and sent copies to every news organization in the world. They say they don't care how the cardinal's friends raise the money. They just want forty-nine million for his release. But the major mystery tonight is this: who are these terrorists? And where do they come from? We have Jim Foster standing by at the NSA."

AT 7:05 PM ON THE GROUNDS OF the National Security Agency in Maryland, Foster told Couric, "Katie, I've been closeted all afternoon with the government's Internet experts, including men from the FBI and the CIA. All they can tell us is that the kidnappers' message came from Malaysia. But that site in Southeast Asia was probably the last in a chain of many intermediate Internet providers. It may take many hours or even days for computer experts to climb back up that chain."

SHORTLY AFTER 10 PM, Bill O'Reilly was confiding to viewers of the *O'Reilly Factor* on the Fox Television Network, "This may well be a hoax, folks. We know the cardinal is missing. But we have no proof that he's been kidnapped at all—other than an e-mail message from Southeast Asia. One of my sources close to the District Attorney in Los Angeles tells me the DA was on the verge of indicting the cardinal for obstruction of justice—for his fifteen-year cover up in the case of Father Michael Baker, a convicted sex predator. So I am wondering if the cardinal didn't stage his own kidnapping, just to buy time—and gain some sympathy."

CNN HAD THE MOST EXPLOSIVE NEWSBREAK of the night. John Allen was reporting from the Vatican—nine in the morning in St. Peter's Square. "CNN has learned," Allen said, "that an organization called the Shining Path—that's an outfit in Peru that hasn't been heard from in years—is putting Cardinal Mahony on trial. They are putting Cardinal Mahony on trial! I cannot tell you my source on this, but it is someone very high up on the third floor of the Apostolic Palace."

Suzy Walker, at CNN's news desk in London, asked Allen, "What for, John? What are they putting him on trial for?"

"Ah, this is the weird thing, Suzy," said Allen. "My source inside the Vatican—he got an e-mail note sometime after midnight here—my source says they are trying Cardinal Mahony for his sins."

"John, what exactly does that mean, 'for his sins?'" She smiled. "For the four cardinal sins?"

At first, Allen was too giddy over his own scoop to get the joke. "Umm, Suzy, we'll just have to wait and see." Then he got in synch with Suzy—and corrected her. "Four cardinal *virtues*, Suzy. Prudence, justice, fortitude and temperance. *Seven* capital *sins*. Pride, covetousness, lust, anger, gluttony, envy and sloth. The sins that cry out to heaven for vengeance are willful murder, sodomy, oppression of the poor and defrauding the laborer of his wages. According to the Catechism of the Catholic Church, there are two kinds of *sin*, mortal sin and venial sin, or two kinds of *sins*, private sins and social sins—"

"John, we have to move on."

"Uh, okay, Suzy. Well, we'll just have to wait and see how they go after Cardinal Mahony, very holy guy as far as the pope is concerned. But you know what? Ha ha. I'd like to cover the trial."

A LITTLE MORE THAN THREE HOURS LATER, *Fox Television News* had a follow-up from its Rome correspondent who had gained his camera crew's admission to the pope's regular Wednesday morning audience inside St. Peter's. They captured the pope's words and the pope's anguish.

"The whole world groans at this latest assault on the Body of Christ, which is the Church," said the pope. His voice quavered, but his words were clear. "We are all sinners. All the children of the Church are constantly on trial for their sins—but before God. Men cannot judge. Terrorists cannot judge. When misguided souls—no doubt they are men of good will—think they can snatch, yes, snatch a cardinal of the most holy Catholic Church and take him off somewhere and put him on trial—we must pray for them, and for our suffering brother in Christ."

ON ONE OF THREE TELEVISION SCREENS in the Oval Office, President George W. Bush had been watching the pope. He picked up a phone and punched a single yellow button. "Bobby? Let's get the Special Forces revved up. We gotta rescue that cardinal from the terrorists. You know anything about this outfit called Shining Path?"

IN THE MORNING, the guard unlocked the cardinal's cell door and María entered with a smile and a tray bearing a pot of steaming coffee, a basket of tortillas and an open jar of honey with a spoon standing in it.

"*¡Hola!*" she said, and though that was the same word she greeted him with on that trail in the High Sierra, he smiled back, grateful to see the only person who had been halfway nice to him during his forced trip to—wherever they were. From the time they spent in the air, he guessed they were in southern Mexico or Central America. He was still wearing the jogging suit he was captured in—minus the jacket, for even at eight in the morning, the air was warm. María wore no shoes and a soft, revealing, royal blue jersey mini-dress. As she stood over him, setting the tray down on the table, one of her perfect young breasts brushed his forehead. He caught his breath.

She said, "They told me to tell you that you will have a day to prepare your defense. Tomorrow you go on trial."

"Defense? Trial?" Mahony pushed his chair back. "What's the charge? Who's the judge? Where's the jury?"

María remained standing. There was no second chair. "Drink your coffee before it gets cold," she ordered. "There's some warm milk in the small pitcher."

He was still fuming. But he did as he was told. He fixed himself a *caffe latte*, no sugar, and bit into one of the tortillas. "Not bad," he said.

"Even better," she said, still standing behind him, "with some of that honey."

He tried the honey and told her she was right. It was better.

By the time he was finished with his coffee, he felt a little calmer. "Tell me more about this trial?" It was less an order than an invitation.

With a dancer's grace, she dropped cross-legged on the floor in front of him. "You will learn more about that at your arraignment this morning. The judge will tell you."

"And who's the judge?"

"Our *presidente*, Iván Díaz."

"*Presidente* of what?"

"We call ourselves *Para los otros*. We are men and women for others. We are followers of Jesus, who came to set us free."

"Free from what?"

"Not *from* anything. *For* something. Free to be all that we can be. So we can be men and women for others."

"And in Mexico, you cannot be all you can be?"

She waved her hand to cancel his reference to Mexico. "Nice try. I cannot tell you where we are right now. And we are not *from* Mexico. Not all of us. We have come together from all of Latin America—and from California, too. I am from East LA."

Mahony knew a good many people from East LA, and María didn't sound like East LA. People from the Mexican neighborhoods in Los Angeles draw out the ell and the ay, and this woman didn't have that drawl.

"You have a school here?"

"Not a school so much as a . . . training camp."

"Training for what?"

"For the revolution."

8

He sighed. "Hasn't Latin America had enough revolutions?"

"This is a different kind of revolution. We aren't training to fight with guns or bullets." She bit her lip. "We're fighting with the most subversive thing there is: new ideas."

"New ideas?"

"Ideas that will help the people of God rise up and win their own salvation—in this life, as well as in the next."

He smiled. "You have an idea gun?"

"Well, duh? We use the media, We use one of your favorite mediums, the Internet. We use radio. We use television. We have our own satellite. Or, rather, we rent space on one."

"You can afford that?"

"We can afford it if our *presidente* can make some deals today."

"Deals?"

"To sell the feed on your trial tomorrow."

"The feed?"

"We are offering your trial, live, to the world's major networks—to CBS and ABC and NBC and Fox and CNN and the BBC and Skynews in Asia. They can do their own commentaries. We hope they will bid on it, like they do for the Olympic Games."

Mahony gasped at the audacity of that idea. "Why, you're using me!"

María gave him a level look. "Yes, I guess we are. As your people have been using my people for centuries."

"My people? What do you mean?"

"Your own father?" she said. "Does he not qualify as one of your people?"

"What about him?"

"On his chicken ranch in the Valley, he used undocumented aliens, did he not? Paid them substandard wages—off the books? No benefits? No Social Security?"

The cardinal said he didn't know about that. "I was just a kid then. I was in the seminary."

She said, "It doesn't matter. Everyone was doing it, just the way everyone has always done it, starting with Columbus. Then, in the seventeen hundreds, the Anglos came in from the East and cheated the *Californios* out of their Spanish land-grants. And in the twentieth century, Okies homesteaded the Central Valley and hired Hispanics to pick their strawberries, their oranges and lemons, their grapes and their artichokes and avocados. We try to call the process by its right name: exploitation."

Mahony's lip curled. "So it's all about money?"

"Money's not important? How could you build your two hundred million dollar cathedral without it?"

Mahony had to admit. This young woman was sharp. He changed the subject. "Ideas are one thing. Violence is another. How can you people justify the violence?"

"What violence?"

"Kidnapping? You stole my chopper?"

She laughed. "We borrowed it. We're just borrowing you, too. To make our point."

"Your point, my neck." He squeezed under his chin. "I still have a sore throat. You could have asked me—nicely—to go on your TV show. I'm pretty good on TV."

"Nice doesn't win audience share. Live action does. And not your phony 'Reality TV' action either. Yesterday wasn't phony. We were playing for keeps. If the U.S. Department of Homeland Security wasn't filled with idiots. They had choppers that could have brought us down." She paused for a breath. "I don't know if I should tell you this, but you will find out sooner or later anyway. We have asked for some big ransom money. For you, we are demanding forty-nine million."

He whistled, pleased to think someone might pay $49 million for his freedom. "Who have you been talking to? Karl Rove? Dick Morris? James Carville?"

"We have clever people of our own."

"I'll say."

María stood. It was almost time to go. "This isn't agitprop theater. It's real. The whole world will be watching this trial. Because the whole world will know we're not competing for—cash prizes, or an all-expenses trip to Paris. We are putting you and the whole damn Catholic Church on trial."

"Now you're going too far! What has the Church done?"

"Nothing. That's the whole point. Words, words, words, words. Lots of say so. Very little do so. If Jesus visited the Vatican today, he would throw up. What you guys have done to his message!" She paused and her voice rose a notch. "What your priests have done to little kids!"

The cardinal flinched, but said nothing.

She glared at him. "The bishops should all lay in a supply of millstones, instead of paying a bunch of smart lawyers to hide you behind the statute of limitations."

"Millstones?"

"Luke seventeen, two? If you harm my little ones, better that a millstone be tied around your neck and you be drowned—"

"Okay, okay," he said, interrupting her. "I get it '—in the depths of the sea.'" Mahony reddened, to think this young woman could quote Jesus so tellingly, and that he needed her to give him the very verse that counted most. As far as we know, Mahony reminded himself, these were the most violent words Jesus ever uttered. And he saved them up for pedophiles. All of a sudden, he had to go. Was it the coffee? Or was this, this mere woman, scaring the piss out of him? He looked at his watch. "What time is it here, María? Do we have to go to my arraignment now? If so, can you tell the guard I have to make a stop before we move on?"

• TWO •

ARRAIGNMENT

MARÍA USHERED THE CARDINAL through a courtyard featuring a simple but melodious fountain to a separate building constructed of heavy bamboo. It had a tile roof and no sides and a dark brown floor that might have been polished clay. Once they were inside, María pointed to his seat at a small wooden table, took the chair beside him and folded her hands.

He had expected a courtroom like this, small and primitive—though he observed it was well lit by six fluorescent lamps that hung from the bamboo rafters. He noted a high-backed, carved wooden chair, but no judge's bench. He saw a witness box to the immediate left of the judge's chair and a jury box to the far left with only six places in it. The jury box faced the prosecuting attorney's table, which was largely taken up by a 27-inch television screen turned toward the jury box. What might have been an area reserved for spectators was filled with a tangle of television cable and three large Sony television cameras and a table full of controls. Mahony saw three cameramen, and several others wearing huge headphones—soundpersons, no doubt, and producer-types.

"No place in this courtroom for the public?" he quipped.

She shook her head, but favored his joke only with a faint smile.

They sat in silence for more than a minute. "Surely," he finally said to her, "*you're* not going to be my defense counsel?"

She whispered, "You'll see."

Then, with no fanfare, a tall lean man with aquiline features strode into the room and took the judge's chair. He had long gray hair tied in the back in a pony tail and deep set eyes under dark beetling eyebrows that said his hair might have once been as black. He looked like he had just stepped out of a painting by El Greco. "Once the cameras start rolling," he said softly, "I would like to start this proceeding with a prayer. To the Holy Spirit."

Mahony was taken aback. Through most of this ordeal, he hadn't been praying at all. Now the terrorists were leading *him* in prayer. He heard the judge intone a familiar Catholic antiphon.

Come, Holy Spirit, enkindle in us the fire of divine love.

He heard those standing by respond—and he joined in, mumbling automatically along with the cameramen and soundmen and producers, too:

And we shall renew the face of the earth.

The judge, who was wearing a severe black suit, a starched white shirt and a black silk tie, said, "I am Iván Díaz. I am a Sephardic Jew. I was baptized by Angelo Giuseppe Roncalli in Venice in 1955. I still consider myself a Jew because, as Roncalli told me, 'By becoming a Catholic, you do not become any less of a Jew.' Three years later, just before he became Pope John XXIII, he ordained me in Venice. I have two doctorates—one in canon law from the Gregorian University in Rome, the other in Church history from Bologna. I was a *peritus* at Vatican II. After the Council, I worked with Cardinal Evaristo Arns in Brazil. When I was brought to Rome in 1990 to explain my writings on liberation theology, I asked Cardinal Ratzinger, the man in charge, for a bill of particulars, and he refused. I took off my collar then and there, laid it on his desk and told him I was going out for a cappuccino. I never went back—to Ratzinger's office, or to the active ministry. Two years ago, I came out of retirement as a professor at UCLA to become the founding president of *Para los otros.*"

Mahony brightened. "I know you. I met you once. It was in Rome many years ago, at the Vatican Observatory at Castel Gandolfo. You were with the Jesuit astronomer, Father George Coyne."

"I remember, Your Eminence. But you do not need to remind me of this in order to get a fair trial. Despite what you may think about your, umm, unusual invitation here, I will see that you get a fair trial. I have appointed an attorney for you, to make sure you get a fair trial. His name is Paul Kelly. He studied law at Georgetown. Before his retirement in Cuernavaca, he was a member of the trial bar in Atlanta, Georgia."

He turned to a huge man in a cream-colored Palm Beach suit who was standing off to his right. "Mr. Kelly, please come in and meet Cardinal Mahony. After this short hearing, when you have both heard the charges, you will have all day, and all night if you wish, to prepare your defense. In privacy, I might add."

Kelly lumbered over to Mahony's side with a smile, shook the cardinal's hand and stood behind the chair just vacated by María. He spoke with a Southern accent, and he had the courtly manners of the Old South. "Thank you, your Honor, sir, Father Díaz, Mr. President."

"For this proceeding, 'your Honor' will do."

"Thank you, your Honor. Now, first thing, we'd like to know what the charges are. Second, we'd like to know what these TV cameras are doing here. Third, we're wondering about the jury. I haven't had time to consult with my client about this, but I kinda think he'd like to have a jury of his peers."

"And he shall have one." Díaz gave a signal, and five men in various stages of decrepitude made their way to the jury box. The judge introduced them in turn as they were seated. The five, he said, were retired auxiliary bishops—from Rio, Recife, Riobamba, Bogotá, Jaramilla. "We have a sixth bishop, Samuel Ruiz, who was once the ordinary of Chiapas. He could not make the trip, but he will be here in a virtual sense. I hope he can watch this proceeding on television. Later, he will be able to confer with his brother bishops on his Blackberry, and he will vote in the same manner."

"I'll be damned," Kelly whispered to the cardinal.

"I hope not," said Mahony. "This is getting good." The amused look on his face disappeared when the judge said, "You asked about the charges. I will let our prosecutor make them. Your Eminence, Mr. Kelly, let me introduce Juana Margarita Obregón."

A tall handsome woman wearing high heels, a black pants suit and a simple silver cross hanging from a silver chain around her neck marched into the room and nodded to the judge, then to Mahony and his defense counsel. "Your Honor," she said, "bishops go way back in the history of the Church, to the early second century at least." Mahony detected a slight Mexican accent.

"Strictly speaking," she said, "according to some theologians, we could get along without bishops. Some reform-minded Christians do not have bishops at all. And maybe they had a point in getting rid of them. Too many of them turned out to be satyrs and scoundrels, more interested in serving themselves and their own pleasure than in serving the people. But, as Catholics, we have gotten used to our bishops. In fact, we love our bishops, partly because they give us the illusion that our priesthood goes all the way back to the Apostles. But we love most especially the simple, saintly bishops dedicated to selfless service of the people of God."

Kelly rose. "I am gonna object right now, your Honor. Before we go any further, I'd like to ask Ms. Obregón—"

Díaz said, "You can call her Doctor Obregón."

"Okay. I'd like to ask Doctor Obregón what standing she has here in this court. In fact, I'd like to ask the court what standing this court has."

Juana said, "I am a member of the parish council at St. Paul the Apostle in Westwood, California, one of the cardinal-archbishop's 287 parishes. I am a member of the same universal Church the cardinal has promised to serve. I am also a member of Christ whose body has suffered so grievously because of Cardinal Mahony's negligence in the performance of his duties to all the people of Los Angeles."

Mahony blanched and uttered a strangled little cry. "Not fair!"

Díaz cleared his throat. "You're out of order, Eminence. You'll have your chance to speak when we give you a chance to speak."

Kelly said, "But your Honor, under what law does this court proceed? Surely not the laws of the State of California? Surely not the laws of the United States of America? We are in—where are we actually? I don't even know what country I'm in! You brought me here blindfolded."

"For security reasons, that's all," said Díaz. "You came willingly, did you not?"

"Yes. When your people grabbed me before breakfast this morning in Cuernavaca and asked me if I would defend the cardinal, there was nothing I could do but say yes—after I got the permission of Mrs. Kelly. But we have to know what legal theory you are proceeding under."

"Doctor Obregón?" The judge was inviting her to answer Kelly's objection.

"Your Honor, we are proceeding according to the canons in Book Seven of the Code of Canon Law entitled "De Processibus" and the section in Book Six on delicts and penalties."

"Excuse me," said Kelly. "I am not familiar with the Code of Canon Law. But I doubt that—"

She interrupted. "Your Honor, I can give you my points and authorities at the end of this hearing."

The judge said, "Very well, Doctor Obregón." When Kelly sputtered, he turned and said, "Mr. Kelly, you can take exception if you want. But we have to get on with this. Doctor Obregón? Are you finished with your statement of the charges?"

"Not quite, your Honor. Thank you. Speaking most appositely for the people of God in Los Angeles, your Honor, we charge Cardinal Mahony with misfeasance and malfeasance. We will prove, your Honor, that Cardinal Mahony has forgotten the sacred duties of his episcopal office, and has demonstrated his forgetfulness by his actions, which we will outline in this courtroom. He has let the unwritten rules of his clerical club undermine the rule of the Gospel itself. He has robbed the patrimony of Christ's poor to enrich crafty lawyers—and keep sodomizing priests out of prison."

Mahony groaned.

Kelly said, "God save us!"

Díaz said, "Mr. Kelly, we don't ask God to undo our own malefactions. We save ourselves." He nodded to Juana Margarita Obregón. "Anything else? No? All right then. Without further objection, I will adjourn this court until tomorrow morning at nine."

"I have an objection," said Kelly, still on his feet. "The TV cameras. I object to these television cameras. They are an invasion of my client's privacy."

Díaz said, "Dr. Obregón?"

"Canon law has nothing to say about privacy. Secrecy, yes. But not privacy. Maybe it should. And nothing about television either."

"All right then," said the judge. "Objection overruled. We'll televise this trial, live, by satellite. In fact, I will spend the rest of my day negotiating with the world's broadcast networks on my secure satellite phone. They will decide whether they want to let their viewers see and hear what we do here." If Iván Díaz had had a gavel, he would have banged it. Not having one, he slapped his knee.

JUANA MARGARITA OBREGÓN was pleasant when she walked over to Paul Kelly's side, but she was all business. "Look," she said. "I am headed to the back of the room now, to put myself on the record."

Kelly said, "I don't understand."

"I am going to tell these cameras who I am. And I am suggesting that you might want to do the same thing."

Mahony hovered, but said nothing.

Kelly said, "But why should I do that?"

"This trial may well be carried live—or on tape—all over the world. But, for obvious reasons, we have not invited any reporters here. If they were here, they would be asking us who we are, and how we got here. Even now, as Iván Díaz is on the phone to the networks, they are more than curious about us. I am going to tell them about *Para los otros* right now, and put our résumés on the feed that will go out at noon. You can do this, too. But only if you want to." She cast a sidelong glance at the cardinal, a man who, she knew, prided himself on knowing as much about the media as any prelate alive.

Mahony told Kelly, "Let's hear what she has to say. I'm curious to know more about Dr. Obregón. And if she's giving you time on their feed, I suggest you better take it."

Kelly shrugged. Damned if he knew why Mahony wanted to cooperate in this legal charade at all. But if that's what he wanted, Kelly wouldn't say no. He was a trial lawyer. He knew the value of a running minute or two on television.

KELLY AND THE CARDINAL AND MARÍA (who, Mahony decided, had been designated his nurse and keeper) watched Juana as she faced into the three cameras and said, "My name is Juana Margarita Obregón. My great-great-great-grandfather's name was O'Brien when he came to fight for Mexican freedom in 1849 and stayed to punch cattle and eventually marry the cattleman's daughter. I received my doctorate in scripture from the Jesuits in Berkeley and my law degree from Boalt Hall. I never took my bar exam. Soon, I was working in the administration of Salvador Allende in Chile. In 1986, I fled to Boston after the CIA had Allende assassinated and my friends started disappearing at the hands of military goons.

"My husband, José Avillán, died in Boston after a short, merciful illness. He was sixty-five. I was forty. I felt the loss, I grieved for almost a year, then

17

I moved on—to a new career. I became pretty good with a mini-cam, and I learned how to win candor from my subjects, even when they knew I was taping them. In 1999, I won an award at the Sundance Film Festival for a documentary on homeless women in Boston. I like television. It can help make us more human. It can change the world."

She looked over to a young woman wearing headphones who was standing beside one of the cameras and smiled. "Okay, Carmen?"

"Tell us more about *Para los otros?*" said the young woman.

"Right," said Juana Margarita Obregón. "I forgot to do that. Okay. We translate *Para los otros* as Men and Women for Others. Our inspiration comes from the vision of the revered Jesuit General Pedro Arrupe, who shared his dream with his colleagues at the Jesuits' Thirty-Second General Congregation in 1972. Out of their devotion to Jesus who had come to redeem the world, the Jesuits had to carry on that work of redemption. They had to change the world, not all by themselves, but by enlisting the help of men and women with the same redeeming aim." Her voice thickened, and her eyes glistened. "What we do, mainly, is find bread for people who have very little of it, and look for justice where we see none."

"Okay," said Carmen. "More than okay. Call it a wrap, boys. Thank you, Juana. That was great."

Juana Margarita Obregón said to her, "Maybe Mr. Kelly would like to have equal time."

Kelly laughed. "Doctor Obregón, if you think I can top that, you're crazy. I'm just a poor little ol' country lawyer."

She smiled.

"Well," he said, patting his paunch, "maybe not so little."

Juana shrugged. "As you wish, Mr. Kelly. If you change your mind, just let someone know. They will find Carmen, and she will set you up."

Kelly looked at the cardinal. "First thing, I think we gotta talk. Maybe you can tell me what in the hail has been going on in LA."

• THREE •

TRIAL

"Well, I never would have believed this, folks." It was ten in the evening in New York, and Bill O'Reilly was trying to backtrack on his charge that Cardinal Mahony had faked his own kidnapping. "But you will be able to see the whole show—I call it a show, not a trial—live on *Fox Television News* tomorrow at 11:00 AM Eastern. You can see your Cardinal Mahony go on trial for his sins. Incredible. For several years now, the media have been calling for accountability from the Church, and we've been pretty much stonewalled by a hierarchy that Governor Frank Keating once compared to the Mafia. But Cardinal Mahony's heard something like this before. Five years ago, a Los Angeles lawyer filed a lawsuit against the cardinal that alleged abuse and conspiracy and cover-up, too. It was filed under RICO, the federal racketeering law, which as you know, folks, was drafted to go after mobsters."

Hannity and Colmes followed the *O'Reilly Factor* on Fox, and they had to comment on the turn this story had taken.

Alan Colmes led off. "I understand, Sean, that Cardinal Mahony blasted Governor Keating for comparing the U.S. bishops to the Mafia. He said Keating's remark was 'off the wall' and Keating apologized."

"No. No," said Hannity. "Keating didn't back down. He stuck to his guns."

Colmes laughed. "He apologized to the Mafia."

"Ha! Pretty good, Alan." Hannity, like O'Reilly, considered himself a good, loyal, right-wing Catholic. But even good, loyal, right-wing Catholics

19

had joined good, loyal, left wing Catholics in their recent reservations about the U.S. bishops.

"So, Sean, do you think Cardinal Mahony should be tried—on international television—for his sins?"

"You—and even my friend O'Reilly—may be cheering all of this," said Sean Hannity. "He may be getting the public trial now that he's avoided so successfully for all these years. But I am appalled—that Fox would make a deal with these terrorists."

Colmes objected. "I wouldn't call them terrorists, Sean."

"The Shining Path are killers, assassins."

"Well we know that, Sean. But who says Mahony's abductors are Shining Path?"

"The Vatican says so. And the Vatican has better intelligence than the CIA."

"That isn't saying much."

Hannity heaved a theatrical sigh. "The fact is," he said, "that these guys kidnapped a cardinal in his own helicopter and whisked him off to some jungle headquarters and put him up for ransom."

"Yes, Sean, but now we hear they may cancel their ransom demands."

"Yeah, because they got the forty-nine million they wanted from our own network." Hannity loathed the very idea of enriching terrorists of any kind. "Our own network!"

"Plus more millions from the BBC and Skynews in Asia. Ten million from the BBC. Ten million from Skynews."

"And didn't they get millions more from Televisa, covering all of Latin America?"

"Yep. Just an hour ago, we are told, they made a thirteen million dollar deal with Televisa."

"My question is how do they think they can get away with this? Where they gonna cash the checks?"

"Didn't you hear? Fox wired its payment to a confidential escrow account in Zurich. Shining Path or not, they're no dummies."

"I still don't get it," said Sean Hannity. "Do they think they can upload their show to a satellite and download it around the world without detection? Sooner or later, they'll be found out. And found, too."

"I understand," said Alan Colmes, "they've been able to cover their tracks with a relay system, leapfrogging from transmitter to transmitter to transmitter. That's easy, these days. And no government seems able to trace 'em, much less control 'em."

Hannity frowned. "Well, they don't know George W. Bush. He'll find a way."

"GENTLEMEN OF THE JURY, your Excellencies, may it please the court?" Juana Margarita Obregón was making her opening statement—to a virtually empty courtroom. But five aging Latin American bishops, and a sixth bishop watching the proceedings on TV, along with an estimated 590 million television viewers around the world, were paying close attention. So was Cardinal Mahony, who was now wearing a red cassock that his captors had provided for him.

Juana Margarita Obregón told the juror-bishops about her background. That she had received a degree in scripture from the Jesuit School of Theology in Berkeley, that she'd written a feminist take on liberation theology, that she had chosen a second career in the law, and then a third in television—"to bring Good News to the poor."

"The Good News," she said, "is that the poor who are almost always voiceless will have their voices heard today." She explained that she'd been gathering the voices of the poor for the past three years in Los Angeles. "I was teaching television writing and production at UCLA," she said, "when the cardinal began raising funds for his cathedral. I could not help but see him in action, mostly in the pages of the *LA Times*. Their editors cheered when the cardinal announced he was going to build his cathedral downtown, not far from the *Times*. And they endorsed his ninety three million dollar fund-raising campaign among LA's rich and famous.

"I was inclined to go along with the popular wisdom. Lord knows, we needed a cathedral. Every great city has one. I started to change my mind when I met the cardinal himself during a fundraising cocktail party at the Bel Air Hotel. He shook my hand. But he never looked at me. His eager eyes were scanning the room to see who else was there. I wondered at his obvious ambition.

"Then I learned the cardinal had entered into a sweetheart contract with the nation's largest death-care conglomerate. The deal helped the company corner a lucrative segment of the funeral market in the counties of Los Angeles, Ventura, and Santa Barbara. Eleven Catholic cemeteries. It also put the archdiocese's *imprimatur* on a company that soon doubled the price of cemetery plots—a company, to boot, that made obscene profits on deceptive sales practices. (It had a habit of selling the same plot two or three times over.) In return for all this, the company made a secret donation of forty million dollars to the cardinal's cathedral fund.

"Was the cardinal doing this all for God's glory? Perhaps. But some of the nuns in Los Angeles—yes, there are a few nuns left—told me the cardinal was going ahead with the cathedral, even as the price tag mounted from ninety-three million to one hundred and ninety-three million, often at the expense of inner-city Catholic elementary schools. He was giving the black and the Hispanic kids short shrift. It was a kind of an ethnic cleansing. My nun-friends told me I ought to go talk to these kids. And their moms. Many of the kids have no dads at all.

"And so I did. I started to do that. I went out with my mini-cam and gathered testimony about the cardinal's obvious neglect. He wasn't paying attention to the needs of his little ones, and I was getting all the sad, simple stories on tape. It was a project that grew in the doing, and soon I was on the move all over town—from the beaches to the barrios—hearing what the sheep were saying about their shepherd. I got it all on half-inch videotape.

"And then one of my students said maybe the cardinal ought to review my tapes. What a great idea! Of course! And so, in one marathon twenty-hour day, my film students and I did our high-speed dubs of these stories, almost one hundred hours worth of testimony, and then I delivered copies of the tapes to the cardinal's residence the very next day. I enclosed a little handwritten note: 'To the Good Shepherd,' I said, 'from one of your flock. When you have viewed the tapes, you might want to phone me.' I gave him my address in Westwood, my phone numbers, my e-mail address.

"I never heard from him."

She glided closer to the jury. "I think I know why," she said, almost in a whisper. "This was February 2002, and the so-called priest-sex-abuse-crisis had just hit LA, like it would soon hit two-thirds of all the dioceses in the U.S.A. 'The sex abuse crisis.' This was a polite, shorthand way of saying that hundreds of men and women had finally started approaching the criminal and civil court system, to get what they couldn't get from their own sacred Church: justice, redress for what their priests had been doing to their children." She paused, and took a full half-minute to lock eyes with each of the juror-bishops in turn and said, "Fucking their children."

She paused, and, for almost a full, silent minute, locked eyes with each of the jurors in turn. Finally, she said, "I know, this is not a pretty word. I have never used it before, and, after today, maybe I never will again. But we have to call things by their right names, so you can be shocked into understanding.

"Priests—the men we were taught to revere and trust as 'other Christs' —were doing little boys and teenagers, too. Their bishops knew what they were up to. And they covered it up. Even worse, if someone blew the whistle on a particular priest, the bishops paid him for his silence and transferred the erring priest to another assignment. You may ask why they did this. I think you know. They did it to avoid scandal. 'To avoid scandal.' Now what did that mean? It meant their first loyalty was not to the people, but to the institution—that is, to themselves and to the members of their clerical club.

"These, your Excellencies, are the facts."

Paul Kelly whispered in the cardinal's ear. "She's bad. And she's not even a lawyer."

The cardinal sneered, "She just plays one on TV."

Juana Margarita Obregón told a story about Mahony's tenure as bishop of Stockton, California, in the 1970s, when he covered up for a priest named Oliver O'Grady, a confessed molester of two brothers and at least twenty other children, an equal opportunity sex maniac who targeted boy children and girl children, while having illicit affairs with at least two of the children's mothers. "It took years," she said, "for that kind of story—and hundreds of other similar stories all around the country—to emerge. Most Catholics just did not want to believe them. Most editors did not want to believe them. They only did so when the *New York Times* finally started to run with them. There is a saying in the United States—that if an event has not been reported in the *Times*, it has not happened. Well, your Excellencies, during a forty-five day period in March and April of 2002, the story started to happen. The good, gray *New York Times* had a Page One piece on the crisis every one of those forty-five days but one. The *Boston Globe* put a half dozen reporters on the trail of Cardinal Law, who, it turned out, had been protecting more than two hundred priests in the Boston area. The *New Times* in Los Angeles did an eight-part series on the sins of Cardinal Mahony.

"At first, it looked like the archbishop of Los Angeles had understood the situation in a way that the archbishop of Boston did not. He protested his innocence and vowed that his Church would pursue a policy of total transparency. When all the U.S. bishops met in Dallas in May of 2002, Cardinal Mahony stepped out in front of his fellow bishops and pushed through a get-tough policy on priest-pedophiles. Zero tolerance, he called it. As it turned out, he did not really mean that. He was just grandstanding. In fact, as we will prove before this court, the cardinal has spent more than fifteen million dollars in legal fees, paying LA's highest priced lawyers to keep his priests and himself out of court, and to help him fight off the efforts of the district attorney in Los Angeles to get information on the malefactors. I wonder if the cardinal ever had time, then, to review the taped testimony I had gathered from the little people of LA?" She looked over to the cardinal, as if to confirm her surmise.

His lawyer turned to him, too, and Mahony shook his head and whispered, "Tapes? I never saw any tapes."

"Now," said Juana Margarita Obregón, "he will have a chance to see them."

She stopped and moved closer to the bishops on the jury. "I am going to ask the judge to give us a ten minute recess here. We will have a long morning."

INSIDE THE THIRD-FLOOR OFFICE of the secretary of state in the Vatican's Apostolic Palace, Cardinal Tarcisio Bertone, the pope's secretary of state—in effect, the sovereign's prime minister—exhaled a mighty breath. He and his staff and three other Curial cardinals were watching this mock trial and they didn't like what they were seeing.

"Television!" said Cardinal Bertone. In his mouth, the word was an expletive.

Cardinal Gianbattista Re used another favorite cuss word in the Vatican: "Americans!"

Cardinal Francis Stafford used other expletives. "Liberals! Reformers!"

"Was His Holiness watching this?" asked Bertone.

Stafford said, "We think so, Eminence. Father Lombardi told me the pope insisted earlier today that someone from the communications office come up to the papal apartment to adjust the reception on his giant TV."

FRANCIS OLIVER GRANDEUR, the cardinal-archbishop of Philadelphia, was watching the trial, too. As a practical man, he didn't waste his time whining. At the recess, he picked up the phone and dialed Cardinal Mahony's chancellor in Los Angeles, the man who had been off skiing on the Fish Creek Trail on the morning of the cardinal's abduction.

"Hawk? Fog here." As a graduate student at the North American College in Rome, Jeremiah Hawkslaw had worked on the 1983 revision of canon law with Grandeur. They were close enough (no one knew how close) to use each other's nicknames, stuck on them by their classmates at the NAC, still sticking in their maturity. "Hawk" was obvious. "Fog" evolved from Grandeur's initials. "I assume, Hawk, that you've been watching the show? Uh huh. Uh huh. Well, look here. They've given us some leads. Did you hear this Obregón woman say she'd sent a copy of her tapes to the cardinal? Along with her address and phone number and e-mail address?"

When Monsignor Jeremiah Hawkslaw said he had never seen—or even heard of—the tapes, Grandeur said, "Well they've got to be around somewhere. See if you can find them. And especially her note. When you do, get back to me. With those coordinates, the FBI can put a trace on her. I'll bet they can find her in twelve hours."

JUANA MARGARITA OBREGÓN fiddled with some knobs on a video playback machine, and invited the judge and the cardinal and his lawyer to take a stand behind the jury so they, too, could see the videotaped testimony. As they were making their move from the defendant's table, Mahony could see the red light blink on one of the large video cameras in the back of the room that was aimed at him, and he thought, *How convenient! While viewers around the world are watching these witnesses and hearing their stories on tape, they can also get a look at my live reactions—and close-ups of the jurors' faces, too, as they take in the testimony. This kind of television will entertain a good many viewers—at my expense.*

Juana presented her first witness, a slim woman named Amelia Rodríguez from Boyle Heights in East LA who cleaned homes for a living in the Hollywood Hills. *Para los otros* was conducting the trial in English, but, for strategic reasons, Juana Margarita Obregón had decided to give the Spanish-speaking jurors their first taste of testimony in Spanish. Let them

25

hear the sincerity of Señora Rodríguez in their own language. Let them hear the choked words and the pathos.

She said she was a single mother with twelve-year-old twins serving as altar boys at St. Martin's Parish on Atlantic Boulevard when they were taken under the tutelage of the new assistant pastor, Father Stephen Wellsprings. She said, "He took them places. To Dodger games and Disneyland and McDonald's. And I was happy, because the boys never knew their father, and I thought it was good for them to have a man in their lives. When the priest asked if he could take Miguel to his cabin at Big Bear during Thanksgiving weekend in 1986, I said, 'Yes, if you take Antonio, too.' He promised he would take Antonio during Christmas vacation, so I said, 'Yes, fine.' I shouldn't have done that, never should have let them go separately. But this man was a priest! I never suspected a thing.

"Ten years later, when the boys were twenty-two, they confessed that Father Wellsprings had used them sexually—and separately—for several years running. Miguel never told Antonio. And Antonio never told Miguel. They never told anyone, until last year, when all the stories started coming out in the *LA Times* about Father Wellsprings. He had been seducing boys for years. The worst thing was that, years before, some parents in his first parish, Good Shepherd in Beverly Hills, had complained about Father Wellsprings and Cardinal Mahony had persuaded them to keep quiet—for the good of the Church. And then he moved Father Wellsprings from Beverly Hills to one parish after another—but always to parishes in the barrio, never back to the West Side."

Here, the woman's voice thickened. She said, "Father Wellsprings made the boys into *jotos*. Last year, Antonio died of AIDS. Then his brother Miguel committed suicide." Here, Juana had used her zoom lens to capture an extreme close up of Señora Rodríguez. She wept, then dug into her purse and produced the last pictures she had taken of her twins. "They were beautiful boys," she said, holding up the photos and looking bleakly into Juana's lens. "So blond, so fair. Now they are in hell, suffering the fires of the damned. And Padre Wellsprings"—she spat out the word *Padre*—"Padre Wellsprings is still a priest."

Kelly turned to see the cardinal's reaction. The cardinal was starting to hyperventilate.

CNN HADN'T BOUGHT THE FEED from *Para los otros*, but that network could make fair use of excerpts from the morning's proceedings, and did. For twelve hours, in fact every hour on the hour, CNN repeated the last running minute of Señora Rodríguez's testimony, tears and all, along with this exchange between CNN's London news desk and John Allen in St. Peter's Square.

"Perhaps you can tell us, John," said Suzy Walker, "what this grieving mother meant when she said this priest, this Father Wellsprings, is still a priest. How can this be?"

"Well, Suzy, she's right. The Vatican—and here I mean the pope himself—is being very careful. The pope loves the priesthood—and his priests. And he won't let anyone sully them—or trash the priesthood. According to Section 1470 of Canon Law, priests who are accused of serious crimes have a right to a trial—in secret of course. That can often mean a delay of as many as ten years."

"You mean they go on being priests?"

"Technically, yes," said Allen. "But often enough, they are sent off to some remote monastery on a mountaintop."

"Wow!"

"But just as often," said Allen, "these priests simply fade away. They get tired of the hassle."

"Okay, John. But one more thing. This mother says she knows her boys are in hell. Is that what the Church teaches?"

"Suzy," said Allen, "the Church doesn't say that. The Church says there's a hell, but it has never officially declared that anybody's in hell. Not even Hitler."

"But a lot of simple Catholics still take comfort believing in hell?"

"Well, Suzy, I wouldn't say comfort."

INSIDE THE CAVERNOUS CONTROL ROOM of the National Security Agency in Maryland, three technicians yanked off their headsets, rose to their feet with a cry of victory, and hustled over to their chief. "Our satellite found 'em, Charlie. We know where they are. Bogotá!"

FOR THE REST OF THE MORNING, Juana Margarita Obregón presented the jury with one videotaped interview after another. The juror-bishops, despite their age, more than managed to pay attention. When Paul Kelly and the cardinal grew tired standing behind them, they were given high-rise directors' chairs to perch upon.

Kelly was riveted by the taped testimony of a priest named Thomas Doyle who had once worked in the Vatican's Washington embassy. He told Juana Margarita Obregón's video cam that he had helped write a report to the U.S. bishops in the early '80s, warning them they could face financial liabilities of a billion dollars within ten years if they didn't enact sweeping reforms. Doyle was a virile, square-jawed Dominican wearing a U.S. Air Force chaplain's uniform. He said, "We told the bishops they had to put priests accused of sexual misconduct on the shelf, report them to law enforcement, never reassign them to new parishes. But that was the cardinal's M.O. He sent one molester on to serve in seven different parishes even after he knew what the man was doing.

"Mahony did send some of his men off for treatment. He sent them to the Paraclete Fathers in Jemez Springs, New Mexico. The priests who were sent there called it Camp Ped. But the Paracletes didn't have a clue. They gave their patients furloughs, sometimes for weeks at a stretch, to fill in as parish priests around the West, and then they turned them loose, so they could get assignments elsewhere, where they molested other kids."

In his director's chair, the cardinal coughed and crumpled and studied the back of his hand.

On tape, Doyle said, "Cardinal Mahony ignored our report, and went right on doing what he'd been doing for the past seventeen years. He's been part of the problem, not part of the solution. He helped set up an ad hoc advisory committee on sexual abuse, but it was just public relations, a joke, a fluff move."

Kelly whispered in the cardinal's ear. "We'll get a chance to rebut all this."

The cardinal gave Kelly a bleary-eyed stare. "Yeah? I doubt it. I doubt that very much."

"You know," said Kelly, "you may be right." He heaved his huge bulk off the director's chair and turned to the judge. "Your Honor, I'd like to cross-examine Father Doyle."

"Father Doyle is not here."

"Exactly. He and all of these so-called witnesses are shadows on a television screen. How can I cross-examine any of them?"

"Obviously, you cannot."

"Then you must allow me some leeway here."

"Leeway?"

"To make an argument to the jury. I know. It isn't time yet for an argument from the defense. But I need to make it now, while these charges are still fresh in the minds of the jury."

The judge recognized Dr. Obregón.

"Let's hear it," she said. "Let's hear Mr. Kelly's argument now. We could all use some enlightenment here."

"All right," said Díaz. "Go ahead, Mr. Kelly."

Kelly stammered in surprise, but continued. "It is unfair, utterly unfair, to judge the cardinal's handling of pedophile priests twenty years ago. He—indeed, most of the bishops—were relying on the best advice of mental-health experts at the time. Now, everyone is taking the matrix of today's knowledge and placing that matrix on what happened fifteen, twenty, thirty years ago."

Díaz listened, then turned to Juana Margarita Obregón.

She said she was dumbstruck over this argument. "Just when did the cardinal learn that it is illegal to have sex with a minor?" she asked. "This had-we-only-known defense is just another type of denial, a rationalization. I have some testimony on this very issue. If I may, your Honor?"

He nodded. "All right."

"Wait a minute," objected Kelly.

"You opened the door," said Díaz. "You cannot object if Dr. Obregón wants to walk through that door."

Kelly threw up his hands. "Jesus!"

"That, I take it," said the judge, "is a prayer?"

Kelly mumbled, "Yes, your Honor, a prayer."

By now, Juana Margarita Obregón had her rebuttal-tape ready. It was an interview she had had with Gary Schoener, a clinical psychologist from Minnesota who had consulted in hundreds of sex-abuse cases involving priests. "Even after it was well-known that a lot of these priests had problems that were beyond fixing," he was saying on tape, "the bishops just kept sending these priests to New Mexico and Maryland and Connecticut for treatment rather than getting rid of them. It gave them a moral out."

• FOUR •

TESTIMONY

HIGH UP ON THE THIRD FLOOR of the Vatican's Apostolic Palace, those meeting in the cardinal secretary of state's office wanted to know more about this Tomàs Doyle. "You say he is a Dominican priest?" said Cardinal Re.

Cardinal Stafford said, "Yes, and he also went on active duty as a chaplain in the U.S. Air Force after the bishops ignored his report."

"The bishops did nothing about that report?"

Cardinal Stafford said, "Some of them read it, and made it operative. When one pastor told his bishop in St. Cloud, Minnesota, that he had a young assistant who was abusing little boys, the bishop said, 'Call the police. The priest should be in jail.' They had no more problems in St. Cloud. Where bishops ignored the report, they had problems. Tons of problems in places like Boston and Los Angeles."

Cardinal Re turned to Cardinal Bertone. "This Tomàs Doyle. He once worked for us?"

"Correct," said Bertone.

"In effect, he was working for your predecessor, Cardinal Sodano?"

"Yes. In the Vatican Embassy in Washington."

"Why did he leave?"

"He was fired."

"Why was he fired?"

"We judged that Doyle's report could only bring shame on the Church. To distance ourselves from the report, we had to distance ourselves from Doyle, too. In Italy, as you know, we do not talk about these matters."

"We didn't talk much about them in the United States either," said Stafford. "Until recently."

"The secretariat should not have let Doyle go," said Re.

"Right!" said Stafford. "As Lyndon Johnson used to say, 'Better to have the polecat inside the tent pissing out, than have the polecat outside the tent pissing in.'"

Re said, "What is polecat?"

Stafford scissored his nose. *Marzetta.* "Skunk."

Re chortled. Then his face darkened, and he said, "This Leen-doan John-soan was a wise man. Doyle was working for us, and we fired him. We are not wise men, your Eminence. We are fools."

Stafford muttered to himself, *If Re only knew the whole story.* One of the Vatican's company men had Doyle terminated as an Air Force chaplain, too, and put pressure on the Dominicans to bar him from living in any Dominican residence. Doyle went on to testify in civil lawsuits all over the United States—to the benefit of the abuse victims, and to the loss of many an American bishop. *Fools indeed.*

IN THE COURTROOM, Juana Margarita Obregón clicked the remote for her video machine and fast-forwarded to another segment of her tape. "This testimony," she said, "comes from a highly respected theologian at the University of Notre Dame. His name is Richard McBrien."

On the video, the jurors saw the image of a large, jowly priest with a five o'clock shadow who said, "The bishops have done little or nothing to address this problem. The proof of that is in the scope and intensity of the current crisis. If they had done something significant, we would not be in the mess we're in today."

Eugene Cullen Kennedy, a famed priest-psychologist from Chicago, told Juana Margarita Obregón's video cam why the bishops hadn't done anything significant. He had spoken to her during the huge Congressman Foley scandal that threatened Republicans facing re-election in the fall of 2006. Kennedy told her, "It is never 'women and children first' when a Titanic like the Church or Congress grazes an iceberg. Hierarchs wear their life jackets as if they were grafted on and never move far from a lifeboat. Their instincts are to preserve themselves and their power and the structure that is the source of that power.

"The bishops want to be pastors just as the members of Congress want to be public servants. They override these good intentions with the acquired hierarchical sense that their destiny is to govern and save from harm a vast establishment. They do not want to see young people endangered but they honestly feel they protect the latter's interests best by protecting their own interests first. Congress helps us understand how the bishops reacted—not out of bad will but out of their nature as men who attained their status by giving themselves to a system whose property, power and privilege they feel they must preserve."

Kelly turned to Mahony. "Is that the way it is? Is that the way it really is?"

Much as he hated to admit it, Mahony nodded. Kennedy had it right.

NEXT, THE JURORS SAW THE FACE of a handsome, middle-aged man identified by letters across the bottom of the screen as David Clohessy. "This man," said Juana Margarita Obregón, "is the national director of SNAP, the Survivors' Network of those Abused by Priests. This clip follows an impromptu meeting between Cardinal Mahony, two other bishops and a group of eight sex-abuse victims during a recess at a meeting in 2002 of the National Conference of Catholic Bishops. Here is David Clohessy's account of that meeting. I am asking the questions, off camera."

Dr. Obregón clicked her video controller and the jurors saw Clohessy, and heard him say, "In private, the cardinal was all business with us, even a bit confrontational. But as soon as the session ended and members of the news media poured into the room to surround the cardinal, I saw a different Cardinal Mahony under the glare of TV lights. Standing three feet from the cardinal, I listened as he told the assembled broadcast and print reporters how moved he was by what he had just heard from us. It felt phony. It was as if he'd switched on an entirely different set of emotions for the cameras. It didn't sound sincere. Then and there this awful feeling crept over me that we were being used."

Doctor Obregón asked him whether Cardinal Mahony had taken leadership on this issue at an emergency meeting of the U.S. bishops in Dallas.

"Big role," said Clohessy. "Mahony made a big deal about pushing his bishops into a new policy, something he called zero tolerance. That meant that one misstep in this area by any priest and he was out of there."

"This was his idea?"

"He told everyone this was his idea. It wasn't his idea. It was forced on him by the terms of a settlement with Ryan DiMaria, a young man from Orange County who'd been molested in 1991 by Michael Harris, the priest-principal of Santa Margarita High School in Orange County."

"Tell me more about DiMaria?"

"By then, DiMaria was twenty-four years old, and a recent law school graduate. He was not so much interested in a cash settlement. What he wanted more than anything was to make a difference, so that other kids might not have to suffer what Michael Harris did to him. Among his demands were a zero tolerance policy, a toll-free victim hotline and the distribution of materials about sex abuse to parishes and schools. DiMaria won a change in the way the archdiocese keeps its internal records. DiMaria even won a commitment that the archdiocese would conduct exit interviews for graduates from its seminary in Camarillo that would quiz them on promiscuous same-sex sex in the seminary."

That caused a stir among the juror-bishops, who whispered furiously among themselves. One of them called out to Mahony in Spanish, "Sodomites in the seminary! For shame!" Everyone in the courtroom shuddered, but Kelly raised no objection, and Iván Díaz pretended he hadn't heard.

So did Dr. Obregón. She put the videotape machine on pause and said, "The next witness you will see and hear, Excellencies, is Ron Russell, the writer for the *New Times* in LA who has become something of an expert on Cardinal Mahony."

From his director's chair behind the juror's box, Kelly raised an objection. "Testimony from a reporter! This has to be hearsay, your Honor."

Iván Díaz said to Kelly and to Dr. Obregón, "Would you please approach the bench." When they paused, he said, "Well, there is no what they call 'bench.' Just come up here."

Díaz whispered to Dr. Obregón, "Is Mr. Kelly correct? Is this reporter, this Mr. Russell, simply passing on second-hand information?"

"No, your Honor. Ron Russell, the writer, will show the jury some documentary evidence of the cardinal's early public relations campaign to hoodwink his Catholic constituency. It began with a pastoral letter in the *Tidings*, the archdiocese's official newspaper. In it, the cardinal pledged to do all that is humanly possible to prevent sexual abuse in the LA Archdiocese."

"Do you have a copy of that pastoral letter. Dr. Obregón?"

"Yes."

"Well, then, why don't you just introduce that letter in evidence? You don't need Ron Russell to read it out loud."

"Your Honor? We're on television, worldwide television. Somebody has to read it."

"Well, then, you had better read it. Lawyer Kelly is right. We cannot allow hearsay testimony in this courtroom. After all, as you've pointed out, we are on worldwide TV, and we cannot let a worldwide TV audience get the impression that we are stacking this deck against the cardinal. We cannot fight injustice with injustice."

"But your Honor," she protested.

"Just you read it," said Iván Díaz.

Juana Margarita Obregón blushed, went back to her counsel table, and riffled through a file box. When she found the copy of the *Tidings* she was looking for, she said, "Here is the pastoral letter. I will read the most important part of it. 'Let me state very clearly,' it says. 'The Archdiocese of Los Angeles will not knowingly assign or retain a priest, deacon, religious or lay person to serve in its parishes, schools, pastoral ministries or any other assignment when such an individual is determined to have previously engaged in the sexual abuse of a minor.' And those are the cardinal's words."

"And what do they prove?" asked Díaz.

"On their face, only this, that the cardinal had cobbled together a tough assault on the malefactors. The implicit message was that other Catholic bishops might appear flat-footed in the face of the worst scandal to rock the church in centuries, but that Roger Mahony was the man with a plan. But the plan wasn't his. It had been forced on him by DiMaria. Mahony's actions amounted to little more than a public-relations campaign designed by Sitrick and Company."

The judge asked, "What is Sitrick and Company?"

"The Enron Corporation's former public-relations firm. Sitrick advised the cardinal to appoint a lay board. He already had a secret board of lay advisors. Now he was going public with a new panel, called the Clergy Misconduct Oversight Board. He said it represented 'another chapter in the efforts of the archdiocese . . . to make certain all churches are safe for children and young people.' But the trouble was this board had no power. The cardinal said he could not surrender that authority 'because only bishops are empowered under canon law to make personnel decisions about priests.'"

The judge said, "That's quite right. That's what canon law says."

Over in the jury box, the bishops whispered to one another. The voice of Recife rose over the others. He was quoting Jesus' words. "Is the Sabbath made for man, or man for the Sabbath?"

THROUGH MOST OF THE MORNING'S TESTIMONY, Mahony's face was a blank. But his stomach began to rumble so loudly that María became alarmed. Twice during the testimonies, she brought him water and a Prozac. When they broke for lunch and siesta time, Mahony told Kelly he didn't want anything to eat. He just wanted to lie down. "I can understand," said Kelly. "I can smell your breath. You smell like a cesspool."

Mahony rose, shaking his head, abashed at Kelly's comparison. María escorted him off, not to the cell he had slept in for the two previous nights, but to a grander room, a room with a flush toilet and running water. That was María's idea. She told *el presidente* that treating the cardinal like a criminal had tamed him. "He won't try to flee."

"Is there something I can bring you?" María said as he hobbled toward his bed.

He shook his head. "You're the only one who dares be nice to me," he said. "I am a worm and no man." It was a quote from Isaiah, often used in the context of the Crucifixion story.

She went to the bathroom, wet a small towel, folded it and brought it back to him. "Here, put this on your brow." He put his head back and let her do it. "I will see if I can bring you some chicken soup."

He nodded, eyes closed, his breath coming in short sobs.

DURING THE AFTERNOON'S TESTIMONY, scheduled to run from three to six, a parade of witnesses recounted Mahony's imperious ways. "I chaired one of his lay committees," said a retired Catholic lawyer named Skip Riley. Juana Margarita Obregón had pulled out his taped testimony and put it before the jurors because it bore directly on the last discussion of the morning. "We weren't allowed our own judgments," said Riley. "We did what he told us to do. We were just figureheads. He made us understand his hands were tied—by canon law."

Retired Irish priests from Los Angeles were the most outspoken. One of them, Monsignor Sean Breen, said Mahony preened himself on public attention. "We weren't a wee bit surprised," said the monsignor, "to see him open the Democratic National Convention in Los Angeles. He looooved the limelight."

Mahony uttered a low groan. Kelly looked at his watch and declared, "Your Honor, we want to say, 'Uncle!'"

Iván Díaz said he didn't understand.

"We give up. This shouldn't go on. This is cruel and unusual punishment. This is—it's un-American." Kelly stammered for a moment, realizing that argument wouldn't carry any weight here, and tried to think of something more telling. He chose a bullfight metaphor. "It's like the picadors have weakened the bull enough. Isn't it time to send in the matador?"

Díaz consulted his prosecutor. Juana Margarita Obregón said, "Cardinal Mahony has spent millions in legal fees to keep this kind of testimony out of civil court. Now we can present it to the court of world opinion. We have seventy more hours of tape."

"Oh my God!" moaned Mahony.

Díaz looked distressed. "I am tending to agree with Mr. Kelly. The bull is reeling right now. And so, I am going to make a ruling, Dr. Obregón. I want you to pick out three more testimonies to help you complete your case. You said you were going to show how the cardinal has forgotten the sacred duties of his episcopal office, how the cardinal—" Díaz consulted his notes—"has let the unwritten rules of his clerical club undermine the rule of the Gospel itself, and how he has robbed the patrimony of Christ's poor to enrich his lawyers. I am particularly interested in knowing to what extent he has enriched his lawyers—rather than help the victims of his cover-ups."

She nodded. "We will try to do that, your Honor."

"Can you get it all completed tomorrow morning? Then we'll let Mr. Kelly and the cardinal decide whether he wants to take the stand in his own defense."

THE U.S. MARINES—fifty men in a half-dozen helicopters—zeroed in on a jungle clearing ten kilometers northwest of Bogotá. They had a simple mission: to break up the mock trial of the cardinal-archbishop of Los Angeles, rescue the cardinal, and bring him back to Los Angeles. Military intelligence told them to expect little opposition from what, they were assured, was a tiny group of wannabe revolutionaries inspired by something called "liberation theology." This news helped their commanding officer, Colonel Robert McCurdy, a 1992 graduate of Notre Dame, conclude that Mahony's captors were Godly people who eschewed violence of any kind. "Our intelligence," he told his battalion, "says this will be a piece of cake."

The oxymoron called military intelligence was flawed. McCurdy and his men had been directed to a marijuana farm that also happened to be the headquarters of Colombia's deadliest drug cartel. Its well-armed private army met McCurdy's approach with withering rocket fire, forcing him back to his base on the U.S. carrier *Enterprise*. He radioed his superiors at Camp Lejeune, "Better recheck your coordinates. We lost two choppers. We're lucky we got four choppers back to the carrier at all."

THE SECRETARY OF DEFENSE picked up the phone and told the President of the United States about the latest military fuckup. "Well," said the leader of the free world, "we gotta use more force. Go in there, Bobby, and kill 'em! Kill 'em all."

"We sent our men to the wrong place. It might help if we found the right place."

"That too," said the president.

WHEN MARÍA BROUGHT THE CARDINAL his evening meal on a tray, she was pleased to find him sitting up in bed, writing on his laptop. "Supper time!" she cried.

He shook his head. "I cannot eat."

"You have to eat."

"It's cold in here."

It was true. At this altitude, in mid-November, the nights were getting cooler. "That is why you have to eat something. Please. Come and eat. Here is some chicken stew, with rice. And I brought you a glass of red wine."

The cardinal grunted. A glass of wine sounded good. He hit the Save key on his laptop computer. He had been composing a list under the rubric THINGS TO DO—if he ever got out of here. He set the Macintosh aside, eased off the bed, and made his way to the table where María had set up supper for him. She helped him adjust the blanket he had wrapped around his shoulders like a cape, then sat down with him. "You're being good to me," he said. "I do not deserve it."

"Not deserve?"

"You've heard what my people say about me. I thought they loved me. Now I know." He looked up at her. "They hate me."

"They do not hate you. They have been disappointed. You could be better than you are."

He scowled. How many times had he said that to his younger priests? Nobody ever told him he could be better than he was. From his earliest days in the seminary, he was a star. As a young priest, working with the farm workers of César Chávez in Delano, he was a star. As a young bishop, testifying before a legislative committee in Sacramento, he was a star. He was always a star. He thought about that as he swallowed a spoonful of stew. "María, when I became a bishop, they said it was possible I would never hear the truth again."

She laughed. "And when you became a cardinal, it was certain."

"On that score, it is not good to be a cardinal."

"On that score," she said, "is it good to be a pope?"

He looked at her with curiosity. She seemed wise beyond her years. He'd known John Paul II for more than 20 years, and, out of fear, he had never told the pope the whole truth about anything.

María pressed on. "I am wondering," she said, "how hard it must be for a pope if no one ever tells him things he doesn't want to hear."

He reflected on that. "Maybe his aides knew it was easier for him to rule as he did, with never a doubt about anything, if he didn't know what was really happening. In any event, he was not the kind of man who listened. I wondered sometimes if he understood his own Church."

"Do you?"

"What?"

"Understand your own Church?"

Her fearless question startled him. He gave it some thought. "More today," he said finally, "than I did yesterday."

"Are you the kind of man who understands yourself?"

That question called for even deeper thought. "I have been very busy serving the Church."

"Which Church? The institutional Church or the people of God Church?"

"I never thought there was any difference. I loved the Church, I loved the liturgy, I loved theology."

She paused. "Have you ever loved a woman?"

"Loved a woman? No." Then he heard himself blurting out words that he had not planned. "But I am beginning to love you." He touched her hand.

She pulled it away. "You only think you do," she whispered. She tried to take the edge off her rejection by smiling. "Did you ever hear of the Stockholm Syndrome? Like, Patty Hearst fell in love with her kidnappers?"

That startled him. He shook his head, finished off his wine, and set down his glass. His eyes filled with tears. He was certainly doing a lot of crying this week.

She rose, took his hand, helped him remove his red cassock, sat him on his bed, and unlaced his shoes. When he swiveled into bed and his head hit the pillow, she circled to the other side of the bed, climbed next to him, her front to his back, and held him in the dark, save for the flickering candle some ten feet away.

"Has any woman ever held you like this?" she asked.

He'd never been this close to a woman. This woman smelled like a peach. "No," he said. "Why are you holding me?"

"Because I am a woman. If a woman knows how to comfort a man, she should do it."

That startled him, too, and he lay there in silence, pondering her words. "If a woman knows how to comfort a man, she should do it." Curious. Why should she do this for him? He began to sob, again, but then, warmed by her touch, he fell into a deep but troubled sleep. In her arms.

• FIVE •

VERDICT

THE JUROR-BISHOPS WERE SHOCKED when they saw and heard the videotaped testimony of Albert Gonzalez, a former archdiocesan official—one of four archdiocesan executives who quit their jobs in Los Angeles on the same day in April 2003. He said that Mahony's blue chip lawyer, Cyrus Cheatham, had already billed (and collected) $15 million for his services over the past five years. Much of the billed time paid for efforts to convince a judge that the cardinal could not turn over the files on several dozen priests who had been accused of tampering with young people, most of them teen-aged boys.

Cheatham argued that Mahony had a confidential relationship with each of his priests, much like the relationship between a lawyer and his clients. The judge denied the argument, and Cheatham appealed the decision. It was denied by the California Court of Appeals, and Cheatham appealed again, to the California Supreme Court, which finally decided against Mahony. But he was still stalling. "Whatever else the appeal did," said Chabolla, "it bought the cardinal some time. And left more than five hundred lawsuits filed by abuse victims in limbo."

Each of the poor juror-bishops wondered what he might have done for his people with Cheatham's $15 million. They sat up a little straighter and craned their necks to get a look at Dr. Obregón's next witness.

On tape, they saw an attractive blonde who identified herself as Justice Anne Burke of the Illinois Supreme Court, and a mother of four. Judge Burke told Juana Margarita Obregón about her appointment to the

American Bishops' National Review Board for the Protection of Children and Young People. "I'm not sure how I got on the board," she said. "I later learned the board was designed by a New York p.r. firm to serve as window dressing for the bishops."

"Window dressing?"

"People got the impression the bishops would be accountable to us. But when the bishops started balking at our questions, we realized they wouldn't stand for that. We couldn't even tell the press what was happening. They forced our chairman, Governor Frank Keating, an Oklahoma Republican, off the committee."

"What was the board supposed to do?"

"As it turned out, nothing. Our mandate was quite vague. We thought we were appointed to oversee what the bishops were doing about the scandal, but we soon realized the bishops didn't want us to do that. They soon forced our chairman out for telling the press their actions reminded him of a criminal organization, not his Church, resisting grand jury subpoenas, suppressing the names of offending clerics, denying, obfuscating, explaining away. I took his place, and was given the title of 'interim chairman.'"

"Didn't the National Review Board issue a report?"

"Yes. Two of them on February 27, 2004. One was an audit conducted by the John Jay College of Criminal Justice in Manhattan, but it wasn't much of an audit. They didn't go out and dig up any facts about priest-abusers, or interview their victims. They sent out a questionnaire and let the bishops make their own reports. Their report said several thousand priests—some four percent of priests in ministry over the last half-century—committed acts of sexual abuse of minors. On the same day, our board also issued our own Report on the Crisis in the Catholic Church of the United States. It said the bishops failed to grasp the gravity of the problem of sexual abuse of minors by priests, made unwarranted presumptions in favor of accused priests, relied on secrecy to avoid scandal, put too much stock on the advice of their lawyers—who intimidated many of the victims—and failed to hold themselves accountable for the mistakes they made. We said they could have used the advice of laypeople."

"Did you make recommendations?"

"We made a number of them."

"How did the bishops follow through on those recommendations?"

"They didn't. They tied them up with parliamentary delays. In March 2004, we had a showdown of sorts at the USCCB's headquarters in Washington. The bishops all sat there in their padded leather seats, each of them with a microphone, like in the United Nations General Assembly. The bishops held us off until they could meet in plenary session late in the year. They didn't really want any more audits. And, so far, they haven't let the board do any more of them."

"How many of the bishops wanted you to continue?"

"Very few. I can count them on one hand. Cardinal Mahony made great sanctimonious statements, but in the end, he voted with all the others (privately of course) to quash a second audit. He continued to tell the public that all priest-predators had been put away, but it turned out that a convicted priest-pedophile was a guest in his own rectory all along.

"These guys are tricky, masters at obfuscation who get tied up in their own wordy evasions. And when they cannot evade, they attack. Henry J. Mansell, the archbishop of Hartford, ripped the board members for 'expanding their competence, responsibilities, activities and studies in a dynamic of autonomy.' "

"What is 'a dynamic of autonomy?' " asked Juana Margarita Obregón.

"I don't know. I guess 'a dynamic of autonomy' is more powerful than simple autonomy. You'd have to ask the archbishop. But it was clear that many bishops didn't like us because we threatened their authority. Archbishop Charles Chaput objected to 'the tone' of one of our letters. 'Your language,' he said, 'is designed to offend. . . . Whatever its goals, your letter diminishes the credibility of the NRB and invites resistance.' Bishop Ignatius Dreedle of Buffalo Tooth, Nebraska, made personal attacks on members of the board. Whenever the bishops spoke, they continued to refer to 'the Church' without ever mentioning their own people or acknowledging that these victims are the Church and that they themselves are their servants rather than their masters."

"What have the bishops learned through all this?"

"Nothing that I can see. They continue to relate to the people by being pompously official rather than simply human."

"And your 143-page report?"

"At this point, it looks like a dead letter to me. The bishops haven't implemented our recommendations. And the bishops continue to insist the board had no right to investigate them."

JUANA MARGARITA OBREGÓN punched up her last tape. It was an interview with a pretty young Filipina named Gloria Verdugo, who told her story haltingly, and, for that very reason, it came across as true. A Southern California priest from the Philippines named Ramón had found her begging and homeless in Pershing Square. He rescued her, set her up in her own apartment off Pico Boulevard, and introduced her to three of his priest-friends, all from the Philippines, whom Mahony had imported to help him deal with his priest-shortage in Los Angeles. She said to Juana Margarita Obregón's video cam, "They took turns with me. In me. Four of them, every day until—" She paused.

"Until what, Gloria?"

"Until I got pregnant. When they learned I had told a social worker about my condition, they slapped me around. When they found I had gone to the police, they went into a panic. Ramón phoned the cardinal's office. Two days later, they were all jetting back to the Philippines on the same flight. When I asked one of them why they were leaving, he said Cardinal Mahony ordered them back to the Philippines—'to avoid arrest.' He paid for their jet fare. Paid me, too, for my silence."

"How do you know it was Cardinal Mahony who paid you?"

"I figured that out for myself. Next day, a lawyer came—a middle-aged woman who told me she worked for the archdiocese. She had me sign a paper, gave me ten thousand dollars in hundred-dollar bills, helped me pack up my things and drove me to a Catholic home for unwed mothers, with the understanding—I had to sign a paper that I would tell no one who the father was."

"Who was the father?"

"I don't know which one. That is how I could promise never to tell who the father was. One of them."

One of the jurors rose and cried, "For shame!" The others nodded in agreement, but urged him to sit down.

Mahony covered his face with his hands.

Juana Margarita Obregón pretended not to notice. She turned to the judge. "That's all we want to put in evidence, your Honor. The prosecution rests."

Iván Díaz asked Kelly if his client would take the stand.

Kelly whispered for almost a minute into the cardinal's ear. Finally, Mahony nodded. "Your Honor," said Kelly, "my client and I need five minutes here."

Juana Margarita Obregón told the judge, "If it will be of any help to Mr. Kelly, I have twenty questions." She waved a sheet of paper. "Twenty questions that I intend to ask the cardinal."

Kelly rose to receive the sheet of paper, then shuffled back to Mahony at the defendant's table. He handed over the sheet and whispered to him. "You want to answer these questions?"

Mahony studied the questions, and said nothing.

"Well?" said Kelly.

Mahony shook his head, thinking, *How can I?*

"How about this one?" Kelly said in a low voice. "Did you or did you not tell the Oliver O'Grady jury back in Stockton that you believed some of Father O'Grady's victims 'liked it?' What would you say to that?"

"If I denied I said that," offered Mahony, "the jurors would know I was lying. If I admitted saying it, they'd see me as some kind of monster."

"Uh huh. Okay. Here's another question. 'In December of 2006, the *Los Angeles Times* reported the archdiocese owned more than four billion dollars in real property. Yet in your public financial statement for the same year, you claim four hundred ninety-four million in total assets. Can you explain this obvious discrepancy?'"

Mahony shook his head. "No."

"Just for my own information," said Kelly, "tell me who was lying? You or the *Los Angeles Times*?"

Mahony didn't reply.

"Well, if that's the best you can do with these questions," said Kelly, "I am going to tell you—insist—you not take the stand. As your counsel, I have a duty to do that."

Mahony gave a shrugging, silent assent.

Kelly waved to Díaz, and the judge called the court back in session.

"Your honor," said Kelly. "We see no point in having the cardinal take the stand. He will accept the judgment of this court, and, of course, the judgment of his fellow bishops."

"All right then," said Díaz. "Enough."

DURING A SHORT RECESS, the juror-bishops repaired to the courtyard and took time out to consult by satellite telephone with Bishop Samuel Ruiz, the retired bishop of Chiapas, who had been watching the proceedings—somewhere—on television. When they returned to the courtroom, Díaz asked them if they had reached a verdict.

"We have, your Honor," said the jury foreman, Francisco Azevedo, retired auxiliary bishop of Recife.

"And what is that verdict?"

"We find the defendant, Roger Michael Cardinal Mahony, guilty on all accounts, as charged."

"Then," said Díaz, "we will move right on to the sentencing."

Mahony whispered, "That's a relief."

Díaz regarded Mahony for a full, unsmiling minute, then told everyone in the court—and more than 590 million television viewers, "We sentence Cardinal Mahony to become a Christian."

"What?" cried the cardinal. "Sentenced to be a Christian! I have been a Christian all my life."

The bishop from Recife spoke up. "Few have noticed," said Dom Francisco, addressing Mahony directly from the jury box in English. One of the TV cameras zoomed in on his face. "You have been something of a crook. Something of a great pretender. You lied during your depositions. You hid priests behind the statute of limitations. You bought the silence of their victims. You listened to lawyers and let them put legalism ahead of the Gospel. You manipulated the media. You made a great show of listening to your people, but you only heard the high and mighty who were in a position to reward you. Try to think of yourself as a servant of the little people, not their lord and master. You will find many ways of doing that. You might consider selling your helicopter and your fleet of cars. When you go anywhere, you might take the bus, like those women who clean the homes of the rich people in Hollywood."

THE JUDGE SAID, "THIS CASE IS CLOSED." The trial was over. The bishops rose and pushed back their chairs. Mahony was whipped. He did not rise. His shoulders drooped and his face showed nothing of the feelings that churned inside him.

Kelly took the opportunity to speak some frank words to his client. "Excuse me, your Eminence," he said, glancing over his shoulder at the juror-bishops as Díaz was thanking them and shaking their hands. "But I think the jury foreman got it right. Try listening to all your people. Don't tell them what you think they need. Find out what they think they need. And give it to them. And see what you can do about abrogating canon law. It's, it's un-American."

Then hell broke loose. Bombs fell all around the compound, and soldiers appeared out of nowhere, throwing grenades and firing automatic weapons. Mahony saw Díaz and Kelly wilt with bullets to the head and surprise in their eyes. He saw the bodies of the juror-bishops and the television people soften and crumple like rows of tall candles in a hot sun.

He did not see Juana Margarita Obregón. Just as he leaped to knock María to the floor and try to shield her body with his, he heard a commanding voice say, "Don't hit the cardinal!"

Then, for him, everything went black.

· SIX ·

REMEMBERING

CARDINAL MAHONY HAD BEEN IN A COMA for four days, lying flat on his back at Our Lady Queen of Angels Hospital in Los Angeles, his head a helmet of white bandages. Five men huddled in an adjacent room, four bishops in black suits and Roman collars and a priest wearing a black cassock cinctured with a red sash of watered silk. As auxiliary bishops overseeing major parts of the sprawling archdiocese of Los Angeles, they outranked the priest, but they deferred to him. Monsignor Jeremiah Hawkslaw looked younger than his age, fifty-nine. His blond hair was close-cropped and in his red-stockinged feet he stood a fit, muscular 5'6"—which tempted people to underestimate him, until they observed him take over a meeting, as he was taking over this one.

"You've done well with the press—so far," Hawkslaw advised them. "You've been affable, but you've told them nothing, because, in fact, you know nothing. The archdiocese wasn't a player in the drama of the past week. We lost our cardinal—for a time—to a gang of terrorists. That's all we knew. And that's all we said we knew."

"Right. We stonewalled all those crazy charges about Roger," said Fred Snyder.

"And now," said Hawkslaw, "our story is that, thanks to our prayers and the prayers of the faithful, we have him back—such as he is."

"'Such as he is,'" repeated Hector Rubio. "In fact, he's a vegetable."

"Uh huh," agreed Ralph Richley. "Nothing going on up here." He tapped his forehead.

47

Hawkslaw cleared his throat. "Your Excellencies, that's why I called you in this morning," he said. "The neurologists have given me the results of two MRIs." He paused, to dramatize his next words. "I am pleased to report they found no brain damage at all."

"A b-b-bullet to the brain and no b-b-brain damage?" stuttered Thomas Dimleigh. "How do they—"

Jeremiah Hawkslaw cut him off. "One bullet—just one bullet, that is all—grazed the cardinal's skull. The MRIs, as I've already said, Tom, show no brain damage."

"But—"

"The doctors say Roger has just had a major shock. The kidnapping, the, the process they put him through, the massacre. It was all too much to take. Something inside him—some protective, inner guidance system if you will—shut down most of his faculties. The doctors say they will be dormant until—until the shock wears off."

"They're saying it is just a matter of time?" asked Rubio.

Hawkslaw nodded.

"He, he, he's going to be a hun-, a hundred percent o-o-okay?" asked Dimleigh.

Hawkslaw said, "They won't go that far. But there's no clinical reason— that is, there's no observable, measurable reason why he won't be okay. He may need a long, long rest, but that's understandable. And we will give it to him."

THE *LOS ANGELES TIMES* had assigned twenty-three reporters to do a complete recap of Cardinal Mahony's abduction and trial, resulting in a total of forty-seven long pieces that took up much of the *Times'* news hole for a week. The *New York Times* reprinted the entire testimony of the trial, courtesy of *Fox Television News*. Two U.S. television networks did ninety-minute documentaries on the entire affair. Mother Angelica's Eternal Word Television Network ran a critical report on *Para los otros* and the small organization's apparent demise when Mexican Army commandos blasted its headquarters in the mountain jungle near Chiapas. The *Wall Street Journal* carried a Page One story on the left-wing organizations that had provided funds for *Para los otros*—based on leaked documents seized by U.S. troops during their raid in Chiapas. On the day the *Journal* story appeared, Dennis Kucinich, the congressman from Cleveland, Ohio, called for a hearing of the House Armed Services Committee to investigate the Pentagon's interest in the Mahony rescue. "Did we have to kill them all?" asked Kucinich on the floor of the House.

AT TEN IN THE MORNING OF HIS FIFTH DAY at Queen of Angels, Cardinal Mahony opened his eyes, turned his head first one way, then another, sizing up his circumstances. He was obviously a patient in a large, luxury hospital room, somewhere. He called for a nurse and told her he wanted a Diet Pepsi. "I'd also like someone to tell me where I am and what I am doing here," he said.

The nurse scurried out, returned with a tray, a can of Pepsi and a glass of ice, and said, "I called Dr. Sargent. He will be here in a minute."

In less than a minute, William Sargent, a wiry redhead wearing his green scrubs and a pair of Ben Franklin spectacles, burst into the room. After ten minutes with the cardinal, he realized that Roger Mahony certainly knew who he was—but didn't recall anything of his ordeal. "The last thing I remember," the cardinal told him, "I went off for a morning hike." He wanted to know who had won the presidential election.

Dr. Sargent grinned. "We don't know. They're doing a recount right now in Florida."

The cardinal's voice wobbled. "What, uh, what day is this?"

"November 15."

"What year is this?"

"Two thousand and eight."

"And they're doing a recount in Florida?" He rolled his eyes. "Again?"

"Yes, again!"

The cardinal said, "Where's the remote for that TV? I want to see what's happening on CNN."

Sargent had heard the cardinal was a news junkie. His words now helped him decide there was nothing wrong with the cardinal's mental faculties. "Your Eminence," he said, "I think I need a few minutes with my colleagues." He looked around, saw no phone in the cardinal's suite, pulled a cell phone from his pocket and hit the keypad twice.

"Gladys," he said, looking at his watch, "see if Dr. Freedman and Dr. Kazarian can cancel any appointments they may have for lunch today and meet me in my office at noon. Yes. Yes. Oh, I'd say you can tell them it shouldn't take us more than a half hour. Then I want to bring them up to meet with the cardinal."

Sargent looked up at the cardinal and gave him an encouraging look and a smile. "I think we're going to let you go home."

At 12:30 PM, the cardinal was finishing a hospital lunch—roast beef and dry roast potatoes and a small dish of tapioca pudding—and watching CNN when Dr. Sargent strolled in with Drs. Freedman and Kazarian in tow. Dr. Sargent informed the cardinal that he'd gone through a horrendous series of events. "I won't even tell you what they were. But you've blocked them from your memory. You're suffering—but we would hardly call it suffering, you're fortunate—from post-anterior amnesia."

"Meaning?"

"When people have a car accident, for example, sometimes they do not only not remember the accident. They do not even remember the events leading up to the accident. It's as if their psyche wants to block out the pain."

"I see." He smiled. "Apparently my psyche has done a pretty good job."

The three doctors chuckled. "We'd like to see how well you can walk," said Sargent. He gave the cardinal a terry cloth robe, helped him out of bed, and held him by the elbow as the two of them headed to the window. The cardinal peered out at the cars below on Sixth Street, then plopped into a seat in an overstuffed chair in the other corner of the hospital suite.

The cardinal said, "I feel just fine."

"Okay," said Sargent. The two doctors stood behind him. "You're tired. That's obvious. But you can go home. We'll call Monsignor Hawkslaw right now. He can come and get you."

AND SO, THE CARDINAL RETURNED to his sumptuous new rectory (with twelve bedroom suites) next to the cathedral, hoping to act as if nothing had happened. But of course something had happened, as he soon discovered when he logged on to the Internet that afternoon, Googled his own name, and found thousands of entries for the week before last, when his abduction and trial was the news of the world. Judging by Matt Drudge's Web site this very morning, his violent rescue was still one of this week's major stories—despite the controversy in Florida over how to proceed on yet another recount.

Yesterday, President Bush, shaky and somewhat subdued because he had no way of knowing whether his handpicked successor won or lost the contested election campaign, had told CNN's Wolf Blitzer that the Army's Special Forces had gone far beyond their orders in their attempt to rescue the cardinal. He apologized for all the bloodshed. "Bloodshed is not what this country is all about," he said.

In today's *New York Times*, his chief at the Pentagon, Robert Gates, was less apologetic. "Sometimes, in our fight for freedom," he said, "we do what we have to do." Which prompted a coalition of Senate Democrats to call for a hearing, a request that the Senate Foreign Relations Committee concurred in. The committee's chief counsel told the Associated Press, "We want to ask Secretary Gates whose freedom he was talking about—other than the cardinal's of course."

For almost four hours, Roger Mahony surfed the Internet, appalled and confused by the cacophony of opinion that raged around the ending of his ordeal—when Mexican commandos had descended on this mountain redoubt near Chiapas and slaughtered everyone but the man they had gone in to rescue. Then, after a Pepsi break and a fifteen-minute stroll around the cathedral plaza, he returned to his desk and started from the beginning by logging on to www.nytimes.com, going to an archive called "Mahony" and reading the *Times*' reports starting with November 5. That done, he walked down to the common room he shared with Hawkslaw and two other priests on the cathedral staff and plucked the current *Time* and *Newsweek* off a shelf, both featuring his face on the cover. *Time*'s headline, "Cardinal Mahony's Trial" seemed more serious than *Newsweek*'s "Roger's Rescue."

He took the magazines with him when he went in to a lone supper with Hawkslaw. "Just give me a minute or two," he said as they pulled their chairs up to the table. He skimmed both cover stories, and agreed with both writers, who concluded that the story was hardly over.

David Van Biema wrote in *Time*, "The wildcatters who put Cardinal Mahony on trial may be gone, but their bill of particulars against him has put the cardinal's credibility on the line. Back in the U.S., he can either say nothing, or he can confess everything. And that will tell us what Mahony is made of."

Ken Woodward wrote in *Newsweek*, "Some Catholics in Los Angeles believe the cardinal's life was spared for some providential reason. But insiders were puzzled last week when they heard the nuncio in Washington had been told by the Vatican to start looking for a new archbishop in Los Angeles."

Mahony waved the copy of *Newsweek*. "Is this true?" he asked his chancellor.

"What?"

"That the nuncio is looking to replace me?"

Hawkslaw opened his palms. "It didn't come from me. But, yes. We were asked over a week ago to put together a *terna*. Cardinal Re wants to see a list of names by the first of the year."

"Over a week ago? You mean before my rescue?"

"Afraid so."

Mahony lip curled. "They thought I was already history?"

"Apparently so."

Mahony drummed his fingers on the table for a moment, then drained his glass of Diet Pepsi. "Are you still working on the *terna*?"

"We've put it on hold."

"I should hope so," Mahony snapped. He rose from the table. "I like the new Mac G-6 you got for me," he said. "And I love the higher-speed DSL. Now I can navigate cyberspace like, like an angel. But I can't do my e-mail on it. Where's my old laptop? The one with all my addresses in it?"

"We didn't find it in your mountain cabin. Did you have it in Chiapas?"

"I don't remember."

"It doesn't matter." Hawkslaw gave a dismissive wave. "We don't want you doing any e-mail. Not for a while yet."

"And why not?"

"For the same reason that we haven't given you a telephone. To protect you."

"From what? From whom?" All of a sudden, he felt like a prisoner in his own rectory.

"From the press, mainly. I have had several reporters from the *LA Times* calling me every day. And your favorite columnist, the guy who has been attacking you for more than four years, Steve Lopez. He wants—they all want to know when they can talk to you."

He tried to hold back his anger. "And you tell them what?"

"I tell them if they want to talk about Chiapas, never. You don't remember Chiapas. Remember?"

Mahony thought that over, and told himself that he might want to talk about Chiapas— if and when he could start remembering.

THAT NIGHT HE DREAMT about a beautiful young Chicana who kept calling for his help. He awoke in a sweat, troubled, because, in the dream, he saw her on a rope bridge that was tumbling into a jungle ravine, and he couldn't save her. He sat on the edge of his bed for some long minutes, wondering who the young woman was. Then he made the obvious conclusion—that she was part of the scenario in Chiapas. But how could he find out?

He said no Mass that morning, but assisted at Hawkslaw's instead, from a vantage point in the cathedral sacristy, where he ran little risk of encountering a Mass goer or a curious reporter. And then, during breakfast, he realized that Pete Noyes, an old friend in the news business who was now working for Fox in Los Angeles, could get him a copy of the entire feed transmitted by *Para los otros*. But how could he get to Noyes? For a time—at least until he could demand that Hawkslaw give him a phone line and e-mail access—he figured he'd be patient.

Patience paid off. For the next few nights, Mahony saw a whole lineup of characters in his dreams, and was even able to put names on them by studying pictures of his captors in *Time* and *Newsweek*, pictures they'd printed off the television feed. With no difficulty, he started identifying them. Here they were in *Newsweek*: the five bishop-jurors, Iván Díaz, Juana Margarita Obregón. And here in *Time* was a short profile of Paul Kelly that gave the details of his work as one of Atlanta's best criminal defense attorneys. Mahony was suffused with a warm, grateful feeling when he regarded Kelly's ruddy Irish face. But the curious thing was that he felt nothing but compassion for his captors, even for Iván Díaz, the judge who sentenced him, and his dogged prosecutor, Juana Margarita Obregón. But he was quite sure she was not the woman in what had become a recurring dream—the Chicana who kept calling for his help.

• SEVEN •

PIKE

IN THE DAYS THAT FOLLOWED, Roger Mahony gave few other clues to indicate where he intended to lead the Church of Los Angeles. He was still under his doctors' orders to take some time off, and to stay away from the archdiocesan headquarters. He followed those orders, and gave some orders of his own—mainly that he wanted to be left alone. He told his finance council they should proceed, of course, with all deliberate speed, to settle—generously—with the victims of clerical sex abuse whose cases were still in a legal limbo. The archdiocese had gone $13 million in the hole in 2007, and would probably do the same in 2008, but he told the council what had been a guarded secret. As corporation sole of the archdiocese, he had $15 billion in assets that he could borrow against if he had to. "We aren't poor," he told them. "Let me know by January fifteenth how much borrowing I have to do. By that time, gentlemen, I'll be back at my desk. I can and will bite the bullet—as unappetizing as bullets are."

He told his aides that he'd be taking no phone calls, or making any other major decisions. Advent was approaching. A good time for all to do penance and prepare for Christmas. Until the New Year, he said, he wanted his chancellor to handle the day-to-day administration of the archdiocese and his pastors (and their parish administrators) to run their parishes.

"In the meantime," he wrote in a brief pastoral letter carried in the *Tidings* on Thanksgiving weekend, "I am going to rest, to read, to pray—and look for ways of doing something about this Church of ours."

54

HE DIDN'T TELL ANYONE that he was still having nightmares—not until that Monday morning when, after answering Dr. Bill Sargent's usual questions about his diet, his exercise, and his sleep patterns, he confessed he was still having a recurring wild dream. It was about a very pretty young woman in distress.

"Is it a woman you can recognize?"

"No. That's the disturbing part."

"How does this dream make you feel?" asked Sargent.

"Sad."

Sargent waited for the cardinal to expand on sad.

Mahony said nothing.

"Just sad, huh?"

"Yes."

It was a relic of his Irish-American Puritanism, perhaps, but Sargent felt uneasy pursuing the subject—a cardinal-archbishop of the Holy Roman Catholic Church and a pretty young woman. Sargent skipped right over the erotic possibilities. He said, "I think it's all a fallout from your ordeal in Mexico. Something happened there, something that made you challenge many of your assumptions—about yourself, about the Church, about the world."

"I know that, Bill," said Mahony. He said he believed the young woman in his dreams might provide some clues—if he only knew who she was, or what she symbolized. "I think I need to do some detective work."

Sargent raised an eyebrow. "About what happened to you in Chiapas? You might be better off if you didn't remember."

"I *don't* remember," Mahony reminded him. "But something inside me makes me want to."

Sargent nodded. "Uh huh. So, what do you want to do?"

"For one thing, I want to watch the trial. I have a friend bringing over a videotape of the entire thing."

Sargent, who had seen highlights of the trial in a CBS documentary, expressed some alarm. "Some of it is pretty rough. It made you sick, literally sick to your stomach, if you'll recall."

"I don't recall. That's part of the problem, isn't it?"

The doctor was embarrassed. "Sorry. I forgot. You don't remember. Of course. Of course."

Mahony said, "I will tell you what I can remember, after I've seen the tape."

PETE NOYES SHOWED UP at the cathedral rectory with a single DVD, not a tape. "We put the entire Fox feed on this disk," he said. "You can pause it at any time. You can freeze any frame, zoom in on a part of it, do slow motion, fast forward. You know the technology."

Mahony nodded. Indeed, he did. Despite the accelerating pace of technological change, he had always found the time to keep up to date on every new electronic toy. "Thank you, Pedro. I'll get this disk back to you."

Noyes said that wouldn't be necessary. "Our little local contribution. Maybe it will make up for the fact that Fox was the network that put your trial out there for the world to see."

Mahony approached Noyes, put a hand on each shoulder and looked down into his eyes. "Pete, you don't have to apologize for Fox. I am glad, in some ways, that Fox had a hand in this, uh, this project. I never would have owned up to my crimes. I've been programmed for more than fifty years, ever since I entered the seminary, programmed to put the institution first, second and third. That made me a very good administrator, but something less than a stand-up guy."

Noyes nodded. "Couple years ago, a Jesuit at Loyola told me, "There are two things I don't like about Roger: his face."

Mahony opened his palms.

Noyes said, "Sorry."

"No, don't be sorry. I am sure that every priest in town laughed over that line, but no one ever had the courage to come and repeat it to me. You did."

Noyes shrugged. "I have nothing to lose."

Mahony thought about the implications of that: anyone telling him the truth was subject to retaliation. He sank into a chair and shook his head. "Now I know," he said to Noyes, "that in my clerical culture, the biggest loser was me. I never expected to hear the truth. Worse, nobody ever expected me to tell the truth either." He consoled himself with the thought that every bureaucratic institution he knew was packed with sycophants. "When I went to Rome, I told the pope what he wanted to hear. At the consistory in May 2001, the pope asked the cardinals to tell him what the Church of the twenty-first century ought to be doing. I quoted the pope to himself. And when a reporter called me on it, I was so furious I sent him an e-mail and told him never to approach me again."

Mahony stood. "I am afraid, Pete, that I will be just as furious when I see who said what about me during that trial. But that will be good for me. Now that I don't have the truth hurdle to cross any more—thanks to Fox and the rest of the media—it will be easier to ask for forgiveness."

IT DIDN'T TAKE LONG FOR MAHONY to identify his mystery woman. She was on the DVD. She was not a major player in the trial, but he was sure she was the woman at his side during every break, and then, at the end of every session, leading him off—somewhere—acting like nothing so much as his nurse. He was distracted during the playback by some key points in the trial itself, masochistically marveling at the way this prosecutor, Juana Margarita Obregón, had skewered his conduct. But to him, now, the main show was only a sideshow. He wanted to study his young keeper, and was able to, by slowing down the action, stopping it, reversing it, freezing a frame, then zooming in on her lively face and flashing eyes. A name! What was her name?

He couldn't remember. Nor could he remember a single word she had ever spoken to him, or he, to her. He tried replaying the entire Fox feed, with the same result. Then, when it was time for lunch, he ejected the disk, turned off the machine and drifted over to his rectory kitchen. "What's for lunch, Monica?" he demanded of the cook.

"Eminence, we have some special chicken soup today, with rice."

The cook was a Chicana. But her accented words, about the chicken soup, with rice, and her speech rhythm triggered the spark the cardinal needed to remember the—name—of—his—keeper. It was María! María! María!

In his confusion, he almost stumbled over to the table. But now, suddenly, he remembered many of the things he and María had talked about, and many of the things she had done for him, starting with the time she gave him his Prozac when his hands had been cuffed behind his back in the chopper. He savored the memory, and remembered especially their conversation the morning of his arraignment, when she had spoken more boldly to him than anyone had ever dared.

He remembered her telling him: "We are putting you and the whole damn Catholic Church on trial."

He remembered his response: "Now you're going too far! What has the Church done?"

And her sassy rejoinder: "Nothing. That's the whole point. Words, words, words, words. Lots of say so. Very little do so. If Jesus visited the Vatican today, he would throw up. What you guys have done to his message! What your priests have done to little kids!"

And then his memory sped him to the end of the story—at least the end of the story as far as María was concerned. He suddenly saw the scene, when he had tried to cover her body with his as the soldiers opened fire, and failed to save her. That memory explained the unresolved conflict in his recurring dream. Now it wasn't so hard to figure out. Life had its mysteries, but it also had its epiphanies, if only we cared to look.

THE NEXT MORNING AFTER MASS, Mahony had an epiphany when he picked up the *LA Times* and found a Page One report that officials from the U.S. Department of Homeland Security had arrested a San Diego attorney and were holding him at Terminal Island in San Pedro on violations of the Patriot Act. His name was Nick Pike and he was connected, according to the *Times'* unnamed government source, to an organization called *Para los otros,* the group that had kidnapped Cardinal Mahony and taken him to Chiapas.

By now, Mahony had persuaded his chancellor that he was recovering well enough to start using the telephone. He phoned Matt Riley, retired but still on active status as a federal judge in the U.S. District Court in Los Angeles. Yes, Riley told the cardinal, he'd seen the *Times'* story. No, he didn't know the status of this man named Pike. "Normally," he said, "the FBI would arraign the man and have a judge set a bail hearing within twenty-four hours. In these terrorism cases, I'm just not sure what they'll do."

"I want to see this man," said Mahony. "Before he posts bail, if possible."

An hour later, Riley phoned back. "Something funny going on," he said. "They haven't set an arraignment date. My source at the FBI says they're not likely to either, not until they find out more about Pike. There's no bail. He could be dangerous. He has a criminal record. Spent three months in federal prison several years ago. At Lompoc."

"Any chance I can see him?"

"No one can see this guy."

"No one?"

"Not unless he has a court order."

"How hard is that?" asked Mahony.

Riley laughed. "For you, not hard at all. I could sign one right now. But I will do better than that. I will drive you down to San Pedro myself, and we'll both see this guy. I am kinda curious. I found out why he spent time at Lompoc. For illegal trespass at Ft. Benning, Georgia, in 1996."

"Prison time? For trespass at an Army base?"

"It was his second offense—demonstrating to close the U.S. Army's School of the Americas. He got a three-month sentence."

Mahony said, "But that doesn't make Pike a criminal in any accepted sense of the word." He knew about the School of the Americas. Manuel Noriega and Roberto d'Aubuisson were trained there, along with thousands of other military men from various Latin American countries, then returned home to kill social reformers throughout the continent. For years, college kids across the land had been trying to close the school. They held annual demonstrations at the Ft. Benning gate to commemorate the martyrdom of three Jesuits in Nicaragua in 1989 who were killed by graduates of the School of the Americas. Those who crossed into the base during those demonstrations got arrested.

"Right," said Riley. "He was a political prisoner, sentenced by an old Southern judge. Everyone in that part of Georgia calls him 'Maximum Bob.'"

Mahony's voice softened almost to a whisper. "Even more, Matt, do I need to talk to Nick Pike. I think he may be one of the good guys."

AT 1:00 P.M., THE SOUTHBOUND TRAFFIC on the Harbor Freeway was moving well. In fact, it took Judge Riley and Cardinal Mahony less time to drive from the cathedral to Terminal Island than it took them to get processed at the federal lockup.

59

"You may be a federal judge," said an assistant warden, nodding at Gate 3 to Riley at the wheel of his Lexus, "and you may be the cardinal-archbishop of Los Angeles," as he pointed at Mahony. "But we gotta follow the rules here." The warden studied the court order, signed by Riley himself, and he examined their California driver's licenses. Then he directed them to a gray building about 100 yards ahead, where they would park their car and then be guided through a set of protocols.

Inside that gray building, in a windowless room lit by a flickering fluorescent lamp, they were each given a one-page list of rules. They were told to sign them, then directed to proceed to a cage enclosed in bulletproof glass where they deposited in separate metal drawers their wallets, their cell phones, the contents of their pockets and the leather belts holding up their pants. Two guards standing behind the glass examined the items, then waved Riley and Mahony on to a set of electronic doors that finally gave them entrance to a long narrow room. Two guards there ordered them to take seats behind one of a half-dozen wooden tables.

"We'll bring in the prisoner now," said one of the guards. His partner spoke into a sputtering walkie-talkie with a line of jargon that only he and the man on the other end of the line could understand.

"Fun, huh?" said Riley.

"It's like a bad movie," whispered Mahony.

NICK PIKE HAD A SMALL POT, a well-trimmed, salt-and-pepper beard, and bright, intelligent eyes. He shook hands, first with Mahony and then with Riley, looked up at the guard who had brought him into the room and said, "Thanks." When the guards had left the room, Pike took a seat across the table.

He pulled at the gray cotton jacket he was wearing and gave them an apologetic look, as if to say if he'd known they were coming, he would have worn a clean shirt and a tie, then asked, "To what do I owe the pleasure of this visit?" His tone was soft, respectful, even deferential.

"We're curious," said Riley. "We'd like to know more about you."

Mahony said, "We'd like to know what you know about *Para los otros.* I have a special interest in the group."

"I imagine you do," said Pike with a knowing grin. "Well, look, first thing I want you to know, your Eminence, I had nothing to do with your kidnapping, or with the action at Chiapas."

"Go on," said Mahony.

"As far as I knew, *Para los otros* was working to reform civil society in Latin America—principally in Mexico and Central America." Pike told Mahony and Riley that its members were post-conciliar Catholics, mainly, with ties to the Jesuits in Latin America. Their name was adopted from a statement that was hacked out at the Jesuits' Thirty-Second General Congregation by their General Pedro Arrupe and others, who set down new directions for the order—and all the people working with them. "They would be 'men and women for others.'"

Mahony asked, "How have the members of *Para los otros* been 'men and women for others?'"

"In general, they were trying—are still trying—to help people in Latin America be all they can be. In this life, not the next. They do this in a lot of ways. They are teaching kids—even girls—how to read. In Third World countries, teaching girls how to read is a subversive act. And they are helping the people get organized. That's subversive, too."

"Organized for what?" asked Riley.

"For bread and justice. They are busy promoting a people's government. In other words, a democracy that would supplant the plutocracy that has ruled in Latin America for centuries."

Pike paused and looked around the room and up to the ceiling vents. "This room is probably bugged. But I never tried to hide this. So I might as well tell you. I helped found *Para los otros*. I have, in fact, raised a lot of money on their behalf. But I raised money for a lot of other people, too. I never knew, until recently, that *Para los otros* had turned from a reform of civil society to a reform of the Church itself."

"You're against a reform of the Church?" said Mahony.

"No. I just didn't think the folks in *Para los otros* had gotten around to it, yet. In retrospect, I shouldn't have been surprised. They were John XXIII Catholics trying to survive in a John Paul II world. They wanted to change that world."

"In Los Angeles?" asked Mahony.

Pike said, "More and more of their members and supporters turned out to be Latinos living in Southern California, I shouldn't have been shocked—

to think that they'd want to reform the Church of Los Angeles. Or that they'd get so creative."

" 'Creative?' " said Riley. "You mean kidnapping the cardinal-archbishop of Los Angeles and putting him on trial? On international television? That's what you mean by creative?"

Pike said, "You'll have to admit it was a brilliant action."

"So," snapped Riley, "these were not just a bunch of dumbass Mexicans?"

"That's a stereotype, Judge Riley. Latinos are in public life all over the state of California. College professors, doctors, accountants, businessmen. Even some judges. When a third of the population in this state are Latinos—. Well, I needn't belabor the obvious."

"But they had to have a leader," said Riley. "Who masterminded this affair?"

Pike didn't respond.

"You telling us you didn't?"

"You saw the man," said Pike. "You saw him on television, Judge Riley. He presided over your mock trial, your Eminence."

Riley and Mahony said in unison, "Díaz?"

"Yes, the late Iván Díaz. For years, he'd been teaching a political science seminar at UCLA, gathering a following there on campus, writing his iconoclastic books."

"Right under my nose," said Mahony. "And I never bothered to meet the guy."

"Well, you did, finally," said Pike. "Though not exactly in a way you might have preferred."

"Well, yes. Unfortunately, I do not have any personal recollection of those days of mine in captivity in Chiapas. What I know about Díaz is what I read about him a few days ago in the *New York Times*. And saw on a recording of the trial. And now he's gone."

"He put something new into play," said Pike.

"What?" asked Mahony.

Pike lowered his voice. "You, Your Eminence. A new you."

Cardinal Mahony wasn't exactly stunned. Ever since he had started making his annual 8-day retreats, he had been accustomed to reviewing his life, and resolving to live it more in accord with his calling—first, in his younger days as an *alter Christus*, another Christ, and then, after he

62

attained "the fullness of the priesthood"—a bishop—he had looked for ways of becoming more and more a teacher and a leader. Trouble was, once he became an archbishop in the nation's largest Catholic diocese, and then given a Red Hat, along with all the adulation that comes with that eminence (they even called him "Your Eminence"), he didn't spend a lot of his time thinking how much better he could be, how much more Christlike. He was already "all things to all men," so what more could he do? What more could he be? Now here he was sitting with this unlikely suspect in a federal prison in the Los Angeles Harbor who was telling him he had undergone a rebirth. He shook his head. What would a reborn Roger look like? If he was reborn, what would that mean to his, to his very identity? That frightened him, and, in his fear, he fell back into the identity he was sure of, the CEO of the Church of Los Angeles. As a good CEO, he had to know his men. At least that was his excuse when he changed the subject, from his supposed rebirth to Pike himself.

He turned to Riley. "Matt, how much time do we have?"

Riley looked at his watch. "About twenty minutes."

"I think I'd like to know a little bit more about Mr. Pike here."

"We can ask him."

Mahony said, "Maybe we can help him out of jail, too. Get the U.S. attorney to drop any pending charges against him?"

"We may be able to do that, too."

"I'd appreciate that, Judge Riley," Pike said, then turned to Mahony. "I really need more than twenty minutes to tell you about me. But here's a short version of the Nick Pike story. At seventeen, I entered the Jesuits. When I was twenty-six, I left."

"Because?" asked Mahony.

"So I could grow up. I did that. When I left the order in 1968, I signed up in the Bobby Kennedy campaign in California. Not a big job. But it helped me grow up. They hired me to help get out the Kennedy vote in East LA."

Riley asked him if he was at the Ambassador Hotel on June 5, 1968.

Pike gave him a pained look. "No. Not one of the million Angelenos who claimed they were there the night Bobby was shot. I wish I had been. In fact, I fantasized about that for years. Told myself that if I'd been there in the pantry, I'd have taken the bullet that was meant for Bobby. Not sure I ever got over it. I'd been invited to the victory party, you see, but I didn't go. I was on top of Mulholland Drive that night, making out in the front seat of my Chevy with this smart nun I met in the campaign, and I felt guilty for a long time afterward. Not for making out. I soon married that smart nun, Anne Murphy, and raised a family with her. I felt guilty because I wasn't in the pantry, where I might have helped Bobby Kennedy avoid an assassin's bullets." He paused, reflecting on what might have been, then refocused on his visitors.

Pike said, "I have had some success in the law. Three years ago, I made almost twenty million. Just my one-third share of four huge cases, that's all—though three of them were years in the making.

"All this time," he said, "I never lost touch with the Jesuits. I helped found an active group of former Jesuits. We're called the Compañeros. Most of us still believe we can make a difference in the world. Some of us are bolder. We say we want to change the world. The General of the Jesuits once told me we are Jesuits who are just a little ahead of our time, the kind of men who can help re-create the kind of Church we had in the beginning."

"What kind of Church is that?"

"A nonclerical Church. A people's Church."

Suddenly, it dawned on Mahony that he'd heard of Pike. "You're from San Diego, right?"

"Right."

"You're the one who built the Newman Center at the San Diego campus of the University of California?"

"Me and my wife, Anne Murphy. She runs the law firm. I just work there. Otherwise, I wouldn't have time to volunteer all over the place. I couldn't have done the actions at Ft. Benning every year—to confront the guys who were training the military goons in Latin America to kill priests and nuns."

"Or fund *Para los otros*?"

"That too."

"But why did you want to take me on?"

"I didn't. Remember? I knew nothing about that. That was Iván's idea."

"Okay. Okay. But why did he go after Los Angeles?"

"Why not? He was living in LA, right? Biggest archdiocese in the country? Because of Hollywood and the media, potentially the most influential Catholic city in the U.S. Maybe in the whole world."

"Except Rome."

"Yes. Except Rome, of course."

"Of course."

Riley shifted in his chair. Time was up. In fact, the guards had just come into the room.

"All right then," said Mahony. "I just have one more question. Did you know Juana Margarita Obregón?"

"Not well. I met her, once. And then, of course, I saw her performance on TV, out of Chiapas. Too bad she had to die."

Mahony said, "Death isn't the end of the story, you know that. It is just the beginning of a new chapter."

"I know. I know," Pike said. "But she was so vital. The one time I met her, I found her so—alive."

Mahony agreed. "Yes, that describes the woman I saw in that mock trial. And what about the young woman who was my keeper in Chiapas? Her name was María. Did you know her?"

Pike frowned. "I'm not sure."

"She said she was from East LA."

"Maybe," said Pike. "We had some volunteers from East LA who signed up to work in Chiapas."

"Anyone named María?" Mahony repeated her name and his voice thickened. "María. Never got her last name. I fell in love with her."

Pike was startled, but gave him a silent nod, encouraging him to go on.

"We hardly touched," said Mahony. "But she touched me. It's hard to explain. "But I will never forget her. I would like to meet her folks, and tell them." He got a far-off look in his eye. "I'd like to tell them—something."

· EIGHT ·
SUNNYHILL

THE NEXT AFTERNOON, Anne Pike drove to Terminal Island, collected her husband, and drove off with him in her antique light green '56 Thunderbird convertible. When they were on the Harbor Freeway, Nick Pike got a call on his cell phone. It was Judge Riley. Not two hours ago, one of Riley's colleagues had appeared before a federal magistrate in downtown Los Angeles, seeking and getting Nick's unconditional release because the feds had no case against him.

Riley said, "You okay?"

"I am out of there," Pike said to Riley, "on my way home. Thanks. Federal prisons are no day in Disneyland."

Riley said, "I called Roger Mahony and told him you were coming out. He was pleased. He wants to see you again. Right away."

"Why me? Why now?"

"He told me he wanted to stop talking and start listening. To a lot of people—different kinds of people. Not the clerics and the professional Catholics he's been talking to."

"What's his angle?"

"He says he wants to start listening—to guys like you who aren't in the Church's career network. He's intrigued with your Compañeros. He says you are a gift to the people of God in Southern California."

"I don't know about that," shouted Pike over the roar of the freeway, "but tell the cardinal thanks. I'll come see him. Day after tomorrow. Tomorrow, I want to spend some time with my family. You should also tell him he may be sorry he ever met this Greek. Tell him to remember that line from Vergil. *Timeo Danaos et dona ferentes.* Beware the Greeks bearing gifts."

THE GIFT THAT NICK PIKE BORE when he entered the cardinal's study two nights later was a Jesuit from Australia that Pike had met and collared earlier that day on the campus at Loyola Marymount University. Pike was that kind of guy. He made friends quickly, and made demands on them just as fast.

"Say hello to Sean Sunnyhill," Pike said. "He teaches Church history at the Greg."

"In Rome?" asked Mahony.

Sunnyhill nodded as Mahony waved him and Pike on to a divan in his sitting room.

Mahony smiled. He knew about "the Greg." The Gregorian University, the Jesuit order's premier institution of higher learning in Rome, was founded in 1601. Bishops from around the world sent their best seminarians there for graduate studies in theology and scripture and Church history and canon law. "I've read some of your books," said Mahony, as he uncorked a bottle of his best Chardonnay, a Chateau Montelena from the Napa Valley. Mahony believed the old Latin adage *in vino veritas.* He had been getting some straight talk out of men like Noyes and hoped to get more of the same from Pike. Now, if Pike was bringing Sunnyhill to see him at this moment—his first real meeting with Pike—he suspected there was something special about this Roman theologian.

"I'm glad you're here," said Mahony. "Both of you. I have a notion. I may want to start doing some things."

"Things?" asked Sunnyhill.

"Things that Rome might not like."

Pike shot Sunnyhill a look that said, *See? I told you this might be worthwhile.*

"What do you have in mind?" asked Sunnyhill.

"We don't have enough priests to go around. A year ago, I had fifty pastoral vacancies, and no priests to fill them. I had an immediate, obvious solution to that problem, but I couldn't go with it." He said he had the names of several hundred married priests living in Southern California who had offered to help out on Sunday liturgies, gratis. He got their names from

CORPUS, an association of inactive priests, most of whom left the ministry to get married.

"They were—and are—good men. They fell in love, often with nuns, and they did the honorable thing. They left the priesthood to marry them. Some of their clerical buddies did the dishonorable thing: they fell in love, too, sometimes with more than one woman, and even had children by them. But they never had the guts to leave the active ministry. These scoundrels are, technically, priests in good standing today. And their brother priests who married are pariahs. They are still priests, but according to canon law, I cannot let them say Mass in my archdiocese."

Sunnyhill said, "Bishops everywhere in the world have the same problem. Canon law is the same everywhere. Except of course in the ancient autochthonous churches of the Middle East. The Melkites, the Maronites, the Copts. As you know, they have two kinds of priests, married priests in the parishes, and celibate monks in their monasteries."

"Doesn't make any sense," said Mahony. "It is not against canon law for me to take in Lutheran pastors and Episcopalian canons, re-ordain them and set them up in Catholic parishes, along with their wives. Rome approves of that. But Rome won't let me recruit all these married priests to serve in priestless parishes on a Sunday morning."

"It takes a little while to understand Rome," said Sunnyhill.

"You've been there for some time?"

"You might say that." Sunnyhill explained that his superiors in Australia had sent him as a young priest to study history at Harvard. After that, the Jesuit General Pedro Arrupe had recruited him to teach at the Gregorian University. That was forty years and a hundred pounds ago. Now, after watching the Roman Curia from his peculiar vantage point at the Greg, Sunnyhill could tell Mahony that the Vatican's vaunted control over one billion Catholics around the world was a myth.

"In huge parts of the Catholic world," Sunnyhill said, "Catholic parish priests take common law wives and raise families. The bishop looks the other way and says nothing and the people are quite happy to have married priests serving them."

Mahony raised an eyebrow. "And Rome never finds out?"

"The men in the Curia know this is happening in small Latin American villages and parts of rural Africa. They just know they cannot do much about the situation. So they do nothing. Oh, they take steps to make sure these married priests do not become bishops. In some places, they can only be sure of that by filling an episcopal vacancy with someone from one of the religious orders that take vows of chastity. You can pretty much figure out where that's happening by looking in your *Annuario Pontificio*. If you see the bishop is a Salesian, or a Dominican, or a Franciscan or a Jesuit, you can make an informed guess that most of the qualified priests in that diocese are family men."

"So," interjected Pike, "the celibacy issue has disappeared in those places?"

Sunnyhill said, "*De facto*? Yes. *De jure*? No. The Vatican clings to the not-so-ancient doctrine, that Roman Catholic priests do not marry."

"But it winks at the situation in Latin America and Africa?"

"Yes, I'm afraid so."

"But it won't wink at a similar situation in the U.S.," said Mahony. He was sure of that.

Pike said he didn't quite get it. "Why should the U.S. be any different?"

Mahony said to Pike, "We could never keep it quiet. The *Times,* or KFI would make a big deal out of it. And if they didn't, some blogger would be telling the story on the Internet."

"Yes," said Sunnyhill, "you have an extremely aggressive press here in America. And now, with the Internet, bloggers' stories go all over the world. A married priest with a family in a Colombian jungle? Who would ever know? But a married priest with a family in Redondo Beach?"

Mahony laughed. "Yeah! He probably gets a profile in the *Los Angeles Times,* and then a knock on the door from *60 Minutes.*"

Sunnyhill nodded. "That's what scares Rome—the American media. It gives the Church in the U.S. too much potential influence—far more worldwide influence than Rome itself has."

Mahony agreed. "Not long ago, when he was running the Holy Office, the pope told me, 'The USA has 6 percent of the Catholics in the world, but it takes up 50 percent of my time.'"

Pike said, "Well, maybe that's a good thing."

Mahony asked Pike what he meant.

Pike said, "The American Church may be able to move the whole Church into the twenty-first century in a way that no one else has been able to."

"I don't understand."

"I already told you. I told you the other day. Make it a people's Church."

Mahony shook his head. "Maybe I didn't hear you. Maybe I didn't want to hear you, because I think that the Church in America has always been a people's Church. That's why American Catholics are the best Catholics in the world."

Pike raised an eyebrow at Mahony. "By what criterion? Thousands, millions of American Catholics have given up on the Church, or to be more accurate, on the hierarchy. You know the second largest denomination in America? Former Catholics."

Sunnyhill was sitting back and sipping his Chardonnay, amused at Pike's near-attack on the cardinal.

"And," said Pike, "the nonaccountability of the bishops has been the last straw."

"What?" asked Mahony. "Don't you remember what we did at Dallas in May 2002? Almost unanimously, we voted in a seventeen-point charter on sex abuse. Abusing priests would get zero tolerance."

"Yeah, once you were caught, you told the people you were sorry the priests did what they did, and sorry you covered up for them, and you promised you wouldn't do it again. But nobody believed you, because you proved you couldn't be trusted."

Mahony flinched.

"Well, can you be trusted?" asked Pike. "Honestly now?"

Mahony sipped his Chardonnay. *What the hell? In vino veritas applied to him, too.* He said, very deliberately, "No. No—one—trusts—us." He looked over to Sunnyhill and gave him a sorrowful glance.

"And why not?"

"I don't know."

"Obviously. If you knew," said Pike, "you'd do something about it. But you've only taken half-measures."

Mahony shrugged. "We are not God. We did what we could."

Pike sat up straighter on the couch. "You leaped halfway across the ditch, and ended up flat on your ass!"

"Sometimes."

"Exhibit number one: you set up a national review board—laymen and laywomen—to make the hierarchy accountable to the lower-archy?"

70

"Yes. It was partly my idea."

"But you didn't give that board any power. And you forced the resignation of your chairman as soon as he put the pressure on to make you accountable."

"Only after he compared us to the mob."

"And that wasn't a good comparison?" said Pike.

Mahony bristled. "In no way are we like the Cosa Nostra!"

Pike let Mahony hear the echo of his own denial, then asked, "In no way?"

"No."

"Have you ever heard of *omerta*? The Mafia's code of silence?" Mahony nodded. "Your canonical secrecy is no different. Correct?"

"Well, canon law—"

Pike interrupted him. "To me that sounds like *omerta*."

"Yes, but—"

"But, what?"

"We're just following the Vatican norms. Canon law makes it very clear—"

Pike interrupted. "The American Church cannot be open with the people of God because of canon law?"

"Yes. No. Well," said Mahony, "we cannot do a lot of things because of canon law. Can't let laymen have any authority over clerics. Can't carry through with the very clear implications of Vatican II—that, yes, we are a people's Church. I'd like to make this a people's Church. You know that. But canon law—"

Pike interrupted. "We just have to scrub canon law."

Mahony scoffed at the very idea. "Impossible," he said.

"That's only because you have never tried thinking outside the box."

"If I'd made a habit of that, I wouldn't be a cardinal today. The Vatican rewards men who get in step."

Pike wondered why anyone who had reached the top as Mahony had would worry about rewards from the Vatican, but he took Mahony's "get in step" as a challenge. "Lockstep?" he said with a snicker. "Or goose-step?"

Mahony shrugged. "For more than twenty-five years, as head of the Holy Office, Ratzinger had more authority than anyone imagined. He talked. We listened."

"If he had the authority, it was only because you—and all the other bishops—gave it to him."

"No. His authority is God-given."

"What isn't?" said Pike.

"What do you mean?"

Pike said, "I think we can all agree that everything comes from God. The real question is *how* it comes from God."

"Well, when Ratzinger was head of the Holy Office, his authority came through the pope, of course."

Pike said to Sunnyhill, "Help me out here."

Sunnyhill said, "Juridically maybe. The pope appoints Ratzinger to head the Holy Office, and suddenly Ratzinger has the authority to clobber any theologian who comes up with a new idea, or even an arresting new metaphor. But ontologically? Teleologically? We have to ask what that authority is for, and who's to benefit from it. Without the people of God, there'd be no need for a Holy Office, or for a papacy either."

"So," Mahony said, "since authority is *for* the people, is it also *from* the people?"

Sunnyhill said, "Good question. It is *the* question. Biggest argument going on in the Church. We've been fighting that battle since Vatican I in 1870. And the battle goes on. The papal party in the Church says Peter's authority came from Jesus himself. Ever stop to look up at the ceiling in St. Peter's? Letters five feet high, in gold, supposedly spoken by Jesus to Peter: I WILL GIVE YOU THE KEYS OF THE KINGDOM. WHATSOEVER YOU BIND ON EARTH SHALL BE BOUND ALSO IN HEAVEN. Awesome."

"Right," said Mahony. "And Peter's successors enjoy the same awesome authority."

"That's what they say," conceded Sunnyhill. "But the scholars are saying the early Church never thought in terms of an Apostolic succession. Later popes cobbled together something they called an unbroken line back to Peter, and laid a claim to absolute power on the basis of some high-class forgeries."

"That's not new news," argued Mahony. "For some time now, we've known the Donation of Constantine and the Isidorean Decretals were forgeries."

"They *were* forgeries, weren't they?" said Sunnyhill.

"Yes," admitted Mahony. "But, so what? For more than ten centuries, the people of God have looked to the pope as the vicar of Christ."

"More correctly, I think, as the vicar of Peter," said Sunnyhill, "but no matter. The best theologians at Vatican II—including Pope John XXIII—rejected those who kept insisting on the papacy as monarchy. It was an emphasis that really got in the way of the message Jesus tried to get across to the Apostles—that he had come to serve, not be served. But those who are served have to have a voice. Maybe even a vote. And not just an advisory vote. That principle can have many ramifications."

"I can think of one," said Pike. "The people might even have a say in the selection of their servants."

Mahony pondered that. He looked at Sunnyhill. "Is he saying the people should elect their own bishops?"

Sunnyhill said, "It isn't an outlandish idea. The early Church did that. For the first six centuries, the people elected the bishop of Rome—that is, the pope—by acclamation. In 1789, the priests of the original thirteen colonies elected the first American bishop, John Carroll of Baltimore."

"So you think the laity should be able to tell the clergy what to do?"

Sunnyhill said, "That's the wrong question, dividing the Church into 'the laity' and 'the clergy.' Vatican II tried to get rid of that dichotomy. Both wings of the council agreed on this—on the radical equality of all the baptized."

"The radical equality of all the baptized?" Mahony had used the expression before in his homilies. But he had never thought to assess its political implications.

Sunnyhill did so. "The Council said every one of the faithful are full and equal members of the Church. But the Vatican keeps insisting that only clerics can make decisions in the Church. That means the people of God don't own their own Church. This has disastrous consequences. We can see the results best in western Europe, where huge majorities of Catholics do not care any more about a Church they do not own."

Pike laughed. "Yeah! In the history of the world, no one has ever washed a rental car."

Mahony said. "The Church is not the Hertz Corporation."

"Or even Avis," said Pike. "Though we do try harder."

Mahony grinned, but Pike didn't. Pike turned to Sunnyhill. "I have a question: if we Americans don't have a hand in writing canon law, why should we follow it?"

Sunnyhill looked to the cardinal.

Mahony said, "We were always told, 'Because it comes from God.'"

"Yeah," scoffed Pike. "God gave canon law to St. Peter—on tablets of stone."

Mahony's voice rose. "You're saying that canon law is just a human thing?"

"What else?"

Sunnyhill jumped in. "Nick is right. Canon law is not only a human thing, but a Roman thing. It was produced out of a Roman culture—starting in the thirteenth century."

Pike said, "I don't want you to think we are ganging up on you, Cardinal Mahony. But I have to tell you that what Americans understand about canon law, they hate. Particularly all the secrecy stuff—with the various Roman dicasteries making up laws as they go along, with the Vatican courts making judgments in secret tribunals, with the pope saying, 'Shut up already about women's ordination. I am the decider.'"

Mahony nodded. Since his seminary days, he'd been conditioned to revere canon law. Now here was Pike telling him he'd made canon law into an idol. He looked at his watch. Pike and Summerhill had given him enough to chew on for one night. He said, "I just want to say this before you go. Whether you realize this or not, you've given me an answer to my first question. 'How do I do what needs doing here without Rome coming down on my head?'"

"We didn't resolve that question," said Sunnyhill.

"But you suggested we might think of challenging canon law?"

"Well," said Sunnyhill. "Maybe just ignore it, then stand back and see what happens. Sometimes we get more things done if we have the guts to just do it. Easier to ask forgiveness than it is to ask permission."

Mahony nodded. That made a rough kind of sense. In this context, he said he had once heard his friend, Oscar Rodríguez Maradiaga, the cardinal-archbishop of Tegucigalpa, Honduras, proclaim, "Between Rome and Honduras is a very wide ocean."

Pike and Sunnyhill shot each other a happy glance. Was it possible that Mahony might help them promote a people's Church in America?

74

WHEN MAHONY WALKED PIKE AND SUNNYHILL to the door of the rectory, he encountered Monsignor Hawkslaw on his way in, looking very sporty in a well-tailored alpaca jacket, silk shirt, and gray slacks. "Jeremiah!" said Mahony. "Lakers win?"

Hawkslaw said they did, but only in overtime on a 34-foot shot at the buzzer by Kobe Bryant. He looked at Pike and Sunnyhill with some curiosity.

Tonight, Mahony felt that the identity of his visitors was none of Hawkslaw's business. He told them. "Say hello to my chancellor, Jeremiah Hawkslaw."

They said hello, nothing more. Hawkslaw nodded, hesitated for a moment, then disappeared up a darkened hall.

On the steps of the rectory, Mahony told them to call him Roger.

Sunnyhill beamed. Pike shook his head. "Couple days ago, I was a jailbird. Now I am on a first name basis with my archbishop."

Sunnyhill handed Mahony a slip of paper. "I think you need to call Jim Kowalski, a former president of the Canon Law Society of America."

Mahony looked at the note. It was a telephone number in area code 574. "Kowalski? The canon lawyer at Notre Dame?"

"Uh huh."

"I've got a canon lawyer. You just met him. Jeremiah Hawkslaw."

"You trust him?" asked Pike.

Mahony hesitated. "Yes."

"I doubt it," said Pike. "Otherwise, you would have introduced us just now."

Mahony frowned and gave Pike a curious look. He'd never known such candor in a layman.

Sunnyhill said, "Call Kowalski. He will tell you that canon law is only law by analogy."

AFTERWARD, MAHONY WALKED ACROSS THE HALL to visit his small private chapel, lit only by a red sanctuary lamp. He genuflected, then knelt and tried a conversation in the dark with Jesus. He said to Jesus, "I am sure that Nick Pike has planted a seed. Maybe you were speaking to me tonight through Nick Pike and his Australian Jesuit from the Greg. They were making pretty good sense." But then Mahony realized this wasn't much of a prayer. What should he say as he lifted his mind and heart to God? Or should he say anything at all? Maybe with God, as well as with the people of God, he should practice the art of listening. He spent the next ten minutes by trying to empty himself of all thought by repeating an ancient sutra: "Lord, be merciful to me, a sinner." That was a prayer.

NINE

RESURRECTION

THE NEXT MORNING AFTER HIS PRIVATE MASS in the sacristy, Cardinal Mahony knelt to pray for no more than five minutes, then straightened up and strode into the nave to visit with some of the 137 saints and non-saints that marched—on tapestries—around both sides of his cathedral. He stopped for some moments to visit with seven of his favorite saints, in turn, then finally stood in front of St. Catherine of Siena, the woman who had once traveled all the way to Avignon in 1376 to tell the French Pope Gregory XI he had to return the papacy to Rome.

Mahony addressed Catherine of Siena, "For the good of the whole Church, Kate, you stood up to the pope. Do you suppose you could stand by me while I see if it is possible for this poor servant to stand up to a pope as you did? Maybe even find me a little help?"

He expected no miraculous answer, but got one only minutes later when he was racing toward the rectory, in a hurry because of the cold January drizzle. On his way, he encountered a handsome woman wearing a trenchcoat—Hispanic, vaguely familiar. She stopped in his path and smiled. He said, "You'll have to excuse me. In my twenty-three years here, I have met so many—"

She said, "Juana Margarita Obregón."

That staggered him. "Dr. Obregón! Are you real? Or am I having a vision?"

"Quite real," she said. She took his hand, so he could feel her warmth.

"But you died on November the ninth—in Chiapas! Along with everyone else, with Iván Díaz and the five bishops and the video crew and—" his voice softened—"María."

She laughed, but there was no mirth in her laughter, only wonder. "It was not a miracle, I assure you."

"Wha, what happened? Tell me."

"All right." She took a deep breath, then another, then plunged in. "Back on that fateful day, as soon as Bishop Azevedo announced the trial verdict, I dashed out of the room. There is no need now for any false modesty. I had a terrible case of diarrhea that day. I had to find relief. I hurried over to the latrine ravine. I was pulling my pants down just as I heard the helicopters overhead. By the time I finished my business, I was able to look up through the foliage and see they were military. When I heard the first explosions, I realized they had come to rescue the cardinal, with lethal force."

Though a cool wind was blowing the rain into Mahony's face, his face was flushed. He took her arm, "Come with me. Let's get out of the wet." She nodded and followed him through the plaza, back to the rectory. He let himself in with a key and led her to one of the visitors' parlors, shaking his head. "I cannot believe this," he said. "Then what happened?"

"I can hardly believe it either," she said, eyes alight with excitement. "Providence, for me, was a pool of—well—shit."

Mahony blinked. "You mean—you just dived in?"

"Well, not head first, I assure you. I just slid in, feet first, closing my eyes and holding my nose. I went under for a few seconds, then realized I could swim my way to the other side, kicking and using a very vigorous breast stroke, until I landed on a kind of shelf under a large banana leaf, with machine gun fire popping all around me. I floated there for almost four hours, up to my ears in excrement. Finally, I heard the helicopters take off."

"American helicopters or Mexican helicopters?"

She gave him a quizzical look. "Helicopters," she said.

She paused, letting the implications of her response sink in, then plunged ahead with her story. "I waited another hour or so, until I heard nothing except the sound of the cockatoos. Then I climbed out of there, covered with—" She grimaced.

"How did you get out of there?"

"I walked out."

"Walked out? Just like that?"

"Well, no. First, I wanted to find out what had happened to all the others. I made my way farther down the ravine, then climbed back up again to the compound. Parts of it were still smoldering. Bullet holes everywhere. At first, I found no one. Then I discovered a large funeral pyre off to the south. I was assailed by a strange combination of smells—kerosene and burned human flesh. There is nothing like it. They had piled up the bodies and incinerated them, probably with their special helicopter fuel.

"I stumbled away from there as fast I could. I found the room I had been staying in, grabbed a shirt and some jeans and a pair of shoes and a towel and went to look for a place where I could bathe. I found a communal shower. It was not working. But nearby, I came upon a kind of wading, or maybe, bathing pool. The water was cold, but it was clean enough. I stripped and immersed myself in that water. Sat there, soaked for a good fifteen minutes and washed my hair as well as I could, then got out and dried myself and put on my clean clothes. Then I moved out. I spent one fearful night in the jungle, then another half day, and I found an Indian village, people who had heard what happened when the choppers had come. They asked me no questions. They took me to the nearest town in a donkey cart and—"

Mahony had sat there in the parlor, silent and astonished through most of her tale. But his impatience broke through. Interrupting, he said, "Why are you here?"

"Where? LA? I once had a house in Westwood. I am told I cannot go back there. The FBI seized that house. But LA is my home now. Where else would I go?"

"Why are you here in my cathedral, my rectory?"

"I have heard you might be getting in trouble. For trying to be a Christian. I want to help you."

He frowned. "Haven't you already done enough?"

She cringed.

He stood and took her hand and lifted her to her feet, then held her in his arms and hugged her to correct her misunderstanding. "Juana, Juana, Juana, don't you see? You've been an instrument of God's inscrutable ways. I want to be a Christian. Maybe you are here to help me do it. Will you help?"

"Yes," she said, eyes glistening. "Yes."

AFTER SEVEN GOOD HOURS OF SLEEP that night, Mahony rose refreshed, too excited to do nothing, as his doctors had ordered. He began to make some radical moves. Two days ago, members of the U.S. Army Special Forces had delivered Mahony's helicopter—in excellent condition—to its hangar at the Santa Monica Airport. Today, he got on the phone, dialed an airplane broker and sold his flying machine for $1 million—and had the check sent to Jeff Dietrich and his wife, Catherine, at the Catholic Worker. He sold his Mercedes, too, and an SUV, then took a walk downtown and bought a bus-and-subway pass from the Los Angeles Rapid Transit District. On his way home, he stopped at the exclusive Jonathan Club on Figueroa and put in his official resignation. He had a small exercise room in the rectory. He could use that, and forego the steam room at the club, and its Swedish showers, and its masseurs.

And then he stunned his bookkeeper at the archdiocesan headquarters by phoning and asking her to get a bank draft for $100,000 and mail it to the pope. He dictated a note: "I will not be able to attend the January meeting of the Vatican's finance committee in Rome, and I will not be attending any more meetings at the Vatican—until, of course, it is time to go and help elect a new pope, which I pray, your Holiness, does not happen soon. I will be busy attending to the pressing needs of the people of God in the counties of Los Angeles, Ventura and Santa Barbara."

What were those needs? First on his list: the people's need for the Eucharist, which came down to one thing: more priests. There were darn few in his own pipeline. Young men weren't flocking to the seminary like they used to in the good old days. Giving up a wife and kids—that was apparently too much to ask of men today. Whatever the reason, his seminary was empty. Almost. One or two young men each year would receive the Holy Oils. And three or four of the old timers would die, so that, each year, he had a net loss.

He'd already tried importing priests from Nigeria. They spoke English, after a fashion, but he'd gotten complaints about them. They were a lordly lot, convinced that the priesthood itself earned them all the perks and the deference due a corporate executive. And their homilies were abstract and moralistic. So imports were not the answer. Not unless he could get young priests from Ireland, as his predecessors in Los Angeles had done for almost a century. Trouble was, there were no more young priests coming out of

Ireland. Last year at All Hallows, the major seminary near Dublin that had sent thousands of priests to America, they had had no ordinations at all.

He phoned Terry Dosh, a former Benedictine, the Southern California vice-president of CORPUS, and said he'd like to set up a pool of good men, married priests who could start saying Sunday Masses all over the LA Basin. "But then," he told Dosh, "before they actually go out and do it, I want to have some listening sessions in every vicariate, to find out how this will go down with the people. How do the people feel about priests who left the active ministry to get married? I want to ask them whether they would like to see these men back at the altar. And if they want that, I intend giving it to them, no matter what canon law says." In a recent flashback, Mahony had recalled the last words of his court-appointed lawyer, Paul Kelly: "Try listening to all your people. Don't tell them what you think they need. Find out what they think they need. And give it to them."

BEFORE SUPPER THAT EVENING, Mahony encountered his chancellor having a martini while he watched Channel 2's evening news. He told him he wanted to embark upon a program of creative listening "to the people of God."

Jeremiah Hawkslaw put his drink down and pursed his lips. "We've already done that," he said in the patient tone of a first grade teacher. "Remember our archdiocesan synod in 2000 and 2001? We *had* a grassroots campaign."

Mahony said he did remember. He had called on every parish in the archdiocese to conduct Town Hall-type meetings where people were encouraged to listen to one another, and to speak up about their Church. Pastors and parish leaders spent hours distilling all the comments down to ten proposals, and then they took those lists to regional meetings. Each of those meetings ended up producing a dozen concrete suggestions—most of them revolving around ministry—for the future of the Church of Los Angeles in the twenty-first century.

Hawkslaw said, "I can give you those concrete suggestions from memory. The first one—"

Mahony wasn't exactly listening. His attention had been momentarily distracted at the sight of Vice President Cheney being interviewed on the *CBS Evening News* about a rumored U.S. raid on a nuclear facility in North

Korea. Cheney would soon be an ex-vice president. He wondered to himself whether Cheney would ever stop trying to make war. Then he turned back to Hawkslaw. "We didn't follow through on those suggestions," he said. "And, anyway, those meetings never got to the heart of the matter."

"Yes," said Hawkslaw, "from the beginning, we had to tell everyone there were certain things the local Church could do, and certain things the local Church couldn't do."

"That was a mistake," said Mahony, "In effect, we crippled that project before it ever got off the ground. "

"Well, yes?" Hawkslaw wondered what point the cardinal was trying to make. To him, the universal Church's worldwide governance was a given— many centuries in the making. "Far as I know, the pope still makes all the rules."

Mahony ignored the implied rebuke. "I'd like everyone to revisit the questions. But this time with no cap on their creativity."

Hawkslaw stared at the cardinal. Further evidence, he thought, that Mahony had lost his mind. "We can't do that."

"Who says we can't?"

"Canon law says we can't. It's given us a whole set of rules and regulations regarding diocesan and provincial synods."

That gave Mahony pause. There was something about Hawkslaw's self-righteous tone, something, even, about the set of his jaw that told him to back off. What was he, stupid? Confiding his reservations about canon law to Hawkslaw, his eminent canon lawyer? "Of course," he said, clapping his palm to his forehead. "Canon law. Forgive me. I don't know what I was thinking." He was thinking, in fact, that canon law was a sacred cow.

"Okay. Okay." Jeremiah Hawkslaw relaxed and forced a grin. But now he started wondering what he'd do about his boss. He suspected the cardinal had been demented by his days in Chiapas—much more than anyone thought.

THE NEXT NIGHT, Hawkslaw had obvious proof. He was standing at the entrance to the cathedral's parking garage next to an LAPD paddy wagon, signing a complaint against the six bums he had found sleeping in the plaza. The cops had come right away, rousted the vagrants and were pushing them into their paddy wagon when the cardinal appeared, his face illumined by the vehicle's flashing red lights.

"What are you doing?" he demanded of the sergeant in charge.

"Just complying with a request by the chancellor here. Monsignor—" He looked at his clip board. "Monsignor Hawkslaw."

Mahony stared at Hawkslaw.

Hawkslaw shrugged. "They were bedded down under some cardboard, just outside the bronze doors. Two of 'em were drinking cheap wine."

Mahony nodded. "Uh huh. Well, we have ten empty rooms in the rectory. There's no need for them to sleep under cardboard. On a concrete slab." He told the sergeant to tear up the complaint. He peered into the back door of the police van. "These men—how many are there, six?—will be our guests tonight."

Soon, the cardinal was leading six grimy bums up to the rectory's guest rooms on the second floor. "You'll probably want to shower before you climb under the sheets," he told them. "It looks like you guys haven't experienced hot water recently."

One of them said, "Recently? Would you believe six months?"

Mahony sniffed and grinned and said he could believe it.

Hawkslaw was agape. He wondered what message he would fax to Cardinal Re at midnight—9:00 AM in Rome. But no. He decided he'd better wait 'til morning, after he had a phone chat with Cardinal Grandeur in Philadelphia.

MONSIGNOR HAWKSLAW REALIZED the Church in Los Angeles was in even deeper trouble than he imagined when the cardinal ordered his press spokesman Harry Gray (in Hawkslaw's presence) to tell the media he'd be making his first public appearance a week from Friday night. "It will be in the cathedral," he said. "And I want to celebrate a Mass of the Resurrection— for my captors. President Bush may have called them terrorists. I call them martyrs. Martyrs for the truth."

If the cardinal's memory was beginning to kick in, it seemed to Hawkslaw like a very selective memory indeed. These kidnappers? These terrorists? He was calling them martyrs for the truth?

"You want to see any of the press before then?" asked Gray. "Give 'em a heads-up?"

Mahony said, "Maybe some of my friends at the *LA Times*? No, I think not. From now on, Harry, I'm not going to play favorites with the press, or try to con them, or manipulate them. They have a legitimate job to do—to tell the truth insofar as they are able. My job is to help them do it—insofar as *I* am able."

Gray lifted an eyebrow.

"I am not kidding, Harry."

"I didn't say anything."

"You looked skeptical."

Gray hesitated, trying to figure out whether Mahony meant what he was saying—that he not only wanted to tell the truth, but be told the truth, too, even by his press spokesman. He took a chance. "Can you blame me?"

"I guess not," said Mahony. "For most of my time here, I only heard what I wanted to hear."

Hawkslaw wondered where Roger had gotten that. The words were certainly not vintage Mahony. But where did they come from? Had his captors brainwashed the cardinal-archbishop of Los Angeles?

THE CATHEDRAL WAS JAMMED. Those who hadn't come early didn't get a seat, and fire marshals asked some of those who were standing to leave and watch the proceedings on two large television screens set up in the plaza.

Before the Mass began, Cardinal Mahony, wearing a simple black cassock, marched out on the altar alone. He surveyed the crowd, then took the several steps down that were necessary to get him on the same level with the congregation.

He began, "In the prophecies of Malachy, the man to succeed *Pastor Angelicus,* Pius XII, would be *Pastor et Nauta.* Those Latin words meant that Pius XII's successor would be a shepherd and a sailor. I think that was a poetic way of saying that that man, John XXIII, would be the kind of pope that Jesus wanted the Apostles to be: a fisher of men.

"Well, I haven't been a very good shepherd, and I haven't been much of a sailor, but I want you all to know that I have undergone a conversion experience, and I have resolved to demonstrate my conversion not with fine words but with daring deeds." He paused, then took two steps closer to the people in the first pews.

"I want you all to know that I fired my lawyers this morning. Then I met with my five-member finance council and gave them a mandate to settle immediately with all the remaining victims of sexual abuse, the men and women whose cases are still unresolved. Those souls, mostly men, a few women, are still haunted by the abuse they suffered at the hands of men they trusted as they would trust Jesus himself.

"At one time, reluctant to lay myself open to my enemies, I played the games my lawyers taught me, played games with the victims, as my lawyers played games—are still playing games—with the victims' lawyers, and with the district attorney himself.

"Now I realize the victims were not my enemies, but simply victims of the clericalism that has shamed the hierarchical Church and, in the process, shamed all of you, the people of God. I also realize that the victims' lawyers—with only a few exceptions—are not the greedy opportunists I thought they were. They had a right—no, a duty—to seek help from our legal system for their clients. They still do.

"And once I realized my own lawyers' strategy, to keep the victims hanging out to dry for more than four years, I should have stopped them in their tracks and worked out an immediate settlement with those victims. You know I finally agreed to a settlement of six hundred sixty million dollars in July of 2007, but the archdiocese got off easy. It only paid out two hundred fifty million. Insurance companies and some religious orders paid the rest. In retrospect, I realized I could have done the right thing years ago, but didn't because I was thinking more about the institution and less about the ongoing suffering of the victims."

Mahony paused and looked out over the audience, and his voice broke a little. "I regret that. Now I want to cut through the legal niceties and help the rest of the victims put an end to this horrible chapter in their lives—insofar as that is possible. My heart goes out to them here tonight, even to those who are insisting on a trial. I'd rather not go on trial, of course, but I will, if that's what it takes to put this all behind us and face into the future as brothers and sisters in Christ—together.

"That said, I want to go back now and vest for Mass. It will be a Mass of the Resurrection for my captors, and for all those who lost their lives at Chiapas trying to hold me accountable to you—and to many others around the world—for my sins. They found a creative way to do that. I admire their imagination, and their follow-through, and their courageous foolhardiness,

85

too." He paused, to wipe his eyes with the back of his hand. "They lost their lives in the process." He paused again, then proceeded, his speech now much more deliberate.

"Please . . . do not blame . . . the entire chain of military command . . . for their deaths. This was just one of those bureaucratic mistakes—poor information, men following orders that were never given, bad communications at the point of engagement. Pray for them. And, please . . . do praise . . . the martyrs, and give thanks to God . . . for sharing them with us before he brought them home in glory. And, if anyone cares, I plead . . . guilty as charged in Chiapas. I confess my sins to all of you, and promise I will try to be . . . a Christian—as I also seek new ways of being . . . a shepherd and a sailor."

He bowed his head, then raised it, and raised his arms, too, and blinked back his tears and tried to smile.

For a few moments, no one stirred, or even breathed. Then, far in back of the cathedral, someone began a rhythmic clap. A few others joined in, and then everyone followed their lead, accelerating to a crescendo of acclaim that ended with a throaty cheer. A male voice rang out, "Do we have a bishop?"

Steve Lopez of the *LA Times*, who was there, wrote a few lines in his reporter's notebook to remind himself that the man in the pew didn't say, "We have a bishop," but posed it as a question, and that someone else shouted, "Maybe!" To Lopez that good-humored "maybe" told him Mahony still had to prove himself to a community that loved him, but didn't trust him.

TEN

PHOEBE

A WEEK LATER, MAHONY PAID A VISIT to the Dorothy Day Hospitality House in downtown Los Angeles, and arranged with Jeff Dietrich and his wife, Catherine, to take up residence in his suite at the rectory—getting their agreement to oversee the conversion of the cathedral rectory into an upscale shelter for homeless pregnant women. At nine in the morning, Hawkslaw was pouring himself a cup of coffee in the rectory kitchen when Mahony informed him that they'd be moving—today.

"Where are we going?" asked Hawkslaw.

"I'm taking up residence in the AIDS wing at Queen of Angels. You can go wherever you want."

Hawkslaw gave him a twisted grin. "Kicked out? Just like that? Any suggestions?"

Mahony shrugged. "Every rectory in town has two or three vacant bedrooms. You might call your, uh, friend, your Opus Dei friend at St. Basil's. It's only a few blocks from the office."

STEVE LOPEZ, WHO HAD ALREADY WRITTEN sixteen seething columns about Cardinal Mahony over the past ten years, wrote on the second front page of the Sunday *LA Times:*

> Yesterday, I watched his Mightiness the cardinal-archbishop of Los Angeles making the rounds among AIDS patients at Queen of Angels. He looked like someone who was not in a hurry, surely not in a hurry to condemn these sorry plague victims, surely

not to rush off for lunch at the Jonathan Club with members of this town's elite.

He sat with many of these AIDS guys, held their hands, gave them their chemical cocktails, listened to their stories, blessed them, asked them to pray for him.

He looked like Christ with the lepers.

Two days ago, he gave up his deluxe suite in the cathedral rectory, which he has made into a shelter for homeless pregnant women and put the name of Dorothy Day over the door. Then he checked into a two-room suite at Queen of Angels. In the AIDS wing.

At last, we have a bishop who is putting the Gospel in play.

I haven't been to Mass in seventeen years.

On Sunday, I am taking my family to Mass at the cathedral.

I understand Cardinal Mahony will be celebrating the ten o'clock.

I want to hear what he has to say. But if he says little, that will be okay.

His recent actions fairly shout.

IN EARLY JANUARY, the cardinal took a phone call from Thomas Dimleigh, his auxiliary bishop in Ventura County. "Wuh, wuh, wuh, we got a problem," stuttered Dimleigh.

"Namely?"

"Up in S-s-s-olvang, at St. P-p-p-priscilla's—"

"That's where we appointed Sister Phoebe McNulty as parish administrator, right?"

"Ruh-ruh-right. Last August. And she's the pro-pro-problem. Without a p-p-p-priest in the parish, as you know, she presides over a Eucharistic serrrrrrr, serrrrrrr, service every morning. Doesn't draw many. Maybe a dozen men and women, mostly reeeeeeeetired p-p-p-people."

"I know." For Mahony, this was not unusual. All over the Catholic world, catechists and deacons were doing the same thing, from the *favelas* in Rio to the Australian outback. When they got a rare Mass-visit from one of their circuit-riding priests, they would ask him to consecrate a large supply of extra hosts, which reserved in the locked tabernacle, then distributed at Eucharistic services in his absence. But parishioners were acutely aware that those prayer services were not the Mass. Some were complaining. Without the Mass, they were beginning to feel like Protestants.

Dimleigh said, "Well, now I h-h-h-ear that Sister Phoebe McNulty is playing p-p-p-priest at St. P-p-p-priscilla's."

"She's saying Mass?"

"Well, not exactly. She t-t-t-takes her place up at the altar, then has everyone in the p-p-p-pews saying all the words of the canon of the Mass in unison. So, in a suh, suh, sense, they are all ceeeeeeel, ceeeeeeel, celebrating together."

"How do you know this, Tom?"

"One of the regulars, a Mrs. S-S-S-Simpson, came to me yesterday afternoon and told me. Wanted to know if this was a vuh, vuh, valid Mass."

"And what did you tell her?"

"I said I didn't think so, but I'd ch-ch-ch-check it out."

"Did you?"

"I phoned Sis-sis-sister."

"Sister Phoebe?"

"Yes. I phoned her and asked her if there was any tuh, tuh, truth to the stuh, stuh, story. She said, 'You don't really want to know, do you?' I said I did. She said I oughta just f-f-forget we were having this conversation."

To Bishop Dimleigh, Mahony didn't appear upset. "Pretty clever, huh?"

"I geh, geh, guess so."

"You ever meet Sister Phoebe?"

"Oh, y-y-yes. Petite little thing. Ruh, ruh, ruh, red hair. Fffffffinely freckled. I think she's a leh, I think she's a leh, a leh, a leh—"

"A lesbian?

"Yes."

"Funny," said Mahony. "One of the women in the early Church who presided over the household liturgies in Corinth was named Phoebe. You believe in reincarnation, Tom?"

"Nuh, nuh, not really."

"Well, before we do anything—and maybe we don't want to do anything—before we do anything, can you give me the names and phone numbers of some of the regulars at Sister Phoebe's daily liturgies?"

"I don't know. I can t-t-t-try Mrs. Simpson. She may have some nuh, nuh, names for me."

"Okay, Tom. Let me know, huh? And Tom?"

"Yeh, yeh, yes?"

"Keep this to yourself, okay?"

WHEN MAHONY GOT A LIST OF SIX NAMES and a dozen phone numbers—everyone seemed to have a land line and a cell phone these days—he called each of them—three men and three women. Those he could reach had a breathless, almost exultant, air about them as they spoke about what they called "our people's liturgy."

"It's the neatest thing that ever happened to me," said the third person he called, memorable to him because she was a young assistant city manager in Santa Maria. "I go to seven o'clock liturgy every morning now, and I arrive at work full of the spirit, ready to change the world. Or, at least, the city of Santa Maria."

Mahony tried two more numbers, got no answer, left voice mail messages, and tried the sixth person on his list, a man named Kevin Stevens, who turned out to be a seventh-grade teacher at a public school in Santa Maria. Mahony asked him if the story was true. "Are you guys having priestless Masses?"

Stevens said, "First thing I'd say, we don't call them Masses. Second thing, these are the most devout, solemn liturgies I have ever seen. When we say the words, we say them in the kind of wonder-filled tones we use when we're reading our nieces and nephews their bedtime stories."

"What do you think is happening at these liturgies?"

"Same thing that's been happening for centuries in every Lutheran church in the world. They believe that at their communion services, they are receiving the Body and Blood of our Lord."

Mahony mulled that. He wondered if anyone except Mother Angelica would dare say they weren't.

Stevens said, "That's what happening here at St. Priscilla's. Sister Phoebe's great. Very spiritual, really awesome. But she has a Schillebeeckx-kind of sacramental theology. She doesn't say she's confecting the Eucharist. She says our little community of loving persons has gathered together in Christ's name. And so, we kinda believe Jesus is there in the midst of us."

"I see," said Mahony. He, too, believed Jesus was there in the midst of them. Instead, however, of asking himself if this could be called a Catholic liturgy, Mahony thought, *If this is an example of Santa Maria's average, seventh-grade public school teacher, the families of Santa Maria are indeed lucky.* "You mention the name of Edward Schillebeeckx, the Dutch Dominican. How do you happen to know Schillebeeckx?"

"I was a seminarian, Cardinal Mahony."

"At our St. John's in Camarillo?"

"At the minor seminary. When it was time to move on up to theology, I dropped out."

"I see. Any particular reason why?"

"I was looking to find my masculinity. For a while, I found it in the penises of other men."

Mahony gulped. This young man's candor took him by surprise, but it helped Mahony speak candidly, too. "Are you gay?"

"No, not gay. I just think I was confused about my sexual identity. A lot of my classmates in the seminary were confused, too. Many of them are priests now. And still confused."

"Did you find your masculinity?"

"Yes. We're all sexual beings. We become men by being men, not eunuchs."

"And priests are eunuchs?"

"St. Paul used the term. 'Eunuchs for the kingdom of God.'"

"Yes, he did."

"But that eunuch system isn't working very well in the Church today, is it, Cardinal Mahony?"

"Depends," he said. "Some priests are very faithful to their promises of celibacy."

"And many are not?"

"Some. I don't know how many."

"In this culture, they're fighting a losing battle. Prayer helps. Daily Mass and Communion helps. But it doesn't substitute for a real woman. A loving woman."

"And not even your daily liturgy helps you control yourself?"

"Oh, it's not a question of control. I have a girl friend now. We sleep together, and she's helping me find my masculinity by being with her. I have no need to control that. I am loving it. In fact, I am exhilarated."

Mahony had to ponder that. At seventy-two, he didn't find himself thinking much about sex. He knew it was the big problem for his young priests, gay or straight. But few of them—maybe one out of a hundred— could talk things over with him as this young man was doing with him now. Kevin's testimony told him he still had a lot to learn about sex, about that important part of being human that he and his fellow clerics found so difficult to integrate in their lives, or even talk about.

He flashed on the image of María, young, high-titted María, and then, with a pang of guilt, switched gears. He said, "I am curious. We banned Schillebeeckx. And yet you found him in your seminary library?" Mahony had met the Dutch Dominican, one of the stalwarts at Vatican II, who was called to Rome three times after the Council to answer charges of heresy. He was never silenced, or even disciplined, but seminaries banned his works.

Stevens said, "That's what made us go out and buy his books ourselves, so we could understand his radical new theology of the sacraments. For us, Schillebeeckx took the magic out of the Mass. Christ doesn't come down from heaven like a bolt of lightning when the priest says, 'This is my body.'"

"Yes," said Mahony. He knew that most post-conciliar theologians had gone along with this view. Christ was present in the Mass, but not because the priest had the power to change the substance of bread and wine into the body and blood of Christ with an incantation. Christ became present in the whole Mass. And, whatever changes came about in the bread and wine during Mass, Thomas Aquinas' "transubstantiation" today was pretty well identified with the change that took place in the people, at Mass, when they were transformed into other Christs, so they could go out and change the world. He wasn't sure how many Catholics understood that. But this Stevens fellow seemed to understand.

"I now have a little collection of Schillebeeckx," Stevens said. "And I share his stuff with some of the folks in our liturgical community at St. Priscilla's. You ought to come up sometime and see what we are doing."

"I should," said Mahony. "But I won't. Not right now. St. Priscilla's is one of those places that I cannot take official notice of. If someone from the Vatican calls and asks me about it—and I am sure someone will, sooner or later—I have to go to Dumbsville."

MAHONY WAS RIGHT. Within a week, Bishop Dimleigh's informant in Solvang, not getting any satisfaction from him, or from the cardinal, faxed a letter to the Congregation of Divine Worship in Rome—with a copy to Cardinal Re, telling them about St. Priscilla's outlaw Mass every morning.

The informant copied Sister Angelica, too, the starchy nun who ran EWTN, the Catholic television network. She assigned a television crew to film Sister Phoebe's daily Mass.

"You must be mistaken," Sister Phoebe told EWTN's assignment editor, who phoned for permission to come and tape at St. Priscilla's. "We don't have daily Mass here. We don't have a priest in residence. As administrator of the parish, I do conduct a communion service."

Her careful words deflected a visit from EWTN. But she couldn't keep her people's liturgy a secret forever in a land where the press's power was now compounded by the signal drums of the global village—the Internet. In three days, the whole world knew how a little nun named Phoebe McNulty had solved the priest shortage at St. Priscilla's in Solvang. And how, emulating her, liturgical communities had sprung up in priestless parish after priestless parish in villages, towns and cities around the world.

It happened like this. A twenty-something reporter for the *Santa Barbara News-Press* did the first feature story on Sister Phoebe's liturgy that ran on Wednesday morning, January 14 under the headline CATACOMB CHRISTIANS REAPPEAR IN SOLVANG. Matt Drudge ran the story on his Web page that night. It got 1,578,000 hits. On Thursday morning, the *CBS Early Show* reported Drudge's pickup. And on Friday morning, the *New York Times* ran a Page One story by Laurie Goodstein, with a three-column picture in color of Sister Phoebe. Goodstein's story not only said that the people of St. Priscilla's Parish had solved the no-priest problem. The people of many parishes and small faith communities, according to *Times* reporters around the globe, were already emulating the example of California's St. Priscilla's.

Goodstein's piece was highlighted by a quote from Sister Phoebe. "No, I do not want to be a priest. That way, I'd just be co-opted in and by the clerical culture, and become part of a dying institution called 'the priesthood.'" Goodstein also reported that, for the last two mornings, an increasing number of teenagers—several dozen the day before—had been showing up for Phoebe's 7:00 AM liturgy. Goodstein said Phoebe said, "I am not sure what that means."

Goodstein drew meaning from one of the kids. She ended her piece by quoting a fifteen-year-old named Heather Scanlon: "Now, we own the Mass. It is ours."

Peter Steinfels did his Saturday column in the *Times* on Sister Phoebe —"the spiritual sister no doubt of St. Paul's Phoebe, who presided over the breaking of the bread in Corinth." He quoted Father Andrew Greeley, whom he reached at his home in Tucson. Greeley said, "In fact, deacons from Chiapas to Borneo have been doing their own Eucharistic liturgies for more than three years. Now Sister Phoebe's little community has just taken the priesthood of the faithful to the next level."

Steinfels also quoted Monsignor Pietro Sambi, the papal nuncio in Washington, who said, "We have known all about Sister Phoebe's wildcat liturgy for some time and have begun a process. The so-called Mass that she's saying is quite invalid, according to Canon 1378 of the Code of Canon Law."

Steinfels pointed out that Sister Phoebe wasn't saying Mass. "As I understand it," he wrote, "the whole congregation is the celebrant." He quoted Keith Pearson, a Jesuit liturgist from New York who was teaching at Rome's Gregorian University. "When the whole congregation says the words of the canon of the Mass in unison as solemnly and as devoutly as I understand folks are doing all over the world this morning, certain Vatican prelates may be frowning. But I don't think God's frowning even a little bit."

MAHONY TOOK A PHONE CALL from his longtime friend John R. Quinn, the retired archbishop of San Francisco, who told him, "Well, Roger, the fat is in the fire, huh?"

Mahony laughed. "You saw the piece in Friday's *New York Times*?"

"Yes."

"And Steinfels' column yesterday?"

"Yes. What was Greeley thinking of?"

"I don't know, John. When does Greeley ever have time to think?" Quinn laughed.

Mahony said, "I think it is safer if priests who are on our side just say they know nothing. If they'd just keep a poker face on this."

"Hard to do that when everyone in the world knows it's happening."

"True enough. Just a minute. I have a fax coming in here." Mahony walked over to his fax machine and peeked at the underside of the note to see if it had a letterhead. It did. It was from the Vatican's Sacred Congregation of Divine Worship. "It's from Cardinal Arinze's office," reported Mahony after he had skimmed the note. "It says I am under the pope's orders to stop this so-called people's Mass."

Quinn said, "Good!"

"You sound fairly gleeful."

"I am. This may be the test case we've been looking for."

"Test case?"

Quinn reminded Mahony of a remark by a ranking monsignor at the Holy Office several years before, uttered one night at dinner in the Villa Stritch. "The U.S. bishops don't need the Vatican's permission to do what they need to do in America. All they need is balls. But few U.S. bishops have them."

"So now," Mahony said to Quinn, "you think this is my chance to show the world I have balls?"

"You're well on the way to doing that," said Quinn.

"I really haven't done anything yet."

"That's the beautiful part. You don't have to do a thing."

"How's that?"

"Give Arinze a taste of the Vatican's own medicine. Tell him you will investigate and report. And then take your sweet time."

"And then what happens?"

"In the meantime, the people at St. Priscilla's will go right on doing what they've been doing. And so will everyone else in the world who has a mind to. All of a sudden, the famine is over."

"Famine?"

"Eucharistic famine."

Mahony thought about that. If you could believe the *New York Times*, Catholics everywhere—including huge numbers of young people who hadn't been to Mass in years—were investigating these people's liturgies. Nothing wrong with that. "*Praxis* trumps *doxis*, huh?"

"Exactly. *Lex orandi lex credendi*. The people's faith comes out of their prayer life."

"How do I tell that to Arinze?"

"You won't have to. In a very short time, I predict, it will be quite obvious, even to those idiots at Worship, that the people have solved the Eucharistic famine *ambulando*."

Mahony understood the allusion to Xeno's theorem. According to the Greek philosopher, it was logically impossible to move from A to B without first going halfway from A to B. But you couldn't go halfway to halfway without first going halfway to halfway to halfway. And so on, forever. Logically, you could never move. The solution, said Xeno, was to start walking. *Solvitur ambulando.* "And what if the men in the Vatican say they disapprove?"

"Of what the people are doing?"

"Yes."

"I think they'd be loath to do that. In the long tradition of the Church, the popes don't usually tell the people what they must believe. When Pius XII declared that the Assumption of the Blessed Virgin Mary into heaven was Catholic doctrine, he did not say, 'This is what you must believe,' but rather, after he had polled the world's bishops, 'This is what we do believe.'"

Mahony said, "We're not exactly talking about belief here. We're talking about a direct order—to stop this people's Mass in Solvang, California."

"But, strictly speaking, it is not 'a people's Mass,' is it? They call it 'a people's liturgy.' You don't have to stop what doesn't exist. So I say just ignore the order, for as long you can."

"And then what happens?"

Quinn said, "Maybe nothing. By the time your answer is due at the Vatican, the issue could be moot."

"Moot?"

"It won't matter," said Quinn, "what the Vatican says or doesn't say. The people will decide what they want to do, and the Vatican will let them. In Italy, red lights don't always mean 'stop.' Everything is open to discussion. It's the Italian way. And if I am wrong, I'll eat my hat."

As Quinn had surmised, the Vatican was slow to act. But, because he left Philadelphia's Cardinal Grandeur out of his equation, he was soon inquiring about the best ways of making his hat into a comestible.

ELEVEN

KEYS

FRANCIS OLIVER GRANDEUR, the cardinal-archbishop of Philadelphia, knew that, left to itself, the Vatican usually dithered. Which is why, on January 23, he was boarding an Air France jet to Rome, to warn the pope and his advisers in the Roman Curia about Mahony's imminent plans to overturn the hierarchical constitution of the Church in America and "give the Church back to the people"—whatever that meant!

It wouldn't be enough to throw Roman canon law at Mahony. Better to mount a campaign against him, gang up on him. If he could just get Rome to call a synod of all the U.S. bishops—dam this river of nonsense with the entire weight of the American hierarchy. Which is what Grandeur told Cardinal Gianbattista Re, president of the Sacred Pontifical Council of Bishops when he presented himself in the Vatican on January 24. "As you know, Eminence," said Grandeur, "the American bishops held three of these regional synods in the 1800s—the First, Second, and Third Councils of Baltimore."

"And now you want a fourth?" asked Re.

Grandeur nodded. "It's the only way to stop Mahony. He's always made so much of the bishops' conference, even manipulated it to do his own bidding on more than one occasion. To turn it against him now would kill him."

"Is that what you want? To kill him?"

"Well, not kill. To save him from himself. He's gone off his head. The poor man. It's not his fault. He fell into the hands of these terrorists, these

97

kidnappers. And he is obviously suffering from some form of the Stockholm Syndrome."

"Fallen in love with his kidnappers?" For once in his life, Cardinal Re did not have a beatific smile on his face.

"I am certain of it," said Grandeur. "A man doesn't change as Mahony has changed—almost overnight. He has moved out of his cathedral rectory and taken up residence in an AIDS hospice, where he spends two hours a day talking to some dying fags."

"We had expected him in Rome this week," said Re. "He sent word that he wouldn't be coming. In fact, he said we shouldn't expect him in Rome until—." He paused. He and his colleagues hardly used the expression. "Until the next conclave."

The words almost stuck in his throat. In the Vatican, they didn't talk about the pope's passing. There, the only time the pope is sick is when he is dead. But now Re was quoting Mahony. "He said he wouldn't see us 'until the next conclave.'"

"There you go."

Re was puzzled at the expression. "Forgive me," he said. "Some of your American idioms puzzle me."

"'There you go' means just one more proof," said Grandeur, "that Roger is off—off balance."

NEXT DAY, GRANDEUR VISITED RE'S OFFICE AGAIN. Three sympathetic American cardinals with Vatican jobs were waiting for him there: Francis Stafford from Denver, and Bernard Law, living in Roman exile since his resignation in Boston, but still very much a power here, along with Cardinal William Levada, the American head of the Holy Office. Re had also summoned two American monsignors who worked in his office.

To Grandeur's surprise, none of them favored a national synod in the U.S.

"Too risky," said Law. "If word gets out we are making some changes in the American Church, we will encourage many—liberals and conservatives alike—to demand changes of their own."

"What do you mean," asked Re, "if word gets out? How can it not? Something like two hundred bishops headed for a meeting, even if it were a secret meeting? You can control the Catholic press in America. In fact, you've been doing that very well. But the *New York Times, Time* magazine...."

"And the *Boston Globe*," said Law. "Don't forget those bastards."

All of them smiled, knowing that stories in the *Globe* had been a major factor in Law's leaving Boston. Lucky for Law he'd been able to buy a job in Rome. Archpriest of Santa Maria Maggiore wasn't a huge sinecure. But it allowed Law to put the best face on his ignominious departure.

Grandeur persisted. "You just have to know how to handle the *Times*—all the press, for that matter." He didn't have to add, *like I do*. He had shown his skill in getting—and maintaining—good press in New York. "No," he said directly to Re, "the reward is worth the risk."

"Reward?" asked Re.

"All over America," said Grandeur, "the natives are restless. Not long ago, some laypeople staged a sit-in in a Polish parish I was closing. I had the cops come and take them off to jail." He turned to Law. "Your successor, the Franciscan? He let protestors occupy his churches, some of 'em for more than a hundred days. I wouldn't put up with any of that nonsense. We need to get tough with the laity. We need to get them back in line."

"And you think you can do that with a Fourth Council of Baltimore?" asked Levada.

Grandeur nodded. But Re seemed skeptical. "A Fourth Council of Baltimore will be like a medicine, the cure for what ails the American layman? I doubt it."

Stafford agreed with Re. He observed that the laity were not so willing any more to take their castor oil "like good little boys and girls."

Law chimed in. "We used to have a lock on the attorney general's office in Massachusetts. On the police department in Boston. Even on the FBI. All good Catholics from the BC Law School, they knew enough to look the other way when our priests got in trouble. Now they can't wait to indict."

That triggered a spate of stories. Everyone had a tale to tell, each of the Americans talking at once.

Finally Re called a halt. "Cardinal Grandeur," he said. "We are simply going to let you handle this national synod idea. You don't need Rome's permission to call a national meeting."

"We don't?" asked Grandeur. "It's in canon law. Canon 443."

"I just read it again last night," said Re. "It says a nation's bishops can initiate a regional synod. Here in Rome, we can only approve your action.

Or suggest you do not have a synod at all. If the American bishops decided to have a regional synod, the pope wouldn't stop them. He might even favor such a move. Prove the Church is not a Fascist monolith."

Stafford pointed out that it would take some time to put together a Fourth Council of Baltimore. "That's not going to help us deal with Mahony today."

"Seems to me," said Law, "that for now we just have to move Mahony aside."

Grandeur thought of his good friend Hawkslaw. "Put the chancellor in charge and bring Mahony in? Let him retire gracefully at Quattro Coronati?" The Basilica of the Four Crowned Saints was Mahony's titular church, one of the most tranquil churches in Rome, first built in 313, to honor four soldiers martyred under Diocletian for refusing to sacrifice to the pagan god Aesculapius.

"No," said Re. "That's premature. Mahony has an auxiliary bishop who handles the northern part of the archdiocese." He consulted his notepad, looking for the man's name. "We will tell Tomàs Dimleigh to simply close down this outlaw parish. That should send a message."

"Duh, duh, duh Dimleigh?" Stafford said mockingly. The others rolled their eyes. "He's not too bright. But he will do as he's told."

"We'll test him," said Re. "Solvang? Danish name. Any Catholics there?"

Grandeur was miffed. He had wanted to level Mahony with an atomic bomb. And these guys wanted to use a squirt gun. He doubted their water pistol would work. And he was angry at himself, jetting all the way to Rome for nothing. Well, not for nothing. He took the time to enjoy a few days at Rome's best hostelry, the Minerva, which was owned by one of his captive American billionaires. The Minerva was the most expensive hotel in Rome. It also had the best kitchen. And the best masseurs.

BISHOP THOMAS DIMLEIGH did what he was told. As soon as he received Re's order by fax, he phoned Sister Phoebe McNulty to give her the bad news. "Sorry," he told her. "And I'll be co-co-co-coming out Monday muh-muh-morning to get your keys. Yes, about ten. And, oh yes, you'll have to find another puh-puh-place to live. In your order's re-re-retirement cuh-cuh-community, perhaps?"

Phoebe phoned Queen of Angels, talked to the administrator there, and got through immediately to Cardinal Mahony. "What do you know," she asked him, "about Bishop Dimleigh coming to St Priscilla's on Monday to shut down the parish?"

This was news to him. But, strangely enough, he was undisturbed. "It's a power play," he told her. "But I think we can block it." He arranged to meet Phoebe in Solvang the next morning at eight. "And I am going to bring my top gun."

"Not Hawkslaw?"

He laughed. "No. Nick Pike. He's a lawyer."

She hummed over that. "A lawyer. There's an old Mexican curse: 'May your life be filled with lawyers.'"

Mahony frowned. His recent experience on trial told him the makers of Mexican proverbs were not dummies. "This is the kind of world we live in. We cannot live without lawyers. The best I can hope for is a no-nonsense lawyer like Nick Pike."

For a moment, Mahony regretted selling his chopper. He could have flown to Solvang in a half hour. Driving would take more than four. But he had a plan in mind, and he wanted to see it unfold. So, wearing a pair of slacks and a sport shirt, he left Queen of Angels well before dawn with Nick Pike at the wheel of his white Ford Explorer. They drove out the Ventura Freeway, sipping coffee from a thermos, mostly in silence, until they passed the turnoff to Lompoc, which prompted Mahony to ask Pike about his time served there in the federal lockup for crossing the line at Ft. Benning. Pike's prison tales lasted until they reached Solvang.

Mahony had no trouble picking out Sister Phoebe in a booth at Paula's Pancake House on Solvang's Main Street. She was what they said she was: fair and freckled with short, carrot-red hair. "This," Mahony said to her, "is Nick Pike. You may be dealing with him more than a little bit in the next few days." They took seats in the booth and ordered coffee and some of the Danish rolls the town was famous for.

She said, "There's no precedent for this, is there?"

"For what?"

"Disobeying, disobeying Rome?"

Mahony recoiled. Just those two words—"disobeying Rome"—went against a lifetime of training. "Well, I'm not disobeying any order given to

101

me. In fact, the Vatican may be out of line here. It had no right to go around behind my back to give Dimleigh any direct order."

Pike said, "We just want to stop Dimleigh from executing it."

"So you are not thinking about going into schism?"

Mahony shuddered. "I could never do that, never, never, never split from Rome. But I do want to do my duty by my flock."

"So what happens when Bishop Dimleigh shows up at St. Priscilla's asking me for the keys?"

"That's why we're here this morning," said Pike. "So we can rehearse our moves."

She nodded. "I am glad you said we. I am with you on this. You know that?"

"As I am with you," said Mahony. "With you on your people's liturgy. You've cut through a lot of our palaver over the priest shortage. We've talked the issue to death. And nothing happened. You did something."

MAHONY AND PIKE sat in the front seat of Pike's white van—about a hundred feet up a palm-lined street from St. Priscilla's, hoping not to be noticed by any of the crowd gathered in front of the little California mission-style church. If this moment was going to signalize the people's Church in action, then the people—not the cardinal—had to be out front. But Mahony and Pike knew this was a historic moment—which was why Pike had tipped off the newspeople, and why the cardinal wanted to make sure he could see the event unfold for himself. Indeed, a Channel 13 news van was parked outside St. Priscilla's. But neither Pike nor Mahony had any way of knowing whether 13 would carry this newsbreak live or on the evening news. As it turned out, they carried it live—as Pike and Mahony could plainly see on the portable TV inside Pike's van.

Dimleigh arrived in a black Mercedes sedan. He had a driver, a youngish man Mahony did not recognize, who parked the car in a red, no-parking zone at the curb in front of the church. They climbed out, both of them wearing their clerical black suits and Roman collars. If they had had an inkling why the crowd—and the TV cameras—had gathered there, they would have stayed in the car and returned to Santa Barbara. But it was too late.

102

Phoebe met the bishop on the steps of the church wearing a white alb and a purple stole. By now, several cameramen and reporters from two local papers and the *Los Angeles Times* had closed in, but Bishop Dimleigh was too flustered to notice. He stuttered through a little canned speech saying he had his orders to take over the church. He concluded, "I ha-ha-have to ask you for the k-k-k-k-keys."

Phoebe stood her ground before him and while the cameras whirred and the soundmen aimed their shotgun mikes at the tableau, she said, "I can't do that."

"I have my or-or-orders," said Dimleigh. "From the Vuh, vuh, vuh, Vatican." He looked to his aide, who was in fact one of the American monsignors working in Cardinal Re's office, dispatched from Rome to help Dimleigh. But Dimleigh was beyond help at this point.

Phoebe smiled, then frowned. "The Vatican doesn't own St. Priscilla's."

"Do you want me to go g-g-g-get the shuh, shuh, sheriff?"

"You needn't *go* anywhere. If you want to talk to him, he's right over there."

"Wha, wha, what do you mee-mee-mean?"

"There's Sheriff Jim Henry. You want to talk to him?"

The bishop turned, glared at the cameras, whispered to his aide, then took some steps toward the sheriff.

The sheriff nodded and moved to the bishop's side. "Sheriff Henry," he said, announcing himself and offering a handshake.

Dimleigh gave the sheriff's hand a flabby, uncertain squeeze. "I have an or-or-or-order from the Vuh, vuh, vuh, Vatican—"

The sheriff nodded. "From the pope?"

Dimleigh stuttered. "Well, nuh-nuh-nuh-not from the pope. From a Vatican dee-dee-dee-dicastery."

"A Vatican—what is it? A Vatican dicastery doesn't have any legal standing here."

Bishop Dimleigh's aide stepped up and informed the sheriff that canon law looks for legal enforcement by what it calls "the civil arm" in every nation.

"That would mean an American court," said Henry. "A half hour ago, I had a conference with our DA. He told me that, since the beginning of the nineteenth century, American courts haven't intervened in many church disputes. You've heard of the First Amendment's no-establishment clause? The sheriff has no power to act in a religious dispute."

Dimleigh said this wasn't a religious dispute. "It's about pro-pro-property."

Henry raised a manila envelope in his left hand, and said, "I have county tax records here saying that Roger Mahony, the archbishop of Los Angeles corporation sole, owns this property."

Dimleigh stammered, "But Cardinal Muh, muh, Mahony works for the puh, puh, the pope."

The sheriff stood his ground. "If you think you have a case here, Bishop Dimleigh, you can file a claim in superior court."

Sister Phoebe said, "I think you ought to know, Bishop Dimleigh, that I have a notarized document from Cardinal Mahony." She waved a legal-sized envelope. "It says I am in charge here. It says the people of God in Solvang own this church, and that the cardinal and I just watch over it for them." She spoke up, so the reporters and the TV soundmen could pick up each word. "If the people don't like what we're doing for them, *they* can get rid of *us*."

Bishop Dimleigh did not speak up. His aide said, "Hey, the Church is not a democracy, you know."

Dimleigh turned and whispered to his aide, "It sure is beginning to loo, loo, look like wuh, wuh, one. Le, le, let's get the he-he-hell out of here."

Neither he nor his aide saw Mahony as they drove back up the street, because, when he saw them coming, he ducked his head. After they had passed, Mahony sat up straight and blinked three times. "I can't believe I did that," he said to Pike.

"It's okay," said Pike. "Dimleigh didn't need to know you were here."

• TWELVE •

KOWALSKI

TWO AMERICAN CANON LAWYERS were guests that night on the *O'Reilly Factor*. Monsignor Albert Rountree, Cardinal Grandeur's chancellor, was in Fox's Philadelphia studio, and Father James Kowalski was in a broadcast studio at the University of Notre Dame, both linked to O'Reilly in New York on a remote hookup. Rountree replied to O'Reilly's first question by saying he regretted seeing the scene in Solvang televised all over the world.

"Legally though, according to canon law," said Bill O'Reilly, "could Sister Phoebe do that to a bishop? Just send him packing?"

Rountree, who was wearing a purple vest under his Roman collar, huffed, "Certainly not!"

"But she did it," said O'Reilly. He turned to Kowalski's broad Polish face on a large, in-studio screen. "Father Kowalski, you're a former president of the Canon Law Society of America. What do you say?"

Kowalski said, "Well, you're right, Bill. She did it. That is a fact. It is also a fact, apparently, that she has the backing of the cardinal-archbishop of Los Angeles. And he is the guy in charge, even in Solvang."

"Most unfortunate," said Rountree, interrupting. "To have this dispute aired on national television."

"International television," said O'Reilly by way of correction. "That news clip this morning flashed all over the world. And our show is now being seen from Rio to Riobamba. It's 4:00 AM in the Vatican, but I am sure this show is also being taped there right now so the pope can see it."

"I hardly think his Holiness is concerned with St. Priscilla Parish in, uh, Solvang, California," sniffed Rountree.

"He should be," said Kowalski.

When Rountree did not respond, O'Reilly asked him, "Shouldn't he be?"

"Well, uh, of course. The pope is the vicar of Christ on earth for all mankind. Humankind."

Kowalski said, "We don't need to get into that. What we learned today by watching that little confrontation in Solvang is that someone inside the Vatican tried an end-around on Cardinal Mahony, and a little nun playing outside linebacker threw him for a fifteen-yard loss."

Reilly said, "Uh, we hope someone in the Vatican can explain to the Holy Father what that means. Outside linebacker, huh?" He shook his head, clearly nettled by a cleric speaking the vernacular as colorfully as he. *Who was the star here anyway?* "Okay," he said to Kowalski. "The pope wanted her out of there, and Cardinal Mahony wanted her to stay. I understand that. But there's something I don't understand. Wasn't Bishop Dimleigh correct? Doesn't Cardinal Mahony work for the pope?"

Kowalski said, "As a cardinal? Yes. As the archbishop of Los Angeles, no."

Rountree stopped him. "Well, just a moment here!"

O'Reilly broke into a big grin. As a staunch Catholic, there was nothing he liked better than a fight between two Churchmen. "Father Kowalski! You're telling us the archbishop doesn't work for the pope?"

"I am."

"Who appointed him archbishop of Los Angeles?"

"The pope."

"So?"

"So what?"

"Well, I should think that the guy that hires you has the right to fire you."

"We're not talking about hiring and firing," said Kowalski. "Popes didn't start appointing bishops outside the Papal States until 1829, and maybe a future pope ought to rethink that policy. But that's another issue. What we have here and now is a difference of opinion. This issue is pastoral, not doctrinal. And some of us think pastoral matters are best left to pastors. The Church has a long-standing teaching on subsidiarity."

"Tell the people out there," said O'Reilly, "what that means?" He implied that he knew what subsidiarity was, but his audience needed some help.

Kowalski said, "Nothing should be done by a higher agency that can be done as well, or better, by a lower agency. That's part of the Church's social teaching."

Rountree said, "What Sister Phoebe is doing *is* against Church teaching. And Cardinal Mahony apparently approves of it."

"Sister Phoebe—and her little community—"

Rountree interrupted Kowalski, "They're breaking Church discipline. Priests—not the people—are the ones who say Mass in our Church. Canon law, number 1378, paragraph two, note one, says that anyone who has not been promoted to the priestly order and who attempts to enact the liturgical action of the Eucharistic Sacrifice incurs an automatic penalty of interdict."

Kowalski picked up on that. "Discipline? Monsignor, you said discipline. Discipline isn't doctrine."

Rountree exploded with a sound, not words, a rippling of his lips.

"This is not a new phenomenon," said Kowalski. "Many religious establishments tend to confuse their own man-made rules with doctrine. Jesus charged the Pharisees with making their own man-made rules into the kind of doctrine they could use to lord it over the people. You can look it up in the fourteenth chapter of Luke."

Rountree insisted, "If Sister Phoebe's defying the pope, she isn't Catholic any longer. In the Catholic Church, the pope makes all the rules."

"That's a pretty big leap, Monsignor. If Sister Phoebe isn't a Catholic in your book, what does that make Cardinal Mahony?"

"Well, I'd hesitate to excommunicate the cardinal."

Kowalski countered. "But you'd find it easier to excommunicate a little nun?"

Rountree made that explosive sound again with his lips.

O'Reilly said, "Gentlemen, we have to move on here. Sum this up, in ten seconds. What's gonna happen here?"

"Unless someone does some furious backpedaling," said Rountree, "I see a schism ahead."

Kowalski said, "I don't foresee any backpedaling. But I don't see a schism."

O'Reilly shook his head in puzzlement. "Folks, I don't think we've heard the end of this. It looks like the American Catholic Church is in for a rough ride."

Rountree tried to correct him. "Don't say 'the American Catholic Church.' Say 'the Catholic Church in America.'"

Kowalski objected. "I'd say 'American Catholic Church' is exactly the right phrase, Monsignor. When we have an American Catholic Church, it will be accountable—to the people. And if it is truly American, it will look more like a democracy than a monarchy. Or a dictatorship."

"We'll have you back," said O'Reilly. "We gotta have you both back."

IN HIS TWO-ROOM SUITE in the AIDS wing at Queen of Angels Hospital in Los Angeles, Cardinal Mahony turned off his TV and sighed at the exchange that had been orchestrated by Bill O'Reilly. He was in huge sympathy with Kowalski's views. He had had two long telephone conversations with Kowalski, and agreed with him: the U.S. Church needed to be more accountable to the people. In the American experience, accountability went hand in hand with a whole host of democratic institutions. Men and women were elected to public service by the people. If they didn't serve, they didn't win re-election. Sometimes, those who served themselves more grandly than they served the people were even recalled in midstream. But he had problems applying that democratic paradigm to the Church.

He told Kowalski, "Making the Church accountable to the people. It all seems so—well, so political."

Kowalski laughed. "Roger! You know who you're talking to? You're talking to a guy who has observed the American bishops in action for more than four decades now."

Mahony grunted.

"Watching you, too, Roger. Are you going to tell me that you haven't played ecclesiastical politics all your life?"

"Well, that's different," he said.

"How different?"

"Well, secular politics and Church politics are two different—"

"The same shenanigans go on. Admit it. The only difference is that in the Church we clerics are the only ones who know what's going on. We play our political games behind a velvet curtain of secrecy and indirection. And keep the laity in the dark."

"What are you suggesting?"

"We could admit the truth—that, wherever men vie for power, we have politics. Let's be honest about it, honest with the people. They have a stake in all this, don't they?"

Mahony shook his head. "I wonder if the people would understand—or even want to get involved in—. Politics is so—" He paused, searching for the right word.

"Messy? Yes, it is," said Kowalski. "And, if it's done right, dangerous, too. Jesus threatened the political power of the Pharisees—urging his followers to hunger and thirst after justice—and they had him crucified for his trouble. And those who followed his lead—some of them got crucified, too. Peter was crucified and Paul was beheaded."

"For being in politics?"

"We don't usually think of Peter and Paul in those terms. But, yes. The Roman emperors saw them as a threat to their power. And that's been the whole history of the world, a struggle for power. I think it is part of being human." He reflected on what he had just said, then added, "What's wrong with being human?"

"People don't expect us to be human," Mahony said. "They like to think that everything out of my office comes from God. Make them part of any decision process and we may have trouble. I wonder if the people of God are all that ready to take a hand in their own governance."

"You've got a number of boards and commissions, don't you?"

"The members are all appointed, not elected. Appointed by me!"

"Well, you might ask the people of Los Angeles to elect them. And give them real, not merely advisory, power."

"How do I do that?"

"Sign 'em up. Make 'em voters."

"Voters for what?"

"You challenge them to elect their own representatives on every parish committee. And you let all the parish committees elect reps to your various archdiocesan boards."

Mahony pondered that. When Pike got him starting to think harder about a people's Church, he hadn't dreamed of going this far. At times, he wondered if he was going too far. Other times, he wondered if he was going far enough. "Who gets to vote?" he asked.

"Anyone who is registered in a parish."

"They tell me half the Catholics in LA aren't registered in any parish."

"I dare say many of them *will* register, if they think this will give them a voice and a vote."

Mahony questioned that, too. "You know what this would mean? This could double the size of every parish."

"Pastors might like that. Double their collections,"

"Double their work, too. Lord help them!"

"He'll have to help them," said Kowalski. "But so will the people. Give the people a voice and a vote, and the people will get to work."

"Work for the Church?"

"Not for the hierarchical Church. For their Church, the people-of-God Church. For themselves."

AS HE LAY DOWN TO SLEEP THAT NIGHT, Cardinal Mahony mulled what Kowalski had been telling him, then pulled his olive-pit rosary out from under his pillow, and started to say five decades—for the people of God, and for himself, praying the people wouldn't drag him under.

But then he caught himself. Drag him under what? He had thoughts like that when he was still a young-priest-on-his-way-up. But he, Roger Michael Mahony, was no longer on his way up. He was the cardinal-archbishop of the biggest archdiocese in America. He couldn't go any higher than that, unless he were elected pope, and there was no chance of that.

He remembered the story about Joe Bernardin, archbishop of Cincinnati in 1976, and president of the U.S. Conference of Catholic Bishops when hundreds of Catholic leaders, mostly laymen and women, but some priests and bishops, too, gathered in Detroit's Cobo Hall for the National Call To Action Conference. The people there got out of hand, caught up in their own enthusiasm for radical change in the American Church. On the final day, Sunday, they voted yes on 86 propositions. One of them called for an end to mandatory celibacy for American priests, another for the ordination of married men, another a request for the Vatican to consider the ordination of women.

Monsignor Joseph Gremillion, the USCCB's executive secretary, who had run the affair from beginning to end, read those propositions from the podium. Afterward, as he was leaving the podium, Bernardin turned to him and said. "Joe, what have you done to my career?"

On Monday morning, Bernardin tried to repair his career at the Vatican by calling a news conference to tell the press, "The American bishops cannot endorse this package." Bernardin soon got his reward for putting down a people's revolt in the American Church. The pope made him the archbishop of Chicago, then a cardinal. Bernardin had saved his career. But, to do that, he had to sell out the people. It wasn't that Bernardin was a bad man. In fact, he was one of the best bishops in America. His troubles stemmed from the simple fact that he had learned from his seminary days that if he wanted a career in the Church, he had to protect the power of the hierarchy.

Mahony came out of his revery just as he was finishing the fifth decade of his rosary. "Holy Mary, Mother of God, pray for us sinners, now and at the hour of our death. Amen." Yes, he thought, we are all sinners.

IT TOOK SEVERAL DAYS for Archbishop Quinn of San Francisco to return Mahony's phone call. When he did, Mahony told him that he would never guess the identity of the newest addition to his growing team of revolutionaries.

"Okay. I give up."

"Juana Margarita Obregón."

Quinn tried to process that information. Finally, he said, "I can't believe it."

"Believe it." Mahony told him how she'd avoided death at the hands of the Mexican commandos—"floating up to her eyeballs in a pond of shit."

Quinn needed to hear all of the details. When he was satisfied he had the entire picture, he wondered whether Mahony had told Nick Pike.

Mahony informed him that Nick Pike already knew Juana Margarita Obregón had come back to town. In fact, Pike had rented an apartment for her. "He was just waiting for her to make herself known to me. He's coming over to see me in the morning. And he's bringing—get this—a community organizer."

"What community you going to organize?"

"Not sure. Pike will probably tell me what to do. We may be in politics up to our eyeballs."

"Yeah. Like Juana Margarita Obregón. In a pond of shit."

"Yes. Politics can get messy."

"And for that, you need an organizer?"

"Politics can get complicated, too. We can't just let things happen. Pike urged me not to do that. That would be dumb. We have to make things happen. Pike reminded me of St. Ignatius Loyola. 'Pray as if everything depended on God. Work as if everything depended on yourself.'"

"Good luck."

"What do you mean, 'good luck?' You're on the team, too."

"I am?"

"John, it is time for you to grow some balls, too."

"What do you mean?"

"You know. After the pope had a fit in 1980—when you called for a rethinking of the whole birth control thing at the synod and the synod secretary called you down for doing that, you retreated. You said you'd been misquoted. Then you came back to San Francisco and did next to nothing, until you took early retirement. You became a spectator."

Quinn was silent.

"Well, didn't you?"

"I did write that book in 2000," said Quinn. *The Renewal of the Papacy.* I took it to Rome and gave the pope a copy. I gave one to Ratzinger, too."

"And nothing happened, right?"

"Very little."

"What do you wish you'd done?"

"I don't know."

"Yes," agreed Mahony. "You really didn't know what to do, except appeal to the pope's common sense."

"Uh huh. What else could I do? I'm no politician. Not like you."

Mahony smiled. In another day, he would have denied it. But now he realized he was indeed in politics. "We all have to be politicians," he said. "We have to be accountable to the people."

"What kind of people?"

"Short, tall, thin, fat, black, white, brown, yellow, gays, straights, and in-between. Everybody. We get the people on our side, the bullies in the Roman Curia will back off. If there's anything these guys understand, it's power.

112

They cozy up to power wherever they find it. In Germany before World War II, they made friends with Hitler. In Latin America, in the 1970s, they were quite cordial with dictators. Two current South American cardinals with big jobs in Rome used to play tennis with Pinochet."

"And how do you get the people on your side?"

Mahony said he knew how to talk to the press. "And I may need a campaign manager."

"Or a press secretary."

"I already have one of those."

Quinn didn't hear him. "Somebody like James Carville?"

"Oh, sure! Bill Clinton's genius, the guy who reduced everything to its simplest elements."

"'It's the economy, stupid.'"

"Right!"

"I'm just not sure," said Quinn, "that you'd want Carville. Southern Baptist, I think."

Mahony said, "Maybe I need someone exactly like Carville. Someone who, the less he knows about the Church, the better."

"Why is that?"

"Because he won't feel his hands are tied by our archaic customs. Or by canon law."

Quinn laughed. "You'd go that far, huh, Roger? Well, good for you. You may not last long. But you'll go down in glory."

· THIRTEEN ·

RACKHAM

MAHONY WAS SURPRISED when he first saw Ted Rackham, motoring into the main hallway at Queen of Angels Hospital in his state-of-the-art wheelchair with Nick Pike trailing behind. Rackham maneuvered with such ease that Mahony guessed he'd been in a wheelchair for a long, long time.

"I got polio when I was a senior at Erasmus Hall in Brooklyn," Rackham explained before he was even asked. "That's where Al Davis started his football career—quite a few years before I showed up. But I never let the polio stop me from being me. At Northwestern, I lettered in football—as an assistant manager. I learned to drive my own special car. I've been married twice, had three kids, lots of girlfriends."

Mahony grinned. He liked Rackham's rugged good looks, shaved head, strong nose, heavily muscled upper body. There was something about a man—or a woman—who suffered severe physical handicaps and went right on living their lives without a whimper. He'd met these people on occasion. He had several paraplegics working in the archdiocesan offices, and he found it easy to work with them because they did their jobs with such alacrity. In fact, Mahony was pleased that when Nick Pike phoned and said he was bringing him an organizer, he never mentioned Rackham's disability. He took that as a cue; he certainly wouldn't either.

After introducing Rackham, Pike took off, pleading another appointment in Hollywood, and Mahony led Rackham into the elevator and up to his small suite on the eleventh floor. Coming out of the elevator with Rackham,

Mahony said, "Nick Pike said you helped César Chávez organize the farmworkers?"

"I had a role there. I had a good tutor, Saul Alinsky, the community organizer from Chicago."

"And you used the lessons you learned from Alinsky for your work in the labor movement?"

"That's all the labor movement is: helping the little guys use the only power they have, numbers."

"I've been reading a piece of labor history," said Mahony, grabbing a book off the shelf behind his desk. "This one was written by George McGovern, before he got into politics. It's all about the coal miners in Colorado, in a battle with John D. Rockefeller, who owned most of the state's coal mines. The miners lost that battle when the Colorado National Guard, paid by Rockefeller's mine managers, opened fire on the strikers and killed more than a hundred of them." He handed Rackham the book.

"*The Ludlow Massacre*," read Rackham. "I remember it." He opened it to an early chapter and found a passage on Joe Hill, by most accounts the father of the labor movement in America. "'Don't mourn. Organize.' That was Joe Hill's slogan. From what Nick Pike told me, this is what the Church in America needs to do."

Mahony tested him. "The Church is already organized, isn't it?"

Rackham said, "We're not talking about that kind of organization. According to Nick Pike, you may be trying to overturn that beautiful pyramidal structure of yours, with the pope at the top and the people at the bottom."

Mahony flinched. This was so unlike him. He used to kiss the pope's ring. And now? "Well, Nick was right. We are trying to do something like that—figure out how to organize the people of God."

"'People of God?' Does that expression have some special meaning? You gotta spell things out for this Jew."

"In fact, Ted, we got the phrase from the Jews. In the Old Testament, the Jews were the people of God."

"God's chosen people?"

"Right! Now, ever since Vatican II—you know about Vatican II?"

Rackham nodded.

"Since Vatican II, we have adapted the expression and made it stand for the notion that the only thing special or 'chosen' about any of us is that we have a greater responsibility to the oppressed."

"I like that," said Rackham. "All my life, I been working with the oppressed."

"Maybe this is why Pike brought you here."

"Yeah, well, sort of. If this is what you really want to do."

"Yes," said Mahony. He told Rackham—and this was the first time he ever said it so clearly, "We want to organize the people of God. How do we do that?"

Rackham gave Mahony a long look. Finally, he said, "Not exactly the way John L. Lewis did it with the mine workers. Or the way Walter Reuther did it with the auto workers We're not talking about jobs and a living wage, are we?"

"No. I have made some moves, Ted, that the Vatican does not like. And they have made some moves, too, moves that I have deflected." He told Rackham about Sister Phoebe turning Bishop Dimleigh away from the doors at St. Priscilla's. "But my theory is that if I have the support of the people, the Vatican will be happy to back off. It doesn't want a schism."

"A split?"

"Right," said Mahony. "The Vatican doesn't want to see a split. Neither do I. So, how do we go our own way without absolutely going our own way?"

"Your Eminence—"

"Call me Roger."

"Okay. Roger. I do not know. But I think I know how to find out. There's gotta be some smart Church scholars out there somewhere. The Church has had such a long history. There's got to be some lesson, some precedent maybe in the Church's history. I will find someone who has an answer."

"Okay. That's a deal. But don't tell them who you're working for."

"Am I working for you?"

"No. Not really. You're not on *my* payroll."

"So I cannot tell them I am working for you, can I?"

"I guess not."

Rackham spun around in his wheelchair, then turned back to Mahony. "Just so you know. Nick Pike is taking care of me, for now. He's a man who isn't happy unless he has a cause. Or, preferably, three causes. He needs men like me to keep him happy. I guess he's also paying a substantial salary to Juana Margarita Obregón. We try to keep Pike happy. Understand?"

RACKHAM DIDN'T FIND ONE SCHOLAR. He found several of them, all authorities on Church history—not only Sunnyhill, whom Pike had told him about, still in temporary residence at LMU, but others, too, in different parts of the world. This was no problem for Rackham. He had a powerful laptop, he'd become good on the Internet and he was not afraid to use a telephone. So being wheelchair bound was more of an asset than a liability: it gave him a good excuse not to travel, or even fight the bumper-to-bumper traffic on LA's freeways in his special van for the handicapped.

And so, Rackham did his research—on the telephone and in cyberspace. There he found all the theoretical underpinnings that any loyal Catholic revolutionary could possibly need.

He found that the Church didn't even think of itself as "lay" and "cleric" in its earliest years. Only half way through the first millennium did "hierarchy" really begin to take hold and give the clerics the notion that they could make the Church their own private feudal kingdom. With some major exceptions such as John Henry Newman's describing the Church as a *conspiratio pastorum et fidelium*—"a breathing together of pastors and the faithful"—this clerical view prevailed from the Council of Trent right up to Vatican II itself. The twentieth century commenced very badly. In 1906, in his encyclical letter *Vehementer Nos*, Pope Pius X said, "The laity have no other rights than to let themselves be guided and so follow their pastors in docility." The Catholic Church set itself apart as something "of the clergy, by the clergy, and for the clergy."

Rackham found something out of Australia called *eJournal of Theology* with an article in its premier issue by a scholar named Peter Price. Price's piece maintained that the Second Vatican Ecumenical Council was supposed to usher in the end of all that, but one of his most stunning finds predated Vatican II. It was a quote from a rather conservative pope, Pius XII, who said in an allocution to the College of Cardinals on February 20, 1946, "The laity *are* the Church." What could be plainer than that?

Price discovered any number of passages in the documents of Vatican II itself that affirmed the same thing. The Council saw the world as a beautiful place created by God and redeemed by the Incarnation of the Word into its material flesh—a redemption that would go on through history through the action of the men and women who lived and worked in that world. Laymen. Laywomen.

Rackham also read parts of other conciliar documents that contradicted this view, passages that reflected a preconciliar view of the layman as a subordinate, a subject of the hierarchy. He phoned Sunnyhill. "How can this be? I thought Vatican II changed all this?"

"Vatican II *tried* to change it," said Sunnyhill, "but the settlements of Vatican II didn't take." It took him an hour to explain how the clerical party at Vatican II had fiddled with the Council documents toward the end of the Council—precisely to blunt their populist thrust. "The majority of the Fathers," he said, "let them get away with it because they were tired and because they thought they'd already won the battle. The upshot is that those who wanted to keep tight control over the people could always cite chapter and verse—verses they'd inserted into the documents at the eleventh hour—to justify their moves."

Sunnyhill said that, after the Council, the pope and the bishops kept urging greater involvement of laypeople in the Church, but always as subordinates. Bishops put laypeople on various committees—as advisors. Pope John Paul II invited laypeople into his synods, but they had no authority there either, even in their own areas of expertise—for example, marriage and the family. They had no voice in the synod of 1980 on the family. And no voice in the synod of 1987, discussing the role of the laity in the Church. At the synods, the nonclerics were simply auditors. After the synod for Oceania in 1998, Pope John Paul II described the relationship between laity and clergy as "deep complementarity—not equality."

Rackham asked, "How does this square with the equality of all believers in *Lumen Gentium*?"

Sunnyhill laughed at Rackham, a Jew and a labor organizer, quoting a key document from the Second Vatican Council. "It doesn't. You've put your finger on the problem. For more than twenty-five years, we had a clerical-minded pope. More than once, he squelched moves to get laypeople more involved in ministry; he said he was worried about what he called 'the clericalization of the laity.' And Cardinal Ratzinger backed him up. Ratzinger kept harping on something he called 'an ontological difference' between the ordained priesthood and the priesthood of the laity."

"What does that mean?"

"It's all smoke and mirrors," said Sunnyhill. "Just designed to maintain a class system in the Church.

"Who's to gain from that?"

"My opinion? No one. The guys at the Vatican, of course, have far more effective control over ordained priests than they have over laymen. Maybe it is all about control."

"Then they can't be serious about wanting to change the world."

"Why do you say that?"

"Simple numbers," said Rackham. "Worldwide, you got a billion Catholics or more, and only two hundred thousand priests. Are the priests saying they don't need any help in getting the job done?"

"This is interesting," said Sunnyhill. "In the beginning, we had some smart Jews running things. Peter was a Jew. Paul was a Jew. Now, maybe this is what we need again, some smart Jews like you. Tell me, what do you think the job is?"

Rackham pondered for a moment. "Well, I've been listening in on a lot of conversations—in cyberspace—among American Catholics. I read them online, on half a dozen forums, right-wing lists, like www.ewtn.com, middle-of-the-road lists, like www.votf.com, left-wing lists, like www.vatican2.org. I see these forums in England, too, in Ireland, even Australia. Far as I can tell, these listers are free to say what they think about their Church. For the first time in history, maybe, we see bunches of Catholics who glory in free speech."

"Yes, But I wonder where their free speech will lead us."

"We'll see," said Rackham. "No one really knows. Free speech? Not the first thing we think of when we're talking about the Roman Catholic Church. I wonder if it's ever been tried. But I ran into another quote from Pius XII. He was not my favorite pope, because of the way he played footsie with Hitler when he was nuncio to Germany. But in some of his papal allocutions, he gave Catholics all the permission they needed to express themselves freely. He said that a society is healthy if it has a healthy public opinion. At Vatican II, *Lumen Gentium* said the same thing, even more strongly."

Sunnyhill was fairly in awe of Rackham, for being so conversant with what a pope had written more than fifty years before, and what the Council had decided in 1966, and he said so.

Rackham smiled. "As a labor organizer," he said, "I got some of my best ideas from the social encyclicals of Leo XIII, Pius XI, John XXIII and Paul VI. Truth is where you find it."

"You were going to tell me what our job is?"

"From what I can see, Catholics want bread and justice. They can get it, they say, by creating communities that aren't afraid to demand bread and justice. Which pretty much come down to the same thing. If men and women get justice in the workplace, they will earn their daily bread, for themselves and for their families."

"What do they think of Sister Phoebe?"

"She's helped the people see they can provide their own Eucharistic bread."

"Without benefit of clergy?"

"Yes. And she's made it very clear she doesn't want to be a priest. She parts company here with a lot of women who want to be ordained. She believes that priesthood itself is a pagan institution, created to preside over barbarous sacrifices that moderns find distasteful—to say the least. Jesus wasn't a priest. In fact, he opposed the Jewish priests. They were the ones who had him crucified. So she calls ordination 'an idolatry'—because it helps set up an adoring relationship between the people of God and the clerics. The people treat the clerics like little gods. And you know where that leads."

Sunnyhill frowned. "I think Phoebe is a little bit ahead of her time. In fact, way ahead. For now, she ought to be pushing for the ordination of married men. That's much more doable."

"But John Paul II wouldn't hear of that."

"John Paul II is gone."

"You're saying the new pope might?"

"Well, maybe my wish is father to the thought. If I were a betting man, I'd bet this pope will stick to the status quo."

Rackham said, "Looks to me, then, like celibacy trumps the Eucharist every time."

"Afraid so, mate. Except in the Eastern autochthonous Churches where they have married priests."

Rackham frowned. "These Catholic Churches?"

"Yes."

"How do they get away with that?"

Sunnyhill said, "Go read up on autochthony."

"Aw what?"

"Another Greek word, not as violent a word as the word schism."

Rackham tried it out. "Aw-TOCK-thu-knee?"

"Right. It doesn't mean autonomy. It means home-grown."

"How do you spell it?"

• FOURTEEN •

AUTOCHTHONY

RACKHAM NOT ONLY LEARNED how to spell autochthony. He also learned the history of the word. He found that there were (and are) twenty-one autochthonous Churches inside the Catholic Church, some of them very ancient, like the first-century Melkites of Lebanon, with a longer history than the Roman Church. They are all in communion with the pope, but they have their own governance, their own patriarch, their own priests (some married, some not), their own liturgies in their own languages.

All aflame, Rackham asked Pike when they could all meet with Mahony.

"You have something for him?"

"A complete solution to the cardinal's dilemma."

"That's all, huh? A complete solution. Tell me, what's the cardinal's dilemma?"

"He wants a people's Church in America. But he doesn't want to go into schism?"

"Right."

"Well, he can take the American Church into autochthony."

"Sheesh," said Pike. "What's that? How do you spell it?"

A WEEK PASSED before Mahony and his A-team—Pike and Sunnyhill and Rackham and Juana Margarita Obregón—could get together. Mahony had been attending a meeting in Sacramento of the California bishops, where he found surprising (but not unanimous) support for his stand on Sister

Phoebe's liturgical revolution. When he returned to LA and met his team at a hamburger joint not far from Queen of Angels hospital, Mahony had to tell them—that at least two-thirds of California's bishops were quietly encouraging other Phoebes to follow Phoebe's lead. "No more Eucharistic famine, they say, in California."

"This is all under the Vatican's radar screen?" asked Rackham.

"So far. But it is only a matter of time—couple weeks maybe—before *NCR* does a story on this development. Or the *LA Times*. Or the *CBS Evening News*. Or all of them."

"So what are the California bishops prepared to do?" asked Juana Margarita Obregón.

Mahony frowned. "They're not sure. Except for Oakland and a few other sees, they're prepared to follow my lead. For now, that means do nothing to stop Phoebe, and all the other Phoebes in California. For the future, frankly, I don't know what I will do."

"You have to lead the American Church into autochthony," announced Rackham.

Mahony almost choked on his burger. After he recovered, he seemed amused at Rackham's naïve enthusiasm. "What makes you think, Ted, that we can become an autochthonous Church?" He snapped his fingers. "Just like that?"

The question caught Rackham with his mouth full. He held up his hand for a moment, then mumbled, "It's not an unthinkable idea."

"Well, *I've* never thought of it," said Mahony. He turned to Pike. "You ever thought of it, Nick?"

"Until a week ago, I never even heard of it. And I am Greek." A waiter hovered. "You guys want coffee?" Then, to the waiter, "Four coffees for them, one green tea for me."

Mahony said, "Juana? Autochthony?"

"I have heard the word before, but I never thought the American Church could go autochthonous."

As the waiter was filling their cups, Rackham said, "Well, you guys don't know your own Church history."

The four others laughed, their house Jew telling them things about the Church they'd never heard before. Pike admitted he had a lot to learn. Mahony told Rackham to get to the point.

Rackham turned to Sunnyhill. "Let the historian answer this," he said.

Sunnyhill wiped some mustard off his chin, taking a moment to marshal his thoughts. "Ted is trying to say that starting up a new autochthonous Church—one that would have a measure of autonomy, but still be fully Catholic—could well happen. In 1925, Cardinal D.J. Mercier of Malines-Brussels proposed an autochthonous Church in England."

Mahony knew of Mercier, an early leader in the ecumenical movement for Christian unity. He asked Sunnyhill, "What did Cardinal Mercier say about autochthony in 1925?"

"He gave a speech at the Malines Conversations called 'United Not Absorbed.' He proposed that the Anglicans come over to Rome 'whole and entire,' with their own patriarch, the Archbishop of Canterbury, their own English language liturgy, their own married priesthood. They'd be just like the Melkites and the Maronites, only different. They'd be English Catholics."

Pike said, "Pius XI must have loved that."

"Hated it," said Sunnyhill. "In fact, when the pope found out the speech was ghosted for Mercier by a Belgian Benedictine named Dom Lambert Beauduin, he had Beauduin kicked out of the Benedictines. For the rest of his life, this monk wandered Europe, effectively homeless."

"How could the pope get away with that?" asked Pike.

"It doesn't matter," said Sunnyhill. "Twentieth-century popes did just about anything they wanted. The point is this: Cardinal Mercier was onto something. He saw that Rome—with all that the word 'Rome' implied back in 1925—was an obstacle to Anglicans and Catholics getting together. And it shouldn't have been."

"But," said Pike, "the idea went nowhere in 1925. What makes it more viable today?"

Sunnyhill said, "It was an idea that seemed to make sense again, in 1998, when the Indonesian bishops came to Rome for the Asian Synod and proposed an autochthonous Church in Indonesia."

"What happened to that proposal? Pope John Paul approve it?"

"No. He also ignored another proposal for autochthony in another synod in 2001. Again from Indonesia."

"Why did the Indonesian bishops keep asking?"

"The Indonesian bishops wanted a measure of independence from Rome's rules because they had made formal requests, at least twice, for permission to ordain married men, and they were turned down."

Pike was intrigued with all this, but, like the good lawyer he was, he needed to take a devil's advocate position. "So Rome said no. That only proves one thing: bishops can propose anything they want. But if the pope doesn't buy it, so what?"

Sunnyhill said, "In an autochthonous Church, they wouldn't have to ask Rome's permission to do that. Not if it's simply a matter of discipline."

Juana Margarita Obregón sat up straighter and announced, "If it is only a matter of discipline, then, in an autochthonous American Church, we would not have to ask the pope's permission to ordain women either."

Mahony said he wasn't so sure about that. "Three popes have said women cannot be ordained. To them, this *is* a matter of doctrine."

Juana Margarita Obregón turned to Sunnyhill. "Is it doctrine—the kind of doctrine that can never change? Or is it a manmade Church rule that can easily change, like they changed the no-meat-on-Friday rule? Or change in some parts of the world, and not in others?"

Sunnyhill said, "It's a manmade rule, made for all the usual reasons that men make rules: control. Most popes like power. They exercise it most effectively in a Church with a male, celibate priesthood."

"You mean with male eunuchs," interjected Pike. Mahony stiffened. "Sorry, Roger, but it's true isn't it? Men without balls?"

Rackham chortled.

Mahony said. "Some celibates have very little courage. I admit that. But maybe it's just easier for a bishop to order a man around if he doesn't have a wife and family. I suspect I'd have a hard time moving a married priest with a family from Beverly Hills to Pear Blossom if he has a wife and kids who do not want to move to the Mojave Desert. And women priests!" He rolled his eyes. "I do not have the slightest idea how I'd handle *them*."

Juana Margarita Obregón said, "I have seen you working with Sister Edith at the education congress in Anaheim. You have no problem working with her."

"Right," he said. "I just let her do what she wants. And she does a great job."

"Did I not once hear you say you would ordain her tomorrow if you could?"

"Well. Yes."

Rackham demanded, "And don't you already have married men in the priesthood, Roger?"

Mahony said, "Well, uh, of course we do. We've got these converts from Lutheranism and Episcopal priests who have come over, with their wives and kids. But that's an exception. This pope—and his predecessors—have made their position on mandatory celibacy very clear. I just don't think we will see married priests in my lifetime. Or women priests either."

Sunnyhill drew some laughter with an old clerical joke. "We won't see married priests in our lifetime. But our kids will."

Rackham broke through the merriment, all frowns. "Roger, aren't you assuming you need Rome's approval on everything? A people's Church in America that made its own rules could change that celibacy thing in a New York minute."

"Which is why," said Mahony with some finality, "Rome would never give us permission to have a people's Church."

"Why do we need permission to have a people's Church?" asked Rackham.

"Huh?" They were all startled at the suggestion.

"I mean," said Rackham, "if you just declared autochthony, you'd be autochthonous, wouldn't you?"

They sat in silence. Rackham's proposal seemed too simple. Then, finally, Pike got it. He said, "You mean, like, the Founding Fathers declared independence from England on the Fourth of July 1776? They didn't need to ask George III's permission. They just told Thomas Jefferson to write a draft, made a few fixes in it, and signed it."

"Yes," said Juana Margarita Obregón. "'Autochthonous' and 'permission' are two things that do not quite go together do they?"

Rackham said, "I think this is why the move by the Indonesian bishops failed. They thought they needed the pope's permission. When they didn't get it, they rolled over and played dead. They should have made a declaration of autochthony and gone ahead with the ordination of married men. And done other things to help them inculturate the Gospel in Indonesia." Rackham smiled at his own words. He was the Chameleon Man in Woody Allen's *Zelig. Hang out with Catholic theologians, you begin to talk like a Catholic theologian.*

Mahony said, "I hear you saying that's what we would do if—" He paused.

Pike completed his statement for him. "If we had balls."

"Or if we were a people's Church," said Rackham.

"What do you mean, 'we,' Jew man?'" joshed Pike.

Rackham's usually severe features cracked into a smile. "I said, 'We.' Now you know: I have joined your revolution."

"I like your spirit," said Mahony. "But, what revolution? I wish we were as ready as you are—to fight."

"Why do you say 'fight?'" asked Juana Margarita Obregón.

Mahony said, "Well, if we're going to follow in the footsteps of the American Founding Fathers, we have to expect a fight. After the Founding Fathers signed their Declaration of Independence, they had to fight a war with the British to make it stick."

"So," said Pike, "are you ready to fight a war?"

"That's not the question," said Mahony. "Whether *I* am ready. The question is, are American Catholics ready? Most of them identify with Rome, and most of them take all their cues from Rome. They think the Church is the pope and the pope is the Church."

Pike was a quick study. It had taken only one pointed question from Rackham, and, to him, the course of action was clear. "That's why we need you, Roger. We need your leadership. If I tried to lead the American Church into autochthony, the people would say, 'Who do you think you are?' But leadership by an American cardinal?"

"Nick, I don't have the guts to lead that charge. Do you know what those guys in the Vatican would do to me?

"What *could* they do?" asked Rackham.

"They'd slap me down. Depose me. Send me to a nuthouse."

Pike grunted. Juana Margarita Obregón studied Mahony's features, then looked at Rackham, then Pike, then Sunnyhill, as they tried to process what the cardinal had said. Finally, Rackham asked Mahony, "Does the Vatican ever do that?"

"In 1990, they did it to Archbishop Eugene Marino of Atlanta."

"Deposed him and sent him to a nuthouse?"

Mahony took a long sip of his coffee. "Yes, I'm afraid so. They told him he had to quit. And he did. I will never forget Eugene's resignation statement. He said he needed an extended period of spiritual renewal, psychological therapy, and medical supervision. He signed himself in to a psychiatric hospital. He was a beaten man. Not many years later, he died a premature death."

Rackham clucked. "What was his sin?"

127

"He was living with—probably married to—a beautiful young woman from his cathedral choir. Supposed to be a secret. But the secret didn't last long."

"Sex!" said Pike, slamming his fist on the table. "In this damn Church, it always comes down to sex."

Mahony smiled. "Afraid so. A half dozen American bishops have had to resign in the last few years."

"Because they had girlfriends?" asked Rackham.

"Yes," said Mahony. "Or boyfriends."

"But they weren't fired," said Rackham, "for wanting to make the Church more, uh, more American?"

Pike said, "The Vatican faced *that* question more than a hundred years ago." He turned to Sunnyhill. "Right, Sean?"

Sunnyhill smiled. "In 1899, Pope Leo XIII wrote a letter condemning something he called 'Americanism.' He was really condemning democracy."

Rackham asked, "What set him off?"

"The pope got all excited when he read the Paulists' official life of their founder Isaac Hecker. To Leo XIII, it looked like Hecker was advocating an American Catholic Church—one that the pope said (with an air of complete disapproval) was 'different from the Catholic Church in the rest of the world.' The pope could hardly object to the way Americans wanted to run their country, democratically. He was just afraid that American Catholics wanted to run their Church in the same way."

"Democratically?" asked Rackham.

Sunnyhill laughed. "Rome has been fighting off democracy ever since the French Revolution at the end of the eighteenth century. For most of the nineteenth century, it was engaged in a process of centralizing all Church power in Rome, under an absolute ruler. The American experiment was a threat to that process. Pius IX once told Hecker there is 'too much freedom in America.' He thought this American idea—the very notion of freedom—might infect Catholics everywhere."

"Leo XIII felt the same way," said Sunnyhill, "He accused the Paulists, or, to be more precise, their founder, Isaac Hecker, of heresy."

"What heresy?" asked Rackham.

128

"Of this thing called Americanism. Can you believe it? Hecker was already ten years in the grave. But the Paulists didn't want to fight the pope. They withdrew their book about Hecker."

"But this all happened more than a hundred years ago," protested Rackham. "Does the current pope think there's 'too much freedom' in the American Church now?"

Pike and Mahony traded glances. "He did before he became pope," said Mahony. "We're not too sure now. We have to wait and see."

"My Jesuit friends are lying low," said Pike. "They have important things to say about freedom in the Church. But they won't publish anything that would test the pope's patience. Right, Sean?"

Sunnyhill said, "He who shoots and runs away lives to shoot another day."

"Exactly," said Mahony, "And I won't do anything that would test him either."

"Maybe," said Rackham, "you already have. When you set out on this new course of yours, you had to know you'd collide with Rome. Some men have greatness thrust upon them, Roger."

Mahony smiled. He recognized the allusion to Shakespeare's *Twelfth Night*. Was Rackham implying he was another Malvolio? Playing to his pride?

He banished the thought when Rackham added an ominous afterthought, "But it will cost you."

MAHONY LEARNED THE COST only three nights later. Shortly after midnight on January 28, Mahony opened his browser's in-box and found an e-mail message from the Rome bureau chief of the *Los Angeles Times*. "Vatican preparing to put California under interdict. What would that mean in LA?"

Grimly, he hit the Reply button, typed four words—"Please tell me more," addressed a blind copy of the *Times'* note and his reply to Kowalski at Notre Dame, and hit Send. He'd expected some action from Rome. Perhaps a summons, to come speak to the pope. But not this. Not an interdict. Indeed, what *would* an interdict mean in 2009? Medieval popes used interdicts to punish entire nations. Was it Innocent III in the thirteenth century who put King John's England under interdict? And California—with 10 percent of the U.S. population and a GNP that surpassed all but five nations in the world—was very much like a nation.

He paced the floor for ten anxious minutes. Too late to phone anyone in California, too early to phone Kowalski in the Midwest. He tried to pray, but his prayers gave him no comfort, only questions. Maybe a midnight walk? Yes. He donned a navy blue jogging suit and laced up his Nikes, then strode out into the corridor. Deserted. No one in the elevator either. Emerging from the hospital unseen, he did a slow jog east on Sixth Street. Five minutes later, he found himself outside the apartment of Juana Margarita Obregón. Not sure why he was even there, he found himself hitting the call button on her apartment's intercom.

After a half-minute, he heard her puzzled voice. "Yes?"

"It's Roger."

"Roger who?"

"Come on!" he said. "It's Roger!"

Long pause. "Okay," she said. "You remember? Take the elevator to the third floor. Three C." Yes, he remembered. He'd been there once before, when Juana Margarita Obregón had invited the A-team over for a Mexican buffet.

When she ushered him in, she was wearing a white cotton sleep-shirt, no shoes, no slippers. No makeup. Flawless olive complexion. Nice bosom. He couldn't help thinking she looked sexy—sexy at sixty. He tamped down the thought. What did that have to do with anything? "I just got an e-mail from the *Times* in Rome," he announced. "An interdict is headed our way."

"*Dio mio*! Interdict. Is that something like excommunication?"

"Something like that. It's a kind of sacramental freeze. The people will be denied the sacraments, as long as the interdict is in place."

"I am not sure I get the point. Is this like a teacher makes the whole class stay after school until the kid who threw the eraser owns up—"

"Sort of."

"That seems extreme." She was in the kitchen pouring them both a glass of sherry.

"Yes."

"Really medieval."

"Uh huh. In medieval Europe, popes used the interdict to make rulers do what they wanted. It was a political move. Under an interdict, the people were supposed to put the pressure on their rulers to knuckle under."

"Who is the ruler here?"

"Good question. In the American Church, it wouldn't be the president of the United States. We have separation of Church and State."

"And in medieval times, did they knuckle under?"

"Apparently so, in Catholic Europe. Those were the days when popes could assert their power over kings and princes. And when the kings and princes let them."

"But today? An interdict laid on the whole U.S.?"

"My e-mail note from the *Times*' reporter in Rome said only California."

"Why the whole state?"

"Earlier this week, most of the California bishops voted to support me in the Sister Phoebe matter. They've all got some Sister Phoebes in their midst. And they like what these Phoebes are doing. They've solved the priest shortage and ended the Eucharistic famine. In the long run, that could mean no more priests for the pope to order about. I imagine he is saying, 'Today, California. Tomorrow, the world.' Maybe he wants to cut off this revolt with as much force as he can?"

She made a face. "Sounds like the pope thinks he has the Eucharistic franchise for the whole world. No one can make Jesus without his permission?"

Mahony frowned and emptied his glass. "I cannot imagine this pope saying anything like that. Or even implying it. He may be cruel. Or may have been cruel at times—when he was running the Holy Office. But he's not running the Holy Office any longer. He's got a different job now."

"Yes," she said. "He is the pope of all the people. More than a billion people. And he is not stupid. But this does not make any sense in America. Who is going to enforce a sacramental freeze in this country?"

"Good question," he said.

"I mean," she said, "the pope does not have any power here unless we give it to him. Do we intend to do that? Do we intend to close down all of our churches?"

"If we don't, I guess I will soon be an ex-cardinal."

Her eyes widened. "Then we would be in schism?"

"I'm not so sure about that. Rackham keeps telling us this is the time for us to just declare our independence."

"You mean our autochthony!"

"Uh huh. But I think I will need some guidance on this. If I can just get my favorite canon lawyer on the phone."

"Kowalski? Why him?"

"Yes. So he can tell me what the Vatican is actually saying."

"How will he know?"

"He has the nuncio's ear in Washington. He can phone him, see whether the nuncio has any solid information for him. Then I can tell you—and the *Los Angeles Times*—what I think it all means and what we are going to do about it." He said no more, caught up in his own thoughts, rose, strolled to the kitchen and asked her if he could pour himself another sherry.

"Of course," she said, holding up her own glass. "I will have another drop, too." After he poured for her, Juana Margarita Obregón gave the conversation a personal spin. "Are you scared, Roger?"

He paused. "A little."

She took his right hand and looked directly into his eyes. "You should be. But are you not simply living out the sentence you accepted in Chiapas?"

He nodded. "I cannot see any bishop who is a real Christian locking his people out of their own churches."

They drifted back to the couch. "You still want to be a Christian?"

"Yes," he said. "I just never imagined what it might cost me. I never thought it would come to this."

"Come to what?" she asked. "We still do not know what will happen. Your boat is sailing along in uncharted waters. But you will not run aground if you pay attention to your helmsman. And your navigators."

"Who? Pike? Sunnyhill? Rackham?"

"Yes," she said. "They are the guys who can think outside the box. But Sister Phoebe and I can help, too. Do you not need women on the bridge?"

Mahony nodded. He wondered if the Church would be in the fix it was in if women had had some say in how it was run. They sat in silence. Finally, Juana Margarita Obregón said to him, "What? What are you thinking?"

He said, "I wonder if the pope realizes how the American press will handle this story?"

Juana Margarita Obregón said, "Does the pope really care what the American press says about anything?"

He shook his head. "He pretends not to. But I do."

She laughed. "Roger, Roger, Roger. You are incorrigible."

He laughed. "Incorrigible?"

"Always so worried over what the press will say."

He looked at her with some puzzlement. "As far as I know," he said, "all the politicos in the land—every city councilman, every mayor, every governor, even the president of the United States—they all consult the press to see how they are coming across to the people. They're all trying to frame their stories. If they frame them right, they get what they call 'the consent of the governed.'"

"And you need that?"

He laughed. "The consent of the governed? You bet I do. And I can only get it if I serve the people with what they need."

"What do they need the most—from you?"

He reflected for some long moments. Finally, he said, "They need to know it is all right to have a voice and a vote in their own Church."

She said, "It is clear the pope doesn't want to give them that. If it is clear that you do, then he will be the villain. And you will be a new kind of hero."

Mahony wasn't at all sure he wanted to be that kind of a hero. But he allowed, "Pike and Rackham would be proud of you, my dear."

"For what?"

"For framing this conflict in a way that the Catholics in America can understand—and support." He added with a frown, "But I don't want to be on a collision course with the pope."

She said, "He is not God, you know."

That gave him some pause. He shook his head. "But I've been—my whole life—I've been acting as if he were. Jesus, what do I do now?"

"Yes," she said. "You are on the right track now."

"What do you mean?"

"You just said an honest prayer. 'Jesus, what do I do now?'"

"Yes, I guess I did."

Juana Margarita Obregón said, "Then he will be sure to answer you."

"I'm sure he will," he said. "You have any good guesses what his answer will be?"

She shrugged. "I have always believed the Holy Spirit speaks to us through history. Including contemporary history."

"Contemporary history? You mean the day's news?"

"Yes. We just have to pay attention to what John XXIII called 'the signs of the times.' That is where we find the Holy Spirit. And where we will find Jesus, too, I think."

FIFTEEN

INTERDICT

ROGER MAHONY GOT HIS MESSAGE from the Holy Spirit at five the next morning when he jogged into the lobby of the hospital to find seven television crews and a dozen radio reporters swarming around him. Contemporary history indeed! Faced with such a news horde, his first instinct was to turn around and run, but he spied Nick Pike in the middle of the crowd, and took three long strides to meet him.

"Thank God, you're here," he said, then grabbed the newspaper Pike was holding, and made for an elevator while he scanned the headline on the right side of Page One of the *Los Angeles Times*.

> **Schism in Catholic Los Angeles?**
> STATE THREATENED WITH PAPAL INTERDICT
> MAHONY IN HIDING, CALIFORNIA BISHOPS MUM

He and Pike grabbed an elevator and got it moving up to Mahony's eleventh floor. Definitely not alone—the car was jammed with reporters firing questions—the two of them said nothing, Mahony reading the story in the *Times*, Pike peering at it over his shoulder, until they arrived at his floor.

Before the doors opened, he pressed the Hold button, held up his hand, called for silence, and tried to speak. "Ladies, gentlemen of the press, you know I'd love to talk to you." He smiled a tight smile. "When have I ever dodged you? Steve Lopez, don't answer that. But you have to give me a few minutes, okay? I need to talk to my people. I need to find out what's going on in Rome."

"You mean you haven't heard from the Vatican?" asked a radio man armed with a large microphone.

"No," snapped Mahony. He waved his copy of the *Times*. "A lot of misstatements of fact here. A lot of misunderstandings. For now, you radio guys—and gals—and you wire service people, you can report this. 'Cardinal Mahony says, "We are not in schism. This doesn't make any sense. And I haven't been in hiding."' I'll see you all in the hospital's boardroom in fifteen minutes, okay? No. I will need a half hour."

A quiver of more questions, one of which seemed to hit a bull's-eye with him: "Cardinal Mahony, where were you this morning?"

For a wild moment or two, he thought of blurting an honest answer —"with a friend." Instead, he said over his shoulder as he made his way to the AIDS wing, "Couldn't sleep. Out walking. In the neighborhood."

Inside the suite, he headed to his Mac and opened his e-mail in-box. Several hundred messages on one AOL account. Perhaps two dozen on his private account, these mainly encouraging notes from his fellow bishops in California, but also bravo messages from Kowalski, Andy Greeley, and James Carroll, and from the bishops of Portland, Tucson, Metuchen, New Jersey, Denver, Des Moines, and Great Falls, Montana.

After skimming most of them, answering none, he turned to Pike, who had been at his side. "Nice surprise. They're all with us. No dissenting voice, not even from Denver."

"They all want to be part of the schism?" asked Pike. He was needling Mahony, and Mahony knew it. He knew Pike knew he wasn't leading a schism. Thank God he had the information he needed to tell the world about autochthony. And the courage.

WITH SEVERAL HUNDRED NEWSMEN crowding the hospital lobby and flowing out the front door, Harry Gray, Mahony's press secretary, sought and got an okay from the hospital administration to move the news conference to the auditorium. In the meantime, Mahony was taking a quick shower. Then he donned a black cassock trimmed in cardinal red, poured himself a huge glass of orange juice, and turned back to his e-mail. He was looking for a message from Sunnyhill, and found one containing something that Sunnyhill called "A Declaration of Autochthony."

"Just a draft," wrote Sunnyhill, the Australian Jesuit with a fondness for America. "You might want to check it out with your team."

> We hold these truths to be evident from scripture and tradition, that all baptized Christians, men and women alike, are equal, that they are endowed by their baptism with certain unalienable rights and duties, that among these are the freedom to be all we can be—in this life as well as the next—and the duty to advance the mission on earth of a Christ who said he had come so that we may have life and have it more abundantly. That to secure these rights, and help us in our duties, we set up a governance in the Church that derives its just powers not from a bureaucracy in Rome that claims to speak for almighty God, but from the consent of the governed on every part of the planet.

No, Mahony thought. This would not do. This was entirely too cheeky, too brainy, too analytical, too wrapped up in the values of law, order, judgment and power. It was too eighteenth-century.

He looked in his personal in-box. Surely other members of the team would have a better sense of what he needed at this moment. He needed to fight, of course. But how? And with what? If the Vatican was forging a hammer to raise against the American Church, he didn't want to fight back with another hammer. His heart leaped when he opened an e-mail message from Sister Phoebe in Solvang.

"Tell them some stories," she said. "Talk to your family."

It leaped again when he opened an e-mail message from Pike, sent apparently at three o'clock in the morning, along with a large attachment. The printout ran a dozen pages. His eyes ran down the text before he put it in the breast pocket of his cassock. It was a well-written compendium of what he and his team had been discussing for weeks, the case for a people's Church in America.

HARRY GRAY HAD SET UP A LITTLE PODIUM on the stage of the auditorium. Mahony spurned the stage, asked for a handheld mike, and took a position at floor level, in the center aisle. He paused, giving the soundmen time to adjust their mikes and their booms, and scanned the faces before him—the press, the most maligned group in society today, vultures ready to tear a man apart at the slightest sign of weakness. He made a rough count of the house—maybe two hundred men and women in the room, and at least twenty TV cameras, three of them marked with the logo of C-SPAN. He thought, *Good, sooner or later, those who care most can catch every word I say here. I only hope people will understand what I am trying to say.*

MAHONY SAID, "If you've been following the horror stories for the past six years, you know it isn't only the spectacle of sex abuse by a relatively few American priests that makes us ashamed of our Church in America. It is the systematic cover-up of that abuse by most of the nation's bishops—including me. I hope that I will someday be able to make up for my part in the cover-up.

"We bishops have covered up because we have labored on the mistaken assumption that this is our Church, a Church that we can run pretty much as *we* see fit." Mahony was speaking now not so much to the press horde, but to the people who were watching and listening, somewhere out there in media land.

"It is, in fact, your Church, one that we must run pretty much as *you* see fit. This means that, although we are in charge, we must be accountable to you, to the people we serve, as Jesus told the Apostles in the twenty-second chapter of Luke. In Luke 22:9, Jesus told the Apostles, 'Let the greatest among you be as the youngest, and the leader as the servant.'

"We have a few servant-bishops today. I wish we had more of them. I would like to be more of a servant-bishop than I have been. But my pastoral team in Los Angeles (and I) would like to do more than wish. We want to push for new laws in the American Church that will make us all accountable to one another, grounding our stand in scripture and the traditions of the primitive Church, and modeling our governance on the American Constitution. In the sixth century, Pope Gregory the Great, who left the contemplative life of a monk before he became pope under protest, laid down a principle that is even more appropriate today: 'Who presides over all must be chosen by all.'"

Mahony paused while his eyes skimmed ahead to Pike's draft. It was too long, so he tried to summarize in his own words.

"In the early 1960s, the bishops at Vatican II wrote a charter to give the people ownership and citizenship in their Church. Then we sat back and waited for our priests and bishops in the United States to implement that charter—to give the people a voice and a vote, American-style. They didn't really do that. But then, it was not very realistic, was it, to expect they would? Few lords willingly become servants.

"It is realistic, however, to come up with our own plan, if only a starting point—to give American Catholics a voice and a vote. We are not calling for a schism nor are we challenging the faith we hold and the beliefs we express in the creed we say every time we go to Mass. We are challenging the way our Church is governed—unaccountably, top-down in a bottom-up kind of world.

"In 1978, Pope John Paul II told millions of Poles, "You can take back your country if you demand it." I am telling American Catholics they can do the same thing. You can take back our Church if you demand it. One way you can do that—you can insist on electing your own bishops. You can do it when I resign—and I will," he assured the cameras with a smile, "when I reach my seventy-fifth birthday.

"I will encourage the four million Catholics in the Church of Los Angeles to elect my successor. I hope you see what I am trying to do, give LA Catholics a voice and a vote. This may not be the only way, but it is the best way I can think of—to make the Church credible once more. This might also reverse the extraordinary outflow of young people from a Church that finds itself stuck, for example, in a theory of ministry that bars half its members from serving as priests at a time when priests are in terribly short supply.

"Once the Holy Father understands how this move will bring millions of alienated Catholics back to the Church, he will have to give his approval. I am not proposing a schism, after all, just a new way of making this Church of ours a Church of the people. I am not saying American Catholics should say goodbye to their bishops. I hope we always have bishops. I am a bishop myself.

"But the American Church doesn't need lord bishops any longer. It needs servant bishops who will act more like the fathers of modern American families. Since Vatican II, mainstream theologians, including Pope Benedict XVI himself, have described the Church as something more like a family. If that's the updated model, then the Church should function in the spirit of modern families, where fathers and mothers share authority, and where even the kids are invited to speak their minds. I think this family model will make sense to American Catholics—who are far more educated than many of their priests and bishops, and won't be treated like kids much longer.

They are adults. They want ownership and citizenship in their Church. I hope we can give it to them."

Mahony dropped his voice and his gaze and made the sign of the cross, as if the words he had just spoken were a prayer. His action was met with what appeared to be a thoughtful silence. No shouts from the press horde, no demands. He looked over the throng, and saw reporters nodding at him, and exchanging glances with one another, but no hands raised. "Okay. I think I have given you enough. You can do some good stories. And that's what it's all about, isn't it?"

Finally from the back of the room, someone shouted. "I have a question, your Eminence. Steve Lopez from the *Los Angeles Times*?"

Mahony smiled. "Go ahead, Mr. Steve Lopez of the *Los Angeles Times*. I think this exchange is long overdue." Indeed it was. Lopez had been seeking face time with Mahony for several years. "Ask your question."

Lopez had gotten what amounted to a graduate seminar in ecclesiology, but what kind of column could he write about it for his audience? "What's next?" he asked. "What's your next move?"

He was disappointed when Mahony told him and the news horde, "We want to make one thing perfectly clear. We're in union with Rome. That means we will abide by the pope's orders. If he wants to put us under interdict, we will abide by that."

"What will that mean?" asked Lopez.

"According to canon law, interdict means that the whole region—in this case, the entire state of California—cannot receive the Sacraments. No Mass. No Communion either. No Catholic who dies can receive a Catholic burial, If I have anything to say about it, we will abide by that order (if, in fact, it is an order), as long as the Holy Father wants it to remain in effect. The people and the priests may protest to the pope. We'll see about that."

"So why is the pope punishing the people of California?"

"You know," said Mahony, "that's the interesting thing. As of now"—he looked at his watch. "As of 8:15 AM on January 28, 2009, we haven't heard a thing from the Vatican, maybe because this is a big holiday in Rome. All we know is what we've read in the *Times*. I don't think that amounts to any kind of legal notice. And, since the men in the Vatican have always been great sticklers for legal correctness, we have to say that, technically, nothing has changed. We haven't been served. Yet. So I am telling all of our parish priests they can celebrate Mass this morning. Until we see an official order from Rome, we cannot consider an interdict in place."

"What about Sister Phoebe? Can she celebrate Mass?"

"Sister Phoebe McNulty, the parish administrator of St. Priscilla's in Solvang, isn't celebrating Mass—and has never celebrated Mass. She and the members of her parish have been saying the words of the Mass in unison together and partaking together of some bread and wine, as Jesus bid all of his disciples to do at the Last Supper. Sister Phoebe and the people of St. Priscilla's aren't doing anything more—or less—than Jesus asked his followers to do in memory of him. We will let the theologians argue over the question—whether Jesus is sacramentally present in this stylized memory or not. The people of St. Priscilla's are quite happy with what they are doing. They feel closer to our Lord. And I feel closer to them."

Another reporter stood, identifying himself as Mark Day of the *National Catholic Reporter*. "Cardinal Mahony," he shouted, "if the people of St. Priscilla are happy with what they feel is Jesus' presence within them in their liturgy, and you're happy that they're happy, why do we need priests at all?"

The news crowd hummed over that one, giving Mahony time to ponder his reply. Finally he said, "Good question. Short answer: we don't. I can give you a somewhat longer answer. Maybe we're just catching up with history itself, which as the good Pope John XXIII used to say, is a good teacher. If we've been paying attention, we might conclude that the ordained celibate male priesthood itself is dying. No one should be surprised if some Catholics who can think outside the box come up with something else to take its place."

A large, bosomy blonde—she looked like a mezzo-soprano from the Metropolitan Opera—rose and challenged Mahony from the front row. "Helga Krankenkrauser from the *Wanderer*, your Eminence." Mahony nodded. He wasn't aware that the *Wanderer*, a right-wing Catholic weekly out of Minnesota, had a correspondent in Los Angeles. He could have predicted the tenor of her question.

"Your Eminence," she said, "according to number 1378, paragraph two, note one of the 1983 Revised Code of Canon Law—" She held up a typescript at arm's length and squinted at it through thick horn-rimmed spectacles. "It says that anyone who has not been promoted to the priestly order and who attempts to enact the liturgical action of the Eucharistic Sacrifice incurs an automatic penalty of interdict."

"What's your question, Ms. Krankenhauser?"

She corrected the cardinal. "Three Ks. Krankenkrauser."

"Sorry," he said, smiling uneasily. "What's your question, Ms. Krankenkrauser?"

"Well, isn't it obvious? You've been supporting Sister Phoebe's priestly pretenses when all the time she and her people are under automatic excommunication. How can you justify that?"

"In the first place, Ms. Krankenkrauser, who says she's acting like a priest? Or that she's attempting to re-enact what canon law calls 'the liturgical action of the Eucharistic Sacrifice?' And in the second place, the canon you are quoting doesn't say anything about excommunication. You are saying she's incurred a penalty that no one has yet been able to define. 'Interdict?' What exactly does that term mean to you, Ms. Krankenkrauser?"

She sputtered. "Well, I don't know. At the very least, I think it means the Vatican isn't happy about what she's doing. And not happy, I'd assume, not happy with what you—and most of the California bishops—are doing, supporting Sister Phoebe and a bunch of other Phoebes up and down the state of California."

"Well, Ms. Krankenkrauser, when you use the word 'assume,' you're using the right word. You assume. I'd like to wait until I see something official on this from the pope. So far, all I know is what I've read in the *Los Angeles Times.*"

Ms. Krankenkrauser cackled scornfully.

"You have another question?" asked Mahony.

"Not really," she said.

Mahony recognized a TV reporter standing next to a news camera.

"Harley Banks of Fox News, your Eminence. Can you tell us just exactly what you mean by a people's Church in America? And why that doesn't amount to a schism?"

"Harley, to make an accountable Church in America, we need to change the way we govern ourselves, not change what we believe. The Church hasn't always governed itself in the same way. For the first six centuries, the people of Rome elected their bishop—who later came to be known as 'the pope.' The first bishop in the United States was elected by a vote of the priests in the new nation. The modern Church has a different polity in different parts of the world, but the same faith. So, for good reasons, we hope we can change our polity here in America. And canon law even tells us how we can do that.

"Canon law talks about a regional, or national synod. The American Church had three of them in the 1800s, the First, Second, and Third Councils of Baltimore, where rules were set for American Catholics by the delegates, all bishops, no laymen. The American bishops are, in fact, now preparing a Fourth Council of Baltimore, scheduled to begin on July 4, 2009, modeled on those early regional American synods. Only bishops attended those synods. No mere priests or nuns, and no laymen. No women, either.

"But times have changed. I am going to urge that my fellow American bishops follow a provision in modern canon law that says a regional synod can include non-bishops—up to fifty percent of the delegates. If those delegates are elected by Catholics in every state (or every diocese) and claim active voice, the synod might take on the character of a constitutional convention, and delegates could end up writing a charter for a people's Church in America, a charter that looks very much like the Constitution of the United States—with an executive branch, a legislative branch, and a judicial branch. That constitution might call for the popular election of two parliamentary bodies—a Senate of Bishops and a House of Commons, an elected president (or executive board), and a judiciary appointed with the advice and consent of both houses.

The Fox reporter said, "What a battle that would be!"

"Sure, " said Mahony, "Just like the Constitutional Convention of 1787 was a battle between men who didn't always agree, and who didn't get it right the first time. You may remember, they had to come back and put together ten amendments, our Bill of Rights.

"I expect delegates to our national synod would wrangle over their charter's specifics. But if they want to lead a Church of and for the people, I think they could come up with rules that would make us all accountable to one another. I think American Catholics would all like to see that happen."

The Fox reporter interjected. "But that sounds very political. Are you trying to bring politics into the American Church?"

Mahony smiled. "We don't know our own Church. We should all realize the American bishops have been playing politics for two hundred years, mainly taking orders from Rome unless they could convince Rome otherwise. But they've always played the game in secret. I should know. I was one of the players. I am suggesting it is high time we bring everything out in the open, and let everyone have a voice and a vote. We are not talking about Catholic doctrine here, but about the way we govern ourselves.

"So why not write a constitution, with three branches of government that operate in the open, covered closely by the media, so everyone can know what's going on? Three branches of government and the Fourth Estate—they check and balance one another. What's so bad about that? Americans are justly proud of the U.S. Constitution, and their free press. And new nations all over the world have been copying our system for more than a hundred years.

"In fact, the Roman Catholic Church itself, the one based in Rome, already has a constitution. It is called 'canon law.' Romans are proud of it, possibly because it is modeled on ancient Roman law and is therefore part of their own Roman culture. Americans do not quite understand it. Nor will we ever. It is a charter for tyranny, actually, designed to make its secret orders stick by the sheer power of an absolute sovereign, who makes all the laws, interprets all the laws, and enforces all the laws. That's one form of governance. One kind of politics, really. But it is not the kind of politics that commends Christ to his people, not any more, not today. Not in California. Not in the United States."

SIXTEEN

GRANDEUR

INSIDE THE THIRD-FLOOR OFFICE of the secretary of state in the Vatican's Apostolic Palace, Cardinal Tarcisio Bertone and his staff and three other Curial cardinals—and Cardinal Grandeur who was visiting from Philadelphia—had been watching the Mahony news conference with fascination.

Cardinal Gianbattista Re said, "The uprising in California becomes very clear. Now."

"Was his Holiness watching this?" asked Bertone.

Cardinal James Stafford said, "I hope not. If he was, he will know that our bluff didn't work."

"Our bluff?" said Re.

Stafford reddened. "We leaked a piece of disinformation to the *Los Angeles Times,* suggesting we might put the whole state of California under interdict. the *Times* story said we had already done so."

"Why?"

"Why what?"

"Why did you resort to disinformation?"

"We thought a Page One story in the *Los Angeles Times* would bring Mahony to his knees. He's always paid more attention to the *Times* than he has to us."

Re said, "It didn't quite bring him to his knees."

"No. Something seems to have made him bolder."

Bertone said, "And it made us look like idiots. *Que brutta figura!* Perhaps you saw the results of your fumbling little move in this morning's *La Repubblica*? A denial from the Vatican Press Office itself, which said it knew nothing of an interdict in California." He raised his palms. "Gentlemen, we got caught leaking a lie."

"Not so fast," said Grandeur.

"Huh?" said Stafford.

"What?" said Re.

Grandeur spoke to them as if they were fourth graders. "I don't think you've read Canon 1378 very carefully. We don't have to *put* California under an interdict. The people up and down the state of California who participate in this liturgical enactment put themselves under interdict automatically." Grandeur repeated "automatically" in Italian. He liked the way the word rolled off his tongue. *Automaticamente.* He smiled at them and said it again. *Automaticamente.* "That means we don't have to promulgate anything."

Bertone turned to his daily compendium of the world press, news clippings that his staff had Xeroxed and compiled for him this morning in a neat stack, six inches thick. He said, "Because of Sister Phoebe's rashness, aided and abetted by the Internet, priestless Catholic communities all over the world are doing their own liturgies today. We're faced with an epidemic of, of, of freedom. No! I will not call it freedom. I call it license! People writing their own Eucharistic liturgies! The Internet is full of new liturgies. New texts have popped up overnight, like mushrooms. People are celebrating something called the 'Thomas Mass' that eliminates what they call 'Roman accretions' and sticks more closely to Scripture."

"Why 'the Thomas Mass?'" asked Re.

Bertone sighed. "Something, apparently, that can appeal to even the doubting Thomases in the Church! *Madonn'*!" He turned back to his notes. "I have an ad from the Internet about another kind of Mass. It says a publishing company in Australia has a text for a new Mass written by someone named Michael Morwood. A defrocked priest!"

"I've seen that text," said Stafford. "It is very poetic and very scriptural. But it doesn't sound much like our Roman Mass."

"Why even discuss it?" asked Grandeur. "It's completely illicit and invalid."

Bertone raised a hand to regain the floor. He wasn't finished. "There's more. The *Washington Post* reported yesterday the existence of ninety-four 'intentional faith communities' in the Washington area that are doing their

146

own liturgies. Without the presence of a priest. If there are that many of these liturgical communities in the American capital, there must be similar communities all over the United States. All over the world, for all I know." He pointed at Grandeur. "So I need to ask you, Eminenza. Have all these people, perhaps hundreds of thousands, perhaps millions, put themselves under interdict?"

Grandeur blurted, "That's what the canon says." He raised his copy of the canon, a single sheet of paper. "How could canon law make it any clearer?"

"Let's not get too legalistic, Fog." This from the American who headed the Holy Office, Cardinal William Levada, who had been a classmate of Mahony in their Southern California seminary "Don't you think we have a duty to tell these folks what they are doing before we tell them they're excommunicating themselves?"

Bertone said, "You mean we should threaten them? You know the faithful don't take very kindly to canonical threats."

"Well, maybe ask them at least what they think they are doing?" said Levada. "We would look more kind, more gentle if we did. More Christlike maybe?"

When Grandeur rolled his eyes, Levada sat up straighter. If the cardinal from Philadelphia wasn't buying into scripture, maybe Levada would meet him on his own ground, canon law. He asked Grandeur for his copy of the canon, and, after he had parsed the language in Canon 1378, uttered a small cry of surprise.

"What?" asked Grandeur.

"Maybe, Fog, *you* haven't read this canon very carefully either."

"Huh?" said Grandeur. He was blushing.

"It says here," said Levada, "that folks come under an automatic interdict if they"—he made little quote marks in the air—"'enact the liturgical action of the Eucharistic Sacrifice.' My question is, Are they really doing that?"

"Not sure I understand," said Grandeur.

"I mean their actions seem Eucharistic enough. But 'Sacrifice?' From what I've read in the *New York Times*, these Phoebe types are not claiming they're offering the Sacrifice of the Mass. They say they are only doing what Jesus told his followers to do at the Last Supper. They say they're following the opinion of some modern theologians like Schillebeeckx, who has written a good deal about the meaning of a Greek word used in the early Church: anamnesis."

Re repeated the word carefully: "A-nam-KNEE-sis?"

"Yes," said Levada. "I can give you a copy of a book on the subject by Bruce Morrill, a Jesuit from New England. Morrill claims that when the first followers of Jesus were engaged in a liturgical remembering of the Last Supper, they were not thinking *sacrifice* at all—not as it was later defined by the anti-Luther theologians at Trent. They were thinking about a meal, a highly significant communal meal, but a meal nonetheless."

Stafford nodded. He had read the same book. "Impressive scholarship."

Grandeur was speechless. After some moments, after he had composed himself, Grandeur admitted he was no theologian. "Just a canon lawyer."

"Aren't we all?" said Re. Re knew there were few real theologians in the higher reaches of the Roman Curia. They had risen to their eminence in the highly juridicized modern Church simply because they had doctorates in canon law. "If we really want to be honest, we are no match for Jesuit historians like Morrill. Or for the Dominican theologian Father Schillebeeckx."

"Theology aside," said Bertone, "we must decide how we respond to these." He reached for a sheaf of e-mail messages on his desk.

"What are they?" asked Stafford.

"A surge of some episcopal support for Mahony," he said. "Seventeen American bishops e-mailed Mahony after his televised news conference and sent my office blind copies." He ticked them off—using not their names but the names of their sees. "Portland, Fall River, Rochester, Buffalo, Cleveland, Toledo, Detroit, Denver, Des Moines, Baton Rouge, Santa Fe, Tucson, Great Falls, Montana, San Francisco, another Portland. You get the idea." He picked up another stack. "Same kind of notes here from other spots around the world: Quite a few from Canada. Montreal. Quebec. Toronto. Bogotá, Cape Town, Jakarta, Yokohama." His voice trailed off.

"Damn Internet," said Stafford. "One news cycle, and everyone in the world knows everything."

Re asked Bertone about Boston, Newark, St. Louis.

"Oh, we got their support. Of course."

"Of course," said Re. "We expect loyalty from O'Malley, Myers, and Burke. I didn't hear you mention Chicago?"

148

"Haven't heard from Chicago."

A rustle of activity at the door of Bertone's office. One of his aides rushed in with a half-dozen copies of *Time* magazine under his arm. He said, *Scuza, Eminenza, ma deve guardare questo.* "Excuse me, Eminence, but you have to look at this." He slapped the copies down on Bertone's desk. Bertone took one and invited the others to help themselves.

The smiling, almost exuberant face of a fair, freckled woman with short red hair graced *Time*'s cover under the headline, "Sister Phoebe McNulty: A People's Church in America."

"Oh my God!" said Stafford. He opened to the middle of the magazine. "They've even got some pictures of her 'at play.' Here's one of her in tennis shorts. *Time* says she was once a tennis star. Played at Wimbledon in 1991. And another, my God, in a bathing suit. Looks like a *Playboy* centerfold." He held up the magazine for all to see.

Grandeur waved his copy of the magazine and cried, "I can't believe this. Roger's lesbian nun!"

"Modernity hits the California convent!" said Re with a chuckle.

I'm going to the pope!" said Grandeur, clutching his copy of *Time*. "He will understand the gravity of this, even if you do not."

GRANDEUR, THE HURRY-UP AMERICAN in a Rome that likes to take its time. He stewed for two days at the Minerva before a Vatican messenger finally showed up at his hotel with a large, ornate envelope, wax-sealed with the papal coat of arms. Inside, he found what he had been waiting for, a hand-written invitation for him—*pranso* in the papal apartment at 8:00 PM Saturday.

GRANDEUR PRESENTED HIMSELF ON TIME. The pope was late, offering his apologies as he strode into the *ingresso* of his apartment. He sighed as he led the way directly to his dinner table, noting the copy of *Time* in Grandeur's hand. "America!" he said. Often enough for him, *Time* mirrored America. "A fraction of the family. But its concerns seem to take up half my days."

Grandeur doubted that, but he conceded it as fact and said nothing. The best he could do was remind the pope that the U.S. also came up every year with 45 percent of the Vatican's financial support.

"Yes," the pope said with a straight face. "That should keep me in Pradas."

Grandeur did a double take. The pope had to be kidding about his expensive, high-heeled red shoes. But if he was, then he was showing a self-deprecating, even wry, sense of humor he'd never manifested before—in Grandeur's presence, at least. In some confusion, Grandeur gave the pope a half-hearted smile. And then as he took his seat at the table, he saw the pope throw back his head in a broad, silent laugh. That didn't make Grandeur any more comfortable. Was the pope laughing at *him*? Not sure what to say, he let the Holy Father have the next word.

The pope didn't speak for some moments. At length, after a small glass of sherry had been served, he asked, "Does this *Time* cover story indicate a swell of popular support for your people's Church in America?"

"*My* people's Church!" protested Grandeur. "Not my idea. You know that!"

"I know." The pope regarded Grandeur with some curiosity. He could never get used to the too-well-tailored American bishops. They exuded an air of prosperity that was quite alien to most of the world's other bishops, with the possible exception of his own German bishops. "It's Roger Mahony's idea. But we have to try to, how do they say it in the American Southwest? 'Judge no man until we walk a mile in his moccasins?' He has had a great deal of stress. Kidnapped. Put on trial before the whole world. And then to be caught up in a military massacre."

Grandeur wondered where the pope had come up with the "walk-a-mile-in-his-moccasins" quote. He nodded agreement. "But does our sympathy for him mean we have to stand by and watch him try to overturn the divinely instituted hierarchical constitution of the Church?"

"There was no hierarchy in the early Church," snapped the pope. "There was no hierarchy at Pentecost. Hierarchy came later. Men set it up, not God."

Grandeur shifted nervously in his seat and toyed with his *pasta in brodo*. Three days ago, he had a new theology of the Eucharist rammed down his throat. Now the pope himself was giving him a new theology of the Church. At his age, and at his eminence, he asked himself, did he have to start learning theology all over again? Not a pleasant prospect.

"I grant you," continued the pope, "we have enjoyed a royal papacy for a thousand years. The question is, can we afford to keep running the Church like this for another thousand years? Or even another ten years?"

This surprised Grandeur. Papa Wojtyla never talked this way. Neither did Cardinal Ratzinger. But now that Ratzinger had become the pope, he was beginning to sound like Hans Küng, his former colleague at Tübingen, who actually dared to write in his recent memoir, "The royalty of Christ means democracy." Grandeur told the pope, "I am not sure what you have in mind." Cautious now. He had to be cautious.

"The Church-as-monarchy," said the pope, "cannot survive. In my youth, which lasted for me until I became pope—imagine, a young man until I reached the age of 78!—I thought numbers didn't matter. I wanted a more controlling Church, and if that meant a smaller Church, that was fine with me, because that would give us a more faithful Church. Now that I am pope, I cannot think this way any longer. I am starting to become something of a missionary."

Grandeur nodded, trying to process this, uh, well, he told himself, he'd have to call this a conversion. "I thought I could count on you," he said, "for your support." They had finished their soup course, and were being served now with a thin slice of veal and some underdone squash. Grandeur thought he might have to stop for a pizza at Il Fornaio on his way back to the Minerva.

The pope put down his fork for a moment, and took a sip of red wine. His cool blue eyes bore into Grandeur. "Tell me, Cardinal Grandeur, what kind of support do you want from me?"

"Well, first, you can withhold your approval of a national synod in the United States. This is not the time for a national synod."

The pope said quietly, "A pity. I remember you were the one asking for a synod only a few weeks ago. I have already approved a Fourth Council of Baltimore for the United States. It will commence this summer."

Grandeur paused, processed the pope's words, and tried to recover. "Well then, you can at least veto Mahony's notion that our national synod has to become an open gathering, with voting delegates there who are not even bishops."

"You want me to tell the American bishops they should hold a gathering of the American Church with only bishops in attendance?"

"Yes. Only bishops attended the three Councils of Baltimore—in 1844, 1866, and 1884. All you have to do is say the word—that we will follow tradition."

"The people-at-large shouldn't concern themselves, then, with things that are none of their business?"

"Exactly," said Grandeur, not quite catching the papal irony. "And you should tell the American bishops to keep the press out, too."

"The press would only arouse public opinion? For no good reason?"

Grandeur stared at the pope. He blotted his lips with a snow-white linen napkin. Was the pope putting him on? No. Not possible. "Exactly," he said. "Press coverage can only hurt us."

A white-coated waiter appeared with two carafes. The pope turned to Grandeur. "Coffee?" he asked. "Decaf?"

Grandeur opted for the decaf.

They sipped their coffees in silence. Then the pope said with some finality, "I will make no rules for your national synod that are not already codified in canon law. I am inclined to let the American bishops work out all the other rules they think they need." He made a lazy gesture with his left hand. "Subsidiarity and all that."

Again Grandeur had a hard time hiding his surprise.

The pope tried to reassure him, "I am sure you can get what you want. You undoubtedly have support from a majority of the American bishops?"

"At last count," said Grandeur, "I have approximately 105 of them— forty percent. That is the number who asked for a national synod a few years back."

"So few!"

"There may be more today."

"I would think so. You are not telling me Cardinal Mahony may have the rest of the bishops?" He did a swift mental calculation. "One hundred and eighty-seven bishops—sixty percent—on his side?"

Grandeur smiled. "I will put my 40 percent up against his 60 percent any day. If he *has* 60 percent, which I doubt. We are much more sure of ourselves. And, you must know, hugely funded, too." He proceeded to tell the pope about the financial help he was getting from Richard John Neuhaus, George Weigel, and Michael Novak.

"I know Novak."

"Yes, of course you do. Well, out of his Washington-based think tank, the Institute on Religion and Democracy—which Novak founded in 1985 with a gift from the Mellon Foundation of several hundred thousand dollars—"

"So little?" asked the pope. "I would think—"

"The Mellon family could have given more? Yes, and you would be right, your Holiness. Since 1985, Novak and company have raised more than forty million dollars in their campaign to overturn the socialism promoted by the mainline Protestant churches in America. Now, Novak and his people have a new campaign—to block this movement for a people's Church. They are kicking it off next week with a black-tie dinner at the Waldorf."

"A black-tie affair?" said the pope. "At the Waldorf? Tell me, will the affluent guests coming to this event even understand why they are there?"

"Probably not. But they love Rome, and they love the Church they have always known. That's enough for them. But when our speakers help them understand how much their Church is in danger . . ."

He waited for a nod from the pope. When he didn't get one, he took the pope's silence as an invitation to tell him the names of the speakers he had lined up to help the $1,000-a-plate dinner guests understand. He pulled a list from the inner breast pocket of his charcoal black cashmere jacket, and proceeded to read out a lineup that might have been culled from a *Who's Who* of the Catholic Church's right wing in America. "Neuhaus. Weigel, and Novak will speak, of course. Robert George of Princeton. Mary Ann Glendon of Harvard. (Harvard *and* Princeton!) Tom Monaghan, the pizza king who is building Ave Maria University in Florida. Patrick Reilly, whose vigilance has kept pseudo-Catholics away from Catholic podiums. John McCloskey, the Opus Dei priest from Washington who stands so strongly behind our nation's militant priests."

The pope raised an eyebrow. "Militant priests?"

Grandeur plunged on. "Yes, your Holiness. Just the other day, Father McCloskey described these American priests as 'the Navy Seals, the Army Rangers, the Green Berets of the Catholic Church.' And, your Holiness, you know how sorely the Church needs militant priests today."

Not sure the pope was convinced, Grandeur continued. "I don't think I have to tell you, Holy Father, there's more than a whiff of revolution here in this so-called people's Church in America? There's something subversive about it, something decidedly socialistic."

"But the early Church was built on a communist model, was it not?"

Grandeur spluttered. Now he knew the pope was toying with him. As Cardinal Ratzinger, he had done all he could to spike the liberation theologians—because he had been persuaded they were communists. "Well, your Holiness, Michael Novak has proven that the future of the world, and the future of the Church, lies in capitalism."

"*Novak* has proven?" The pope frowned. "I thought history itself has already delivered its verdict on the future of communism? I also thought the future of the Church did not lie in any, ummm, -ism, but in our following Jesus, who loved us and wanted us to follow his way, his truth, and his life. 'I have come that you may have life, and have it more abundantly?'"

"Of course," said Grandeur, with an impatient wave of his hand. "But that abundant life statement could mean anything. I think Mahony might want to turn it into some kind of socialist manifesto, or maybe I should say a call for liberation."

"Perhaps." The pope took a sip of red wine, and stared at Grandeur, and marveled at his efforts to manipulate him with the word "liberation." Grandeur knew he had never liked the so-called liberation theologians, because they always seemed to care more about liberation than they did about theology. He changed the subject, now tired, perhaps, of sparring with his capitalist cardinal, whom he liked even less than the liberation theologians. "Perhaps you could get Mr. Novak's publisher to send me a copy of his latest book? *Blessed Are the Rich for They Shall See God*?"

As he rose to leave, Grandeur remembered the hundred dollar bills he had brought as a little gift for the pope. Most bishops from affluent western nations did this as a matter of course on their periodic ad limina visits. The cardinal-archbishop of affluent Philadelphia brought greenbacks on every visit. He reached into his cashmere jacket, produced a large, long white envelope, waved his gift, handed it over, and said, "Peter can no longer say, 'Gold and silver have I none.'"

"No," said the pope, taking the envelope and, without looking at its contents, slipped it into a pocket of his cassock. "And neither can he now say, 'Rise and walk.'"

Grandeur wondered what the hell the pope meant by that. Nevertheless, he, Grandeur, did rise and walk—right out of the room.

• SEVENTEEN •

PRESS

ON FEBRUARY 2, BILL MOYERS AIRED a public television special on "A People's Church in America." It was a panel show that featured two principal guests, Roger Mahony and Cardinal Ted McCarrick, retired archbishop of Washington, D.C., along with four Catholic commentators, two sitting on Mahony's side of the podium, and two sitting on McCarrick's side.

After Moyers' introductions, Mahony seized the first word. "Bill, I have to take issue with the title of this show. This isn't a people's Church yet. The people—and the bishops—will have to decide on a lot of things before this becomes a people's Church."

"When have the people ever decided?" demanded Moyers. "I thought Catholics always did what they were told." He winked at Mahony, then invited McCarrick to respond.

McCarrick was there because Grandeur wasn't. Moyers had invited Grandeur to appear on this show, but Grandeur declined without an explanation—though he confided to his aides and to Monsignor Jeremiah Hawkslaw, his spy in Los Angeles, that he didn't want to engage Mahony in public debate. That would only give his cause more publicity. No, Grandeur was going to operate like an incumbent governor with a big lead in the polls; why debate the challenger when there was nothing to gain, and everything to lose? Grandeur couldn't help citing a principle from canon law as well: *possessio juris*, which, roughly translated, meant that rules governing the American Church were "in place." To him, that meant that anyone who wanted to change the rules had to prove they needed changing.

Grandeur was quite sure Mahony couldn't do that. His side could knock down whatever arguments the Mahony forces could muster, simply by referring the faithful to "the way things have been in the Church for more than a thousand years." No arguments necessary, except one: people who didn't like the ancient rules could simply leave the Church. And if arguments were eventually needed, Grandeur had the money behind him to buy a good deal of p.r.—everything from subway advertising in New York to television commercials in Los Angeles. Grandeur knew he could bury all this talk (that's all it was at this point, nothing but talk, and a *Time* cover story) about a people's Church.

Getting turned down by Grandeur hadn't bothered Moyers' producers. They knew they could always get the affable Ted McCarrick. McCarrick, who never met a TV producer he didn't like, said he'd be happy to come on the Moyers show and explain "where the Church stands on this idea of 'a people's Church.'" So now, with a honey voice and a winning smile, McCarrick told Moyers and his national TV audience, "The Church, as you know, Bill, is not a democracy. But the American bishops are also Americans. They cannot help thinking about better ways to serve their Catholic constituents. It is no accident that we have chosen the Fourth of July to begin our national synod in Baltimore."

"The Fourth of July!" exclaimed Moyers.

"Exactly," said McCarrick. "It will be a time when we all come together to do what we have to do to create a more faithful Church."

Moyers asked McCarrick, "Do you mean all the bishops? Or will we see some laypeople there?"

McCarrick said he expected every bishop-delegate to bring a lay representative with him to Baltimore.

"How will those representatives be chosen?" asked Moyers.

"That will be up to each bishop," said McCarrick. "The bishops know who their good loyal Catholics are."

"Loyal to whom?" asked Sister Joan Chittister, who was sitting at the Mahony table.

Moyers beamed. He'd brought Chittister onto his show because he knew this Benedictine sister—widely known as America's super-nun—wasn't afraid of McCarrick, or of any other American bishop. And she asked good, feisty questions.

"Well," stammered McCarrick. "Loyal to the Church."

"Which Church?" said Chittister. "The people's Church or the hierarchical Church?"

"There's only one Church," said McCarrick.

"The pray, pay, and obey Church?" prompted Chittister.

While McCarrick considered how he could offer a courtly response to Chittister's hostile question, Moyers recognized Nick Pike, introducing him as "a leading Catholic lawyer in California who has been working with Cardinal Mahony."

Before Pike could speak, Richard John Neuhaus, the priest-editor of a conservative monthly called *First Things*, challenged Moyers. "Bill," he said to Moyers, "you don't give Mr. Pike enough credit. He is, in fact, working for Cardinal Mahony as his campaign manager, is he not?"

"I don't know," said Moyers. "Is he?"

"He's right here," said Neuhaus. "You can ask him."

Pike bristled. "I'm not working for Cardinal Mahony."

"But you are managing his campaign, are you not? A frankly political campaign?"

Pike counterattacked. "Let me ask you a question, Father Neuhaus. Do you think there's something shady, maybe even something sinful, in trying to overturn the Church's old pyramidal structure?"

"You mean," asked Neuhaus, "what John Paul II called 'the divinely instituted hierarchical constitution of the Church?' Yes, I'd say there's something wrong with that. Something fairly heretical."

"'Divine institution,'" said Pike, "means it was founded by Christ. But if Jesus founded our Church, he certainly didn't found the hierarchical Church that we know today. Claiming Jesus founded the kind of authoritarian, unaccountable Church we have today can have only one purpose: to keep us in our place."

Neuhaus didn't try to answer that. Instead, he launched a personal attack on Pike. "I find it very curious, Mr. Pike, that you, a founder of *Para los otros*, the terrorist organization that kidnapped Cardinal Mahony in November and put him on trial in Chiapas, should end up in Cardinal Mahony's camp. I am surprised that he should want you to be a spokesman on this show for his 'people's Church in America.' I am even more surprised to see Cardinal Mahony running a frankly political campaign to advance this so-called 'people's Church.'"

"And you're not part of a political campaign against it?" This from Mahony himself.

"Only out of self-defense," said Neuhaus. "Only out of loyalty to the Holy See."

"Gentlemen!" said Moyers. "Let's get back on track here. We were talking about the upcoming Fourth Council of Baltimore. Will it help make a more accountable Church in America or won't it?"

Neuhaus said, "It will as long as that Council remains loyal to Rome."

Pike countered. "I'd say accountability, not loyalty, is the big issue in the American Church today. We're all loyal Catholics. All loyal to the pope, too. But if delegates are appointed by the bishops, who can say they will come to the convention as anything but yes-men to the bishops? Or yes-women?"

Sister Joan Chittister said, "I don't think many bishops would bring a woman to Baltimore."

Pike said, "They might if their people elected women delegates. They'd have to."

"What do you think of that, Mr. Novak?" said Moyers, who knew that Novak had once written tellingly about the need for more democracy in the American Church. "Should delegates to Baltimore be appointed by their bishops or elected by the people?"

Trying to come across as a voice of reason, Novak said, "There's no need for a battle here, between the priests on one side and the laity on the other."

"Right, Michael," agreed Pike. "In their battle to have a voice and a vote in their own Church, the people are learning that a good many priests are on their side. Many of those priests could well win a delegate's spot in Baltimore. In a free and open election, the people of Erie, Pennsylvania, could vote to send Sister Joan. Or the people of Brooklyn could send Father Neuhaus."

Neuhaus and Chittister both smiled, happy to think they might be elected delegates to the convention in Baltimore.

Moyers asked Cardinal Mahony, "Does canon law say we have to have a vote?"

Mahony tried to clarify the process. "Canon law doesn't say how delegates must be chosen. It does say up to 50 percent of the delegates can be non-bishops." He said he hoped to see some outstanding laypeople at the meeting—especially history professors who had an understanding of the primitive Church (which operated like a commune), and of the early

Church in America (where the churches were owned by lay trustees). He also expected to see some priest-delegates in Baltimore—theologians, major religious superiors, even some canon lawyers.

Cardinal McCarrick confirmed Mahony's guess. "Canon 443, paragraph three, says "up to 50 percent non-bishops." Doesn't say up to 50 percent laypeople. This could still turn out to be a very clerical gathering." He couldn't resist a dig. "In which case, I'd doubt the Fourth Council of Baltimore will endorse a people's Church."

"So," demanded Chittister, "the Fourth Council of Baltimore will give us more of the same-old, same-old, a new kind of clerical Church? That's just what I was afraid of. That's been the root of our sex scandals in the American Church—priests covering up for their clerical buddies. The root of our financial scandals, too, priests helping themselves to the collection. We need lay people there in Baltimore. Lots of them."

Mahony interjected. "Sister, it all depends on what laypeople we're talking about. Do we want yes-men and yes-women there? I don't think so. Why not some thoughtful people of all kinds? Scholars and thinkers and mothers and fathers of families. Nuns are laypeople. I'd like to see some nuns there. I'd like to see some college kids there as well."

"Any chance of that?" asked Moyers,

Pike said, "So far, we don't even know if there will be an election of delegates."

McCarrick agreed with Pike. "I don't think we will have enough time for an election campaign. I think we just have to rely on the bishops to appoint good people."

"Who makes that decision?" asked Moyers.

McCarrick said, "The American bishops. They'll come together for their quadrennial retreat in March. In Phoenix. They'll decide then."

"Do you have any idea—now—what they'll decide?" asked Moyers.

"My guess," said Mahony, "is that some bishops will want to pick their own delegates, and some will want their people to do that. I should tell you I already have an election commission at work in Los Angeles to set up some voting protocols. Before people can vote, for instance, they have to register to vote."

"Where will they do that?"

"The easiest way? Through their parishes. If they're registered in their parishes, they can vote in their parishes."

159

"But half of the Catholics in America are not registered," said Michael Novak. "How will they cast a ballot? Will they even want to?"

Mahony laughed. "I didn't plan it this way, but I predict a lot of pastors will start smiling—when the currently unchurched start showing up to sign on to the parish rolls."

"Just so they can vote?" Neuhaus sneered.

Mahony smiled. "I would hope they might stick around for Mass, too, and drop some folding money in the basket."

Pike said, "Cardinal Mahony may not have planned this. But I don't see how it can not happen. Give the people a voice and a vote, and they will have a sense of ownership."

Moyers challenged. "A *sense* of ownership, Mr. Pike? What about real ownership? When will they have that?"

"That," said Pike, "is one of the things the delegates will have to work out at the Fourth Council of Baltimore. If the Council gives real legal title to the laypeople—I am talking about the churches and schools and hospitals they've already built—then the bishops will have to listen to their people."

"Wow!" said Moyers. "Then you'll be just like the Baptists."

"Or," said Neuhaus, "like the Episcopalians. What a mess they've got, with everyone voting on everything."

"Yes," said Chittister. "Just like one big, unhappy family. But they do know they are part of a family. What's wrong with that? It's real. And it's human. In many of our Catholic parishes these days, we've lost our humanity."

Moyers asked, "What happens if, say, the bishop of Buffalo Tooth, Nebraska, decides to bring his own yes-man to Baltimore?"

The panel—and the small studio audience—laughed. Every one seemed sure that Bishop Dreedle of Buffalo Tooth would bring his own lackey to Baltimore. "Some bishops," said Mahony, "will no doubt do that. In which case, we might end up with a few delegates at the convention who will vote as their bishops tell them to. We'd have to learn to live with that. That's part of being human, too."

"What if the people of Buffalo Tooth got together—somehow—and elected their own delegate? What then?"

"If that happened," said Pike, "we could end up with a fight before the credentials committee."

Chittister rubbed her hands gleefully. "A good political convention always has a credentials committee, doesn't it?"

Pike said, "Yes, and a rules committee, too. We don't want an unwieldy convention. There are 193 dioceses in this country. If we had one delegate from every diocese, we'd have 193 non-bishop delegates and 193 bishops. A body like that needs some rules of order. Quite a crowd. Exactly 386 delegates."

"But not as big as the House of Representatives," said Moyers. "Could this convention handle 386 delegates?"

Pike said, "I'd expect the delegates would try to form a rules committee right from the start."

"Who'd be on this rules committee?" asked Moyers.

Pike said, "I should think the pro tem chairman—or chairwoman— would call for nominations from the floor. Then the delegates would adjourn and caucus together with their friends."

"Two caucuses? Maybe a liberal caucus and a conservative caucus?" asked Moyers.

"Probably," said Pike. "Maybe we'd even see a two-party system emerge before our very eyes."

Moyers smiled. "This could be fun."

Michael Novak raised his hand. Novak, a young liberal at Vatican II, and an aging conservative during the reign of John Paul II. "How will you know, Bill?"

"How will I know it's fun?"

"No. I mean, what makes you think you will be privy to the proceedings?"

"I don't understand."

With some exasperation, Novak demanded, "What makes you think this Fourth Council of Baltimore will even be open to the press?"

"Why wouldn't it be?"

"I should think Rome will have something to say about that," said Novak. "There was no press at the First, Second, or Third Councils of Baltimore. For all of its openness, Vatican II wasn't open to the press."

"And maybe you didn't know this," Neuhaus chimed in, agreeing with Novak's point. "The Founding Fathers kept the press out of the Constitutional Convention of 1787."

Moyers said he had always assumed members of the press in colonial America reported on the progress of the Constitutional Convention from inside Philadelphia's Independence Hall—simply because it was American. "But now that you bring it up, I do recall that press freedom in America came gradually, and not without a fight. The editor John Peter Zenger spent some time in jail for things he'd written in colonial New York." Moyers turned to his right, then his left and addressed both cardinals. "Where would you stand on that issue, your Eminences? Press or no press in Baltimore?"

"I'm all for giving the delegates some freedom here," said McCarrick.

"Freedom?"

"The bishops," said McCarrick, "will be freer to speak their minds if they know they won't be quoted in the *Times*." Laughter from the audience.

"Or seen on television?" said Moyers. "I'd expect the networks might want to be there. Or at least C-SPAN."

McCarrick shuddered. "Television would kill any serious deliberations. I can see a lot of delegates trying to grandstand."

"Bishop delegates, your Eminence," joshed Pike, "trying to grandstand? Horrors!"

"I didn't mean the bishop-delegates," said McCarrick, blushing.

"Who then?" asked Pike. "The elected laymen and laywomen?"

McCarrick squirmed. "I withdraw my comment," he said.

Moyers turned to Mahony. "You've been silent on this, your Eminence."

Mahony laughed. "I'd expect everyone of the delegates at Baltimore— clerics and non-clerics—to behave at Baltimore."

Moyers asked him, "So, do you want to see the press there, or not?"

Mahony said, "I don't see how the Fourth Council of Baltimore can have any credibility with the people of the twenty-first century if it proceeds in secret."

"It needn't be secret forever," said McCarrick. "We could present the people with complete reports after the council is over." Groans from the audience.

"I'm sure that's what you'd like," snapped Chittister. "After the meeting's over? No way. The people will want to know what's happening while it is happening. So they can express their opinions on the issues."

"But the Church isn't a democracy!" insisted Neuhaus.

"Are you saying, Father, that the delegates shouldn't care what the people-at-large think?" demanded Pike.

Neuhaus set his jaw. "Catholic doctrine," he said, "is not determined by a popular vote."

"Who said anything about Catholic doctrine?" demanded Chittister. "We're talking about changes in the way we govern ourselves, so we can create a more accountable Church. In the beginning, bishops were not lords. They needn't be now."

"That's only a liberal assumption!" shouted Neuhaus. "If I am not mistaken, the bishops have already set an agenda for the Fourth Council of Baltimore. It'll be about restoring the priesthood, making it holy, putting it back on the Jesus track. Nothing in that agenda about changing the Church's governance in the United States. That's why we still call our Church the Roman Catholic Church."

"We have to stop calling it that," said Mahony. "That's been a major part of the problem. The Church is too Roman and not nearly enough Catholic. Catholic with a small 'c,' huh?"

"What about that agenda, your Eminence?" asked Moyers. "Does it deal with governance issues?"

"An agenda has already been drafted," Mahony conceded, "and it does center on 'restoring the priesthood, and making it holy' again. But they didn't set that agenda in stone. At Vatican II, the bishops-at-large objected to the council's conservative agenda, the one that was drafted in advance by the forces of no-change inside the Roman Curia. The bishops from outside the Curia opened up that agenda, and the rest is history. I'd expect the same kind of group dynamics to take hold in Baltimore. Especially when the people-at-large have a chance to study the agenda in advance."

"They won't have a chance to do that," said Neuhaus. "The agenda will be *sub secreto*, You can count on that."

"Not after it's leaked," said Mahony. That created a stir at both tables. "And Father Neuhaus, *you* can count on *that*."

"You'd leak the agenda? That's outrageous!" shouted Neuhaus.

Mahony laughed. "Father Neuhaus, didn't you just do that?"

"I did not!"

"A minute ago, didn't you give us the first leak? I think you said the synod would center on 'restoring the priesthood, and making it holy' again. And I commented on it. There'll be other leaks."

"Well *mea culpa!*" said Neuhaus. "*Mea maxima culpa!*"

Mahony smiled. "If Ted McCarrick will absolve you, Father, so will I."

McCarrick laughed and made a generous sign of the cross in Neuhaus's direction. "*Ego te absolvo, Ricardus.*"

Mahony said, "I'll absolve you after the show, Father Neuhaus, after I hear your confession."

Neuhaus snorted, and Mahony continued. "Earlier tonight, there was some discussion about which Church will show up in Baltimore—the people's Church or the clerical Church? I say that for the health of the American Church, whether the delegates are elected or appointed, the people of God have to be there. That's why we have to let the TV cameras in, so everyone in America can be there, virtually at least. And if C-SPAN is there, the people can have gavel-to-gavel coverage."

Hullabaloo. Everyone talking at once. Moyers finally calmed everyone down and turned to Mahony. "You're not serious, are you? You want to see gavel-to-gavel television coverage of the convention in Baltimore?"

Mahony said, "TV is part of the press, Bill, and the very future of the American Church will depend on the press being there. Not because it is the press (the press in itself has no special privileges here) but because the press will make it possible for the people to be there. If the people are there, and if the people like what they see happening, they will say, 'Yes, this is my Church.' They will want to own it. When they do, many of those folks who left it in disgust will come back, and, I hope, attract a great many new people, too, who will want to be a part of a people's Church in America, fully American, and fully Catholic, too."

"That's an optimistic view," said Novak. "What if the people out there don't like what's happening on the Council floor?"

"What do you mean?" asked Mahony.

"In the Constitutional Convention of 1787, members were at each other's throats. They battled over the slavery issue. And never did solve it. We're going to have battles, too."

Neuhaus said, "And do we really want to put those battles on display?"

Pike's retort dripped with sarcasm. "No. Let our holy bishops cover 'em up."

McCarrick tried to mediate the battle that was going on right here with a joke. "Whoever said the bishops were holy?" He chortled, and gave

Mahony a friendly wink. Murmurs from the audience, not knowing whether to laugh or cry.

Moyers tapped his microphone. "We'll have to wind this down, gentlemen."

"And 'lady,'" said Mahony. "We do have one woman on this side of the room. We should have more of them."

Moyers apologized for slighting Sister Joan Chittister, then tried to proceed. "By way of summary," he said, "let me ask Cardinal Mahony a question about the pope. What place will he have in your people's Church? Will Americans just forget about him?"

"Hardly," said Mahony. "An autochthonous American Church will need a pope more than ever. He will still be the Vicar of Peter, still someone we can rally around on a host of international issues, and still the first among the bishops of the whole world. We'll also continue to support him financially—as well as, or better than ever."

"How do you figure that?" demanded Neuhaus.

Mahony laughed. "Because there will be more Catholics in the pews."

"So you want to have it both ways?" asked Moyers. "You want an American Catholic Church that is also loyal to the pope?"

Mahony said, "Bill, I don't think you understand autochthony."

"Aw what?"

Mahony pronounced the word very carefully. "Aw-TOCK-thu-nee. It doesn't mean autonomy. It means homegrown, homespun, homemade. An autochthonous American Church would be Catholic. And it would also be American. Just like an autochthonous Chinese Church. It would be Catholic. And it would also be Chinese."

Neuhaus and Novak responded together. "You mean communist?" they demanded. Murmurs from the audience.

"That's unfair!" cried Pike. "How rotten is that?"

"It's not unfair," retorted Neuhaus. "A people's Church in America? Unfortunate phrase. Sounds to me like the People's Republic of China."

More uproar—from the panel, from the audience.

"Gentlemen, gentlemen," chided Moyers. He turned to Mahony. "I'm intrigued with this thing you call autochthony. How do you spell it?"

EIGHTEEN

STANDOFF

FROM MARCH 17 TO MARCH 20, 2009, the American bishops met for their quadrennial retreat at the Phoenician in Scottsdale, an exclusive oasis in the Arizona desert, expensively landscaped with hundreds of palm and banana trees, an occasional saguaro cactus, and a thousand flowering plants—yellow birds of paradise, begonias, chaparral sage, and red yucca.

The Phoenician boasted nine heated swimming pools including a 165-foot water slide, a twenty-seven-hole championship golf course, twelve tennis courts, a bowling green and a croquet lawn. It had a health center with a gym, professional fitness trainers, a meditation center, and a spa. Some of the best chefs in the world presided over the Phoenician's eleven restaurants, most of which had spectacular views of the desert and the mountains that surrounded the resort—built at a cost of almost a billion dollars, money stolen from investors in a savings and loan run by a former governor of Arizona (who went to prison for his crimes). It was now owned and operated by some oil sheiks from Dubai.

The word "retreat" was a cover. At the Phoenician, the bishops did what they had been doing at some of America's finest resorts for decades: they kicked off their meeting with a grand St. Patrick's Day banquet, then spent three days gossiping in the sun, eating well, drinking well and (many of them) playing eighteen holes every day. They attended a mid-morning Mass at nine every morning, then hit the links. They held one business meeting at 11:00 AM on March 20—where they voted down a proposal by Cardinal Mahony that the Catholics in every diocese in America elect a single delegate—with full voting rights—to accompany his ordinary to the Fourth Council of Baltimore.

Under the direction of NCCB president George Niederaurer, the bishops followed *Robert's Rules of Order* to amend Mahony's proposal. In its redrafted form, the proposal called for each ordinary to select a delegate of his own choosing. He could bring a priest or a nun or a layperson, anyone but another bishop, to Baltimore. But that delegate would be a mere observer, with no voting rights.

That proposal won by a huge show of hands. Someone later estimated four out of five bishops voted aye. At that point, Mahony rose to address his colleagues, and Niederaurer, a former classmate of Mahony in the seminary at Camarillo and someone who halfway sympathized with Mahony's new cause, gave him the floor. "You want to come up here, Roger?"

Mahony said he didn't need a mike, stayed in his seat, and proceeded to give voice to his disappointment—and put his own twist on the bishops' vote. "Gentlemen," he said, "I am gratified by this decision to bring some other perspectives to Baltimore. I'd like to think this decision will bring some fresh air, too. I see this move as a step—a baby step, but nevertheless a step toward a people's Church in America." That drew some negative murmurs from his fellow bishops.

Mahony ignored them and continued. "For the entire history of this body, dating back to 1917, we've been seen as the high and mighty spokesmen for an exclusive clerical club. We do what we do out of our own private, and largely secret, considerations. Often enough, we've been more worried about what Rome thinks than what our people think. Rome has even demanded the right to approve, or disapprove, whatever we do. And we've let Rome have its way. To me, this has been a very unpleasant kind of political arrangement that makes us hugely unaccountable to the people we're vowed to serve. And most of you have long recognized another real flaw in this system. We cannot make any rules that are canonically binding on any particular bishop. Bishops who don't like what we've decided can thumb their noses at us."

From off to Mahony's left, someone guffawed. It was Ignatius Dreedle, the group's bad boy from Buffalo Tooth, Nebraska, who had derided and dismissed every element of the bishops' Charter for the Protection of Children and Young People, and had given the bishops' lay Review Board none of the cooperation it needed in order to do its job.

Mahony acknowledged the outburst with nothing more than a wry, resigned smile, like a teacher who had long ago decided to ignore the class clown. He went on. "I won't say I am not disappointed by your vote this morning. I *am* disappointed. We need a real *metanoia*, and not only a change in the way we think, but a change in the way we feel. We need to rid ourselves of what I can only call a bad habit—of continuing to impose our top-down rule in a bottom-up kind of world.

"This is a world that doesn't much like hierarchy of any kind, but does have a great respect for authority, the kind of authority that is fashioned by a consensus, and by the consent of the governed. To get that kind of authority, we don't need to reinvent the wheel. We're Americans. Over the course of our nation's history, our elected leaders in America have learned how to come to a consensus on some of the great issues that have faced us as a nation. And how to win the consent of the governed, who, in the end, almost always come up with solutions that work—which has generally meant solutions that are fair as far as they go. Americans fought a war over slavery, and we fought another kind of battle over the civil rights of all of our citizens, a battle that continues to rage. The fight for liberty and justice in America never ends. But when will the fight begin for liberty and justice in our Church? When have we ever worried about our accountability to the people of God?"

More murmurs from the crowd. "This is nonsense," cried Dreedle. Others shouted him down.

"Let Roger speak!" said Archbishop Niederauer.

"As many of you are aware," said Mahony, "I've been thinking very hard about the need for inculturating the Gospel in the United States. I look forward to some deep discussions at the Fourth Council of Baltimore on just exactly how we can do that. Some of my advisors insist we need three branches of Church governance to bring that off, a legislative branch, a judicial branch, and an executive branch. I look forward to hearing your opinions about that —in Baltimore, not now. I am sure we will work out something that answers the needs of our American Catholic Church at this time. But I'd like to bring all the people of God into our deliberations. If all the people cannot be there in the flesh, then we can give them a virtual presence there. That means a Council that is open to the press. And so, with George's permission, I am going to offer another proposal for your consideration. That we let the print press into the Council—and the broadcast media as well."

"Second the motion!" cried Paul Bootkoski, bishop of Metuchen, New Jersey.

"Moved and seconded," said Niederaurer. "Discussion?"

No one spoke up. The last vote had told the bishops where the power in this body resided. Certainly not with Mahony. What need to talk about it? They were going to vote him down again, no matter what. Niederaurer picked up his gavel, ready to call for a vote.

Mahony leaned over to one of his supporters, Leonard Paul Blair, bishop of Toledo. "I don't think we're going to win this one either."

Blair whispered, "I agree. What were you thinking of anyway, bringing the issue to a vote so quickly?" He shouted to the chair, "Table the motion!" According to *Robert's Rules of Order,* that did it. Mahony's motion was put aside, for now at least. Maybe there would be other innings.

Niederaurer, knowing many had tee times starting at 12:30, adjourned the meeting. And the bishops moved off to lunch.

Mahony opened his laptop, got online immediately (the whole resort had wireless connections to the Internet), and started tapping out an e-mail message to Nick Pike.

PIKE DIDN'T TAKE THE NEWS WELL. Just before 1:00 PM on March 20, he was reading Mahony's e-mail from Phoenix, and groaning over it just as Rackham was wheeling into the back room office in the campaign headquarters.

"What?" demanded Rackham.

"Note from Roger in Phoenix. Four out of five bishops just voted down his proposal."

"To bring elected delegates to Baltimore?"

Pike was all gloom. "Yes."

"Just like that, huh?" Rackham snapped his fingers.

"Well, they decided they *may* bring delegates—but need not. It'll be up to each bishop—to bring his own appointed delegate, as an observer. "

Rackham mulled that for a moment. "Well," he said, "that's some progress."

Pike measured an inch with the thumb and forefinger of his right hand. "Very little. Each bishop will bring his own lackey."

"With some exceptions," said Rackham. "Remember, almost every diocese in California has a campaign going—for the people to elect their own delegate for Baltimore. A dozen other dioceses around the country are doing that, too."

Pike shook his head. "So we will have maybe a dozen or two delegates in Baltimore—presumably, but not necessarily, on our side. And most of the bishops and their appointees on the other side."

"We need more support than that."

"Yes. Makes me feel a little silly. We've got a national campaign headquarters here." He waved toward the large empty room of their Wilshire Boulevard storefront. "And no real campaign." He nodded toward the screen of his laptop. "And, to make things worse, Roger says they tabled his proposal to allow the press into the Baltimore meetings."

"Shit," said Rackham. "We need the press there."

"The press will be there," said Pike. "But they'll be on the outside looking in. That'll make our job ten times harder."

"Or maybe it will piss off the press. Put 'em on our side. The press could help us."

"Your lips to God's ears, Ted."

"Maybe," said Rackham, "the Holy Spirit will think of something."

Pike, who was in no laughing mood, laughed. "Ted, you don't even *believe* in the Holy Spirit."

"Well," he said with one of his rare smiles, "if She comes to the rescue here, I could believe in Her."

Pike shook his head. "You're too much. Let's go to lunch. I'm buying."

• NINETEEN •

MOORE

THE HOLY SPIRIT SURELY HAD a sense of humor, coming to the rescue as She did through the instrumentality of a comedian named Michael Moore.

In the hit documentary *Roger and Me,* released by Warner Bros. in 2001, Moore had chronicled his unsuccessful pursuit of Roger Smith, the board chairman of General Motors, who eluded him and his camera crew for months on end after GM closed its plant in Flint, Michigan, terminating some 40,000 workers, and turning Moore's hometown into a wasteland. Moore got few words from Smith, the runaround from Smith's lieutenants, and a lecture on capitalism from one of GM's p.r. people (who later lost his own job). Moore demonstrated that GM gave less of a damn about its poor fired workers in Flint than it did for its corporate profits. By implication, *Roger and Me* also skewered America's ruling class.

In a project with the tentative title *The Bishops and Me,* Moore intended to skewer the American Church's ruling class, but now, eight technology-driven years later, he could do so much more than he did in *Roger and Me.* He didn't need a camera crew with him when he visited the American bishops' retreat at the Phoenician in Scottsdale in March 2009. He was outfitted with a mini-cam the size of a quarter; it looked like a button on his denim shirt. Under his shirt, a wire ran down from that camera to a three-by-five-inch transmitter in the pocket of Moore's baggy jeans—which sent his material to a command truck parked a half-mile away, where an associate recorded every sound, every image.

Moore did not record the bishops at prayer, of which there was very little on this so-called retreat. He caught them at play, in a venue they had chosen for its privacy. Only when Cardinal Grandeur and a few of his helper-bishops in Philadelphia saw Moore's rough cut some weeks later—given them by a friend at *Fox Television News*—did they realize that Moore had been able to wander around the Phoenician with his hidden camera for almost two hours before he was found out by four security guards and thrown off the property.

The networks, which had copies of Moore's rough cut, refused to buy—no matter how much editing he might promise to do on it. They had what they called "ethical and legal and commercial reasons." They were probably right. The bishops hardly ever appeared in public without their medieval costumes, their funny hats, and their tall curved sticks called "crosiers." Moore caught them in their Bermuda shorts with their golf clubs and their tennis rackets and their dry martinis—a self-satisfied, pompous lot relaxing in the kind of splendor enjoyed only by America's corporate elite.

A producer at PBS told Moore, "You invaded the bishops' privacy in Scottsdale. We cannot risk a lawsuit. Or a Congressional inquiry either." A vice president at CBS told Moore, "You can do kamikaze journalism on the president of General Motors. You can do attack journalism on the president of the United States. But you can't do that to the cardinal-archbishop of Philadelphia. Do you know that one out of every four Americans is a Catholic? Seventy-five million Catholics in this country?"

"I'm a Catholic, too," protested Moore. "That's why I can have a little fun at the bishops' expense. I think at least half of that seventy-five million will laugh along with me."

"Half?" said the man from CBS. "The other half will kill us. We can't risk that."

Moore did no better with the other networks. A friendly p.r. man at ABC told him, "In September 2006, we spent thirty million dollars on a two-night docudrama about 9/11 and produced something that alienated half our audience. We'll never, ever do that again." Bill O'Reilly confessed to Moore—off the record—that Fox had lost $38 million in advertising revenue after he presented his show with Monsignor Rountree and Father James Kowalski, a show that helped kick-start the movement for a people's Church.

"How did you lose thirty-eight mill?" asked Moore.

O'Reilly said Fox had ad contracts with most of corporate America. Pillsbury. Procter and Gamble. Exxon. Ford. "Apparently, most of these big companies all have conservative Catholics on their boards. We don't have their ad business any more."

Moore rolled his eyes. In the capitalist world that supported Fox, what could he expect? Well, he could be a capitalist, too. The hell with the networks. He could distribute his ninety-minute documentary to movie theaters across the land. He'd done that with two of his other productions. One of them had even won him an Oscar. But a theatrical release would take months to mount. And this subject was hot right now, wasn't it?

MOORE DIDN'T KNOW HOW HOT until he was invited to visit the Wilshire Boulevard campaign headquarters of the people's Church in Los Angeles—and told to bring a copy of his tape. Moore remembered that Bill O'Reilly had told him something about a movement for a people's Church in America. He had considered that a quixotic dream. The bishops were as thoroughly entrenched as any corporate board, and nothing, he thought, would ever move them toward a sharing of their power with the people, who weren't even stockholders. But now, as he was parking his SUV along the curb on Wilshire and noting a red, white, and blue sign in the window that read CAMPAIGN FOR A PEOPLE'S CHURCH, he was wishing he had been paying more attention to what was going on—in the Church of Los Angeles, at least.

Juana Margarita Obregón met him at the door and brought him through a huge almost empty outer room to a single windowless inner office in the back. It had a bare linoleum floor, a flickering fluorescent fixture in the ceiling, and was furnished with one desk, one telephone, one small TV, and four chairs.

"I guess you know who this is?" she said to Pike and Rackham and Sunnyhill. How could they not? Amply overweight with a scruffy brown beard, Moore was wearing his trademark costume—baggy jeans, an oversize Navy blue jacket, Nikes on his feet, a John Deere cap on his crown.

With a straight face, Pike looked up at Juana Margarita Obregón and said, "Does he have an appointment?"

Rackham turned his wheelchair toward Moore. "If you'd like to fill out this form," he said with a frown, "we'll see if we can get you on our schedule. We'll take it under advisement."

Moore's face dropped. Then when Pike and Rackham roared with laughter, he got the joke—that he wasn't going to get the same reception here that he had received at General Motors when he was trying, in vain, to see Chairman Roger Smith. But then, this bare campaign headquarters didn't much resemble the chairman's suite at General Motors.

Pike offered Moore one of the chairs, introduced him to Rackham and Juana Margarita Obregón and Sunnyhill—only their names, no titles—and got right to the point. "We've heard you can't sell your documentary," he said.

Moore didn't bother asking which documentary. "Where'd you hear that?" he said.

"On the Hollywood grapevine," said Rackham.

"The grapevine has it right. TV networks won't touch it."

Pike asked, "How about cable? HBO?"

"HBO is Time-Warner. Time-Warner won't touch it either." Moore spread his hands. "None of the other cable outfits would even look at it, not when I told 'em what I had."

"Can we look at it?" asked Pike.

"It's only a rough cut. I got this tape." He waved a small plastic bag at them. "You got a VHS player?""

They turned their chairs toward the TV in the corner of the office and watched Moore's tape. It started out with a slow, nostalgic look back at the Church Moore had known as a skinny Irish kid growing up as part of a large Catholic family in Flint, Michigan. His camera lingered on family snapshots—close-ups of the smiling nuns who taught him at St. Bridget's, his Irish pastor wearing a Detroit Tigers baseball cap, and a portrait of the St. Bridget's eighth-grade basketball team. Thirteen-year-old Michael Moore knelt in the front row, next to his nun-coach standing over her charges in a black serge habit and starched white wimple.

His opening narrative featured interviews with old-timers who fondly remembered the discipline and the devotion of the Church they knew, and it recalled Hollywood's reverent treatment of a long line of Catholic heroes and nun-heroines, as played by some of its most beloved stars—Loretta

Young in *Come to the Stable,* Ingrid Bergman in *The Bells of St. Mary's,* and Audrey Hepburn in *A Nun's Story.*

Moore's tape followed those shots with footage of Bing Crosby in a Roman collar crooning a lullaby in *Going My Way,* of Barry Fitzgerald, an Irish-brogue pastor in the same movie, and, no surprise, Spencer Tracy in his classic role—as Father Flanagan in *Boys Town,* slapping around a snotty orphan played by Mickey Rooney. He also had a clip of Pat O'Brien as Knute Rockne, giving a fiery pep talk to George Gipp (played by Ronald Reagan) and his teammates at Notre Dame. "Rockne wasn't a Catholic when he got to Notre Dame," observed Moore in his voice-over, "but his presence on the campus at Notre Dame showed how smart those Holy Cross priests were, to hire a guy who knew how to inspire winners on the gridiron."

The film cut to a close-up of Moore himself on camera. "But then," he said, "something happened to the Church in America. Many of the nuns and priests we knew and loved quit their orders. And some of the priests who remained at their altars turned out to be scoundrels. Worse, much worse, their superiors and their bishops who knew they were abusing children covered up for them.

"One of the scoundrel priests was Paul Shanley, a member of NAMBLA, the North American Man Boy Love Association, who was convicted of raping several young men before he fled Boston to set up a gay bed-and-breakfast establishment in Palm Springs, California." Here Moore's viewers saw a police mug shot of a shifty-eyed Shanley, then footage of a handsome, white-haired Irish priest outside the fence of a children's playground. "This is Oliver O'Grady, a priest from Stockton, California, now living in exile in Ireland. In California, he was found guilty of raping young children in his rectory, one as young as nine months old. A court found that his malefactions were covered up by the man who was then bishop of Stockton, Roger Michael Mahony." More quick shots of O'Grady, then of Mahony.

"What happened?" asked Moore. "These priests and bishops forgot who they were and why they'd taken their sacred vows in the first place, not to dominate over their flocks, but to serve them. The bishops were afflicted with an Edifice Complex, building lots of churches and schools, but acting more like CEOs of General Motors, aloof from the people, and unaccountable, very unaccountable for their actions."

The camera cut from Moore to a series of police mug shots, all confessed or convicted priest-pedophiles. Then some shots of bishops in their purple.

"Several bishops were indicted for raping young boys, and one archbishop was found paying four hundred fifty thousand in hush money to a former gay lover. He didn't use his own cash. He had none. He was a Benedictine abbot with a vow of poverty, but he was able to sign a check out of a slush fund given him (perhaps unknowingly) by the good Catholics of Milwaukee. Other priests were caught with their hands in the collection plate. One pastor in Santa Barbara stole more than a million from his affluent parish in Montecito. And when an independent auditor went over the books at a parish in Darien, Connecticut, he found the pastor had racked up hundreds of thousands of dollars in credit card charges (billed to the parish) for vacation trips to the Bahamas with his lover. The bishop suspended the priest who turned him in, telling him he'd only made the situation worse by blowing the whistle."

How did the whistle-blower make the situation worse? He said to Moore's camera, "The bishop told me I was suspended because I made the system look bad."

"Better, I guess," said Moore, by way of comment, "not to let the people know they were being screwed by the system. For more than four years now, the bishops haven't done much to fix the system. Many young Catholics haven't lost their faith in Jesus. But they have lost their faith in the bishops, whom they do not trust, and in the Church, which puzzles them. They're less and less likely to show up at Mass on Sunday, and even less likely to drop any money in their parishes' collection baskets. Meanwhile, the bishops keep on trying to pass state laws prohibiting abortion and same-sex marriage. A few bishops threaten their people who insist on voting for Democrats with excommunication.

"On a personal level, they look like a comfortable lot, carrying on with business as usual. To show you how they carry on in fine style, I visited a meeting of the American bishops recently in Scottsdale, Arizona, where they were on one of their quadrennial retreats. They met in a palmy resort called the Phoenician."

On the screen, Pike, Rackham, Sunnyhill, and Juana Margarita Obregón saw lingering cameo shots of the Phoenician. Its yellow birds of paradise, begonias, chaparral sage, and red yucca, its heated swimming pools, its twenty-seven-hole golf course, its twelve tennis courts, its bowling green and croquet lawn, its health center and spa, its eleven restaurants, its spectacular views of the desert and the mountains surrounding the resort.

"Thanks to the latest video technology," Moore was saying, "I rigged myself with a miniature lens no bigger than a quarter. " Close-up of a button-sized camera. "This little button-camera made it possible for me to slip into some places that I could hardly visit with an old-fashioned camera crew."

On the screen: a ten-second shot of an unidentified bishop covered with a tiny towel as his pink corpulence was being kneaded and pummeled by a young, bosomy, blonde masseuse.

The camera cut back to Moore, mischievously smiling at his own button-camera, held out at arm's length. He was in a sort of disguise. Freshly barbered for the occasion. Hair cut. Close shave. Trim button-down shirt. "More significantly," he said, "I was able to get candid interviews from some of the bishops."

The screen cut to the face of Raymond Burke, the archbishop of St. Louis, coming off the Phoenician's practice-putting green in a screaming Hawaiian shirt, pink Bermuda shorts and a pair of pink leather sandals. Burke thought Moore was the new auxiliary bishop from Detroit. Moore knew who Burke was, from the name tag pinned to his Hawaiian shirt.

When Moore ambled up to him, he was surprised by Burke's friendly nod and, sizing up the situation, decided to see if he could draw Burke out. Moore asked him what kind of reactions he had gotten for excommunicating all those who had voted for the Democrat in the November election. Burke said, "My people supported me on that. That was a no-brainer. Catholics cannot vote for candidates who are pro-abortion."

"As I understand it," said Moore, "The candidate wasn't pro-abortion. The candidate was pro-choice."

"Same thing," said Burke.

"Right!" said Moore, as if in agreement, though he couldn't have disagreed more. He changed the subject, asking Burke for an update on the Polish Catholics in St. Louis whom he had excommunicated for refusing to give him the deed to their church and school and hand him some $12 million in savings they'd accumulated over the years. It was the kind of shop talk, Moore correctly imagined, that bishops engage in when they're "on retreat." He carried it off quite well.

"I haven't seen the twelve mill yet," Burke assured him. "But I'll get it. You'll see. These Polacks are good Catholics. They won't challenge my authority forever. They know why. I have my name on the deed of every other church in my archdiocese. Why not *their* church, too?"

Moore nodded and smiled, hoping Burke would think he agreed with Burke's highhandedness. "But what do you tell your Polacks when they say they've owned their own church for more than a hundred years?"

"That doesn't make it right," he said. "They have no reason to expect I will deal with them any differently than I deal with all the other churches in St. Louis—with absolute power to teach, sanctify, and rule. As a new bishop, you ought to know that. That's the way it is in the *Roman* Catholic Church. Always has been. Always will be."

"But Ray—" To carry on with the charade, Moore decided to call the bishop by his first name. "But Ray, what do you say when reporters remind you about Lord Acton's famous remark about absolute power corrupting absolutely?"

"Acton!" exclaimed Burke. "The same Lord Acton who opposed the declaration of papal infallibility at Vatican I? Well, you know who won that battle? The infallibilists." It was a difficult word, but it rolled smoothly off Burke's tongue. "The infallibilists won. After Vatican I, in fact, some of those in Acton's crowd who opposed them were excommunicated for their cheekiness."

Moore realized that his next question might make himself less than affable. But what the hell? No telling how Burke might flame forth. Hoping he would, Moore asked his question. "Are American Catholics cheeky for wanting accountable bishops?"

Burke growled, "We're accountable to God—and to the pope."

"But don't they have a right—"

Burke cut him off. "American Catholics *are* being cheeky when they start demanding their rights. Pius X put it quite well way back in the first part of the twentieth century. 'The laity have no other rights than to let themselves be guided and so follow their pastors in docility.'"

"Some say the laity ought to have a voice and a vote."

Burke flared at this. "The Church is not a democracy. But you know that, don't you?" He looked at Moore, now more curiously than he did at the outset of this conversation. "Have we met yet?"

Moore extended his hand. "Moore of Flint."

"Oh yes," said Burke, not flashing on the name, but offering his right hand anyway. "The new auxiliary in Detroit, right? Now, if you'll excuse me. I have to change for dinner. See you later?"

Moore said he hoped so. "Maybe at cocktails."

In the documentary, Ignatius Dreedle, the bishop of Buffalo Tooth, Nebraska, appeared in a white, no-collar, clerical shirt, black shorts, black knee-high socks, and black shoes. He was playing gin rummy and having a preprandial martini with another bishop at a small table alongside one of the resort's swimming pools.

Dreedle was downright hostile. "You're Michael Moore, aren't you? How did you get in here?"

Moore said he was hoping he could have fifteen minutes with him. He looked at his watch. "Maybe before dinner? Or after breakfast in the morning?"

"What for?" demanded Dreedle.

"I'm doing a documentary on the American Church," said Moore. There, he wasn't hiding anything now. He was being quite upfront.

"For whom?" asked Dreedle. "CBS? NBC? ABC?"

"Not sure yet. We'll have to see."

"Uh huh. Hoping to sell us to the networks? Good luck with that." He took a nervous sip of his martini. "Now if you don't represent anybody, you'd better scram out of here. Or do I have to call security?"

His gin-partner said, "Of course we call security. This is a private meeting." He rose to his feet and raised a fist. "Michael Moore?" he said. "Michael Moore! You've got a lot of damned nerve coming here. You're a Democrat, aren't you? Member of the party of death? The party that advocates abortion, buggery, contraception, divorce, euthanasia, radical feminism, genetic experimentation, and mutilation?"

Moore smiled. Some days before, he had seen this tirade on the Internet, part of a pastoral letter penned for Catholics in Rockford, Illinois. Now he was overjoyed to get the author of that postroal letter on tape. "I didn't get your name, your Excellency?"

"None of your damn business," he growled. He'd obviously forgotten he was wearing a name tag. In Moore's rough cut, he was clearly identified by a super at the bottom of the screen. "BISHOP THOMAS DORAN ROCKFORD, ILLINOIS."

The bishop's picture faded as Moore retreated, but Pike, Rackham, Sunnyhill and Juana Margarita Obregón didn't need to hear any more to appreciate what Moore had done. The bishops' words were quite enough. Great sound bites. And the visuals weren't half bad either. Doran was wearing a black T-shirt with white lettering that said:

ROPE. TREE. JOURNALIST.
SOME ASSEMBLY REQUIRED.

MOORE HAD ONE MORE ENCOUNTER ON TAPE—with Francis Oliver Grandeur, the cardinal-archbishop of Philadelphia. Moore found him near the entrance of the resort, strolling out of the main building wearing charcoal slacks and a Hawaiian shirt. He was looking toward a line of limousines parked at the curb.

"Going off campus for dinner, your Eminence?" said Moore.

Grandeur nodded. "One of these chariots is mine," he said, waving at the line of limos.

"Just wanted to ask you," said Moore. "Is Cardinal Mahony here?"

Grandeur regarded Moore with some curiosity. "Have we met?" he asked.

"Don't think so," said Moore.

"You look familiar." Grandeur paused. "You look something like Michael Moore."

"Yeah, I guess I do."

"Are you Michael Moore?"

"Yes, your Eminence, I am." Moore rubbed his nose.

Grandeur glanced to his right and to his left, looking for, maybe, a camera in the distance with a long lens. Seeing none, he proceeded. "Tell me why you're interested in Cardinal Mahony."

"He's been a spokesman for the American bishops for some time."

"Have you talked to Cardinal Mahony?"

"No," said Moore. "But I'd like to. Is he here?"

"He is. But I don't think he'll want to talk to you. He's on retreat here with the other bishops." Grandeur's limo was pulling up to the curb, but he couldn't help asking Moore whether he was here on business or pleasure.

"I'd like to do a story on the Church in America. It's going through some hard times."

Grandeur said he had to agree with that. "But why focus on Cardinal Mahony?" *Grandeur knew it was a little vain of him. If Moore wants to interview an American cardinal, he ought to interview me, Fog Grandeur." Why not me?"*

"Well," said Moore, "I wanna do that. How about tomorrow morning?"

Grandeur paused, briefly tempted to take Moore on. "I'll think about it. Call me. Call me about nine? We should talk. You could tell me—"

"Exactly," said Moore.

"—tell me what areas you want to explore. I don't want to talk about pelvic issues. You press people always want to talk about birth control, abortion."

"No, no, no. I want to ask you what you think about a people's Church in America."

Grandeur frowned, then laughed. "Where'd you come up with that line? The Catholic Church in America has always been a people's Church. What's there to talk about?"

"Well, for one thing, the Church's financial situation."

"What's wrong with it?"

"Some say few dioceses could stand an honest audit. Some say, 'The people don't know—'"

"What people? I am transparent to the best possible people. So when you say 'the people don't know,' I say, 'Well, my people know.' Some of the best financial minds in Philadelphia. The rest of the people don't need to know."

"Other bishops have published their financial reports. Chicago, Boston, Brooklyn. Cardinal Mahony has done it in Los Angeles. For his Church, which he says is 'a Church of and for the people.'"

"Cardinal Mahony!" Right then, Grandeur could have ended the encounter by stepping into his limo, but he didn't want to offend Moore, and he felt he needed to make a point. "I know what Cardinal Mahony's been saying. Well, he can probably create a Church of and for the people. But let me tell you this. To do that, he'd have to wipe out canon law. Good luck with that." He laughed as he climbed into the limo and said, just before he slammed the door, "Cardinal Mahony could have an American Church all right. But it wouldn't be Catholic."

"THAT'S WHAT I'VE GOT SO FAR," Moore told the quartet. "But I have one more bit to show you." He hit a button on the controller. "Here's some footage. Security guards surrounding me. You can see 'em, hear 'em, watch 'em patting me down until finally, they find my button-camera and rip it off, and yank the transmitter out of my pocket."

The quartet watched the assault with fascination, with laughter, and with tears as the screen went to black.

"Make a great ending," said Moore. "Action. A little violence."

"Agreed," said Rackham, spinning his wheelchair back to face Moore, "as long as the violence doesn't take away from the message."

"What do you think?" Moore asked Pike. "*Will* the violence take away from the message?"

"No," said Pike. "With the right musical score, you can make the seizure into a piece of comedy. Comedy violence is okay."

Moore raised an eyebrow and said to Pike, "You aren't as dumb as you look!"

"Aw shucks," said Pike. "But let me give you a compliment in return. You really nailed these bishops."

"Well," Moore said, "they sorta nailed themselves. That's what people tend to do when I show up anywhere asking my innocent questions."

"Sometimes not-so-innocent questions," said Rackham.

"What you did, mate, really worked," said Sunnyhill.

"Almost," said Pike.

Moore said, "Almost? You think maybe I was too hard on Mahony? Saying he was one of the cover-up bishops?"

"No," said Pike. "He'll be good with that. He's already confessed his complicity in the sex scandals. He was only one among many. And our whole campaign is designed to make clerical accountability more than a mere word."

Rackham said, "But your documentary doesn't go nearly far enough. You're mostly telling an old story."

Pike said, "You were just starting to get into the real story during that exchange with Cardinal Grandeur."

"You mean the stuff about a people's Church?"

"Precisely," said Sunnyhill. "Cardinal Mahony wants to give ownership of the Church back to the people."

Moore said, "But how's he gonna do that? The Church isn't his to give away, is it?"

Pike said, "It is in Los Angeles. Legally, the cardinal owns all the churches and most of the schools. And he's taking steps right now to turn over the management of all that to the people. Giving ownership of the parishes to the people of the parish, promoting elected boards and commissions in every parish—and in the archdiocese as well. If they're elected by the people, these boards and commissions will be accountable to the people in ways that the cardinal isn't accountable right now."

"Okay, if you say so. But that's only in LA. What about the rest of the country?"

"That's the political task ahead," said Sunnyhill. "Roger has to persuade the rest of the hierarchy to do the same thing."

"Oh," said Moore, snapping his fingers, "just like that, huh? Where and when will he do that?"

"At the Fourth Council of Baltimore," said Pike. "Big battle ahead there. It'll be something like the Constitutional Convention of 1787 in Philadelphia. Your documentary will help frame the struggle."

Moore whistled. "I had no idea. I started out to make some fun. Now you want me to make some history."

"Hell of a story, isn't it?" said Pike. "A movement for a people's Church, led surprisingly enough by the same Roger Michael Mahony who was protecting that priest-rapist in Stockton, California, as we just saw on your tape. The same Roger Michael Mahony who had a miraculous conversion after he was kidnapped by some liberation theologians, put on trial for his sins, convicted by a jury of his peers, and then almost killed by Mexican commandos—with some help from the U.S. Army Special Forces. You can tell most of that story in your documentary. You can buy some of the trial footage from Fox."

"Sheesh," said Moore. He pushed back the bill of his cap and studied this group. A guy in a three-piece suit, another guy in a wheelchair dressed as casually as he was (but with no John Deere cap), a priest with an Australian accent in a Roman collar, and a Chicana with nice tits in high heels and a pants suit. "Who are you guys anyway? What's your interest in this?"

Pike said, "Look around you. What does this place look like?"

Moore scratched his nose. "Like a campaign headquarters, I guess."

"Yes. We're trying to launch a campaign. Frankly, a political campaign."

"Yeah, I see," said Moore. He gestured toward the large room, mostly empty floor space, its walls and plate glass windows hung with red, white, and blue banners that read:

CAMPAIGN FOR A PEOPLE'S CHURCH.

TAKE BACK OUR CHURCH.

AN AMERICAN CATHOLIC CHURCH.

"We are just getting started," said Juana Margarita Obregón. "We do not even have our phones yet, or our computers."

Moore looked dubious. "Tell me. Is Cardinal Mahony backing you on this?"

The group exchanged glances. Finally, Pike said, "We're backing him. This was more our idea than his. He's just getting comfortable with the revolution."

"Well," said Sunnyhill, "I wouldn't exactly say comfortable. He's under a great deal of stress."

"Who are *you*?" asked Moore, curious about the priest's accent.

"Sean Sunnyhill. I'm a Jesuit from Melbourne."

"Cardinal know you? Know what you're doing here?"

"The cardinal knows me," Sunnyhill allowed.

Pike said, "Sean can give you some very necessary background on Catholic history. In the beginning, the Church looked something like a democracy."

Moore laughed. "Okay, fine. But I need some face time with Cardinal Mahony—on camera."

Pike shook his head. "We don't want anyone to think he set you up to do this documentary. Or even cooperated with it."

"He's leading this movement for a people's Church. I need him on camera saying that."

"He's already on record saying that."

"On film?"

"On tape. C-SPAN recorded all of the cardinal's news conference on January 28 when he gave his rationale for a people's Church. You can get the footage you need from C-SPAN."

Moore gave Pike a long look. "You ever think of becoming a TV producer, Nick?"

Pike ignored that, and turned to the others. "Any other thoughts for Mr. Moore?"

"At the Phoenician," asked Juana Margarita Obregón, "did you talk to any of our friendly bishops?"

"No," said Moore. "Who *are* your friendly bishops?"

"We'll set you up with some of them," said Pike. "Bootkoski of Metuchen, New Jersey. Aymond of Fort Worth. Weigand of Sacramento. Kicanas of Tucson. Good idea, Juana. We don't want people to think all the bishops are against a people's Church."

Sunnyhill had a footnote to that. "They will also tell you they have one job—to serve the people. They may be ready to go on the record with you."

Moore rubbed his hands together and nodded. "Good. This is gonna be even better than I thought."

Rackham said, "I only have one question."

"Yes?" said Moore.

"Who was the naked bishop you got on tape?"

Moore laughed. "The fat guy getting the massage? I don't know! I'm not even a hundred percent sure he *was* a bishop."

Juana Margarita Obregón said, "To me, it looked like the bare backside of Ignatius Dreedle."

Moore did a double take. He said to her, "How would *you* know?"

Juana Margarita Obregón winked at him. She was kidding. The fat ass could have belonged to any of a hundred bishops. Or maybe not to a bishop at all. *Obviously, this whole room was full of kidders.*

"So you liked what I did?" asked Moore.

"As far as it goes," said Sunnyhill. "You're an answer to prayer."

"Okay, thank you," said Moore, "Nobody ever told me I was anyone's answer to prayer. But hey, that won't mean a damn thing if I can't get this show on the air."

"Have you thought of a theatrical release?" asked Pike. "Like you did with *Roger and Me*?"

"Warner Brothers put up some big financing for that. But Warner Brothers isn't going to finance *The Bishops and Me*." Moore paused. "None of the other studios either. The Jews in Hollywood—" Moore made a face—

185

"have never put up big money to finance anything that even remotely looked like an attack on the Catholic Church."

"But this is not an attack on the Church," said Juana Margarita Obregón. "On the hierarchy maybe. But the hierarchy is not the Church!"

Moore said, "Hollywood doesn't know that."

"We may have a better idea," said Rackham.

"We could go straight to DVD," said Pike.

"What do you mean, 'we?' " said Moore.

Rackham said, "What would you think about giving us distribution rights for a DVD? For starters, we can dub a million DVDs overnight for less than fifty cents a copy. We have the man-and-woman-power to put a disk in a million Catholic homes every week for the next twelve weeks. We'll sell twelve million of 'em at nineteen ninety-five a copy for a gross of two hundred forty million dollars."

"Could be a lot more," said Pike, "if things go as we hope they will. Sales will soar when bits from the documentary start getting passed around on the Internet."

Rackham said, "We could net a half billion."

"Well," said Moore. "I don't know. I'm not sure if—"

Rackham said, "We'll give you half of the net."

"Of the DVD rights?"

Pike said, "And we'll take half of the theatrical rights, too, if there is a theatrical release. Share and share alike on the promotional costs."

Moore turned to Pike. He seemed like the guy in charge. "The cardinal knows you want to distribute this DVD? Some of his brother bishops will want to kill him if they find out he's behind this."

"His office will not be distributing the DVD," said Pike.

"Better," said Juana Margarita Obregón, "that the cardinal not even know—everything. We like to give him some deniability. With his brother bishops."

Moore smiled. "So Church politics is a lot like presidential politics!"

Rackham gave Moore a smiling, middle-finger salute. "And the horse you rode in on!"

Moore laughed, then asked, "So, what's your hurry? You got a deadline?"

"We've got a crisis," said Pike. "The bishops are headed to the Fourth Council of Baltimore. It ought to be a meeting of the people's Church.

Instead, it's shaping up like a meeting of the clerical Church. Under some pressure, the bishops voted to bring their own appointed lay delegates."

Rackham said, "We can't have an open convention of the people's Church with 193 bishops and 193 yes-men. Not unless we can stir up the people and get a tsunami of support to send some independent-minded Catholics to Baltimore."

Pike added, "As delegates with a voice and a vote, not just observers."

Moore said, "And you're all thinking this documentary might just start a tidal wave of public opinion?"

"Well, duh!" they all said in a loud chorus.

Moore reflected for more than a few moments. "I will need some help to do a final cut, produce a musical score."

"How much help?" asked Pike.

Moore said, "A million bucks? No more than that. I'd like Bob Dylan and maybe Sting to do a few songs for us."

Pike, Rackham, and Sunnyhill turned to Juana Margarita Obregón.

"Bob Dylan?" she said with a smile. "Sting? All right! Yes. Yes, I think we have a million for Mr. Moore."

"Okay," Moore said. "Deal."

187

• TWENTY •

TSUNAMI

MOORE'S FINAL EDITS caught the spirit of the campaign. After he added extensive footage of Cardinal Mahony's trial in Chiapas, and his impassioned news conference at Our Lady Queen of Angels Hospital on January 28, Moore ended up with a new title, *The Bishops and Me: A People's Church*. His score, which included three songs by Sting and two by Bob Dylan, had half the nation singing the message. Three of the songs became hits in their own right. In an MP3 format, Apple downloaded eight million copies of Sting's "It's Our Church, Too," thirteen million copies of his "God's Human Hands," and six million copies of Dylan's "American Catholic."

Needless to say, the film also did wonders for the campaign. In fact, at first, Moore's documentary *was* the campaign. Once the DVD was finished, Pike asked Sister Phoebe McNulty to handle the distribution.

As a *Time* magazine cover subject, Phoebe had no trouble recruiting volunteers. "Celebrity has its costs," she told Pike, thinking of the vicious e-mail notes she had fielded from Catholics who were outraged to see a nun in tennis shorts in the pages of *Time*. "But it has its benefits, too. I did a recruiting video and put it out on YouTube, billing myself as 'the take-charge nun.' I got almost three thousand youngsters want to sign up. So many I can hardly use 'em all. They want to take charge—of themselves and of their Church."

Phoebe ordered a hundred desks delivered to the campaign headquarters, a hundred phones, and fifty computers.

From the length and breadth of California, and then from all over America, orders started to pour in, and DVDs sailed out, a million the first week, then two million the second week, partly because *The Bishops and Me: A People's Church* became the media flavor of the month. A review in *The Hollywood Reporter* before the film's release said it "achieved notes of pathos and high passion." Pieces from the film ended up being beamed all over the world on YouTube. For at least three days, thousands of kids on MySpace. com were buzzing about it, and planning film parties to see it together.

For their own ethical and commercial reasons, the TV networks didn't carry the documentary. But commentators on their news and feature shows couldn't help talking about it. Fairness aside, its popularity alone made it, simply, news. And, once the film became news, it accelerated the campaign for a people's Church, indeed, the news accelerated time itself. A new idea, or a cause that might have taken weeks or months to penetrate the nation's consciousness in Woodrow Wilson's America (before the broadcast media and long before the Internet) now flashed across the country in milliseconds. Editors and broadcast producers trained to see trends long before they became trends gave the spinning top of American Catholicism some extra twists of their own.

CNN ran cuts from the show. *Entertainment Tonight* did a special on it, and *NBC Dateline* produced a profile on the mischievous Michael Moore for holding yet another venerable institution up to his good-natured scorn. On April 19, Daniel Schorr did his Saturday morning commentary on National Public Radio about Moore's documentary—and its aftermath. He summed up the situation in a few choice words that raced through the Internet. "Kamikaze journalism has never been employed in a better cause, the democratization of the Catholic Church."

BY NOON LOS ANGELES TIME, Cardinal Grandeur was on the phone to Hawkslaw. "You heard what Daniel Schorr said this morning on NPR?" he asked.

"Yes."

"Hawk, the Church is *not* a democracy."

"Uh huh." Hawkslaw was cautious, wondering what the cardinal would ask of him now. He was uncomfortable enough serving as Grandeur's spy in LA. He just couldn't afford any exposure as a spy.

"We can't have people like Daniel Schorr saying it ought to be. This does great harm to the Church—Dan Schorr calling this 'a cause.'" Schorr's words rolled off Grandeur's tongue. "'The democratization of the Church!'"

Hawkslaw surprised himself by defending Mahony. "Roger never uses the word 'democracy.' Neither does his team."

"Well Dan Schorr's using it."

"We can't exactly stop Dan Schorr. He says what he wants to say."

"Not suggesting we should, Hawk. We do have to stop Roger Mahony. There wouldn't be a cause at all if your boss wasn't leading the charge."

"So how do we stop him? The pope's already said he wouldn't put California under interdict."

Grandeur sputtered. "We've got to be a little more creative. Get something personal on Mahony."

"Something personal?" Hawkslaw stiffened. This was something that could backfire on him. "What do you have in mind?"

"Have him followed? What about your friends in LA? The supernumeraries from Opus Dei who work for the FBI?"

"They don't have any heart for that."

"If they found he had a girlfriend. Or a boyfriend?"

"He's seventy-three years old for Godsake. And he's not well either. Goes at least once a week to this clinic on Wilshire Boulevard—just down the street from my apartment."

"Treatments?"

"Uh huh."

"For what?"

"He says dialysis."

"Kidney condition?"

"That's what he says."

"You believe him?"

That gave Hawkslaw pause. He wondered what Grandeur was driving at. "Yes," he lied. "But let me see what I can find out at the clinic."

THE CHATTERING CLASSES were all having their say about Michael Moore's documentary, pro and con. But to Pike, the important thing was this: that everyone had an opinion about a people's Church. Newspapers carried critical comment—"a piece of advocacy journalism at best," said an editorial in the *Minneapolis Star-Tribune*, and readers reacted both pro and con. Jan Novotna of Eden Prairie, Minnesota, wrote a letter to the editor. "Thank God, Moore had the courage to look in on the bishops at play. How refreshing to know they are not little gods." Another reader, Patrick O'Connell, wrote: "Fantasy, pure fantasy. A people's Church is not in God's providence."

John Harrison of the *Washington Post* sneered at "Moore's Freak Show Theology." Giuseppe Capodano wrote in *First Things*, "Michael Moore hasn't been to Mass in years. Need we say more?"

Editors of the *Wall Street Journal* came out against the film's "intrusion on the bishops' sacred space," and wondered what other hallowed institution Moore might be aiming at next. "Watch out for this guy," the *Journal* told its business readers. "He's a menace." *Time* reviewed the show with grudging approval, not for what it revealed about the affluent lifestyle of the American bishops, but for "the strong case it made for a people's Church." Jon Meacham of *Newsweek* said it was "high time Catholics started rebelling against their clerical Church."

For a time, Rush Limbaugh didn't know what to think. But his populist and largely blue-collar audiences finally won over their host. "Folks," announced Limbaugh, "it looks like the people are speaking up. Catholics! Catholics who used to say there's nothing they could do about their Church's medieval ways. They're demanding a voice and a vote." Over on the left-hand side of the radio dial, Al Franken, to his chagrin, couldn't think of any reasons to oppose Limbaugh on this one. He said he particularly liked their battle cry, "Take Back Our Church." In a commentary on April 21, Franken said he had detected something new in the air—a spirit of exasperation with the way things are. "People feel they've lost something precious and they want it back."

Maybe, he said, this was only an echo of the "take back our country" movement started by John Mellencamp, the recording artist, and his wife, Elaine, appealing to people to take back their country from political agendas, corporate greed, and government lies. There was a movement to "take back our kids," another called "take back our time," another called "take back our rights," and yet another called "take back our media." Franken said, "Maybe this 'take back' rhetoric started with Howard Dean's bestseller back in 2005 called *You Have the Power: How to Take Back Our Country and Restore Democracy in America*." Whatever. He noted that Barack Obama picked up on Howard Dean, and talked throughout his campaign about the need for people "to take their country back."

A NOTE IN *PUBLISHERS WEEKLY* said Howard Zinn had just signed a contract with Doubleday to write *A People's History of the American Catholic Church*.

CRISIS MAGAZINE gave its Internet readers "Ten Reasons Why We Can't Have a People's Church in America." *Commonweal*'s editors ran long, thumb-sucking demurrers to Mahony's platform, and the Jesuits at *America* magazine, unsure what their own general in Rome would think about this people's revolt in the U.S. (for that's what it was becoming), carried not one word about it, or about Moore's documentary either.

But the Jesuits could hardly claim no involvement. Sean Summerhill, an Australian Jesuit, made the cover of *People* magazine and *CBS Sunday Morning* did a feature on him, giving him time to talk about the democratic structures in the Church during its first ten centuries. "The Benedictine monks have always elected their own abbots," said Summerhill, "and the youngest monks were given active voice in their community deliberations on matters great and small." Medieval masterpieces provided a backdrop for Summerhill's talk, illustrated by paintings of some of the most famous abbeys in Christendom. Then, while the CBS cameras cut to a long shot of a cathedral in Switzerland, viewers heard Summerhill's report: "In Switzerland, the people in at least two cantons elect their own bishops, and the Vatican accepts them. The Swiss government won't let the Vatican interfere."

LOCAL NEWSPAPERS EVERYWHERE soon decided to start reporting on their cities' reactions to the campaign for a people's Church. Local television news shows produced a great many man-in-the-street stories. And local Sunday morning television started airing earnest panel discussions with Catholics debating the pros and cons of a people's Church. Program directors were pleased they could get rabbis and Protestant ministers to come on these shows with Catholics, a move that staved off most demands for equal time, except of course from their cities' atheists, who didn't know what to think, or say, about all the time being devoted to—well, not to God—but to Church politics. Presbyterian pastors, Episcopalians, Methodists, even Unitarians, pointed out that, as far as they could remember, their congregations had always had a voice and a vote.

The History Channel featured an interview with Mark Noll, a respected American evangelical, an historian, who told its upscale viewers that the Catholic Church was finally catching up with a trend that began among American Protestants early in U.S. history. "Almost from the beginning," he said, "the Protestants were developing a theology of democracy. By 1830, Alexis de Tocqueville was already noting that American Christianity almost always took the side of democracy. This was in marked contrast to what had happened in Europe, where Christianity most often identified with the political status quo, with established churches (both Catholic and Protestant) loyally supporting monarchical government and aristocratic values.

"But American theologians moved in another direction. They reimagined Christianity in a democratic context as they built a Christian civilization in the American wilderness." Noll noted that, for a variety of reasons, mainly out of loyalty to the Holy See, Catholic theologians weren't doing that—until 1964, when the Jesuit Father John Courtney Murray succeeded in getting the U.S. Constitution baptized at Vatican II. "Now, more than forty years later," Noll said, "it seems that American Catholics are finally getting the message—that they can be in communion with Rome and run their Church on democratic principles, from the bottom up, not from the top down."

HISPANIC TALK RADIO JOINED IN to promote the cause of a people's Church. Those listening to the populist commentators on Mexican radio stations in Southern California had always known that Cardinal Mahony (even before his conversion) had been reaching out to Hispanics, whether documented or not, in all their needs. Out of simple loyalty to him, the radio guys encouraged the Chicanos of Los Angeles (who relied on radio more than on any other medium) to support Roger Mahony's new moves to give the Church back to the people. They passed the word to their aunts and uncles and cousins in Arizona, New Mexico, Texas, Illinois, and New Jersey. They, too, started approaching their pastors and bishops with petitions for an *iglesia popular*.

INEVITABLY, A HOST OF BLOGGERS weighed in with carping comments about a people's Church. The people's Church was "a cant phrase" that was "too facile" for Rocco Palmo, whose blog, *Whispers in the Loggia*, had a host of fans in every American chancery. Anne Coulter wrote, "Now we see that Cardinal Mahony is finally living up to the name Pope John Paul II gave him years ago: 'Holy-vood.' He's worked out an imaginative, unreal theology. I'd call it Disneyland theology."

On the Fox Network, Bill O'Reilly scorned what he called "the new American Catholic revolution"—and reported some gossip that alarmed Pike. On April 1, he told his viewers, "Sources say Mahony's revolution is being funded by *Para los otros*, the very outfit that kidnapped him in November. Sources say the Los Angeles lawyer who founded *Para los otros* and a Chicana who might have escaped the massacre at Chiapas have key roles in the management of Mahony's populist uprising."

Rackham told Pike about O'Reilly's comment. "I heard about it," he snapped. "I can hardly wait to see what comes next." He was even more alarmed when Matt Drudge logged 1,345,746 hits on his relay of O'Reilly's revelation—ending with the ominous note ". . . developing."

PIKE TOOK HEART, HOWEVER, when Phoebe brought him the news that people were watching Moore's DVD two and three times, and then bringing friends into their living rooms to watch the documentary for themselves, to discuss it, and to sign petitions demanding ownership and citizenship in their Church. They were signing two different petitions—signed with names and ages, and e-mail addresses. One asked the bishops to transfer legal ownership of the parishes to the parishioners, with laypeople sitting on every parish board, and on the boards and commissions of every diocese as well. The second petition urged that each bishop take a delegate—elected by the people, not appointed by the bishop—to the Fourth Council of Baltimore.

RACKHAM HAD WONDERED how much cooperation they could expect from the pastors of every parish. "If the pastor doesn't get the petitions into the hands of the bishops," he asked, "what good are they? What if the pastors just burn 'em?"

Pike said, "When they see 'em, they won't burn 'em."

Pike was right. Many pastors pored over hundreds, sometimes thousands of petitions, and saw names they didn't recognize, and the names of parishioners they did recognize who hadn't been to Mass in years. Pastors compared notes and expressed surprise over the ages of many petitioners, men and women in their twenties and thirties, who they surmised, had given up on the Church long ago. Now they were coming back to Sunday Mass.

"They're filling up seats that have been empty for a long long time," Pastor Sean Maley of St. Stephen's Church in Sacramento told a reporter for the *Los Angeles Times*. "And filling up the baskets, too,"

"Are collections up?"

"Thirty percent! For the last three Sundays, they're up thirty percent over the previous Sunday."

"Are you getting their names on the parish rolls?"

"That, too."

"What do you hear from the other pastors in town?"

"Same deal."

"And they're sending the petitions in to the bishop?"

"No. Not sending them. They're taking them downtown themselves, in person."

AT THE BEGINNING OF MAY, Mahony, who had yet to visit the campaign headquarters on Wilshire, paid a call on his team. He was surprised by the buzz of activity in the big room, more than a hundred men and women of all ages on the phones, but he said nothing at first, until finally his curiosity overcame him. In the back office with his team—Pike, Rackham, Sunnyhill, and Juana Margarita Obregón—he asked, "Who's paying for all this?"

"All volunteers here," said Pike. "Recruited by Sister Phoebe. She's out there." He waved toward the big room in front.

Mahony said he hadn't seen her when he walked in. "Great! But who's paying the rent here? Paying for all the desks and the computers and the telephones?"

The team members exchanged glances. It was obvious to Mahony that no one wanted to speak up. The others seemed to be looking at Pike. Mahony turned to Pike. "Well?"

"We've got some funds," said Pike.

"Funds from where?"

Pike didn't reply. Finally, he said, "You don't need to know."

"I don't?"

"Let's say, better you not know."

Mahony turned to Juana Margarita Obregón. "You know?"

She glared at him, eyes burning, and said nothing.

"You *do* know!" he said. It was almost an accusation. Like, *Why didn't you—of all people—tell me?*

Rackham had some tough words. "Much as you hate to think this, Roger, we're in a game here. It's called 'politics.' A new kind of game for you, maybe, but not for me, and not, I think, for Pike either."

Pike's words were softer. "You need deniability, Roger. You need to be able to say honestly, if anyone challenges, 'I don't know. I never knew.'"

Mahony frowned and shook his head. "I see trouble ahead."

"When have you not seen trouble ahead?" asked Pike. "You jump-started this uh, this revolution (there's no better word for it) and you recruited us to lead it. So, we're leading it. You have to let us lead it."

"I recruited *you*?" demanded Mahony. "Looking back now, I wonder if you didn't actually recruit *me*?"

Pike was piqued. He said, "As I recall, first time we met, you came to visit me at the federal prison on Terminal Island. I didn't invite you there. I'd never seen you before. And then all of a sudden you were asking me for my help."

Mahony sighed. "You're right. I did come to you first. Sorry."

Juana Margarita Obregón smiled her approval, and Mahony nodded. That broke the tension in the room.

She changed the subject. "Tell them," she said to Mahony, "about the e-mail messages you are starting to get from many of the bishops who had voted against you in Scottsdale?"

Mahony brightened. "Cardinal George tells me he already has more than a million signatures piled up in his office in Chicago demanding 'people's reps' at Baltimore." He said he had a report from Bishop Michael Morrissey of Davenport, Iowa. His people, who were aghast when he had to declare bankruptcy toward the end of 2006, are demanding the diocese hold an election to send "a man we can trust" to Baltimore. Mahony waved printouts from George and Morrissey. "I like your strategy," wrote Morrisey. "Now, when I need the financial support of my people more than ever, what better way to get it than tell them this is their Church?"

Pike was not pleased with that. He grabbed Morrissey's e-mail note and almost shouted. "He's saying *tell* the people this is their Church? We don't just tell 'em this is their Church. We give them ownership of it, and citizenship in it."

Rackham said, "I think the time has come to tell all the bishops—the good guys at least—what we are doing in the Archdiocese of Los Angeles to drive that message home. Tell 'em we've started a voter-registration drive, signing up Catholics from Santa Barbara on down to Disneyland. Tell 'em how we're getting the word out—not only in our parish bulletins, and in the diocesan papers, but in the general media as well."

Pike said, "This is important. The people who aren't going to Mass any more have to know. We want to give them a voice and a vote. Then they'll know. This is their Church."

"But get this," said Rackham. "If they want a voice and a vote, they have to sign in on the parish rolls."

"And this is working?" said Mahony.

"Rather well," said Sunnyhill, who had been delegated to supervise the campaign outreach to the pastors in the LA Basin.

"Our campaign is less than eight weeks old," said Juana Margarita Obregón, "But spot checks tell us that some LA parishes have already doubled in size. They do not have enough priests to say the Masses." She laughed. "But they do have a great many Sister Phoebes to lead them in their own people's liturgies."

Pike said, "I wish we could take credit for planning it this way. We wanted to give the people a voice and a vote. Once we started doing that, they started coming back to Mass. That will mean a lot to Cardinal George—and all the other bishops—those, at least, who want to know. We hope they will follow our example."

"Then what?" asked Mahony. "Electing delegates to Baltimore is going to be fairly complicated."

"Not any more complicated than electing reps to the Sacramento legislature," said Rackham. "In fact, for us, it will be simpler. Eventually, we're going to register everyone online. And let 'em vote online, too."

"We've already worked out a simple one-two-three formula for the guidance of the pastors and their associates," said Juana Margarita Obregón. She took Mahony over to her computer in the main room. Over the hum of a hundred voices, she told him, "Step Number One. We get the pastors to ask their people for their nominations, people they trust—good, intelligent people of faith. Step Number Two. Town Halls in every parish, where the nominees speak up, one by one, and tell their parishioners who they are and what they think they can bring to the table in Baltimore."

Mahony said, "Hey, we had Town Hall meetings in every parish back in 2000 and 2001."

"But if I'm not mistaken," said Juana Margarita Obregón, "you put constraints on them right from the start. The people never felt free to say what they really wanted."

"True enough," said Mahony.

"We're giving these Town Hall meetings some power, power to cast their votes for Baltimore. Each parish Town Hall will vote for the delegate they want."

Mahony said the plan seemed too daunting, "Okay. We have 287 parishes in the archdiocese. Every parish picks one man, or one woman. What then?"

Juana Magarita Obregón said, "That takes us to Step Number Three. Then we have those 287 nominees come to one of six Town Hall meetings, one in each of our six vicariates. The nominees will have another chance to speak up—a little less than fifty of them in each Town Hall. Then those fifty folks each vote—for the one man or woman who can best represent them. Six vicariates. Six representatives. Those are the people you take with you to Baltimore."

Sunnyhill said, "First time I heard of this plan. I thought we decided on one delegate per diocese. Now you're saying Los Angeles would have six delegates?"

"Sorry," said Pike. "We've got so much going on, it's hard to keep everyone informed on every new development. But, Sean, Ted Rackham made a pretty good case the day before yesterday. This is the only fair way to proceed. Big Catholic cities will have a number of delegates based on their Catholic population. Smaller cities will have one. What's evolving here is a rough approximation of the U.S. House of Representatives, one Congressman for so many registered voters. If this makes sense, the other bishops should follow our plan—insofar as they can."

"No reason," said Rackham, "why Chicago can't follow our plan."

"Or," Pike said, "they can come up with their own plans. We won't presume to tell any bishop what to do."

Mahony laughed and clapped Pike on the back. "Nick, it would do more harm than good if we even tried."

ON MAY 14 A *CBS NEWS*-GALLUP POLL reported that 74 percent of the nation's Catholics were urging the bishops to bring laymen and laywomen delegates (not priests) to the upcoming convention in Baltimore. Among Catholics who regularly attended Sunday Mass, the number rose to 81 percent. They were asked a second question: "Should the delegates be appointed by their bishops or elected by the people?" Some 38 percent of the respondents chose "appointed," 35 percent opted for "elected" and 27 percent were "undecided."

"What does this mean?" asked Sunnyhill.

"It means," said Pike, "that American Catholics are split on this issue. Nothing new about that. For decades now, Catholics have been split on a lotta things."

They were eating burgers at their hole-in-the-wall on Third Street— parked at Rackham's favored spot in a corner of the restaurant, where he could keep his wheelchair out of the foot traffic. Juana Margarita Obregón and the cardinal were still putting lettuce and tomato slices on their hamburgers at the condiment table.

Pike shook his head and frowned. "We may be split, but not split as before, on conservative versus liberal lines. There's something new going on. We've got seventy-four percent of the Catholics in America opting for something that wasn't even a possibility a few weeks ago. Think about it. Almost three-fourths of the Catholics in America don't want the bishops at the Baltimore convention making all the decisions themselves."

"Maybe the respondents in this poll," said Rackham, "never knew it was a possibility until Gallup asked 'em about it."

Sunnyhill said, "Those people are accounted for in the results of the poll. The people who never knew? They're the undecided twenty-seven percent."

Pike said, "If they read the papers or watch television, even some of that twenty-seven percent will know more when they go to bed tonight than they did last night. The very fact that CBS and Gallup are asking this question tells even the 'don't knows' this is an issue."

Rackham was skeptical about the sudden turn things had taken in this campaign, "If they even care," he said.

"Yes," said Pike. "Maybe some don't care—now. But that's our job. To make 'em care."

The three of them were still noodling the question when Juana Margarita Obregón and the cardinal joined them. "What's *this* argument about?" asked Mahony. He rather enjoyed his team's disagreements. They generally led to more enlightened action.

Pike said, "We're talking about the CBS-Gallup Poll. What's it really mean? Ted says it doesn't mean anything. I say it's an important barometer of Catholic opinion. It means that, for the first time, Catholics are thinking their opinions can matter."

"*Can* matter," said Mahony. "Need not matter if the bishops aren't listening."

"How can they not be listening?" asked Juana Margarita Obregón.

Mahony shook his head. "Some bishops have a habit of not listening. It makes their lives easier."

"So tell us," said Juana Margarita Obregón. "What *will* the bishops think about this?"

Mahony took a few moments to ponder his reply. Finally, he said, "This could be a turning point for the American bishops. Most of them 'made bishop' (as they say) because they demonstrated a remarkable ability not to think for themselves, but to get along by going along."

"Going along in this case," said Pike, "means obedience, a virtue when the institution is good, and wise, and just, but a vice when that institution is corrupt."

Mahony bristled. "Out of touch, maybe. But not corrupt."

Sunnyhill disagreed. "When the official Church is more interested in protecting its institutional interests than it is in serving the people, it's a corrupt institution."

Mahony said, "I don't think most of the bishops would admit that."

Sunnyhill said, "With all due respect, Roger, I think most of the bishops have been kidding themselves."

Mahony reddened.

Pike agreed with Sunnyhill. "The people of God are forcing the bishops to take a look at themselves, and at something much more concrete than Rome's authority. They're listening to the people. And when they start doing that, they will give the people a new kind of authority."

"If you want to call that 'authority,'" said Rackham. "Maybe the bishops are just caving in to public opinion."

Pike said, "I don't care what we call it. What matters is what the bishops do right now. The CBS-Gallup Poll gave them a nudge. They can ignore the message. Or they can join the revolution."

Mahony clucked over that. "Nick, I don't think many of the bishops will join anything called 'the revolution.' Bishops aren't built that way."

"Okay," said Pike, "you know 'em better than I do,"

"I know them," said Mahony, "because I once thought and felt as they do. Until I had my crisis. And my conversion. And I have to confess I keep wondering if I've done the right thing."

Juana Margarita Obregón gave him a look of dismay.

"I'm sorry," said Mahony. "But you don't know all the pressure I am under—from my fellow bishops. None of you can really know how I feel."

Pike nodded. "Okay, Roger. I'm glad you can admit this now. We need to know how you feel."

"You have to keep telling us," said Sunnyhill.

MAHONY'S FEARS DIMINISHED on May 28, when he received a news note from the monsignor in charge of the National Conference of Catholic Bishops. Surprisingly enough, about half of the U.S. bishops had decided to bring elected delegates to the Council. Pike suspected their decision had been dictated by a strong shift in public opinion. Michael Moore's documentary— Hollywood pundits said it would win an Oscar nomination—had triggered a swell of popular support for a people's Church, an idea whose time had come, for the people, and for the more-pastorally-minded bishops, whose sense of crisis over the shaky state of American Catholicism compelled them to start "thinking outside the box." It was a cliché that worked for them. A number of these bishops met at an exclusive site in cyberspace called "OUTSIDE THE BOX," where many of them agreed to work along the lines of something they started calling "the Mahony Plan"—one elected delegate for every U.S. diocese under a million members, and one extra delegate for every additional million Catholics in larger U.S. cities.

Cardinal Grandeur had access to the site, of course, which told him there was a sea change among the American bishops. He reacted with an angry e-mail note to colleagues who were still on his side. "Everyone knows the Church is not a democracy. Everyone except Mahony and his crowd. If they get their way, they will bring to the Council of Baltimore everything that's wrong with American politics: deceptive sloganeering, lobbyists, maybe even television ads full of blatant deception, wild claims, and outright lies. And dirty tricks."

Grandeur's reaction was a classic case of paranoia—his forefinger pointing at another, his other three fingers pointing back at him. He had already launched his own plan to derail Mahony's movement for a people's Church with his own department of dirty tricks, recruiting members of the FBI who were also supernumeraries in Opus Dei to start snooping into the banking records of the Campaign for a People's Church. "Only one way to keep control," Grandeur told Jeremiah Hawkslaw. "Bring this movement down, whatever it takes."

· TWENTY-ONE ·

BLACKMAIL

GRANDEUR'S SPOOKS FROM OPUS DEI soon gave him the information he needed. He phoned Jeremiah Hawkslaw immediately with the good news. "Archimedes once said, 'Give me a lever long enough and a fulcrum on which to place it, and I shall move the world.' Well, I think we have the fulcrum and the long lever that will make Roger give up this silly fantasy."

"Fulcrum? Lever?"

"My guys found documentary proof that Nicholas Pike and Juana Margarita Obregón are the sole signatories on several numbered accounts in Zurich. They add up to more than seventy-five million dollars."

Hawkslaw said, "Where would they get seventy-five million?"

"Think about it," said Grandeur. "Seventy-five million sounds like just a little less than the networks paid to that terrorist organization back in November 2008."

"*Para los otros?*"

"It has to be, because my spooks also tell me that exactly five million recently moved out of one of those accounts in Zurich into an account at the People's Bank in Los Angeles. The name on that account is Organizing Committee, Campaign for a People' Church."

"Who are the signatories on that account?" Hawkslaw thought he already knew the answer.

"Nicholas Pike and Juana Margarita Obregón! And on April 12, 2009, one of their checks, for a million dollars, went to Michael Moore Productions.

Hawk, I hope you know what this means. This damn movement for a people's Church is being financed with blood money, pulled together by one of the boldest kidnapping plots of all time."

Hawkslaw shivered with glee, happy to hear that Grandeur had found the ammunition he needed to fight these—these outsiders who had taken over the Church in Los Angeles. But he knew Grandeur didn't want to hear about his joy. Grandeur was a practical man, a man of action. "What's next, Fog? What can I do?"

Grandeur wanted Hawkslaw to confront Mahony with the facts. "Tell him we're ready to bring this entire matter before a federal grand jury in Los Angeles. Once a grand jury gets this documentation, it will have no other choice. It will have to indict Pike and the Obregón person."

"On what charges?" asked Hawkslaw.

"God, I don't know! Kidnapping, extortion, most of the things prohibited by the Patriot Act, I guess, and the Terrorism Act as well. Enough to send Nick Pike back into the U.S. federal prison system for life. And the Obregón person along with him. Unless—" He paused.

"Unless what?"

"Unless we decide *not* to take this to the grand jury."

"And why wouldn't we want to do that?"

"We strike a bargain with Roger. Option one—either he walks away from this campaign for a people's Church. Or, option two—his friends go to prison."

"Sounds like blackmail, Fog."

"I'll pretend I didn't hear that, Hawk."

"Why would he pick option one? Why wouldn't he let his friends go to prison?"

"He's in love with this Obregón person, isn't he?"

"Is he?"

"You were the one told me he was spending three nights a week at her apartment."

"Yes, I guess I did."

"You've been having him followed?"

"Yes, I was. Not any more, though, once I confirmed my suspicions. But I still don't see him walking away from the movement. He can't do that. Not without giving the public and the press a damn good explanation."

"With your help, he can make up a story. "

204

"The movement may go on without him."

"I doubt it. Who will take his place? No bishop I know."

Hawkslaw said, "Nicholas Pike is the real brains behind this campaign. He could keep leading it, with or without Mahony."

Grandeur sounded very sure of himself. "People won't follow a layman. If they don't see an American archbishop at the front of the parade, they'll know this movement isn't really Catholic. And if it isn't Catholic, it'll be just one more damn Protestant Church."

Hawkslaw pondered that. His good friend Fog was probably right. The movement needed Mahony. "So, when will you tell Roger?"

"Hawk, I was thinking you should tell him."

"Me?"

"He wouldn't have to know you've been spying for me. You're just my messenger."

"He might buy that," Hawkslaw conceded. "He knows we worked together in Rome for three years, but—"

"Right."

"But he will be very angry when I bring him this news. He may want to kill the messenger who brings it."

Grandeur chuckled. "Well, if he kills you, he'll really be in trouble, won't he?"

ROGER MAHONY AND JUANA MARGARITA OBREGÓN.

Her apartment.

He in his navy blue jogging suit, his face dark with anger.

She in a bright blue, floor length, jersey robe, buttoned down the front, her face frozen with fear.

She sits motionless, poised on the edge of her couch.

He has grabbed a kitchen chair, planted it ten feet away from her, turned it around and straddled it, using the back of the chair as a kind of shield. He leans toward her and says in a hoarse whisper, "How could you?"

"What? How could I do what?"

"You and Pike planned this whole thing." He tells her all he knows about *Para los otros* and its numbered Swiss accounts, news delivered to him not an hour ago by Jeremiah Hawkslaw, along with Grandeur's threats to expose her—and Nicholas Pike—unless he resigns his leadership of the movement for a people's Church.

When he is finished, she says nothing. She raises her palms and shrugs.

He shrugs, too. "Well?"

She rises, walks over to the window, opens it to the cool night air, and returns to the couch. "Where do I start?" she says. "This has been so—. We never planned it this way. We thought we would hold our mock trial and send you home. The Mexican commandos and the U.S. Army Special Forces—" She shakes her head and shrugs. "We never thought—"

"You never thought? You never thought?" he says, cutting her off, hardly wanting to hear what he is sure will be another lie. "That's obvious. All those people dead! Iván Díaz. Paul Kelly. Five bishops. Your entire film crew. And María."

This news has numbed him. It ties so well into his suspicions about Pike. He should have known—that Pike has been using him all along. How stupid he was, not to realize. How stupid, too, not to realize Pike has been using Juana Margarita Obregón. Or maybe she has been using him, who knows? He rises from his chair, pushes it back, presses his palms to his temples and closes his eyes. Pike was his friend. And he thought he was in love with Juana Margarita Obregón. He can taste the double betrayal, a mouthful of lye. He strides toward the door.

"Where are you going?" says Juana Margarita Obregón,

"Out!"

"What are you going to do?" she cries.

"Frankly," he cries, just before he slams the door behind him, "I don't know. I just don't know."

Juana Margarita Obregón bursts into tears.

MAHONY DOESN'T HEAD BACK to his room at the hospital. He strides east on a deserted Sixth Street all the way to MacArthur Park, turns south on Alvarado, turns west on Wilshire, his mind a blank, his soul a jumble of conflicting emotions. If he were an elevator right now, he'd be plummeting in free fall. He wonders when he will hit bottom. *Juana Margarita Obregón looked intelligent. She just "didn't think." Didn't think . . . what? Was anybody else thinking? Not so much as anyone could notice.* An hour later, he finds himself ringing the buzzer at Juana Margarita Obregón's apartment.

"Roger?" she says.

"Yes," he croaks.

"You coming up?"

"What do you think?" he cries.

She replies by buzzing him in.

When she opens her door, he notes the redness in her eyes. "You have to tell me more," he says, taking a seat in the straight back chair, closing his eyes, as if to gather his thoughts. He opens them and gives her a level, unblinking look. "Who thought up the kidnapping and the trial?"

She perches on the edge of her couch and blinks. "Iván Díaz. Me. A few others."

"Brilliant!" he cries. "Pike, too?"

"Pike? No. He helped found *Para los otros*, but that was to bring bread and justice to Central America. We never told him we had a plan for a people's Church in the United States. At the time, we didn't even have a plan."

"But Pike's name is on that Swiss account!"

"That only came later, long after I had escaped the holocaust in the jungle and made my way back to LA. Then, after we hooked up with Michael Moore, he jetted with me to Zurich so we could straighten out our numbered accounts with the banks."

"Get his name on them, along with yours?"

"Yes, to take the place of Iván Díaz. We had quite a time doing that."

"I can imagine."

"We had to prove that Iván Díaz had died, prove that was indeed my name and my signature on the accounts that Iván and I had opened a year before our adventure."

Mahony shakes his head, amazed at all the planning that had gone into their caper. "And then when you made Nicholas Pike a signatory on the accounts, you jetted back to LA and started working on me?"

She nods and bites her lip. "No. We were 'working on you' long before that. But the plan was never that clear-cut. Things just sort of evolved. Nick wanted reforms in the Church—the reforms chartered at Vatican II—but he had never even thought it possible to create a people's Church in the United States, never heard the word autochthony before."

"Neither had I."

She says nothing, tries not to move a muscle while he mulls all this. Finally, she says, "You have to admit. A people's Church in America is still a good idea. No matter what happens to me and Nick."

He nods, heaves a sigh, lumbers over to the couch, and drops to his knees, his forehead to her breast.

She leans into him, dropping her head to his neck. She goes on, still teary-eyed, spilling her words, needing to pour out the rest of the story. "And then our Aussie, Sean Summerhill, joined the team. And then Phoebe McNulty rose up out of the hills of Solvang with her people's liturgy, and pretty soon we had an idea, an idea whose time, we thought, had come."

"Yes, autochthony. It was a brilliant idea. And if I am not mistaken, its final form came from our tough friend Rackham, the union organizer."

"Not even a Catholic." She smiles through her tears.

"No," he nods. "Just one smart Jew." Mahony mulls that, too. His silence is almost more than she can bear.

"So," she says finally, "that is pretty much the way it happened."

He sighs. His voice is now a whisper. He has to believe her. He has no other choice. He loves her. "Okay. I guess that's. How. It. All. Happened."

"You believe me?" she says, pushing his shoulders back so she can look into his eyes.

"It is all such a fantastic story. I shouldn't believe it. But—I—do." He kisses her on the neck.

Blinking back her tears, she returns his kiss, first on the neck, then shifting to his lips. It is not a sexy kiss. In the past few months, they had become intimate in almost every way a man and a woman can be intimate without having sex. They weren't going to start now. Her obvious, chaste love for him had given him the courage to mount this campaign. His reliance on her, for her intuitive advice through one crisis after another, made her feel important again^in yet another kind of career. They hug for a long silent minute, then stand and walk over to the open window and breathe deeply of the cool night air.

"Now," says Mahony, "I cannot do what I thought I had to do only two hours ago."

"Two hours ago?"

"That was when the Hawk brought me the bad news. And gave me Grandeur's ultimatum."

"Specifically? Tell me again?"

"One, he wants me to trash the whole project, the people's Church idea, the Fourth Council of Baltimore, everything. Or, two, trash you and Pike. Send you both to federal prison for life."

"And?"

"I cannot do either."

She smiles. "I am certainly glad to hear that!"

"Only an idiot would think I'd go for either of these two choices."

"So, what other choices do you have?"

"I don't know. But there has be a twist somehow, somewhere, in this wacky plot."

"Great!" She laughs at his solemnity.

"We need a good screenwriter. Or a team of them."

"Well, yes, I should hope so. Something that will stop Grandeur. You think he could go ahead with his threat—to put me and Nick Pike away in prison for life?"

"I don't know. Hawkslaw says Grandeur wants to hear from me by Monday. Until then, we have to see how we can stop him."

THE TEAM MET THAT EVENING—Friday night at Judge Matt Riley's five-bedroom beach house in the Malibu Colony. Riley had told Mahony, *Mi casa es tu casa.* "My house is your house. If your group needs to talk most of the night, there are more than enough bedrooms for all of you. Tess and I will get out of the way—go stay with our son and his family in Encino."

And so, after they had barbecued some prime steaks on the deck overlooking the Pacific at sunset and poured themselves some California red, a Benovia 2005 Russian River Zinfandel, Pike took the lead. "Grandeur's blackmailing you, right, Roger?"

"That's an ugly word. " Mahony frowned. "Let's just say he gave me an ultimatum."

"Let's analyze this," said Rackham. "What does Grandeur really have on Pike? Or on Juana Margarita Obregón?'

"You mean what can he *prove*?" This from Pike.

"Well," said Mahony, "he can prove you have all this money in a Swiss bank."

"So?" asked Rackham.

"The feds could trace the money," said Mahony.

"To the TV networks?" asked Rackham. "So what?"

"They paid for the rights to televise the trial."

"Exactly," said Rackham. "Nothing illegal about that. Not on the part of the networks, not on the part of the folks who were conducting this trial. It was a mock trial, for the entertainment and the enlightenment of people all over the world. No crime there."

"Kidnapping's a crime," said Mahony.

"So who can they prosecute for that?" demanded Rackham.

Pike agreed with Rackham. "The kidnappers are dead."

"That's what I mean," said Rackham. "They've got nothing on you, Mr. Pike."

Pike pointed to Juana Margarita Obregón, "What about this lady?"

"What proof do they have," said Rackham, "that she did anything more than play a prosecuting attorney on a bit of reality TV."

"Hey," objected Juana Margarita Obregón. "I helped plan the whole thing!"

Rackham laughed. "You shut up! You're innocent until you're *proven* guilty. You don't have to testify against yourself."

"Great!" said Summerhill. *Nemo se accuset.* St. Thomas Aquinas. No one is obliged to incriminate himself."

Pike held up both hands. "Halt!" he cried. "Best case scenario, Juana Margarita Obregón and I get acquitted in a public trial. But we're in the middle of a political campaign for a people's Church, remember? We simply don't want any kind of trial."

That gave Rackham pause. He spun his wheelchair in a complete circle. Twice. Then he said, "You're right. Of course."

Pike said, "We just have to figure out a way of turning Grandeur aside."

Rackham asked, "Can we get something on him?"

Mahony grimaced. "We need to stop him. But 'get something on him?' I don't even want to think about it."

"Better you do think about it," advised Rackham.

Primum est vivere, said Summerhill. "The first law, mate, is the law of self-preservation. That's a free translation. And you're fighting for your life here."

Mahony still couldn't quite feature this. He said he felt guilty, plotting against a fellow member of the Sacred College of Cardinals.

Summerhill said he had to get over that. "Maybe it's the word 'sacred' that holds you back. But it isn't holding Grandeur back. In the long history of the Church, cardinals have done people in, and been done in, in a great many interesting ways, for good reasons and bad. Leo X had some cardinals beheaded for plotting against him. One cardinal was defenestrated—pushed to his death on the cobblestones below. But not by another cardinal—by a jealous husband."

"You mean," said Pike, "this guy pushed the cardinal out the window?"

"Out of his own bedroom window, mate, after the man found him bonking his wife!"

"The human element in the Church of God!" laughed Pike, raising his glass to all.

"So," said Phoebe, "we have to go after Grandeur."

"Defenestration?" joshed Rackham. "We gotta push him out a window?"

"No," said Pike. "But we might look for a skeleton in his closet."

"The end specifies the means," said Summerhill.

"Cheers for the Jesuits," said Phoebe, raising her glass of orange juice on the rocks.

"Let's stop fooling around," said Pike, "and start thinking."

Somehow, the group proceeded to brainstorm, just ignoring Mahony's objections. And he let them do it. He was strangely exhilarated now, despite his reservations about planning a counterattack—and launching it against a cardinal who had no apparent scruples at all.

So the group fantasized together, about Grandeur and the life he led in Philadelphia. After a good deal of open speculation, the group concluded it didn't know much about Grandeur's private life, or much about his public life, either. He ran a big archdiocese, one of the richest in the land, and that was pretty much a full-time job. He visited different parishes, one after another, on Sundays, and didn't consort with anyone outside of his own circle. If he had any friends, they were most likely his auxiliary bishops.

"I guess that means we wouldn't find any of Grandeur's inner circle willing to tell tales out of school?" said Rackham.

Mahony said, "His own auxiliaries? He made them bishops. They are much more likely to back him than buck him."

"How about his pastors?"

Blank looks all around. To sound out all the pastors in the several hundred parishes of the Archdiocese of Philadelphia, surmised Phoebe, they would have to start dialing up these pastors one by one. "And we'd have to do it all in two days."

"Good luck with all that this weekend!" said Summerhill.

Pike waved his right hand. "Let's forget that idea. Even if we could reach ten percent of them, we'd have zero chance of getting any pastor to gossip about his archbishop—with someone calling from LA, someone he doesn't even know."

For an hour, the group discussed other ways and means of getting in with Philadelphia's many pastors, in enough to do them much good. "I give up," said Pike. "We're pumping away in a dry hole."

"What about the other bishops around the country? Grandeur have any enemies among them?" This from Summerhill.

Mahony said, "They hardly know him. Some can't stand his lordly ways, but—"

"We're going at this from the wrong end," interrupted Rackham.

"Meaning?"

"We start with what we know. How do we even know Grandeur is the one who has come up with this ultimatum?"

"Well," said Mahony, "Hawkslaw said so."

"Exactly," said Rackham. "But how do we know Hawkslaw is telling the truth?"

"What do you mean?"

"I mean, maybe we should focus on Hawkslaw first. Maybe this is all about him, not Grandeur. I've never trusted the Hawk."

"Or about Hawkslaw *and* Grandeur," suggested Summerhill. "Maybe they both have special reasons to stop us." He pointed out that Grandeur and Hawkslaw worked together for more than three years in Rome.

"You think they were sweethearts?" Rackham had a twinkle in his eye,

"Or," suggested Pike, "still are?"

"Now, mates, that's a thought," said Summerhill.

But it wasn't a very productive thought. They agreed; they didn't have much time to check out that possibility either.

"Let's keep brainstorming this," said Pike. "Let's ask a different kind of question. 'What does Hawkslaw have to lose if our people's Church moves ahead?'"

"Power?" suggested Phoebe. "Lot's of power?"

"Okay," said Pike, "that's good, Phoebe. But exactly what kind of power?"

They all looked to Mahony.

Pike said, "Tell us something, Roger, about Hawkslaw's duties as chancellor of the Archdiocese of Los Angeles?"

"In effect, he's our corporate counsel. He informs us what we can do and cannot do under canon law. Under civil law, too, sometimes."

"That doesn't sound like much power," said Rackham.

"He look over contracts?" asked Pike.

"Building contracts?" suggested Rackham.

"No," said Mahony. "We have a whole department doing that. Our building department wouldn't call in Hawkslaw unless it was having a special problem with canon law."

"What about purchasing?" asked Rackham. "Lotta room for graft there."

"Oh, I see," said Juana Margarita Obregón, "you're looking for a money angle?"

"What else?" asked Pike. He recalled a mantra from Bob Woodward's Watergate story. "Follow the money."

Impatient with the turn this conversation was taking, Mahony said, "Forget the money angle. Our money is all handled by our purchasing department. All good people."

"All your purchasing?"

"Yes."

"Construction?"

"I already told you. Our building department handles all that. And the money all goes through central purchasing."

"How about textbooks?"

"Textbooks," said Mahony "go through central purchasing at the archdiocese.

"Who decides what textbooks? A committee, I imagine."

That gave Mahony some pause. "Wait," he said. "In 1985, when I arrived here from Stockton, Hawkslaw was already in charge of selecting textbooks for all our schools, K through twelve. I let him go on doing it. He didn't want textbooks that were teaching heresy."

"Uh huh," said Pike. "That's understandable."

"Lotta money there?" Rackham looked at Mahony.

"More than ten million a year."

"You say your schools buy ten million dollars worth of books every year?"

"Yes. At least that. But the money all goes through central purchasing."

Rackham's eyes brightened and his bald pate took on a kind of shine. "Have you ever heard the word 'kickbacks,' Roger?"

"I never thought of kickbacks," said Mahony. "Kickbacks from the publishers?"

Pike's voice rose. "What kind of lifestyle does Jeremiah lead?"

Mahony measured his words. "Fairly affluent," he said, "for a diocesan priest."

"Doesn't come from a wealthy family?"

"No."

Phoebe said, "He wears tailor-made suits, alligator loafers."

"Alligator loafers!" exclaimed Pike. "Those come at two thousand dollars a pair."

Mahony remembered, "When we moved out of the cathedral rectory last year, he didn't go to a nearby rectory. He found an exclusive high-rise apartment building at 9999 Wilshire Blvd."

Phoebe said, "And he bought a yellow Mercedes 650-SL convertible."

Mahony said, "You knew about that?"

"Every nun in town seemed to know about that," she said.

"Those only run about two hundred thou," said Pike.

"Mercedes, huh?" asked Rackham. "He have a girlfriend?"

"We don't think so," said Mahony.

"He gay?"

"Maybe. But some of my best priests are gay."

Pike said, "My impression is that the Hawk is asexual."

Mahony said, "You may be right. You've seen how stiff he is. With everyone. But he has two apparent passions. The Dodgers and the Lakers. Somehow, he manages to see every game from the owner's box."

"Dodgers or Lakers?"

"Both. If he's got any friends outside the clerical club, they're likely to be the upper-crust friends of Frank McCourt. Or Jerry Buss."

Sotto voce, Phoebe explained to Juana Margarita Obregón, "McCourt owns the Dodgers. Buss owns the Lakers."

"Doesn't matter who his friends are," said Rackham. "We gotta get a look at his financial records. Checking accounts. Savings. Investments."

"How will we do that?" asked Pike. "Banks are closed on Saturdays and Sundays."

"Go to his bank?" asked Mahony. "I wouldn't want to do that. I wouldn't want to ask him to show me his bank accounts either. I don't feel comfortable with this."

Rackham rolled his eyes. He wanted to tell Mahony that his comfort didn't have anything to do with anything. "An eye for an eye," he said.

"No," cried Mahony. "We follow that course, and the whole world is blind."

They were all stunned at Mahony's vehemence. After that, the meeting fizzled. People were tired. Mahony suggested they sleep on the problem, and pray over it, and talk more in the morning. "There are plenty of beds here."

"Okay," said Pike, "you guys can talk—or pray—in the morning. But I need to drive to San Diego tonight. I haven't seen Anne in days. I'll phone here at noon tomorrow. See what you've decided. Everyone okay with that?"

Agreed.

AFTER PIKE ROARED AWAY in his Ford Explorer, after everyone else went off to bed, Rackham and Phoebe continued to talk. Phoebe helped herself to another glass of orange juice on the rocks. "You want some port?" She waved a bottle at Rackham that had been nesting among some other liqueurs on a sideboard.

"No."

She raised an eyebrow. She knew Rackham liked the port.

"I've had enough wine," said Rackham. He wheeled his motorized chair closer to her. "I need some clarity to discuss what I want to talk about now."

"Okay?"

"I have a hunch Hawkslaw has the information we need to spike his guns. Or Grandeur's guns. And I need your help."

"Why me?"

"Because you're a gal with gumption—and a nice pair of legs."

"What do my legs have to do with it?"

"Because we're gonna do a little caper. I don't have the legs for this,"

"A caper?"

"A burglary. But I can't do it alone."

"Burglary? You must be joking."

His urgent tone told her he wasn't joking. "Hawkslaw's apartment on Wilshire. Where did Roger say?"

"At 9999 Wilshire! The Hawk won't thank you for breaking and entering there."

Rackham pretended he didn't hear that. "We'll have to go into his apartment tomorrow night. But it will take us all day tomorrow to get ready."

She looked at her watch. "You mean tonight? It's already tomorrow. It's after midnight."

He nodded. "Yeah, yeah. I am talking about Saturday night."

"What are you after?"

"You mean 'we.' What are we after. Are you in or out?"

"I'm in," she said. "I think." She waited for him to answer her question.

"We're after his desktop computer."

She nodded. "We're just going to steal it?"

"Not steal it. Download its entire contents into my laptop. Take ten minutes. Maybe fifteen."

"And where will he be while we are doing all this?"

"Dodger Stadium's my guess. Dodgers and the Giants. Game time's at seven. That'll give us all day to case the place, get a key made."

"Whew! Sounds like you're a pro at this."

"In another life."

"I guess. But, uh, how do we know he'll be at the game? He might want to watch it on TV."

"We're gonna *assume* he is going to the game. But we can check that out when the time comes. We'll need his phone numbers. Cell phone number. Land line. Can you get 'em?"

"I know someone at the chancery. A nun in my order."

"Good! Can you get 'em by noon tomorrow? I mean today?"

"Yes, of course." Phoebe was trying hard to understand Rackham's plan, and shoot holes in it, if she could. "And what if he stays home, simply not answering any calls? We break and enter and find him there, watching the game on TV?"

"No. We park across the street from 9999 Wilshire until he leaves—in his yellow Mercedes convertible. Then we go in."

"And how do we get in?"

"Good question. Those luxury high-rise apartments along Wilshire usually have underground parking, and doormen, and a security staff. There's gonna be some risk here."

"Risk? That's okay. We can take risks, if we have a high probability of reward. What do you hope to find on this laptop?"

"God knows."

"'God knows?' That's not good enough."

"Let's just say I got a hunch about Hawkslaw. He's hiding something. We just need to take a look. As a great philosopher once said, 'Sometimes you can see a lot just by looking.'"

"Yogi Berra?"

Rackham cracked a smile. "I like smart nuns. Nuns with gumption."

She laughed. "And good legs?"

WHEN THE TEAM ASSEMBLED for breakfast the next morning at Malibu, it hardly had a quorum. Pike was in San Diego. Rackham and Phoebe were nowhere in sight.

"Rackham's van is gone," reported Summerhill. "But Phoebe's Chevy is still here."

"We will assume they left together," said Juana Margarita Obregón. "But why?"

"I'll try Rackham on his cell," said Mahony. He dialed him, got nothing but an invitation to leave a message. After trying Phoebe's cell phone, he said, "Ditto for Phoebe. I wonder where they went?"

"You worried about them?" asked Juana Margarita Obregón.

"I don't even want to imagine," said Mahony, "what they might be doing." In the past few months, Mahony had found it in himself to feel a genuine affection for both of them, Rackham, his paraplegic, outspoken Jew, and Phoebe, his try-anything nun. They were such—well, he had to fall back on an ancient term of endearment. They were such pistols. He just hoped that, whatever these pistols were doing, they didn't get shot down.

• TWENTY-TWO •

CAPER

TEN AM. At 4222 South Sepulveda Boulevard, not far from his own apartment, Rackham visits a ramshackle lock shop called Keys. One man on duty there, a friend of a friend of Rackham named Gonzalo. For a fair price, with no questions asked, Gonzalo will make him a key. To do that, he will sell Rackham a black box about the size of a pack of cigarettes. The black box is a camera, fitted with a tiny fiber-optic lens on the end of a bristle-like probe. Gonzalo tells him that techies developed the lens so surgeons could look inside a patient's heart. Others had found legal and illegal uses for it. "Call it the ambiguity of human progress," he says. Then Gonzalo shows Rackham how to hook the black box up to a laptop computer and take a picture of the inside of any lock, through the keyhole. "You brought your laptop?" he says to Rackham.

"No. But I have one at home."

"Okay," says Gonzalo. "I can show you with my laptop. I have a program in it called Sesame. Like in 'Open Sesame?' You just plug this black box into your laptop—after it is loaded with Sesame—then take the rig to your keyhole, any keyhole, and the probe takes a picture of the inside of the lock." He demonstrates the operation while he is speaking, walking the instruments over to the front door of his shop.

"Now, here, I insert the bristle-probe into the keyhole of this Yale lock, and we can see the picture pop right up on my laptop screen. See the pins and the key cuts inside the lock?"

Rackham nods. "I'm impressed."

"You wanna try it yourself? Let's start all over."

"Looks easy enough," says Rackham. He tries the operation. It works for him. He can see the inside of the lock on Gonzalo's front door, right there on his laptop. "Then what?" he asks.

"Then you click here, and save the picture, just like you save a Word document. Save it on your desktop. Or anwhere. Anywhere you can find it easy. Then bring it back to me this afternoon before four and I make you the key."

"How much?" asks Rackham.

Gonzalo squints at him "A thousand."

"A thousand pesos? For one key?"

Gonzalo laughs, knowing the man in the wheelchair is kidding, reminding Rackham that for a thousand dollars, he will get the key and the black box, too—"for future jobs." Rackham rolls his eyes at the thought he might ever volunteer for another job like this. He extracts ten one hundred dollar bills from his wallet and hands them over. "This include the software, too? Sesame?"

"Absolutely. Here is Sesame. On this data key. Just plug it into a USB port on your laptop and you are in business. Don't forget to download Sesame into your laptop."

ELEVEN AM. From the van, parked across the street, Rackham and Phoebe are watching 9999 Wilshire. It is a neighborhood of high rise apartments, no commercial real estate, no shops, no foot traffic, and, this late on a Saturday morning, no heavy auto traffic either. He and Phoebe keep an eye on the exit of the high rise's parking garage. "He's gotta come out sometime today."

"You hope."

"Shopping. Haircut. Some kind of Saturday errand."

"Unless he shopped and got a haircut yesterday."

"Uh huh." Rackham hunches over the wheel and frowns and rubs his neck.

Phoebe sees he is feeling some tension. She reaches over, massages his neck and upper back muscles. "Feels good," he says. "Thank you." Rackham briefs her again on her moves. One more time. And then one more time after that. By 1:00 PM, Phoebe is also feeling the tension. Rackham reaches over and rubs her neck. No sign yet of Hawkslaw's vehicle.

At 1:33, they smile when they spy a yellow convertible spinning out of the garage. It is Hawkslaw, driving with the top down, wearing a blue and white Dodgers cap.

"Okay, girl, there goes the Hawk. Now we park on the other side of the street." Rackham starts his van.

Phoebe says, "We're just going to wait for another car to come out?"

"Uh huh. Or see a car coming in. Then we slip in before the gate closes."

In less than five minutes, Rackham perks up. "Here's a Lexus, coming from Westwood, slowing up here." The Lexus makes a left turn into 9999 Wilshire, the driver punches in on a key pad, the gate rises, and he guns his Lexus in.

Rackham is five seconds behind him, easing his van into the garage, parking in a space near the elevator bank marked VISITORS, and waving with a smile to the man walking toward the elevators from his Lexus. Rackham takes two minutes getting his motorized wheelchair out of the back of his van. By the time he and Phoebe reach the bank of elevators, the Lexus guy is gone, and no one else is in sight.

He punches a button that says LOBBY and she punches one that says PENTHOUSE.

While Rackham engages the doorman in conversation, mainly to distract him, Phoebe, well-briefed now, proceeds to Hawkslaw's door, Penthouse B, carrying Rackham's black nylon computer bag. She kneels to extract Rackham's laptop and the little black box, then inserts the probe into the lock. She snaps several pictures of the lock's interior, remembering to save them to the desktop.

The whole operation takes her less than a minute, but, even so, she is trembling at the thought that Hawkslaw could be returning at any moment. According to the plan, she takes the elevator directly to the garage and waits for Rackham.

In less than five minutes, he is wheeling his way out of the elevator, all smiles. Phoebe is all smiles, too. She watches Rackham get into his van, fascinated with the way automakers have designed this vehicle for the handicapped.

"You obviously got it," said Rackham, over the whirr of the motor that raises the van's tailgate and draws his wheelchair into the back of the van and then eases him forward to a spot behind the steering wheel. By then, Phoebe has climbed into the front passenger seat. When he locks his wheelchair in place, she hands over Rackham's black nylon computer case. "Do I have to look at this?" he asks.

She shakes her head. "I got the pictures. Slam dunk."

He opens the laptop anyway and finds the image of the inside of the lock, and a second and a third. "Perfect," he says.

"Good. I don't want to have to go up there again. He could have come up the hall and caught me in the act. This is crazy."

"Espionage is not for the faint of heart."

"I'll say. What unbelievable story did you tell the doorman?"

"I told him I was working with the caterers who are doing the party tomorrow."

"What party?"

"I was hoping there'd be a party."

Phoebe grins. "*Is* there a party tomorrow?"

"As it turns out, there is."

"The doorman buy your story?"

"Not at first. But when I took offense—I was loud and I was profane, complaining that no one can ever believe I am gainfully employed because I am wheelchair bound—he backed right off, with apologies. 'That's all right,' I said. 'Now I just wanna make sure we can get in to set up our party tomorrow night.'"

According to Rackham, the doorman consulted his clipboard and found a notation for the "Bornstein party Sunday night."

"That's it, the Bornstein party," Rackham fumed. "But, damn it, no one told us how to get our van into the garage. I think they were supposed to give us one of those cards—you know, with a magnetic strip."

The doorman, a young Hispanic who was overcompensating for his initial rudeness, was more than helpful. "You won't need a card," he said. "Just enter our four-digit code and you will get right in."

"And what is that code?"

"On Sundays, it is 9991. It's the address on the front of the building, except for the last digit, which changes every day. On Mondays, it is 9992. And so on."

Phoebe smiles, marveling at Rackham's good luck.

"The harder I work," he says, "the luckier I get."

As they pull out of the garage, Rackham says to Phoebe, "Just to make sure, why don't you just hop out and give that keypad four little punches. It's Saturday, the seventh day of the week. Try 9997."

She does that. And as the gate starts to rise, she hustles back to the van.

"This is too easy," she says. "Worries me. How easy will the rest be?"

Rackham chuckles. "Crime is easy. Comedy is harder."

AT 6:00 PM, THEY INVADE the garage again. Rackham takes a complete turn around the garage, up one aisle and back down the other, looking for Hawkslaw's yellow Mercedes convertible. "Not here," he says. "So far, so good."

Rackham parks the van near the elevator bank as before, backing into a handicapped space near the elevator bank. It takes him two minutes to exit the van. "Okay," he says finally. "You got the rake?"

He is referring to a three-foot bamboo rake, which Phoebe will use when they leave Hawkslaw's apartment, to cover up the tracks of Rackham's wheelchair on what they imagine will be the apartment's wall-to-wall carpet. "Yes," she laughs. "I got the rake." She shows it to him, then halfway hides it under her denim jacket. Soon, the two of them are in the elevator heading up to Hawkslaw's penthouse.

Strangely, no one challenges them—which is probably because no one sees them.

Rackham is humming. "Saturday night security isn't very secure," he says.

Phoebe nods. "How much time do we have?"

"We could assume a couple of hours, at least."

"If, that is, the Hawk is really *at* the game."

"Uh huh."

"So why don't I call him on his cell?" asks Phoebe. "I can probably tell where he is, by the background noise."

"Wait," he says. "Is your cell phone secure?"

"Secure?"

"I mean is your ID blocked?"

223

"No. I don't think so."

"Well, then, don't call him on your cell phone. Take my Treo. It's secure. And call the landline in his apartment first, just to make sure." Her knees buckle at the thought that Hawkslaw could be sitting there in his apartment. He laughs. "Just teasing. But, I mean, his car *could* be in the shop."

Phoebe punches up Hawkslaw's home number, lets it ring until the voice mail comes on, and hangs up.

"Now try his cell," he says.

She does. Hawkslaw picks up on the third ring. She knows his voice. "María?" she says.

"No," he says. "What number are you calling?"

She can hear other voices in the background, but it doesn't sound like he's at the ball game. He is polite enough not to hang up, and she is glad of that because she needs to hear more, and so does Rackham. "I'm sorry," says Phoebe, trying to affect an Hispanic accent. "Is thees seven seven three four seex four seex?"

"No," he says, "you're close, but you have two of the numbers turned around, okay?"

As he speaks, Phoebe is handing the cell phone to Rackham, so he too can listen to the background noise. He listens for a moment and hands it right back to her. "Okay, *muchas gracias*," Phoebe says, "I hope I deed not disturb you." She hangs up.

"So where is he?" he demands. "Ball game?"

"Sounds more like a restaurant. I heard some voices and the tinkle of some glasses, and faint music in the background."

"So did I," says Rackham.

"Could be the sounds in the owner's box. They serve dinners there, don't they?"

"I have never been in the owner's box. Sure, I guess they dine elegantly in the owner's box. But I doubt they pipe in music. I heard violins."

"Then," she quails, "we have to assume he is not at the game? Maybe out for dinner?"

"I'd say that's a pretty good guess." He pauses. "This makes things more risky." He looks at his watch. 6:44 PM. "If he's doing an early dinner, he could be home by eight, eight-thirty."

"So, let's move it!" she cries.

THEY EXIT THE ELEVATOR on the top floor, Phoebe almost sprinting up the hallway in her tennis shoes, Rackham whirring along behind her in his motorized chair. At the door of Penthouse B, they slip on some cheap surgical gloves, and turn off their cell phones. Phoebe tries the key. Gently. Softly. It fits. She turns the key. "Open Sesame," she whispers.

The door opens, and they are in. Rackham says, "Let's not turn on the lights in the foyer, or in the living room either." He wheels around the apartment. A great room with a big picture window looking to the north, an unobstructed view of the Santa Monica Mountains, a large kitchen, a master bedroom with the same mountain view, and a medium-size second bedroom, which Hawkslaw has turned into an office furnished with a desk, a blue Aeron swivel chair and a Hewlett-Packard computer and printer sitting on an adjacent table. A soft black briefcase sits on the floor next to the chair.

Rackham pushes the chair aside, maneuvers his wheelchair into position in front of the computer, and turns it on. But he cannot log on without Hawkslaw's password. Terrific. He checks the Post-its tacked to the computer, the desk drawers, the bottom of the keyboard, the underside of the desk, looking for any anomalous number-letter combination that might be a password (or passwords). Nothing.

The passwords are probably around somewhere. People are told these days to create passwords of random numbers, letters, and symbols so no hacker can crack into their privacy. Trouble is, few can remember their own high-security combinations, so they write them down. But where? He scans Hawkslaw's Rolodex, flips through the pages of a comic calendar (*Far Side* cartoons, one for each day of the year), looks in the desk drawers. Still nothing. He checks the satchel, finds the usual junk—pens, pencils, some business cards, a pair of sunglasses, Hawkslaw's passport and, tucked away in a pen slot, a USB memory key on a neck strap. Aha.

He sticks the key into his own laptop's USB slot and dumps the contents of maybe one megabyte onto his hard drive.

"What'd you find?" asks Phoebe, looking over his shoulder.

"Maybe nothing. I don't know. Let's see."

He sees a good deal of churchy correspondence with e-mail addresses like <archdiocesedenver.org> and a good many recent ones <archdiocesephilly. org>, but opens none of them. "We can review these later," he says. "We need to get into his HP."

"We've been here twenty minutes," Phoebe says. "We're pushing it. People notice lights. People come home. We have to leave."

"Can't leave unless and until we can say, 'Mission accomplished.'"

"Oh great. We stay here until Hawkslaw comes home and finds us here. The cardinal will die if he gets a call from Hawkslaw telling him he's found us snooping in his apartment and has called the police."

Rackham shakes his head. "I'm thirsty. Can you get me a glass of water?"

She finds water bottles in the refrigerator, brings him one, and one for herself, too. They are both thirsty, and the cold water calms them down a little.

"Look," he says. "I have to at least try to guess some possible passwords. You have his coordinates in your iPhone?"

She does. He tries variations on Hawkslaw's phone numbers. Nothing, He tries <msgr123> and then <msgr345> and <msgr678>. Nothing. "You have his social?"

She does and reads it out to him, and he tries any number of words linked to the last four digits of his Social Security number, which is 1723. Nothing. A half-hour later, still nothing. He rubs the back of his neck. "I am almost ready to give up," he says.

"What do you mean, 'almost?' It's after eight. I'm getting so nervous I am going to pee my pants."

"You, too?" he says. "I think we both better go to the bathroom. You first. It takes me more time, getting out of, and back in, this damn thing." He rattles his chair.

"WHAT ARE YOU DOING NOW?" she asks.

He is back into his laptop. "I am taking another look at the downloads from this memory key. Gotta be something hidden there."

She moans. "Five minutes. I am giving you five more minutes. That's all."

"Okay, okay," he says. "Now I have to look inside his documents, look for some anomalies."

"Yeah," she says, "but which one?"

"Some one thing that is not like the others."

226

She cannot help looking over his shoulder. "Do I make you nervous?" she asks.

"I am already nervous. Please rub my neck while you are looking, okay?"

"Here, in his My Documents directory, something different. Looks like he's writing a novel. A crime novel?"

Phoebe, rubbing his neck muscles and staring at the screen: "Hey, this isn't *his* novel. It's a Father Brown mystery. He must be reading it on-screen."

"What's a Father Brown mystery?"

"G.K. Chesterton, famous British convert to Catholicism, journalist and author of about a hundred books, including several crime novels centering on a priest who is also a pretty good sleuth. Sort of a Sherlock Holmes in a Roman collar."

"Jeez. Who reads novels on their computers?"

"Apparently Hawkslaw does. You can download lots of 'em these days off the Internet, particularly the classics that are already in the public domain, which these are. You can download 'em into your computer, or into a reader, even into your Palm Pilot."

"Doesn't make any sense," says Rackham. "You can get these books in paperback, can't you? Lot more portable than a laptop, or even a text-reader. I'd go blind trying to read a novel on my Treo."

"You're right. Doesn't make sense. So why is Chesterton lurking in Hawkslaw's memory key?"

Rackham brightened. "Hang on a minute," he says. " 'Lurking.' You just used the word 'lurking.' Maybe something else is lurking, or hiding, in this novel." He types the numeral 1 into a Find box, gets a single irrelevant hit, then gets another irrelevant hit with the number 2. But with number 3, he gets <38@3frt8*q*>.

"That's got to be a password," cries Phoebe.

He types the number 4 into the Search box, and the Find function comes up with <46&5984*qrr4*>.

"Another password!" squeals Phoebe.

"Pretty damn smart," he says. "Instantly accessible, and completely portable with the data key, and totally invisible."

"Invisible?" says Phoebe. "Not to us."

RACKHAM TAKES THE NEXT STEP, swiveling over to Hawkslaw's HP, trying the first password. "Shazam!" he says. From there, the rest is easy. He cables his laptop into the HP and proceeds to download the entire contents of Hawkslaw's main directory into his Macintosh Powerbook. "Both computers are fast," he tells Phoebe, "but this will take about five minutes." He watches the names of the folders whiz by, pleased to see that a whole series of them are named FINANCIAL—starting with FINANCIAL 1986, and ending with FINANCIAL 2008.

Still looking over Rackham's shoulder, Phoebe points out another directory on the computer's desktop. "Have you checked on that?" she asks.

He tries, but he is blocked with a prompt for a new password. "Damn!"

"You've got another password, remember? The second one with the fours in it?"

Rackham shakes his head and grins. "Right! Forgot we had that." He types in <46&5984*qrr4*> and he's in. Only three folders there, one called CHILD PORN, another labeled PRETTY YOUNG MEN, and a third called FOG.

"Let's not even look," she says.

"We don't have time to look," he says as he downloads the contents of the second directory. "We get his stuff and we get ready to scram out of here."

"Thank God," says Phoebe, with a glance at her watch. It is 8:37.

"You got your bamboo rake?"

She nods. "Right over near the door." While Rackham disconnects his cable and stuffs his laptop into his little black tote bag, she rakes over the wheel marks throughout the apartment, even drops to her hands and knees to wipe the tiled bathroom floor with wads of Kleenex, which she flushes down the toilet. When she returns to the office, she finds Rackham peering into his own laptop. "What're you doing? We have to get rolling. Now!"

He grins. "I couldn't resist looking at this last folder, FINANCIAL 2008. Look here, he's recorded hundreds of thousand dollars worth of receipts from some of the major textbook publishers in the land. Along with explanatory notes to himself. Apparently, he was not only getting kickbacks for business he was conducting on behalf of the Archdiocese of Los Angeles. Looks like he has been getting credit for business the publishers were doing in Boston,

New York, Philadelphia, Baltimore, Cleveland, St. Louis and New Orleans. Whatever you say about Hawkslaw, he wasn't selfish. He shared the loot with his colleagues in some the country's major cities."

As intrigued as Phoebe is, she is also fuming. "We have to get going. What do we do with these?" She holds out two empty water bottles.

"Here," Rackham says. "Put 'em in my bag." He is still peering into his laptop.

"What are you doing now?"

"You want to take a look at the other folders?"

"No!" she cries. "You should send 'em to the Trash."

"We'll see, Phoebe. We'll see.

"What do you mean, 'we'll see?'"

"We won't use 'em if we don't have to. Depends on what kind of reaction we get when we tell Hawkslaw what we have."

"What do you mean, 'we?' *We're* going to tell him?"

"Well, maybe Roger might want to do that."

RACKHAM WHEELS OUT of the apartment first, Phoebe right behind him with her rake, hyperventilating all the way. "It's 8:43," she says in a whisper. "What'll we do if Hawkslaw comes out of the elevator right now?"

"He know you?" He is whispering, too.

"I was on the cover of *Time,* remember? He knows you, too, doesn't he?"

"I've only seen him twice."

"Well, his memory won't need much jogging if he sees you now. How many other men does he know who go whizzing around town in a motorized wheelchair?"

Phoebe dumps the rake down a trash chute in the hallway, and, seconds later, they are scooting into the elevator. Phoebe punches the button marked GARAGE and heaves a sigh of relief when the doors close and the car descends.

But the elevator stops at the first floor, where a security guard says he needs to talk to them. His name tag says he is Julius Jackson. He says he has seen them on his closed circuit television monitor, coming down on the elevator from the penthouse floor. No telling why he didn't see them when they were on the way up, but maybe he feels guilty now that he didn't, and he wants to cover his behind.

"Hey," says Julius Jackson, "you want to tell me what you were doing up on the penthouse floor?"

Without a beat, Rackham tells him something close to the truth. "Visiting Monsignor Hawkslaw in Penthouse B. We work with him down at the archdiocesan headquarters."

"Your car in the garage?"

"My van is."

"How'd you get in?"

"Monsignor gave us the code. Nine nine nine seven."

"He up there now?"

"I imagine so. We just left him there."

"Just a minute, huh?" The guard saunters over to his station, turns some pages in a directory of some sort, and dials a number on his phone.

Phoebe whispers to Rackham, "I am having a heart attack."

The guard lets it ring. "All I get is a voice mail message."

"I guess he turned his phone off," says Rackham. Phoebe has to hand it to him. *He certainly knows how to keep his cool.* "We had a lot of work to do tonight. He was tired. Said he was going right to bed."

The guard looks dubious. "Well," he says after giving the situation some thought, "I am not gonna go up there and disturb him. And I am not gonna call my superior on a Saturday night. But, do you mind if I see your IDs? Driver's licenses maybe?"

Phoebe says, "Sorry, I don't drive."

Rackham says to himself, *Good girl. She can lie and smile while she lies. But if they can only get out of here tonight with his laptop, his own identity won't matter. Hawkslaw will know about this caper soon enough—after the fact.* "Sure," he says to the guard, "I drive a special van. Here's my license."

The guard takes Rackham's California driver's license over to his station and copies it on a Xerox machine. It takes him a minute, but to Phoebe, it seems like an hour. "Thank you very much, Mister uh Mister Rackham. And you, too, Miss Uh . . . Uh."

She wants to scream. "Jones."

"Right. Have a good, uh, good night. Mister Rackham. And, uh, Miss Jones."

Rackham is careful not to call him Julius. "You too, Mister Jackson."

RACKHAM HAS JUST COMPLETED the two-minute drill to launch him into the back of his van, onto the motorized tailgate and on up to the front of the van, which is facing out into the garage.

Just as he locks himself behind the wheel, they hear a car whizzing into the building and heading to a parking place in the far aisle.

From her place in the front seat, Phoebe says, "I think that was a yellow Mercedes convertible."

"Let's duck," says Rackham, For him, that is easier said than done. He has to fall out of his chair and try to hide under the dashboard, and do it quietly, too.

"Is he coming over to check us out?" whispers Phoebe from under the dash. "Or is he just headed to the elevator?"

"I don't know. And I am not going to rise up and look."

"I can hear him coming our way," she says. "Lucky it's pretty dark in here."

Rackham can hear the man's footsteps, then sense his hesitation when the footsteps stop right in front of the van. Long pause. If they can read his mind, they suspect he is saying to himself, *Now where have I seen this van before?*

Finally, they hear the footsteps again quickening past the van. Twenty seconds later, Rackham raises his head in time to see Hawkslaw trotting toward the elevator bank.

Rackham gives it twenty seconds more, then tells Phoebe, "He's out of sight. Probably waiting for the elevator. We better not move yet."

"We can't stay too long," says Phoebe. "What if he stops to talk to the guard on the first floor?"

"By then we gotta be long gone." Phoebe helps him struggle back into his chair, and, once he is in, Rackham doesn't wait another second. He starts the engine and heads for the exit gate, congratulating himself for parking in a getaway mode.

"Uh oh," cries Phoebe, peering into the rear-view mirror on her side of the van.

"What?"

"The Hawk. He's coming after us." She sees Hawkslaw's figure moving into a shaft of light coming from the elevator bank.

Rackham guns it, knowing he doesn't have to key out for the gate to open. It will start automatically as soon as a vehicle comes within ten feet. *But the gate better not be sluggish.*

Phoebe cries, "The security guard is right behind him. They're both running now."

The van approaches the gate, which begins to rise. Rackham edges up to the gate as close as he can. He wants to go, but he can't risk crunching the gate, which is moving too slowly.

"Hey, stop!" cries Hawkslaw, slapping the back of the van just as Rackham clears the gate, and pulls up the incline, laying rubber and a trail of smoke on the driveway. He makes a hard right on to Wilshire Boulevard, dodging a VW bug in the right lane and fishtailing into the left lane.

Phoebe, who has been holding her breath for the past twenty minutes or so, exhales, then laughs. "Nice going, Clyde."

"Okay," says Rackham with a maniacal grin. "Thanks, Bonnie."

THEY ARE HEADED SOUTH on Westwood Boulevard. "I wonder," asks Phoebe, "if Hawkslaw or the guard got your license number?"

"In a way, I hope the guard *was* getting my number. Better that than drawing his gun."

"If he got your license number, the cops will probably have an APB out on this van inside thirty minutes."

"That's enough time for me to get you to your convent. And enough time for me to get to my place off Pico."

"You better not go to your place," says Phoebe.

"And why not?"

"Because Officer Julius Jones has a copy of your driver's license, remember? It's got your current address on it, doesn't it?"

"Damn," says Rackham.

"So where will you go?"

Rackham ponders, but only for a moment. "Gotta get to Roger sooner or later. Might as well be tonight. Judge Riley's beach house. Roger's still gotta be there. With the others."

"He's probably been phoning you."

Rackham turns on his Treo and finds he has a dozen messages, nine of them from Roger Mahony, and three from Nick Pike. He listens to the first message from Mahony, then hits the repeat button so Phoebe can hear it, too, and hands it over to her.

She listens, then listens to the rest of the messages. "Roger is really pissed off. And he doesn't even know what you've been doing tonight. You're in big trouble, Ted."

"What do you mean, '*you're* in trouble?' What have you been doing tonight?"

Phoebe nods. "You're right, Ted. I'm in trouble, too. We're in trouble. We'd better face the music together. I'm not going back to my convent. Make a U-turn here and get us on the I-10 headed west—to Malibu."

• TWENTY-THREE •

MUSIC

MAHONY ADDRESSED RACKHAM, not Phoebe, because he had a hunch Rackham was the guiltier of the pair and anyway he intended to take her aside later. "Okay, Mister Eye-for-an-Eye," Mahony said, "What have you done?" He was livid, and the others on the team didn't look very happy either. They were sitting at a 20-foot oval oak table in the great room of the Riley beach house when Rackham and Phoebe dragged in at 9:30, both of them exhausted.

"Yeah," interjected Pike, "when you didn't return my calls, I drove all the way back from San Diego. What the hell you been doing? You look like shit."

Rackham wheeled his chair to the far end of the table, heaved a huge sigh and said, "You better take a look at the contents of this laptop." He motioned for Pike to come down and take his tote bag. "In the meantime, I need a glass of gin."

"Yes, we have no gin," said Summerhill. "Settle for a glass of beer?"

Rackham said a beer would be fine.

"Me, too," said Phoebe. "I need a glass of beer."

"You don't drink," said Juana Margarita Obregón.

"I do now. And can I have a salami sandwich or something? I am starved. Ted, we forgot to eat today."

"Turkey okay?" said Juana Margarita Obregón.

"Me too," said Rackham. "I'm starved too. Turkey sandwich and a glass of beer."

"What's in your laptop?" asked Pike, unzipping the bag.

"Just the entire contents of the Hawk's desktop computer."

That drew cries from the whole crew, all of them except Mahony talking at once.

"The Hawk?"

"Monsignor Hawkslaw?"

"His computer?"

"Outrageous."

While Pike was opening Rackham's laptop, he said, "I need your password."

"RACK321. Upper case R-A-C-K. Open a directory called Hawkslaw. Look at all the documents marked 'TODAY.' Among them, you should find the records of under-the-table kickbacks the Hawk has been getting from the textbook publishers since 1986."

Pike took several minutes to look while the others watched in silence. Finally, Pike announced, "Hundreds of thousands of dollars each year! Along with explanatory notes to himself! They're kickbacks all right."

Now more curious than angry, Mahony asked Rackham, "How'd you get all this?"

Rackham shot back, "You are more interested in the how than the what?"

Mahony backed off. Now not so livid, he said, "Okay, first tell us what you have. Then you can tell us how you got it."

"I just told you. The Hawk has documented his thievery, going back more than twenty years."

"Looks like it," said Pike, keeping his eyes on the computer screen. "It also looks like Hawkslaw has been helping other chancellors pursue the same kind of tricks."

"How many chancellors?" asked Sunnyhill.

"I see ten others," said Pike, "from the largest archdioceses in the country."

Rackham took a long sip of Heineken's, straight from the can. "Hawk only demanded five percent of their annual take, which, for him, meant another half-million a year. I think we can conclude he taught most of 'em how to canoodle with the textbook people. Otherwise, why would he expect a cut from them? You can see all the numbers right there."

Pike was scanning another folder, a list of deposits in a Geneva bank. "Yes, I can. Hawkslaw kept good records. Four bank accounts that add up to, let's see, seven million and some change. And a lot of e-mail traffic from chancellors in Boston, New York, Cleveland, New Orleans, St. Louis, Denver, Detroit."

Summerhill said, "But not Philadelphia?"

Rackham said, "It appears that Grandeur himself took the kickbacks in Philadelphia."

Still scanning the computer records, Pike announced, "Hawkslaw has been quarterbacking the whole thing."

Rackham called down the table to Pike. "Take a look at the directory called CHILD PORN."

Pike did so, then hooted. "This came from Hawkslaw's personal computer, too?"

"Uh huh. Phoebe saw me download it all. Also the folders called PRETTY YOUNG MEN and FOG."

"A folder on Grandeur?" asked Mahony. "You don't mean?"

"Yes, I do," said Rackham.

"This changes everything," said Mahony.

"You still want to know how we got all this?" said Rackham.

Mahony paused for ten seconds. "No, not really," he said.

"Good," said Rackham, "because Hawkslaw could go to the LAPD and have me arrested in a New York minute."

"For what?"

"Breaking and entering. Burglary. Theft."

Mahony laughed, but with a pained look. "My bishop friends will never believe I had nothing to do with this."

"They'll never find out," said Rackham.

Mahony shook his head, "I've learned that whenever anyone says, 'They'll never find out,' they always find out."

ON MONDAY MORNING, Hawkslaw showed up as planned at Roger Mahony's office in the archdiocesan headquarters, dressed as smartly as always, but without his usual strut. "Okay, Roger," he said, almost in a whisper. "Let's have it."

"Last week, I think, you were reporting some demands from Cardinal Grandeur," said Mahony. "You said he wanted us to fold up our plans for Baltimore. Or else."

"I don't think he's in a position to make any demands at all," said Hawkslaw. "Not now." He shook his head. He took a seat and folded his hands. "He can't withstand your counterattack."

"What counterattack?" Mahony was all innocence.

"You've got plenty of ammunition to launch one."

"Ammunition, maybe, but I haven't locked and loaded."

Hawkslaw had been holding his breath. Now he exhaled. He knew his apartment had been burgled on Saturday night. He'd noted activity on his computer for almost two solid hours from 6:49 to 8:27. He even knew who the burglar was. He had a copy of the man's driver's license. It was Ted Rackham, the cardinal's organizer, a man who had now seen too much. Hawkslaw said, "You're not going to shoot Grandeur down?"

"No," said Mahony. "Nor you either."

Hawkslaw looked like he wanted to cry. "Not me either?"

"I could, you know."

"Uh huh."

"You've been spying on me for months now. I have proof of that."

"It was for the good of the Church, you must realize that?"

Mahony laughed. "You sound like the kind of cleric I used to be. Save your tears, huh?"

"Well, you could throw the book at—"

"I *am* going to ask you for restitution, Hawk. Those kickbacks—millions in kickbacks—should go right into our textbook fund, for the kids who can't afford textbooks."

"You know how much I took. I can't argue that."

"I know how much you've invested, too." Mahony slid his own G6 Powerbook over to the middle of his desk, and, with one tap of the space bar, brought up some of Hawkslaw's financials. "Pretty nice portfolio. General Mills, General Motors, General Electric." He looked up at Hawkslaw and smiled. "You like the Generals, huh?"

Hawkslaw shrugged. "Blue-chip. Little risk. Except maybe for General Motors, now."

Mahony put his palms together, as if in prayer. "How much of your investments, Hawk, do you need to keep?"

Hawkslaw didn't respond, because he didn't know where the cardinal was going with this.

Mahony said, "You're going to resign as chancellor, of course. And then you can find a place to retire to. Maybe get a chaplaincy at some convent. Your choice."

"You're going to take everything I have?"

"No." Mahony did some mental calculations. "You'll have your pension from the archdiocese, of course. It's not generous enough to keep you in that penthouse on Wilshire. But let's say we give you a retirement bonus in addition to your pension." He grabbed a yellow legal pad, and wrote a number on it. "An annuity to keep you in somewhat the style to which you've become accustomed." He slid the pad across his desk.

Hawkslaw said. "That's a generous number, Roger."

Mahony smiled. "I just don't want to see you working with Cardinal Grandeur."

"Oh, you won't, you won't."

"You talk to Grandeur? Tell him what happened?"

"I had a long chat with him yesterday. He said to tell you, he'll be good—if you're good."

"What does 'good' mean?"

"He's not asking you to give up the fight. But he will fight you, fair and square."

"He expects me to be in Baltimore?"

"Uh huh. As he will."

"So, tell me, what's Grandeur going to do in Baltimore?"

"He'll oppose your people's Church, that goes without saying. He's more Roman than the Romans."

"Okay. I understand that. I couldn't expect him to do anything else. Where two or three are gathered together in Christ's name, politics is there in the midst of us. And we don't share the same politics. I understand that. So, on political issues, everything is negotiable. I just expect him to fight fair. And he can't fight us on the media issue. We want the press inside. Or else." Hawkslaw knew what "else" was. His computer incriminated Grandeur in so many ways. "I want Grandeur's word on that right now." Mahony pushed his desk phone toward Hawkslaw. "Call him."

"I'll do it on my cell," said Hawkslaw.

"Do it on my desk phone. I want to talk to him, too."

Hawkslaw got right through to his friend Fog, and summed up Mahony's only non-negotiable position. He told Grandeur, "I'm here with Roger right now. He understands. There'll be a legitimate political battle in Baltimore, and he's okay with that. He just wants the media there. Gavel-to-gavel coverage, if he can get C-SPAN to do that. In fact, he even wants your men and women in the Philadelphia chancery to handle accreditation for the media. Yes, he knows it'll be a big job. Yes. Yes. Several thousand of them."

Now Hawkslaw was listening and nodding. He looked up at Mahony. "Cardinal Grandeur says okay on the media thing, kind of glad you will let his office handle the accreditation. Will help give him some status with the media. But he wants to talk to you, privately, on a couple other things." He handed the phone to Mahony.

"Good morning, *Eminenza!*" Mahony was trying to be cheery.

Grandeur skipped the small talk. "You going to Olmsted's last rites in Phoenix tomorrow?"

Mahony punched the calendar on his Treo. "Yes, if tomorrow's Thursday. Yes, as a matter of fact, I am. Will I see you there?"

"Yes. We need to talk."

"About a lot of things."

"I think I understand," said Mahony.

CARDINAL BERTONE RAISED HIS EYEBROWS when the pope's *maestro di camera* phoned to say the Holy Father was on his way over to see him in his office on the third floor of the Vatican Palace. Normally, when the pope wanted to talk to him, Bertone walked the several hundred paces to the papal apartment. Subjects called on the sovereign. The sovereign didn't call on them. That was the protocol, at any rate, and he could only wonder why the Holy Father was doing it differently today, June 30, 2009.

But then, as Bertone thought about it, he was learning to expect the unexpected from Benedict XVI, who had been acting strangely for more than a year.

He had put a halt, for instance, to the granting of indulgences—no more free passes through purgatory, because, of course, His Holiness had told the world he doubted anyone, including himself, believed in purgatory any more. Benedict also reversed himself on Turkey. As Cardinal Ratzinger, he had opposed Turkey's admission to the European Union; that move would surely hasten the de-Christianization of the continent, which had become de-Christianized enough, thank you very much. Then a quick trip to Turkey in the spring of 2006, and Ratzinger, assaulted by a worldwide uproar over an offhand remark he made about Mohammed at an academic seminar in Germany, changed his position so he could make a *bella figura* on his trip to Istanbul.

Then there was the Hans Küng affair. Benedict had just announced he was going to give the proud Swiss theologian a Red Hat. Hans Küng had been on John Paul II's enemies list for more than thirty years and as far as Bertone was concerned, Küng should stay on the list. Why didn't the pope consult him (or indeed anyone) before he made the announcement? And why did he suggest the German bishops award Küng their highest prize, the Cross of St. Boniface?

Many of the Church's staunchest and richest supporters, including the John Paul II biographer George Weigel, had complained to Bertone about the Vatican honoring Küng, the darling of Vatican II. But what could Bertone tell Weigel, except remind him that he had called Benedict's accession to the papal throne *God's Choice*?

Suddenly, the pope swept into Bertone's office, his white cassock flapping a bit around his knees. Bertone gave thanks to God when he noted Benedict wasn't wearing his high-heeled Pradas. Those red shoes made the pope tower over Bertone by more than a half a meter.

They embraced. Bertone tried to kiss the papal hand, a move that drew this pope's customary resistance. The pope smiled. Bertone hesitated, not sure which chair he would offer the pope, his own, the one that sat on a platform behind his desk (so he could look down on everyone who came to visit), or another grander, low-slung chair across from his desk? The pope settled that dilemma by planting his right buttock on a corner of Bertone's desk and waving Bertone to his platform chair.

"I received your report on China this morning," said Benedict, smiling again, waving a sheaf of paper.

Bertone had trouble with Benedict's smile. He couldn't tell if that smile indicated pleasure or pain. Sometimes the pope smiled like that at the beginning of a concert. Sometimes, he broke into the same smile just before he signed off on the Holy Office's latest *Notificazione*.

Bertone nodded, not sure whether the pope had come to praise Bertone or pain him. Recently, he had learned to let Benedict have the first word. And the last one.

"I think this is all wrong," said Benedict, waving the paper. *Well, good,* thought Bertone. *No more suspense.* "Am I to understand you and your diplomats walked away from a concordat with Beijing— just like that?" The pope snapped his fingers.

"We were stuck on—"

"That same old sticking point?"

"Yes, Holiness. Through all our talks, Beijing has never seemed to understand—that, in the Roman Catholic Church, *we* approve all the bishops."

" 'Approve,' but not necessarily 'appoint.' "

"I thought we went over all that last month. We decided the Church in China was getting out of hand. Beijing ignored us again. Ordained four new bishops without our prior approval. Didn't even check out the new men with Cardinal Zen in Hong Kong."

The pope grimaced. "Cardinal Zen!"

"We know," said Bertone. "He sometimes takes a too-hard line with Beijing."

"And a foolish line, too. Tell me, *Eminenza*, what this 'hard line,' as you call it, will mean to the future of the Church in China?"

"Quality control," said Bertone. "This is obvious. You ought to see some of these new bishops tapped by Beijing."

"If I did, what would I see?"

"Well, for one thing, they're not theologians. They never studied in Rome."

"Few Chinese bishops have studied in Rome, even those who are most loyal to Rome. For more than thirty years, most of the bishops in both the Underground Church and in the Open Church have been very careful to communicate with us, to assure us they want to be in communion with Peter. And that is the main thing. We have more than six thousand bishops around the world. And few dare call themselves theologians."

"True enough."

"Just before he died," said the pope, "John Paul II, of happy memory, seemed ready to make a deal with Beijing. He seemed quite content to let the Chinese people pick their own bishops."

"If it were only the Chinese people!" exclaimed Bertone. "Today in China, the people have no say in the matter. A few senior bishops put their heads together with the Bureau of Religious Affairs in the Beijing government, and, *voilà!* they create a new bishop."

"Almost the way we do it in Italy, Spain, France, Germany?"

"Well, I suppose so," Bertone conceded. "Before we announce new episcopal appointments, we do confer with those countries' governments. In some Swiss dioceses, we have no say at all."

"So why don't we let well enough alone in China? If they're all Catholics—"

"But are they really Catholics? How many Chinese Catholics can explain the doctrine of the Real Presence?"

"You mean transubstantiation?"

"Yes."

"How many citizens of Rome can do that?"

Bertone raised his palms. "*Madonn'!*"

The pope smiled at Bertone's frustration. "Look," he said, "as much as I hate to ask you to go to the documents of Vatican II, I am going to ask you—and your capable staff—to study what the Council had to say about inculturating the Gospel in mission lands. The Church in China must be Chinese. If this means we have to go along with their doing things their way, then we let them do things their way. We have to trust the people to do the right thing." He handed Bertone the document he had come in with.

Bertone took it. "So it's not acceptable?"

"Too Roman, not enough Catholic. And not enough Chinese. Go take a look at my 1969 essay "Primacy and Episcopacy." It appeared in the book *Das neue Volk Gottes.* It was about the need for autochthonous Churches in missionary lands. The Church in China must be Chinese."

Bertone nodded. He knew it was time to quit when Benedict started to repeat himself.

"My guess," said Benedict, "is that when we make it clear to the people of China—who need a spirituality in the midst of all their new prosperity— that they can have a Church that is both Catholic and Chinese, they will love us. And come flocking in."

The pope was so impressed with his own words (words that surprised even himself) that he found it agreeable to repeat them in a somewhat different form at his Wednesday audience in St. Peter's Square. Ian Fisher of the *New York Times* was there.

In reporting the pope's words, he made the easy connection—from China to the United States, and, more specifically, to the upcoming national synod in the United States where he knew the liberal majority was determined to push for the popular election of bishops in America. Fisher quoted an anonymous Jesuit theologian in Rome: "If they can have an autochthonous Church in China because it is 'a mission land,' then why can't they have one in the United States? Who would say the U.S. isn't a mission land, too?" The anonymous Jesuit was Sean Sunnyhill, summoned to Rome by the new General, who wanted to know from Summerhill, first hand, about the move toward a people's Church in the United States, and what role Summerhill was playing in it.

IN THE SACRISTY at St. Mary's Basilica in Phoenix, Mahony and Grandeur, side by side and in silence, vested for the last rites of the bishop of Phoenix, Thomas Olmsted, both of them surprised to find they were donning black vestments. They hadn't participated in a Solemn High Requiem Mass since before Vatican II.

Then they joined another hundred bishops in solemn procession up the center aisle, while the choir intoned the lugubrious *Dies Irae*, which they hadn't heard since Vatican II either. The two cardinals marched together, wearing their pointed hats and holding their crosiers in their left hands, but exchanged no pleasantries. Grandeur got right to the point. "About those pictures of me and the Hawk in the Bahamas," he whispered. "What will you do with them?"

"I wanted to talk to you about those pictures," said Mahony. "I wanted you to know we dumped them all into the trash. Keeping them as ammunition would have been unfair."

Grandeur bobbed his head, almost giddy with relief, and gave Mahony a friendly tap on the shoulder with his shepherd's crook. "I think you're crazy. Roger. But you're a gentleman."

Mahony changed the subject. "Let's talk about something of more substance?"

Grandeur nodded with some enthusiasm.

Mahony asked, "Will you oppose a people's delegation to represent the people of Philadelphia in Baltimore?"

Grandeur grumbled.

"You know, don't you" said Mahony, "that there *is* a people's delegation? Five delegates from Philadelphia and its suburbs, two laymen and three laywomen—all elected by the people?"

"My office had nothing to with that," snapped Grandeur. "A few Philadelphia pastors helped make that election happen. My office didn't. I've appointed my own delegates, all priests I can trust. They will assume the five seats Philadelphia has coming to it."

"Maybe not."

Grandeur asked Mahony how he could stop them.

"We already have control of the rules committee."

"And of the credentials committee, too?"

"They haven't formed that committee yet. When they do—it will probably be the first order of business when the convention opens, if delegations from the same diocese are demanding a voice and a vote—we plan to control that committee, too."

"You have the votes to do that?"

"My floor manager tells me we do."

"Floor manager? Who the hell's that?"

"Nick Pike. Ever heard of him?"

"Heard enough about *him*," said Grandeur. "I could have had him in Leavenworth for life. You're pretty sure of yourself, aren't you?"

They were being seated now in chairs on the left side of the sanctuary. Mahony smiled at the nun serving as master of ceremonies. Grandeur fidgeted and gave her a dark look. He didn't like nuns when he saw them prancing around a sanctuary. "In this scenario," Mahony told him, "we assume nothing. We can only wait and see."

Grandeur advised Mahony, "The pope's legate may have something to say about the legitimacy of a credentials committee."

"Did you see Ian Fisher's story in the *New York Times* this morning? About the pope's encouraging an autochthonous Church in China?"

"I saw it on the plane," said Grandeur.

"So I doubt the pope's legate will be leaning on us at all at all," said Mahony with a slight put-on-Irish lilt in his voice. "He'll be wanting us to rebuild our Church, I think, American-style."

"Don't count on it," said Grandeur. "One story in the *Times*? Nonsense! I'll believe the pope will approve an autochthonous Church in America when I read it in an encyclical. He will never give you permission for that!"

"Somehow, your Eminence, 'autochthony' doesn't go with 'permission.' If the Fourth Council of Baltimore wants the American Church to go autochthonous, it won't need permission. And the pope will then be faced with a choice, to accept a people's Church in America, or say we're all in schism."

"He's capable of doing that, I think."

"As Cardinal Ratzinger, he might have been capable. As the pope, I don't think so. Seventy-five million Catholics? You think he wants to lose them? Seventy-five million affluent American Catholics who provide almost half of the Vatican's annual support?"

Grandeur said, "Well, he may not have to make that choice, Roger. I'll fight you on this.

"I'm ready to do battle," said Mahony. "And judging from the advance stories I've been reading in the press, I'd say the media will be on our side."

Grandeur grimaced. "You'll love that, won't you? You're pretty good before a media horde. And I do mean horde. My office tells me it's already issued almost three thousand press credentials for Baltimore."

"They won't all be against you, Eminence. You know that, don't you?"

"Right," said Grandeur. "Bill O'Reilly's on our side."

Mahony smiled. "There you go. The fair and balanced Bill O'Reilly, who has decided to cast his vote against a people's Church. He ought to even things up, right?"

• TWENTY-FOUR •

BALTIMORE

"WELL, I NEVER WOULD HAVE believed this, folks." It was ten in the evening in New York, Thursday, July 2, 2009, and Bill O'Reilly was trying to give his audience an update on the battle raging in the American Catholic Church. "The Catholic Church has looked like a feudal monarchy for more than a thousand years, but on Saturday afternoon the forces of monarchy will meet the forces of democracy in Baltimore to determine the future of the Church in America. Or, rather, the future of the way the Church is governed in America—no matter what the pope says."

He reminded his audience how the battle began, right here on the *O'Reilly Factor*, when O'Reilly had one of the first reports about the kidnapping of Cardinal Mahony by a group of liberation theologians who looked like terrorists putting him on trial for his sins. "Millions of you saw that trial right here on Fox. Incredibly enough, many of you sympathized with the terrorists. They came off as gentle souls who were only conducting that trial to win support for a people's Church. You sympathized with them even more when U.S. Special Forces tracked them down and the Mexican commandos killed them all—all except Cardinal Mahony, who underwent a conversion when he was taken back to LA and started leading the charge for a people's Church in America."

The camera pulled in here for a tight close-up on O'Reilly, and he assumed an intimate tone. "I'm not at all sure I like the sound of that. 'A people's Church in America' sounds like the People's Republic of China.

Red China is still red, folks. Bunch of communists there, still communists, despite their new affluence and their new prosperity.

"Now I'm not saying Roger Mahony is a communist, far from it. But I fear this outpouring of populism and all this *politics* in the Church of God. Mixing up politics and the sacred—well," he shrugged, "I just don't know."

"And, not to oversimplify too much here, but just look at the kinds of folks who are coming to a preconvention rally on Friday night." His camera pulled back to reveal a huge in-studio television screen displaying news footage—a dozen stars of stage, screen, and the music world arriving that evening at the Downtown Hilton in Baltimore—while O'Reilly launched into a rant. "Look, folks, there's Ellen DeGeneres! She's going to emcee the rally at the Baltimore Arena. They expect a crowd of more than forty thousand there to support a revolutionary movement of Catholics who are agitating to—well, they have an organization called the Campaign for a People's Church, which is pushing for 'a voice and a vote and ownership' in their Church."

The screen filled again with a tight close-up of Bill O'Reilly while he told his audience how he really felt, as a lifelong Catholic and former altar boy, that he was not used to this kind of revolution inside the Church. In the past, he said, Catholics who weren't thrilled with the Church as they found it just left the Church and found other places to say their prayers. "Martin Luther, for instance. He just started his own Church. Me, I go along with the Church I've always known, the Church that stood on the side of discipline and devotion. Now, it looks like a bunch of radicals and gays and lesbians want to take it over."

O'Reilly's producers cut away here to their huge in-studio television screen—a photo montage of Phoebe McNulty in action, while O'Reilly's voice-over told viewers what they were seeing. "Take Phoebe McNulty, for example. Phoebe McNulty's the Wimbledon star who became a nun. Phoebe McNulty's the woman who started these people's liturgies all over the globe. Phoebe McNulty's the gal who made the cover of *Time* magazine in January. Phoebe McNulty's the one who produced this rally tomorrow night."

O'Reilly looked pleased with himself, but allowed himself a moment of modesty. "I advised against this, but then management doesn't listen to me very much. So, I hate to say it, but Fox will televise this Baltimore rally—

8:00 PM Eastern tomorrow night. Phoebe McNulty says she has some big stars lined up. Even got Bob Dylan and Sting to warm up the audience.

"Warming up the audience for what? Well, folks, the headliner at the rally, you guessed it, is none other than Roger Michael Cardinal Mahony, who will give a pep talk to this crowd—which will include a good many delegates already committed to what they are calling 'a people's Church.' You may wonder, as I do, why all this hoo-ha for a Church meeting? It sure as hell doesn't look much like a Church any more. I guess we'll have to get used to this—the new political climate in the American Catholic Church." He paused and cocked his head. "I wonder: whatever happened to the 6:00 AM daily Mass? In Latin!"

ON FRIDAY MORNING, Phoebe realized her team would have to move the rally. Advance intelligence from Catholic groups around the entire Baltimore-Washington area told them to expect at least four hundred thousand at the event—half of them kids who had heard that the American Dance Contest people had begged to hold its national finals competition on the stage at the Baltimore Arena as part of the rally for a People's Church. "The Arena's not big enough," Phoebe told Pike. "We have to find another venue."

Pike rang Mahony's room at the Intercontinental. "Roger, you know anyone in Baltimore with clout?"

"What kind of clout?"

"Political clout." He explained the problem, one they could solve if they could get the City of Baltimore's permission to take over the giant green in a large downtown park that had been the venue for many a rock concert.

"What's the name of the park?"

"Carroll Park. It's three blocks away from your hotel."

"Named after Baltimore's first Catholic bishop, John Carroll?"

"I don't know. Would it help if it was?"

Mahony said, "Let me call someone with a little clout."

BALTIMORE IS A CATHOLIC CITY. It was the nation's first Catholic city, and the residence of America's first Catholic bishop, John Carroll, who was elected by a vote of the new nation's priests in 1789. Mahony imagined the archbishop of Baltimore, Edwin O'Brien, had a little clout. So he phoned O'Brien, asking him if he could help secure Carroll Park for the rally.

248

"I could, but I won't," growled Archbishop O'Brien. Period. End of call.

Mahony wasn't surprised. O'Brien was one of the Vatican's company men. In his previous post as head of all the chaplains in the armed forces of the United States he had had Tom Doyle cashiered out of his chaplain's post in the Air Force, just months before Doyle might have qualified for retirement. And he had put his blessing on the war in Iraq.

Mahony turned to O'Brien's predecessor, William Cardinal Keeler, now retired and living in Palm Beach, Florida, to explain the problem. "O'Brien just hung up on me," he said to Keeler. "So I am asking you. You know some people on the City Council?"

Keeler said, "I do. I will call you back." He did, three minutes later. "Roger," he said, "if you—or your friend Nick Pike—can make an appearance at noon today at City Hall, I'm told you can have Carroll Park tonight."

MAHONY SENT PIKE to an emergency meeting of the Baltimore City Council, where he got the permit he needed for the rally—over the initial objections of one council member, an atheist, who objected to the use of a public park for a religious service.

"Not religious," Pike told the council. "It's Catholic."

After the laughter in the chamber died, Pike said, blushing a bit, "I mean, of course, catholic with a small 'c.' Catholics, as I am sure you know, believe in the sacramentality of everything. Which is why the rally will be a secular entertainment—secular in the best sense of the word, 'of this world,' the same world that God pronounced good when he created it.

"Except of course when Cardinal Mahony takes the microphone for five minutes to explain the historic significance of Saturday's meeting of the delegates to the Fourth Council of Baltimore. I won't call his talk exactly secular, or entertaining either. He won't mind if I don't call his speeches entertaining. I'm the guy who helps writes them.

"Other than the cardinal's talk, the whole program will be an entertainment. Pop music, three bands, Dylan, Sting, the men's glee club of the Naval Academy, who will be singing a medley of patriotic songs to commemorate the two hundred and thirty-third anniversary of the Declaration of Independence, plus the finals competition of the American Dance Contest. Fox TV will be there for a television special focused mostly on the men from Annapolis and the dancers. Most of the finalists, I am told, will be African American teenagers."

"African American teenagers?" said the council's atheist, a Baltimore politician with a sense of humor. He made the motion to give Carroll Park to the Campaign for a People's Church. It was seconded immediately and passed without discussion.

ACROSS THE NATION ON TALK RADIO, starting at 1:00 PM that day, Sean Hannity groused about the rally—managing to stir up thousands of the nation's rule book Catholics.

Hannity said he had a few problems with what looked like "politics, pure politics, in the Church of God, the Church I knew as a kid," though he did concede, "The bishops have been getting away with murder. They've gotta be accountable, just the way we make our mayors accountable." But Hanniity said he wondered about the entertainment that promised to dominate the rally. "I ask you what are Bob Dylan and Sting doing there? And what do all those hip-thrusting kids have to do with a reform of the Church?"

Those calling in to Hannity's show tended to agree with him. Josephine Rabert of Fond du Lac, Wisconsin, said, "I'm afraid this new push for an American Catholic Church will drive an even bigger wedge between Catholics."

Steve Cronin of Missoula, Montana: "These people want to see democracy in the Church. Don't they understand it's not their Church, but God's?"

"Why don't all these protesters just become Protestants?" asked Joseph DeVera of Bridgeport, Connecticut.

Sean Rockfield of Chicago said, "I can't figure out if Cardinal Mahony is a liberal or a conservative."

"In response to that last caller," said Mary Hargrove of Scottsdale, Arizona, "I will help him figure it out. Mahony's not a liberal and he's not a conservative. He's just simply a heretic. That's all there is to it."

AT THE MAHONY CAMPAIGN HEADQUARTERS in a penthouse suite of the Intercontinental Hotel, Phoebe McNulty switched on a clock radio and brought the Hannity show to the attention of Nick Pike as he was wolfing down a club sandwich. "You want to phone in and make some kind of comment?" she asked.

Pike listened for a time to Hannity's rant, and to the yahoos that seemed to live on Hannity's airwaves, then, after he had finished his lunch, he picked up the phone in the suite and dialed in to 1-800-277-4653.

Hannity's screener put Pike on the air right away, once he realized Pike was who he said he was.

Pike was cool. He didn't argue with Hannity. He just tried to point out that —whatever else this movement for a people's Church was—it was bringing some fun into a Church that had been in a state of depression for more than seven years. "And we have to give the rally's organizers some credit for that."

"Who," asked Hannity, "are the organizers?"

Pike knew how to deal with a bully. "Me and Phoebe McNulty and the rest of Cardinal Mahony's team," he asserted. "You got a problem with that?"

Hannity backed off. He said he didn't.

Then Pike took charge of the show, if only for a minute. He said he had only one point to make—to Hannity and to his thousands of listeners across the nation. "Jesus told us to 'have life and have it more abundantly.' And that's what we're doing. Bringing in Dylan and Sting and the Annapolis glee club and the kid finalists in the American Dance Contest adds to the life here, you see, and the fun. There's something very proper about that. Saints are not sad."

Hannity sneered, "Who's a saint? Dylan? Sting? You? Saints do not go about leading the faithful astray." He looked at the clock on the studio wall. Only ten seconds left 'til signoff. He wanted to make the most of those seconds, with one last word that would fire up the rule book Catholics in his audience. "Saints don't go around," he said, "leading people into schism."

GOD ONLY KNOWS how many rule book Catholics got fired up after Hannity told them Pike and his high-profile cardinal were leading people into schism. But at least one sad, rule book Catholic in Baltimore named Barney Mulvey, a janitor and a former seminarian, took Hannity to heart and decided to do something about Mahony. That afternoon, he caught a bus downtown, bought himself a $79 Iver Johnson .22 revolver at K-Mart, took a taxi to a gun range near the bay, practiced shooting for two hours, then hung out for the rest of this Saturday afternoon in the storefront headquarters in downtown Baltimore of the Campaign for a People's Church. There, he picked up some campaign brochures, seven campaign buttons, and a red, white, and blue plastic bowler, along with the information that the Mahony people were staying in the Intercontinental Hotel on Fifth Street, not far from Carroll Park.

After a hearty meal, two Big Macs and a large Coke, Barney Mulvey wandered over to the Intercontinental, and watched Fox's coverage of the rally on a huge flat screen television in the bar. He felt sad that he wasn't a part of the happy crowd in the park, some half-million strong, according to the local television commentator for WBXY in Baltimore. Folks had filled up the lawn, enjoying the balmy evening and one another, schmoozing with their neighbors, feeling good about being with people who wanted to have life, as Jesus had advised, more abundantly, feasting on fried chicken and cold lobster and imbibing a great deal of wine.

Barney couldn't quite understand them—why they felt so good listening to Bob Dylan and Sting, singing their heretical songs, Dylan belting out his hit song, "American Catholic," and Sting up there on the stage, too, singing the songs that had made all the charts that spring: "It's Our Church, Too," and "God's Human Hands." Or why it was that almost everyone in the crowd knew the words to those songs (he didn't), and why they all wanted to join in, especially on the choruses.

> We lift up our hands.
> Me and you.
> Our human hands.
> Me and you.
> Our loving hands.
> Me and you.
> Our helping hands.
> Me and you.
> They're God's hands, too.
> They're God's hands, too.

Barney had three highballs—Jack Daniels and Seven, as the bartender later told the police—then left the bar after the rally was over and took up a position on the sidewalk in front of the hotel, looking for all the world, with his bowler and his buttons, like an avid fan of the people's Church. He noted that those leaving the rally had jammed the downtown streets, eager to mill around and continue partying with—anyone and everyone who didn't want the night to end. He kept an eye on some one hundred prune-faced protesters who were marching in front of the Intercontinental with banners and sandwich boards attacking Cardinal Mahony as a traitor and a schismatic and a heretic. Barney was happy to see the police roust the protesters down the sidewalk and away from the hotel—happy because he was not among them. His disguise was working.

NOW NICK PIKE AND HIS WIFE, ANNE, have become separated from Cardinal Mahony and his entourage, walking the three blocks from Carroll Park to the Intercontinental. They have missed a traffic light a block back, and are headed to the Intercontinental on a parallel course with the Mahony party on the other side of Fifth Street. Anxious to catch up to the Mahony group before they hit the hotel entrance, Pike tells Anne he will see her later in the campaign suite, then sprints ahead, laughing to himself at how well the evening had gone.

A half-million at the rally in the park, a spectacle that would surely put part of the Mahony speech on the networks' late news shows. And, now that the fundies have been rousted—he can see the cops shoving them farther south on Fifth Street—Pike knows there will be no embarrassing confrontation in front of the hotel, where television news teams have already taken up a vigil, ready to capture the cardinal on camera as he enters the hotel. He wants the cardinal to get a good night's rest, maybe even sleep in before the gigantic liturgy on Saturday morning. What a coup, he thinks, to open the Council with the black Gospel choir—a hundred heavenly voices—from St. Augustine's Church in Washington, D.C.

Pike is still on the wrong side of Fifth Street when he notices one of the cardinal's fans, wearing a red, white, and blue People's Church bowler on his head and We Are Church buttons pinned all over the front of his denim shirt. Even in the relative darkness, there is enough light from the surrounding neon signs and the passing cars for Pike to note something freaky about him, something suspicious. And when he sees the man step out of the crowd and make an awkward move up the sidewalk toward the cardinal with both hands in the pockets of his baggy overalls, he is sure of it.

In his mind's eye, in fact, Pike does not see Barney Mulvey, but, flashing all the way back to the Los Angeles Ambassador Hotel in 1968, Sirhan Sirhan.

God damn it! Not again! Here is Pike's chance to redeem himself for failing Bobby Kennedy way back in 1968. He leaps into the street, sidesteps two passing cars and is slammed to the ground by a braking taxi. In a second, he bounces back on his feet and continues his rush toward the cardinal.

"STOP!" Pike shouts, hoping to distract the freaky figure with his hands in his pockets.

He does, for a moment.

Barney turns on Pike, now ten feet away, pulls out his revolver, and fires, hitting Pike in the palm of his raised right hand. Then he does a quick about-face and, from a squatting position, pops off five more rounds toward Cardinal Mahony before Pike tackles him down.

THE COPS GRAB BARNEY, of course, but, by then, Roger Michael Mahony lies on the sidewalk, one bullet lodged close to his spine and another in his neck, a thin trail of dark blood running down the sidewalk. He can speak, but his words cannot quite keep up with his racing thoughts.

On the threshold of, of wherever he is going, he is sure the Trinity father son and holy mother will attend his arrival, nothing in this world Los Angeles California Baltimore Maryland where is he United States of America planet Earth nothing means very much now funny how your perspective changes on your deathbed only it isn't a bed it is a gritty piece of concrete in Baltimore Roman Catholic Church autochthonous American Church and all the ships at sea. Nothing's that important.

Except, of course, Juana Margarita Obregón. When he opens his eyes he sees her there, kneeling at his side and holding his head while the emergency medics are hooking up an IV for him, taping a needle to his left arm and raising a bottle of clear fluid. He smiles at her presence there and he wonders where the others are, *those happy few, those brothers and sisters who fought with me it has been less than a year battling in a beautiful, laughing, crying cause show me a man (or a woman) without a cause and I will show you a man (or a woman) who is less than a man (or a woman).*

As they are lifting him onto the stretcher, he tries to say their names. They come out in a mumble. "Nick, Sean, Ted, Phoebe."

Juana Margarita Obregón tells him, "They're right here, all except Sean Sunnyhill who's in Rome right now. Do you want to see them?" And of course he does, nodding yes, *I want to tell them not to give up the fight, no matter what, because because well he doesn't have to tell them why—they are the ones who have had to tell* him *why in the first place.*

Phoebe follows the stretcher on its short rolling run to the waiting ambulance. So does Rackham, who has somehow managed to angle his wheelchair next to the ambulance, a foot or two away from Phoebe and Anne and Nick Pike, holding his right hand high with an improvised tourniquet wrapped around his wrist, a strap from Anne's leather purse.

The cardinal is glad they aren't blubbering, not even speaking, but just . . . there. He doesn't have any more to say either. There is so little left to say—except thank you. Which he does. "Thank you and bless you." His final words, just audible enough for them to hear, and respond, "Amen" before the ambulance pulls away, its lights flashing, its sirens screaming.

ARCHBISHOP PIETRO SAMBI, the papal nuncio in Washington, begins working on a terna—a list of three candidates for the next archbishop of Los Angeles. The Catholics of Los Angeles, demanding the right to elect Mahony's successor, start to work on their own list of candidates.

THE FOURTH COUNCIL OF BALTIMORE does not commence as planned on July 4, 2009. The American bishops postpone the Council indefinitely, possibly for another full year. Archbishop George Niederauer tells a news conference at Baltimore Washington International Airport it isn't fair for the Council to proceed without Mahony. He says, "Cardinal Mahony was the leader of the change party in the American Church. That party represents something good in the American Church. It is not only leaderless now but pretty much in mourning and confusion."

Nick Pike is in mourning, too, but he is even more confused when Rackham wheels into the campaign headquarters in Los Angeles on July 15, shouting and waving his laptop. "Just happened to be browsing yesterday

255

in the Hawk's old e-mail archive," he tells Pike. "Seems our friend had a friendly correspondence going with a Barney Mulvey at Yahoo dot com. Not sure if this is the nut who shot Roger. But in April, look here, the Hawk got this Mulvey a janitor's job—at the archdiocese of Baltimore."

"Jeez," says Pike. "Look at this story from yesterday's *New York Times*." He hands Rackham the paper and Rackham shakes his head over the headline:

FBI REPORT: MAHONY ASSASSIN ACTED ALONE
DEFENSE TO PLEAD INSANITY IN MULVEY TRIAL

"We'll see about this," says Rackham, slapping the *Times* on Pike's desk. He points to his laptop. "I gotta go to the FBI with this."

For a long moment, Pike cannot speak. Finally, he says, "Can you even go to the FBI?"

"Why not?"

Pike frowns and shakes his head. "You gonna tell the FBI how you got the Hawk's e-mail correspondence? This will incriminate you. Could put you in jail."

"Uh huh."

"And if this is the same Mulvey who shot Roger, you gonna tell the FBI the Hawk had something to do with the shooting? This could put the Hawk in the gas chamber."

"And maybe some people in Baltimore, too!"

"Jesus!" says Pike.

"Is that a prayer?"

"Huh?" Pike looks dazed. "I guess it better be. Lord help us."

AUTHOR'S NOTE

Stand by for the sequel.

Robert Blair Kaiser
rbkaiser@takebackourchurch.org